ALSO BY
AHMET ALTAN

Like a Sword Wound
Love in the Days of Rebellion

DYING IS EASIER THAN LOVING

Ahmet Altan

DYING IS EASIER
THAN LOVING

Book Three of the Ottoman Quartet

*Translated from the Turkish
by Brendan Freely*

Europa
editions

Europa Editions
27 Union Square West, Suite 302
New York, NY 10003
www.europaeditions.com
info@europaeditions.com

Translation by Brendan Freely
Original title: *Ölmek Kolaydır Sevmekten*
Translation copyright © 2022 by Europa Editions

Library of Congress Cataloging in Publication Data is available
ISBN 978-1-60945-829-4

Altan, Ahmet
Dying Is Easier Than Loving

Art direction by Emanuele Ragnisco
instagram.com/emanueleragnisco

Cover image: John Singer Sargent,
Nonchaloir (Repose), 1911, oil on canvas.

Prepress by Grafica Punto Print – Rome

Printed in Canada

I'm going to tell you a great secret
Close the doors
It's easier to die than to love
That's why I take such pains to go on living
My love.
—LOUIS ARAGON

DYING IS EASIER
THAN LOVING

Index of Characters

Osman

A middle aged man who lives alone in modern-day Turkey except for his frequent visitors from a century ago, who bring along their personal versions of a family history that only the dead can remember and tell.

Sheikh Yusuf Effendi

Osman's great grandfather. The leader of a prominent *tekke*— a monastery of dervishes—in the late 19th century Istanbul, whose wisdom is sought by people from all corners of the vast Ottoman land.

Hasan Effendi

A former commissioned officer of the Imperial Navy; both a loyal disciple and son-in law of Sheik Yusuf Effendi.

Mihrişah Sultan

An Ottoman princess related to the Khedive of Egypt and the estranged wife of the late Reşit Pasha, personal physician of the Ottoman Sultan.

Hüseyin Hikmet Bey

The only child of Mihrişah Sultan and the late Reşit Pasha. Trained as a lawyer in Paris and formerly married to Mehpare Hanım, he is now Dilevser's husband.

Mehpare Hanım

The daughter of an Ottoman Customs Director and a two-time divorcee, who has a daughter from her first husband Sheikh

Yusuf Efendi and a son from her second husband Hüseyin Hikmet Bey. She now lives alone in Istanbul.

Nizam
The only child of Mehpare Hanım and Hüseyin Hikmet Bey, he spent most of his life in Paris but now is back in Istanbul.

Rukiye
The daughter of Mehpare Hanım and Sheikh Yusuf Effendi, she is married to Tevfik Bey.

Tevfik Bey
A clerk at the Grand Vizier's Office.

Ragıp Bey
Osman's grandfather. An officer in the Ottoman Army, childhood friend of Hasan Effendi and married to Hatice Hanım, one of Sheik Yusuf Effendi's daughters.

Cevat Bey
Ragıp Bey's older brother and a leading member of the Committee for Union and Progress.

Dilara Hanım
Poland-born and well-travelled widow of an affluent Ottoman Pasha, she now resides alone in Istanbul.

Dilevser
Dilara Hanım's daughter and Hikmet Bey's second wife.

Anya
A Russian pianist who plays at a gaming den in Istanbul.

Monsieur Gavril
The owner of the gaming den where Anya works.

Efronia
An Armenian nurse who tends patients at the French Hospital in Istanbul.

Stéphane Lausanne
A journalist who has come to Istanbul to cover the Balkan War for the newspaper *Le Matin*.

Major Rasim
Hüseyin Hikmet Bey's friend and a member of the Committee for Union and Progress that had overthrown Abdulhamid, he had been commander of the military unit assigned to guard the former sultan during his years in exile.

Abdulhamid
Sultan Abdulhamid II ruled the Ottoman Empire from 1876 to 1909, until his dethroning by a military coup. A major figure in the first two volumes of the Ottoman Quartet, Abdulhamid has spent years in exile in Salonica and is now back in Istanbul.

Why would a person carry around a letter his whole life if he was never going to read it?

Osman sought the answer to this question as he wandered through this old mansion where the curtains were closed and the shutters were lowered, listening to the endless winds, the sounds that changed with the season and the day, and speaking to his dead, an extended family that had scattered over the course of a century, mixing themselves up in all of those wars, uprisings, coups, murders and anguished loves.

He kept repeating the same question to himself again and again as he wandered from room to room and hall to hall in this wooden mansion that groaned liked an aged invalid, wearing an old nightdress that had belonged to his grandfather and that he'd found in one of the old chests with rusty hinges.

He never went outside, never looked out the window, never set the decorative wall clocks that had long since stopped, he knew the time only from the sound of the wind; when it rang like little bells it was spring, when it howled it was winter, when it became irritable it meant autumn had arrived, and when it turned into a whisper it was summertime.

He'd almost entirely cut off his relationship with the present. One of the family's faithful retainers stopped by once a week, saw to all of Osman's and the house's needs, put away the food and then left without seeing the owner of the house.

He'd been living in this vague murkiness for a long time. He'd found his dead in this mansion, he'd begun speaking with them and had passed to a different life in which time and place had been lost. The dead told him their stories, sometimes lying, sometimes putting a spin on things, sometimes making mistakes, sometimes getting the dates mixed up, sometimes shaken by the confessions that came from the heart, recreating a past life here.

Osman had flowed into the past through a crack in time, after he'd done so the crack had closed and he'd remained in the past. For those who live in the present, time always flows in the same direction, towards the future, but behind Osman's magical crack it stretched in every direction but didn't flow anywhere, sometimes it moved forward and sometimes backward.

He lived surrounded by fog in an elastic, slack and disordered time, listening to his dead, speaking to them, gossiping, asking curious questions in a struggle to solve their mysteries.

Every question that got stuck in his mind seemed like the most important question in the world, he would fall in pursuit of that question in the belief that when he found the answer he would have solved the mystery of life.

He'd recently learned that it was not one but three unopened letters that Ragıp Bey carried close to his chest. Dilara Hanım had written him three letters in a row and had not received a reply to any of them.

Those letters had travelled from one front line to another, from one city to another, growing tattered and yellowed in the inner pocket of Ragıp Bey's jacket.

For Ragıp Bey, who didn't value possessions and cared nothing for goods and property, those three letters were the most valuable things he owned.

What is it that makes a letter valuable, Osman kept asking himself.

He couldn't say "the contents" because Ragıp Bey, who'd carried those letters in his breast pocket from the moment he'd received them, had never once opened the envelopes and didn't know what was written in them.

If he said, "the person who wrote the letter," Ragıp Bey said that he didn't ever again even want to meet the woman who wrote the letters.

Ragıp Bey hadn't opened the letters, he didn't want to see Dilara Hanım again, but during the Balkan War, when a village house in Çatalca just beyond the emplacements was hit by Bulgarian cannon fire and started burning, and he barely managed to scramble out alive, he realized that the jacket with the letters in it was still inside, he shook off the sergeant who has holding him back, crawled in through the flames and rescued the jacket and the letters.

Remaining on the thin line between life and death without touching either side, his clouded mind wandering among the fragile waves of time, he'd heard so much about that war from his dead, he'd seen scenes from the war on the broad, empty walls of the halls so many times, had watched them so many times.

He never forgot the way Ragıp Bey stood above the trenches on that strange, rainy day.

As the clouds mingled together in restless confusion it began to rain, and as it fell to the ground rent by the spooky and inauspicious phosphorescent lavender, orange, purple and green glow, the thousands of dead and the piles of mud in which they were buried began to change color from moment to moment.

A powerful light was emanating from the drops.

The trenches, the piles of mud in front of the trenches, the cannon carriages, the shell casings next to the carriages, the wet hair of the dead whose faces were hidden by the mud, the moustaches of the men who waited for a new attack and the rifles they were holding were swathed in the constantly changing color of the rain, sometimes lavender, sometimes purple, sometimes blue, sometimes yellow.

As the colors of the sky changed, the trenches and craters filled with rainwater, dead horses, broken wheels, one or two empty shacks with thatched roofs, the lone trees that stood here and there and the naked plain that stretched as far as the eye could see were all undulating with them like a soft cover, seen from a distance it gave one the feeling that the entire plain was moving in an incomprehensible and unnerving harmony.

The bodies of the soldiers, twisted in their grey, military cloaks, hunch-backed, their legs drawn up to their bellies from their final agony, became a part of this motion with the changing of the colors and were moving with the plain.

The infantrymen were watching the sky in terror, they were trying to hide in the trenches as if to protect themselves from the assault of this roaring of colors they'd never seen before, they believed that these gushing colors that tore the sky were an omen, but they feared it was a bad omen.

Ragıp Bey, who was standing alone above the trench watching the sky and the plain, seemed to grow larger and taller with every color that struck him, he was the only person on the entire plain who was standing up and as his fur cap, hair, moustache and uniform were painted in the fiery colors reflected by the clouds, he looked like a flaming torch. He could have been struck by a bullet or torn apart by shrapnel at any moment, but the tranquility on his face as rainwater streamed down it from his fur cap made one think that he'd forgotten he was on a battlefield.

As he later told Osman, "In fact in those days I'd forgotten about death, and about life as well."

Not being given the absolute love he'd yearned for from the woman he loved, his belief that there was something lacking in Dilara Hanım's love, had torn from him the feeling of happiness that he'd always desired, that he yearned for with a strange bashfulness, that he'd always dreamed about and that he'd believed he was certain to find one day, he'd lost his trust in people, and indeed in life. There was nothing left of what the future had promised him, as he told Osman, "Life and people are always a little incomplete, I have neither the power to complete what's missing, in life and in people, nor the tolerance to consent to accept them with their imperfections."

After the Dilara Hanım "affair," "incompleteness" became the word that defined Ragıp Bey's life, it was as if this word could explain everything, make everything comprehensible. Even Osman, with his clouded mind, could grasp that this word was the key not to solving the meaning of life but on the contrary that it served this bellicose-souled man to lock the thick door with which he'd closed himself off from life.

He'd once thought that this soldier who'd spent his life on the shores of death had sought in life the absoluteness of death. He'd thought he'd wanted life to have that poignancy, that dark wholeness as well.

Much later, as they spoke, he'd realized that this word expressed a helplessness, an impasse, an inability to talk about what troubled him. Ragıp Bey had arrived at the opinion that the woman he loved didn't love him with the same degree of strength and he assessed everything that happened in light of this opinion of whose truth no one was certain, and he'd begun to find life and people lacking.

It was as if his belief that he would never again find happiness had become an affliction that cut him off from the whole world and from people, he both looked down on people who were willing to live out a life that was incomplete and envied them for the ease with which they failed to see this incompleteness as an affliction.

In any event, in those days all of his emotions were battling one another as if they were enemies, his soul was a battlefield like the one he was looking at. Wherever he went and whatever he did, he always carried Dilara Hanım's letters in his pocket, but he never once read them, he could neither part with them nor look at them.

He was like someone who loved a woman who had died, but the woman he loved was alive. He knew that if he went, if he knocked on her door, she would invite him in, he could reach the woman he loved whenever he wanted, but the woman he reached wouldn't be the woman he loved and wanted.

He wanted the Dilara Hanım he'd created in his imagination, who his thoughts and feelings had made unique, who he'd set apart from all other people and kept in an unreachable place, someone with weakness that made her like the others wouldn't be enough to fulfill his dreams and hopes.

Every time he looked at Dilara Hanım he would see a sign of incompleteness on her face, and when he saw this he wouldn't be able to bear it; to accept not being loved as he wanted as a natural part of his life would cripple his entire life, his future and his existence, it would make him weak. Despite all his love, he felt that to accept Dilara Hanım's inadequate love would destroy the last chance in his life for happiness, no matter how much he lived as if he'd given up on life, he had hope that one day he would find absolute love, absolute happiness and in order not to lose that, he was struggling to put up an almost instinctive resistance.

He wanted an ongoing dream, a hope that he could hold on to, he was unwilling to give the last hope of happiness he possessed even to the woman he loved in exchange for something that only resembled happiness.

He now knew that there was an obstacle between him and the woman he loved that couldn't be overcome or removed. He loved the woman he'd created in his imagination with such a strong passion, the woman who was the source of this dream now seemed pitiful and lifeless in comparison to the dream. In those days Ragıp Bey was learning that losing an imaginary woman was more painful than losing a real woman; he could have found another woman to love, but it wasn't always easy to create a dream out of a woman.

He was like a sculptor who'd found the best marble in the world and then made a bad statue from it, he didn't like the statue but he'd also lost the marble. The marble he liked was hidden within the statue he didn't like and every time he thought of the statue, he remembered the marble he'd lost and would never find again, he grieved for the times when he'd created that magnificent dream and Dilara Hanım had been a supreme and perfect woman for him. He was imprisoned in the past.

The clouds had slowly begun to regain their dominance of the sky, but the phosphorescent colors that shone through them like a volcano that had erupted in the depths of the universe continued to mix, gilding the edges of the clouds that were trying to obscure them; the rain, quickened by the sharpening October wind, seemed to be spouting from the ground to the sky, the edges of the plain had grown dark, but the center was illuminated like a forest fire.

For whatever reason, the Bulgarians had stopped their cannon fire two hours earlier, and the silence worried the soldiers, they suspected the Bulgarians were preparing a night attack. Ragıp Bey could sense that they were frightened, for so many years he'd been in and out of so many battles, so many times he'd walked towards death with the men, but for the first time he saw how daunted and timorous the army had become. They outnumbered the enemy's units, but they didn't possess the enemy's desire to fight, they didn't believe they were going to win this war, they trusted neither the officers, the generals, nor the Sultan.

Ragıp Bey thought angrily about how they'd lost the war, it was as if it was over before it had even begun.

When, after a boom, the soldiers saw a shell whooshing

towards them as it tore through the rain they plastered themselves to the trenches, but Ragıp Bey didn't move. The shell buried itself in the earth with a hollow sound about ten meters from the trenches, splattering mud as it did so. Ragıp Bey squinted his right eye and looked towards the Bulgarian trenches as if he was disgusted by the enemy artillery's needless shot and inept targeting.

For a moment he wondered whether or not he was going to die in this strange war, but his anguish, like a well full of venom, demolished any thought, any feeling, including the fear of death, the moment it appeared. Later he told Osman, "I can tell you this from experience, the feeling of happiness and the feeling of anguish have the same way of making a person indifferent in the face of death and life"

Before leaving for the front he'd visited his former father-in-law, Sheikh Yusuf Efendi, to get his blessing, and as always he'd been welcomed as an old friend. Due in part to the admiration and gratitude he felt for Sheik Efendi, he'd married his youngest daughter Hatice Hanım, they'd had a child too, but in fact the marriage had come to an end before the child was even born, the great love for Dilara Hanım with which he'd been smitten ended the marriage. When the child died of meningitis at the age of six months, their last bond was severed, the young woman married a department head at the Ministry of Sharia and Foundations. He'd been far from Istanbul when he heard about the child's death and he hadn't mention it to anyone, he hadn't been able to fully grasp the reality of the death of a child he'd only seen once. Because Sheikh Efendi was the kind of person to understand that what had happened was because of helplessness rather than ill will, he'd never reproached Ragıp Bey, hadn't held him responsible, had forgiven him, and had never spoken of the matter again.

As they wandered through the *tekke* garden that day, Sheikh Efendi, in the manner that always amazed Ragıp Bey, it was as if the man knew what was going through his mind, said, "One shouldn't expect too much of people, it can diminish a person, Ragıp Bey."

"If we were all created with so many defects, how did we learn to want so much, Your Excellency the Sheikh?"

"Wanting," said Sheikh Efendi, "Shows us our own shortcomings. You mustn't forget that sometimes what we want most from others is what we are least able to give them."

Ragıp Bey shook his head stubbornly.

"What you say is true, your excellency, but that's not for me, I can't accept my shortcomings so calmly."

"Courage is what you know most about, Ragıp Bey, sometimes it can be necessary to display the courage to endure, God's love is absolute, yet when you love one of God's creatures you have to love them with their faults and shortcomings . . ."

Sheikh Efendi stopped suddenly, sighed, repeated his last sentence and continued speaking.

"Ragıp Bey, you have to love God's creatures with all their faults and shortcomings. If you ask me, to love is to accept defects. Intolerance shown to the defects of others is a person's love for themselves. If the Great Lord loves the countless people he called into being with their sicknesses, sins, and shortcomings, we must demonstrate the power of loving one person with their weaknesses."

"I don't have that power, Your Excellency. This is my shortcoming . . ."

"This shortcoming hasn't prevented other people from loving you."

Ragıp Bey responded with an almost pained laugh.

"Perhaps that's so . . ."

"You're pursuing something impossible," said Sheikh Efendi.

Ragıp Bey shrugged his shoulders resignedly.

"Perhaps . . ."

Sheikh Efendi realized his words weren't going to be of any use, but he talked as if he wanted to give a final warning.

"Those who don't tolerate shortcomings can suffer a great deal."

"When it comes to the pain of shortcomings, I'd prefer the pain of absence. There shouldn't be any half measures."

"Ragıp Bey, arrogant people poison their own lives, they destroy the God-given capacity to love, it makes a person the enemy of his own happiness. Those who don't move past their arrogance see only shortcomings, faults and weaknesses, to see what's really there and to love it requires humility. A person should be a bit forgiving . . ."

"Excuse me, but it's not my place to forgive anyone. But I want what's coming to me to come to me in full . . . Otherwise I'd rather it didn't come at all."

Sheikh Efendi realized that Ragıp Bey would never defeat his own arrogance, he would not forgive, he would be in search of a dream all his life and would never accept anything less than that dream.

When, as they were parting, he said, "You have my blessing, may God help you," he hoped God would help him in life rather than in war and give him the happiness he so sincerely yearned for.

At that time he didn't know that his prayer would be effective.

The black clouds swelled quickly like large animals jumping on top of each other, besieging the last beams of light, leaving in the middle of the plain a column of light whose colors changed by the moment, everything outside this illuminated patch had grown very dark. Ragıp Bey was still standing above the trenches, watching the last darkening of the plain. The little shacks, the trees, the piles of mud and the puddles were quickly disappearing, they still existed but would soon be swallowed by nothingness and would be invisible until the morning light appeared.

Suddenly, red flames began spouting one after another from the Bulgarian trenches, the dusk was suddenly cut into slices by bright red beams as the shells shot out of the cannon barrels, the plain was shaken by a frightful booming, the shells were exploding in front of the trenches. One landed behind the trenches. Ragıp Bey heard the soldiers' screams and as he leapt into the trench he shouted to the sergeant, "Go take a look, see how many casualties we have."

A little later the sergeant came running doubled over through the trench.

"There are three wounded, but not seriously," he said.

The cannon fire continued.

The plain had become pitch black, the light that seeped through the small gaps in the clouds didn't reach the ground and remained suspended in the air.

"Are they preparing for a night assault, I wonder," said the sergeant.

"Make sure the men are ready, have all of them fix their bayonets."

"That's already been done, sir . . . It's just that the men are hungry . . . The mess wagons didn't come at noon, and now with this shelling they won't come in the evening either."

"No one ever died of starvation from missing two meals, I see you've forgotten about the war, seeing as you're thinking about the mess wagons . . ."

"No sir, it's not about forgetting . . ."

The sergeant lowered his voice and continued.

"The men's morale isn't so great, sir. They're already like drowned rats after the rain, and now they're hungry . . ."

Ragıp Bey turned and gave the sergeant a look that even in the darkness was enough to shut him up.

The Bulgarian artillery bombarded the trenches constantly

until midnight, the men held tightly to their rifles and pressed themselves into the mud, waiting for the bombardment to subside. The worry that the bombardment would be followed by a night attack seemed more daunting than the shells.

The army seemed wearied by the series of upheavals that had shaken the empire, the men's spirit had long since been broken, a sense of defeat had spread from the first day of the war, the mess wagons failed to arrive on time, supplies didn't arrive at all, the units failed to establish proper channels of communication, sometimes the cannons were sent to one place while the shells were sent to another, relationships between the lines had been lost, the officers were irritable, there were disagreements among the generals, a number of generals believed before the war even began that it would end in disaster, the army was done for before it even went into battle.

Ragıp Bey sensed that the empire was facing the greatest military disaster in its history, he was angry, he would rather get the order to attack at once and charge the Bulgarian artillery than witness this great defeat.

He was covered with mud from head to toe, muddy water dripped from his eyebrows, his moustache and his two-day beard that had a few strands on white in it, he burned with anger and anguish under the hail of shells. It was as if his life had been besieged by impossibilities, he didn't have the strength to change either the outcome of the war or his own future. He saw his life as an enemy, it wouldn't begrudge him even the smallest consolation, shattered every kind of hope and destroyed his dreams, he felt belittled, defeated and abandoned, without realizing it he longed for an honorable death that would free him from all of this, for the fatal wound he would receive on the battlefield.

He spent the night in those muddy trenches. Occasionally he dozed off, and shook himself awake as if he was tumbling into darkness. Even though he sensed that the reason he was so aggrieved had less to do with the outcome of the war than with losing Dilara Hanım, he grew increasingly angry. If Dilara Hanım could come to him as the woman he wanted and expected, if he could turn back time, if he could return the marble to an untouched state, he might not have minded defeat on the battlefield so much, but the hammer had descended and the marble had been ruined.

He'd surrounded himself with impossibilities to the extent that he was like a poor scorpion surrounded by a ring of fire it couldn't escape, his own being prevented him from reaching the woman he loved, he was making it impossible to be united with the woman he loved and strangely enough this impossibility he'd created increased his longing even more. If he'd thought about reuniting with Dilara Hanım, if he'd overcome the impossibility, perhaps he'd miss her less, perhaps he'd feel less anguish, but being stuck between his love and the insurmountable barrier he'd created bound him inexplicably closer to his love.

Osman, surrounded by a crowd of the dead, looked at the trenches in which the soldiers who would soon die were lying, at Ragıp Bey, wracked with anguish, at Dilara Hanım, who was standing next to him, at her transparent and fragile body and the mocking smile she wore even in death.

When Dilara Hanım saw that Osman was looking at her she began to speak without losing her mocking smile, but Osman sensed the pain beneath the mockery.

"I," said Dilara Hanım, "loved Ragıp Bey very much, but I loved him as myself, he wanted me to love him as himself, he never understood that everyone can love in their own way, he ruined my life and his own life."

When Osman heard this, that almost antagonistic smile peculiar to half crazed people appeared on his face, because he knew that despite the deep anguish Ragıp Bey was experiencing at the moment, his life was not ruined, and he would find his happiness at a time when he least expected it.

For a moment he thought about telling this to Dilara Hanım, but then he changed his mind.

He decided it would be more fun to do this at a time when Dilara Hanım's mockery made him even more angry.

When the ship rounded the point and the city emerged from behind the fog, Nizam looked at the city that was awaiting him the same way his father had looked at it years ago, as if he was looking at a beautiful woman he knew from the start he was going to abandon, keenly, but with the secret disdain of knowing that she would have no place in his life. The city didn't at all resemble the city that had awaited his father, the city that had looked like lace under the white snow and smelled of flowers, the sea, fruit and tar; now the elegant silhouette of domes, minarets and hilltops was darkened by a dirty rain and torn by oily smoke, the sea had lost its light and taken on a pale silver tone, everything was enveloped by the smell of sickness, death, and caustic lime, the streets and bridges were filled with tumbrels carrying the sick and the dead, the roar of the crowds was crushed beneath a suffocating silence.

The city was sick.

The handsome face that combined his mother's beauty with his father's nobility and the likeableness that came from the selfish and nonchalant geniality in his soul gave Nizam an appeal that drew every type of woman to him. Beneath the detachment that asked nothing of people and didn't promise them anything was an innocent and childish greed that he felt because he wanted take hold of all of life's pleasures, this strange contradiction, like all contradictions, led people to take an interest in him; that handsome face, polite amiability, amusing nonchalance, the free soul that gave the impression that he could drop everything and leave at any moment, and indeed he could, evoked a feeling that behind this shallow and polished appearance was an elusive darkness, and people who met him, led by their strange and inexplicable instincts, couldn't help but flock around him in order to possess what they couldn't reach.

Even as he watched from the ship's railing, feeling the city's death-scented wind on his broad and radiant brow, there was a crowd of mostly beautiful women around him. Usually he would have entertained those women with a mixture of the niceties he'd picked up while living with his grandmother in Paris, the toughness he'd gained wandering the back streets of that sinful city and the cheerful jokes that expressed his disposition, but as the chain rattled while the ship dropped anchor he looked at the city somewhat pensively and quietly, as if he could smell the fate that was awaiting him and the horrible murder he would commit.

As he was looking at the harbor he saw his father, who had come to meet him. Hikmet Bey had come to meet his son in the same way that his own father had come to meet him when he returned from Paris, he waited for his son next to the carriage in the same way his father had waited for him; the way the son looked at the harbor from the railing and the way the father waited was exactly as it had been in the past, as if the past had been reflected into the present, everything about the two winter mornings seemed so much alike; everything was the same, and this similarity carried with it so much that was not similar, someone who had witnessed both events might have found some disquieting things in the way these similarities and dissimilarities emerged together, intertwined.

When Hikmet Bey saw his son, who was now a young man, walking towards him wearing a fez that had been given to him on the ship and that was lopsided because he was unaccustomed to wearing it, a long, black coat with an astrakhan collar and chamois gloves, foppishly twirling a silver-handled cane and smiling brightly he felt, at the same time as he felt the delight of a father seeing his son, a disquiet, he realized he'd been waiting hopelessly for his son to be something more than a dandy and that he was saddened that this wasn't the case. He was saddened both by this reality and by having nourished feelings like this for his son, but he realized that his father had felt the same emotions upon seeing him again after many years, remembering how mercilessly time had passed for him and what he had lived through during that time made him melancholy, but at the same time he became hopeful that his son could change the way he himself had.

When they stood face to face they looked at each other awkwardly for a moment because they didn't know what to do, as Nizam reached out to shake his father's hand Hikmet Bey, forgetting his feelings of a moment before, embraced his son with true fatherly love.

"Welcome son . . . How are you? How was your trip?"

"*Merci*, I'm fine . . . The trip was fine. The sea got a little rough off the coast of Sicily, but other than that it was generally fine."

"Come, let's get into the carriage. It's cold."

As he was climbing into the carriage, Nizam turned around as if there was something he wanted to see, "What's this smell?" he said, "What a strange smell."

"The smell of death, my son. There's a cholera epidemic in the city, but even though everyone knows about it we're forbidden to talk about it as if it was a secret. All of the hospitals, parks, and indeed even mosques are full of cholera patients . . ."

"What are you saying?"

Hikmet Bey patted Nizam on the knee and affectionately tried to calm him.

"Don't be afraid, we've taken all the necessary precautions, anyway the epidemic has been mostly in this part of the city. Where we are is much safer . . ."

As they spoke, the driver was supervising the loading of Nizam's luggage onto the carriage. As they were getting under way, an infantry unit trudged past the carriage, the men could barely walk, their cheeks were sunken, their faces had taken on a blackish yellow color, they were on their way to the station to board a train for the front lines. When Hikmet Bey saw his son looking at the soldiers he explained.

"They're going to the front . . ."

"I think it would be better for them to go to the hospital . . . They don't have the strength to walk, how are they going to fight . . ."

"Unfortunately most of the other side are sick too, my son. In any event the epidemic spread from the units that were mustering in Istanbul to go to the front."

"They're sending them to the front when they're this sick? But father, how can they allow this . . . Do your commanders think that the battlefield is a hospital and that the Bulgarians are doctors? To tell the truth, when they called the Ottoman Empire a sick man I thought they were speaking figuratively, it never occurred to me that it could be true."

Hikmet Bey didn't answer his son, he kept silent because he was ashamed to tell Nizam that it could be dangerous to speak this way, that words like this could get you into deep trouble in the Ottoman capital, and he waited for his son to stop speaking as well. He was surprised that his son could have even the slightest compassion for those sick soldiers.

To change the subject, he asked the question that had been stuck in his mind since he received the telegram informing him of Nizam's arrival.

"What happened between you and my mother, why did she send you here so abruptly in these most hazardous of times?"

Nizam smiled and shrugged his shoulders.

"My grandmother got angry with me because the Comte de Serebrack came home early."

Hikmet Bey looked at his son in surprise.

"When the Comte returned I still hadn't left his bedroom . . ."

Hikmet Bey bit his lip and stared straight ahead to keep from laughing, but after the desire to laugh came an uneasiness that disquieted and distressed him, he found Nizam's witticisms a bit too egotistical and savage; he knew very well that this air of selfishness and nonchalance that he made so obvious came from not having suffered any blows in life, he sensed he could speak so mercilessly because he sincerely believed he would never fall into the predicaments of the people he mocked. He saw how weak this belief could make a person, how vulnerable to the vicissitudes of life, but he wasn't going to tell his son this and he could guess his son wouldn't heed this kind of talk.

He could see how, as with all young men, Nizam thinking himself untouchable and invulnerable could put him in harm's way, how he could be left unprotected against all kinds of blows, how he wouldn't be able to find time to protect himself, how much the first slap would knock him off balance, how he would tumble from his present degree of confidence into a great self-doubt. He made himself believe that these apprehensions were exaggerated by his fatherly feelings, he tried to forget what he'd seen and he succeeded.

They started moving quickly through the city's wet streets, which had been darkened by rain and anguish, the horses threw themselves forward of their own accord as if they were fleeing something, as if they wanted to get off these streets as soon as possible. Sick, pale-faced soldiers in tattered uniforms lay moaning in burnt-out buildings, mosque courtyards and parks, they looked with pleading eyes at the passing carriages as if they'd brought someone who could help them, as the carriage passed they tried to sit up a bit, then lay back down after it had passed.

As they barreled along, splashing mud, through the smell of death that enveloped the city, the cobblestones, the bare trees that had shed their leaves, the buildings, the walls and covered the sea like a dirty yellow cloud, Hikmet Bey, inside the swaying carriage, looked his son over without letting on, trying to grasp what it was that had upset him so much during this brief meeting. Nizam sensed his father's disquiet and what was passing through his mind. Later on, Hikmet Bey would discover his son's eerie talent with a disquiet that combined surprise and admiration.

Nizam could intuit all the feelings and even the thoughts of the people around him, as if people's every emotion emanated from them like a secret wave of color and he was the only one who could see these hues, he could sense everything the moment he saw their faces, and sometimes even before seeing their faces. It was as if his soul had been cracked in places by a violent tremor, forming channels through which the feelings of others could flow into his soul. Even in the first days Hikmet Bey was astounded by the contradiction of someone who seemed so indifferent yet at the same time able to feel every emotion around him with such a keen power, but as time passed he saw that his son was a ball of paradoxes rolled together from many distinct contradictions. A fatherly intuition frightened him. He was spooked by the seething chaos that lay beneath an ordinary, foppish appearance.

He thought about his own father Reşit Pasha, Sultan Abdulhamid's physician and confidante, who'd died after going into exile with the sultan, he thought about himself and remembered that even though they didn't seem at all alike there had been similarities between them. Nizam, though, didn't resemble either of them, even though they came from the same roots, they'd become cut off from each other, while he'd been expecting a cycle to keep turning out people who resembled each other, the cycle had been shattered and someone completely different had emerged. As Hikmet Bey remembered his former wife Mehpare Hanım, he tried to figure out if his son took after her; he resembled her in his selfishness, his impudence and his foppishness, but these were superficial resemblances and he couldn't find anything beyond that.

In fact Nizam didn't resemble anyone Hikmet Bey knew, he was like a stranger who had suddenly appeared in the house one morning, he didn't resemble anyone, he had nothing in common with anyone, he didn't make any effort to find common ground or to grow close, but amazingly people found him easy to like.

He wasn't concerned about anything, he didn't value anything, he didn't struggle for anything, he was indifferent to people's ambitions, but he was so likeable that it was impossible not to like him, he fluttered through life like a brightly colored bird that didn't care which branch it perched on, he concerned himself with whatever took his interest at that moment, he would suddenly make a person or an object that took his interest the center of his world.

He rolled along without caring which direction he was going in life, he seemed ready to slide down any slope, it didn't matter to him where he was going, he didn't have any preference regarding the paths that presented themselves to him, he didn't forbid himself anything, for him everything was possible in life.

Once when, as was their habit, Hikmet Bey and Dilevser were having a heart-to-heart discussion before going to bed, he'd sighed and said, "What makes people strong is having a goal, a belief, standards that they value, things they hold untouchably sacred and other people they're bound to, if we hold on to these we can avoid losing our grip and making mistakes we'll be ashamed of, but Nizam doesn't have any of these things, nothing is sacred or precious to him, he has no branch to hang onto, this leaves him very weak, this frightens me a great deal, I live with the worry that I could receive bad news at any moment."

When he said this Hikmet Bey was speaking from his experience, from what he'd lived, he was convinced that his faithfulness to the ideas he believed in and the commitment he felt to his family's good name had saved him from a shameful end after all he'd lived through, from losing his honor, had constituted a fence that prevented him from stumbling and falling when he came too close to the edge of the cliff. He and his father Reşit Pasha had created important purposes in order to overcome their weaknesses, they'd saved themselves from falling into the traps set by their weaknesses through these sacred purposes, but Nizam had no purpose, no belief, to hang on to. He didn't find anything more valuable than himself, he took all of the emotions he could and granted himself the freedom of life with an almost obscene pleasure.

He was a difficult person to understand, he never spoke of his emotions or his thoughts, he only joked around and spoke of trivial matters, at first Hikmet Bey's son had seemed to him to be like a desert with vague boundaries, somehow he couldn't figure out what standards to use to gauge him.

The worries that had appeared within him at their very first meeting had not been eased, with a strange foreboding, Hikmet Bey sensed that there were difficult times ahead for them.

When they arrived home they found Dilevser waiting for them in the living room with a book in her hand, as always she'd put her finger in the book so as not to lose her place, when she stood like that it seemed as if the book was a part of her body.

The moment they met, Nizam said "*Bonjour* Dilevser" with a broad smile as if they'd only parted a few moments before, then put out his hand and walked towards the young woman, but Hikmet Bey saw in the middle of the smile that spread across his son's handsome face and in his eyes, which seemed to have grown larger and to have gained a strange depth, that he was looking at Dilevser as if he wanted to be able to read her entire soul. There was an alien expression in his eyes like that of a being that had come from another planet, an expression the like of which Hikmet Bey had never seen and that made those who saw it want to hide.

Dilevser was somewhere in the middle of her transformation from a dreamy young girl to a mature woman who was the lady of a mansion, her slender body had broadened slightly and become more womanly, there was a confidence in her face reminiscent of her mother Dilara Hanım, aristocratic politeness had not yet settled into the lines of her face, the way she held her back straight and her head high made it clear that she was accustomed to giving orders.

There could be seen in her expression a slightly childish pride that carried a teasing playfulness, the kind of expression seen in young women after they marry and find themselves responsible for a man and a home; one could sense in her manner the affectedness of an actress who hadn't become accustomed to her role and was ready to giggle at any moment; Nizam saw all of this at the same moment, even though most of these were expressions he'd never seen or encountered, he comfortably grasped everything he saw, but under the waves of expression that could be seen passing from one personality to another, he could the sense a stirring of uneasiness, there was no sign of it, but Nizam was certain that this emotion was present in the woman before him.

Dilevser said, "How are you Nizam?" and shook her stepson's hand, even though they were about the same age, there was a superiority in her manner that suggested she believed she was older than Nizam and that she regarded him as a child.

"How was your trip?"

"It was fun, but to tell the truth I realized I don't really enjoy travelling. Especially not on ships. You can't say you want to get off here, you can't change your mind, you can't escape being part of a crowd, I don't mind being in a crowd but I prefer to preserve the freedom to choose which crowd I'm in."

Nizam paused and then added,

"That was a long answer to a short question, isn't that so? When I'm tired I tend to go on and on like that. With your permission I'd like to rest a little, then I'll be calmer."

Dilevser smiled like a mother being tolerant of her child.

"Of course, indeed your room has been prepared, make yourself at home. I invited my mother to dinner as well, I hope you won't find four people too much of a crowd."

Dilevser regretted that she hadn't been able to keep herself from uttering this last sentence, a flush spread across her face.

Nizam pretended he didn't understand the insinuation.

"I'm afraid that at such a distinguished gathering I'm the one who would be superfluous, I hope you'll be patient with me."

Even though for a moment Hikmet Bey found this sarcastic talk alarming, he was glad that there was a young person in the house with whom Dilevser could spend time, be sarcastic, and joke without fear and without being slighted. She'd spent her childhood like a recluse, keeping everyone away from her and not feeling the need for friends young or old, but now that she'd been suddenly thrust into real life and become the lady of a mansion, she missed, without knowing quite what it was she missed, all of those youthful conversations she'd never known, those rambling discussions, joking around without anyone getting offended.

She wasn't bored by the conversations about literature and discussions about philosophy she had with Hikmet Bey, nor by the political arguments they had when her mother joined them for dinner, she liked these conversations, and she was amused by the unexpected witticisms Hikmet Bey injected into his talk to entertain the young woman and make her laugh, but still, from time to time, she felt as if something was missing. Dilevser wasn't aware of it, but while she enjoyed playing the role of the demure young woman in this new life she'd been given, she sometimes wanted to be able to run down the stairs, imitate the Albanian gardener's accent, make fun of Hikmet Bey's aristocratic refinement, but she held herself back. Sometimes, like a kitten, she wanted to abandon herself to games with people her own age, to chase after a ball of yarn, she didn't make an issue of not doing this because she was by nature a demure young woman, Dilevser had enjoyed having a rambling conversation with someone her own age. She was glad there was finally someone with whom she could have those inane conversations, amusing because they're so inane, that are particular to young people.

When Nizam entered his room, he saw the dark blue and pink tiled stove, reminiscent of a giant candy box, in the middle of the room. The stove was burning, and even though he knew it was hot he touched it lightly with his fingertips, then quickly pulled his fingers away when they burned. He walked over to the window. The trees in the well-kept garden had shed their leaves, the flowers had taken on the color of the rain, there were a few roses on the saplings in the rose beds that had withstood time, they'd taken on a melancholy air as if to remind everyone that they were in Istanbul, they would die soon, he thought, it was as if the smell of death he'd caught the moment he arrived in the city had worked its way into him, he found the city, the house, the room and even his father to be strange, he already missed Paris, its amusements, well-lit avenues, warm cafes that smelled of cognac, women, cheerful soirees, it had nothing in common with this city or with the people who lived here.

He was accustomed to being alone, he lived alone even when he was in a crowd, he kept himself hidden from everyone in a castle of seclusion, but like many recluses he wanted to see around him the house, the streets, the city and the people that enveloped his loneliness and had become part of it. They didn't decrease his loneliness, they positioned loneliness in his life in a safer manner; now that he'd been torn from the place to which he was accustomed, it was as if he'd lost his loneliness as well, he felt as if he'd lost himself too, as if he was diminished and weakened.

He sat in the large leather armchair by the window, stretched out his legs and smiled to himself, someone watching him might have thought that he liked the room and his surroundings and that he was pleased with his life, but Nizam was secretly mocking the powerlessness he felt at that moment, his own powerlessness, like the powerlessness of others, struck him as both pitiful and laughable.

Powerlessness was not a feeling he could tolerate, he became as angry as an eagle that saw a snake in its nest, he would prepare to attack, when he didn't find anyone else to attack he would denigrate, mock, and castigate himself, sometimes speaking to himself aloud. Being strong had no importance to him, but he found weakness ugly.

Later he told Osman, "At that moment I wanted to flee that place, if I'd had any place to go I wouldn't have stayed there a moment, I would have left, I wouldn't have hesitated for a moment to trade several years of my life to be in Paris again."

Just as he didn't know that his father had had the same feelings and experienced the same loneliness when he returned to Istanbul from Paris, he didn't know at that time that Istanbul would draw him in and make him a part of it.

The calm and happy mood he'd sensed as soon as he entered the house also deepened his loneliness. Just as unhappiness is prepared to invite all strangers in, the doors of happiness are closed to others, and this made him think that he would remain outside, that he would not be a part of this happiness, that he would be superfluous.

Suddenly he missed his older sister Rukiye, he didn't feel alone when he was with her, he didn't feel alienated, he could bear his own weakness, she was the only person he could take shelter in without taking offence, since childhood he'd been bound to his sister by a strange admiration, that they were not at all alike made this bond stronger, Rukiye's decisive, head-strong and combative personality and Nizam's nonchalant, unrestricted personality, his sense that it wasn't even worth struggling with people or with life, completed each other.

He decided to lie down and take a nap, as was his habit when he was feeling a bit down, he lay on the bed in his clothes, he knew that he would sleep soon and that later when he woke he would feel better, since childhood sleep had been the safest and most durable sanctuary, when he felt oppressed that's where he fled, he hid in his dreams, he always returned to life strengthened after these journeys through that fairytale land in which he lived a thousand and one adventures.

When he woke it was dark, the darkness in the room was tinged with red from the light that came from the lid of the stove, he put his hands behind his head and looked at the ceiling, he felt his loneliness keenly for the first time, and he was feeling this in his father's house, perhaps he wouldn't have felt this loneliness so intensely in a strange house, getting out of there in the hope of reuniting with friends and relatives, sharing, having fun, might have lessened the loneliness, but here, in the home of the person he was supposed to be closest to, to see the unbridgeable distance between him and his closest relative pushed him away from other people, from friends, from almost all of life, created a sense of helplessness that he knew wasn't quite real.

This time even sleep hadn't soothed him. "It seems that all

children want to flow towards their fathers like rivers into the sea, to be reunited with them, to be made whole, to feel their strength next to them," he said to Osman later, "being distant from your father seemed like being distant from life. You either disavow your father and feel the strength of this within you or you merge with your father and add his strength to yours, there's no middle way, establishing a connection with your father outside of this is tiring, it makes you feel lonelier."

In fact he'd grown up in a family were any demonstration of closeness was considered "unnecessary" and impolite, he was accustomed to distant relationships, he was even accustomed to sensing the love that was felt for him at that distance; indeed to feel love that had been disguised like that had since childhood given him a confidence in the power of that love, but now with his father he felt restless and alone, he was trying to understand the reason for this.

In fact he'd long since found the real reason, the disquiet that had settled into his father and Dilevser's happiness had made him anxious, the way they kept all of their uneasiness closed up inside them like a globe that didn't let out any light gave one the sense that they wouldn't let anyone in and this made him feel alone, but he was still trying to find another reason, one that had to do with himself.

He thought his father looked down on him, like all children he confused the worry his father felt about him with disdain. Strangely, when love and attachment were involved, his intuition lost its strength and keenness.

As he lay in the dark he heard the faint sound of a piano, diminishing as it rubbed past the stairs, carpets, decorations, and furniture of the mansion and almost disappearing altogether as it went through doors. A trained ear could tell from the notes it heard that it was a Polonaise and that the person who was playing it was adding their own melancholy and yearning to the melancholy of the song.

He knew how his father played the piano, this wasn't his playing, the strokes had a more feminine feeling, he guessed that it was Dilevser playing the piano. At that moment, in this city that seemed so foreign to him, in the room he found so strange, the sound of the piano was like the voice of a friend, of someone he knew. He jumped out of bed, put on the jacket he'd left on the armchair and rushed out of the room in haste, as if to be late would be to miss the chance of finding a friend he'd seen in a large crowd, a friend he'd lose if he didn't find him.

The sensation akin to panic that people have when they feel very alone, the desire to embrace someone he knew, enveloped him in a way that surprised him, he wanted to get there before the music ended, as if it would be unlucky if the music ended before he got downstairs, as if he would be trapped forever in the loneliness of that moment.

When he reached the head of the stairs the sound of the piano had grown stronger, it grew brighter with each step he descended, he could hear the youth and the anguish in the notes more distinctly, he almost ran into the living room, after he entered the living room he slowed down, he caught his breath, moved forward slowly and stood next to the piano. After looking up in surprise, Dilevser continued playing, perhaps because she sensed the loneliness in Nizam's eyes, or perhaps in fact because she was so caught up in the piece she was playing that she didn't sense anything.

By the time Dilevser had played the last note, Nizam had calmed down, as if he'd forgotten what he'd just experienced, he was quick to forget incidents that didn't please him, "too quick" according to Hikmet Bey.

As Dilevser closed the lid of the piano and rested her hands on it, Nizam said, "*Merci*, Dilevser, you played very beautifully."

Because Dilevser had no idea about the emotions Nizam

had just experienced, and didn't know why he was thanking her, she looked in surprise at her strange stepson who was the same age as her. Quickly abandoning the gratitude he'd felt a moment before, Nizam said, "The way you play seems a bit sorrowful," with the meaningful smile that spread across his face and gave him a strange allure, and that Dilara Hanım later told Osman was "reminiscent of Mona Lisa's."

She denied this so vehemently, saying "Nooo," that if she'd said, "Yes, I'm very sad" Nizam would not have been as convinced, but even more strangely, it was the vehemence of her denial that led her to become potently aware for the first time of the emotion she'd secretly been nourishing within her.

It was as if with the vehemence of her denial, the anguish that other emotions had surrounded and concealed had suddenly cracked her shell and emerged, not finding any obstacles in the darkness in which it was concealed, it had grown, become stronger, had become almost unmanageable.

Someone else might have been shaken and frightened by an emotion that appeared so suddenly like this, but Dilevser's passion for self-knowledge was so strong she examined every emotion like a jeweler, assessing its value, measuring whether its value was consonant with her own value. She lowered her head and began thinking as if Nizam wasn't there, she wanted to find the reason for this anguish, she wanted to understand its source. It was very strange, but when this young woman encountered an anguish that yellowed her face, she didn't know the reason for this heartache she'd been experiencing for so long.

"Was it very sad?" she asked Nizam.

"Yes, it sounded very sad to me."

As Dilevser leaned against the piano thinking, Nizam asked with his genial tactlessness:

"Is my father making you sad?"

"Noo, not at all, it would be very unfair to say that. On the contrary he makes me very happy, but yes, you're right, there really is a deep sadness within me, but if you can believe it I don't know why."

Perhaps it was because they were so close in age, perhaps because at that moment they felt so alone, perhaps because they sensed that they could speak to each other comfortably, a fraternal closeness between them became manifest during that brief conversation, Dilevser sensed that she could trust Nizam.

If she'd known the reason for her anguish she would have told Nizam then, but she didn't know, there was no visible reason, she truly did love her husband, and he loved her.

"Do you know what I want most?" she asked in a childish voice.

"What?"

"To become a character in a novel and to read about my life and emotions as they were written by someone else. Sometimes I don't understand anything. No one would believe it, how could I tell anyone that I don't know my own feelings, they'd think I was an idiot . . ."

She looked at Nizam and smiled, then continued.

"Sometimes I think the same thing of myself too."

"But you're not . . ."

"No I'm not . . . Well, perhaps sometimes . . ."

Nizam was also leaning against the piano, they looked at each other like two children examining the new toys they'd just received.

"What kind of woman is your mother?" asked Dilevser.

"A very beautiful woman . . ."

"I know that. That's not what I was asking. What kind of woman is she?"

Nizam took a deep breath.

"What kind of woman is my mother . . . If you want the truth, I'd like to read about my mother in a book too. When you asked me that now I realized that I don't know my mother well enough to describe her to someone else. My mother is very beautiful, she has an imposing manner, she's cheerful, it's strange, but when you asked me it occurred to me that my mother could be a very sad woman."

"Is she a tender woman?"

Nizam laughed.

"Look, it would never occur to me to say that about my mother."

"Is she stern?"

"No, she's not stern either, I've never heard her shout, she never scolded me or Rukiye, but still I'm somewhat cautious around my mother. I don't know why. There's something about my mother that gives you the feeling that if you don't make her happy she's just going to leave. As far as I can see, that's why everyone always tries to make her happy."

"Was your father in love with her?"

Nizam squinted his eyes and looked at Dilevser. Dilevser suddenly felt embarrassed.

"Excuse me, please forget I asked that, I was tactless, to tell the truth I'm embarrassed about asking that question."

"It was a peculiar question but I don't think it was tactless . . . Yes, my father was in love with my mother. What do you say, did you know that he shot himself because of her?"

"I know . . . Why do you think a man would want to kill himself over a woman, because of love, I suppose, could a man forget a woman he'd loved so much, such a beautiful woman?"

Nizam suddenly began speaking in an earnest tone.

"Dilevser . . . Will you permit me to address you by name?"

He suddenly let out a laugh.

"If you like I could address you as mother, but that would feel a little strange."

Dilevser laughed as well.

"When other people are present I would prefer you address me as mother, but when the two of us are alone you may address me as Dilevser."

Nizam became serious again.

"When I entered this house I felt a kind of peace and happiness that I never felt in my own home, there's no doubt about
it, my father was definitely in love with my mother, but he was
never happy, if he'd been happy would he have shot himself?"

"People don't just remember the people who make them
happy, they also remember the people who break their hearts.
Indeed perhaps heartbreak leaves more traces than happiness . . . Your father wouldn't have shot himself for me, would
he?"

"Would you want him to shoot himself?"

"Of course not, God forbid . . . That's not what I wanted to
say . . . Whatever, I'm talking nonsense."

No matter how much she was suffering, Dilevser would
never open up to anyone except Nizam about her anguish and
the poisonous curiosity that nourished it deep in her soul, she
would never reveal her inner feelings and her curiosity in this
manner, she would never ask that kind of question; she would
see it as an unforgiveable betrayal to speak of the man she
loved to someone else, to reveal her feelings about the man she
loved to someone else. Of course Nizam was a part of the man
she loved, but the only reason she'd suddenly opened up to
someone she didn't in fact know very well, the only reason the
anguish within her came out into the open in such an over-
powering manner, was not because he was Hikmet Bey's son.
That secret, incomprehensible communication between people, the coded information that's transferred from one person
to another without a word being uttered, told her that he
wouldn't betray her or her secret, that he wouldn't judge her
for her suffering and her curiosity.

For reasons unknown, Dilevser had heard and seen this
code, these complicated vibrations that perhaps other ears
wouldn't have heard and other eyes wouldn't have seen, she'd
decided she would trust this person on account of a brief

exchange of glances, she'd chosen him as a brother, she'd spread the questions in her mind before him.

Nizam's soul was like the closet of a wealthy woman of good taste, there was an emotion suitable for every occasion, he could find and chose the most appropriate emotion without even having to think about it. In fact Nizam could wear these emotions without actually quite feeling them. When he sensed that Dilevser possessed a much deeper anguish than she could put into words, he felt a pain and sense of friendship that was very close to the real thing, he felt a desire to help, like an older brother seeing a younger sibling in distress.

When he spoke there was a gravity in his tone that was reminiscent of his father.

"People's pasts always seem to me like a dark cave full of monsters," he said. "I think it's better to avoid entering. I don't know why, but the past always frightens me, it doesn't interest me, perhaps because I don't like things I can't change . . . Thinking about the past, wondering about it, is like taking a sharp sword out of its scabbard, someone who brandishes a sword is bound to get into a fight and someone is definitely going to get hurt . . ."

Dilevser pressed her fingers against the piano lid, she lowered her head towards the piano as if she was looking for something there, as if there was something she wanted to see, without raising her head she asked in a somewhat hoarse and bashful tone,

"Have you ever loved someone very much?"

When Nizam was faced with this question, which he had perhaps never asked himself, he seemed surprised and drew in his breath.

"Not in the way you mean, no."

"If you had, you would know that you are curious about everything to do with the person you love, their past, their memories, their future, you learn this when you love someone.

This isn't a feeling you can control with reason . . . I'm not afraid of being hurt, I'm afraid of something much worse, of embarrassing myself, but I still can't stop myself. As you see, I feel embarrassed talking even to you, and I know I'll feel much more embarrassed when I'm alone . . . I don't know, perhaps it would have been better not to have brought up the subject."

"I think you know that you don't have to be embarrassed with me."

"It's not about you, I know that I have to feel embarrassed for myself . . . I'd never have thought I'd say this one day, but at the moment being embarrassed isn't even important . . . I saw you for the first time today but I know you, I know, I've heard so many stories about you from your father, and perhaps the most significant thing for me is that you're the son of the man I love, you know so many things about him that I don't know. So many things that I've been curious about . . ."

Dilevser suddenly fell quiet. Nizam saw that the knuckles of the fingers she was pressing against the piano had gone completely white. When Dilevser raised her head from the piano and looked at him, he knew that he was going to see there, on that face, the weary expression of someone just coming to after having fainted.

The young woman felt the embarrassment and weariness that appears in people when they suffer a great deal, when they become helpless, and are surprised that they can't prevent themselves from speaking like a stranger whose behavior and words didn't resemble their own. Her face, splotched here and there with red, reflected this weariness in a pensive expression. She was looking at Nizam as if she was surprised to see him there.

In a calm voice, as if they'd never had this conversation, Nizam asked, "Where's my father?"

"In his study. I suppose he's reading news about the war in the newspapers. Go to him if you want, I'll go supervise the preparations for the evening."

As she was leaving the room, Dilevser turned back.

"Thank you very much, Nizam," she said.

"For what?"

Even Nizam hadn't guessed that Dilevser could laugh in such a mocking manner.

"For the life lesson . . ."

As soon as she'd said this she almost ran out of the room like a little girl running from a garden where she'd stolen plums.

3

E ven though he'd grown up with two women who possessed such magnificent beauty that whatever city they
went to, the entire city would soon turn to look at them
and talk about them, Nizam had been bound since childhood
not to his mother and grandmother, whose names were mentioned throughout the Ottoman Empire, but to his step-sister,
who was not as beautiful as they were and seemed lusterless in
their presence, the feelings, admiration, love, devotion and
faithfulness that he denied all other people he nourished in his
soul for Rukiye alone.

This young man, who could face even the greatest disasters
with a selfish nonchalance, without being shaken, indeed with
a mocking smile, would panic when his older sister was even
slightly upset or had a mild illness, in a situation like that he
wouldn't hesitate to travel a thousand miles just to be with her.
When it came to Rukiye it was as if Nizam was another person,
all of the feelings and attitudes he was known for changed,
even though they were aware of this they both found it natural, they saw nothing surprising or strange in it.

It was as if there was something undeveloped in Nizam's
emotions, he could manage to take an interest in people in the
place where he was, he could feel love and friendship for them,
he wouldn't even remember the people who weren't there, he
carried his feelings around like a little bag that he would open
wherever he was, then when he left without leaving even the
smallest feeling behind and then, carrying no trace or memory,

he would forget everything. He could barely feel emotions for the people who were very close to him. His emotions didn't have the strength to overcome distance and reach other places.

Indeed Dilara Hanım later said to Osman, "How people could love someone so much who loved people so little, this has always been a mystery to me."

The only exception to this was Rukiye, wherever he might be, he missed her, thought about her, worried about her. The bond between the two siblings, which made other people uneasy because they couldn't explain it and didn't understand it, was the most important bond attaching them to life and to life's realities.

At breakfast on the first morning he woke in Istanbul, he told his father that he wanted to go see Rukiye.

"Of course, my son," said Hikmet Bey. "Let's tell them to get the carriage ready."

The previous night, at the dinner at which Dilara Hanım had joined them, he had seen the friendship that was developing between his son and Dilevser and was pleased, and, thinking that perhaps this time he might be able to experience the warmth of a family home that he'd always longed for, he felt a vague gratitude to his son. And perhaps now that he was beginning to get older he wanted things other than love, he wanted a reliable peace that enveloped him, to be surrounded by people who loved one another, unhurried tenderness; what he wanted was to live within the friendly warmth of affectionate conversation, witty remarks, intellectual arguments, to leave behind the suffering, disappointments, and betrayals that had shaken his unfortunate life and to settle into the warm cocoon created by the love he felt for those around him as if he was settling into a soft bed.

The dinner had passed pleasantly despite the way Dilara Hanım, who of late wore a distracted expression during even the fieriest arguments and whose voice had for some reason become harsher despite the disappointment she'd experienced, taunted Nizam in a manner that could be considered rude.

At one point Dilara Hanım said to Nizam,

"You're a very charming young man, but I always regard charm with suspicion."

Smiling in his most charming manner, as if he hadn't noticed the sudden cold silence at the table, Nizam answered,

"What is there that shouldn't be regarded with suspicion?"

He said this with such affable nonchalance that any kind of argument was rendered meaningless. In a strange way it granted him immunity. While charming people, as Dilara Hanım felt, generally use this as a shield to protect themselves from other people and from life, one could sense that Nizam's charm didn't arise from this kind of anxiety or weakness. People thought that he could step over the edge of a cliff with the same carefree smile, that he really didn't care about life.

This strange, unfamiliar, inexplicable nonchalance awoke in every intelligent person who met him the desire to dig into what lay hidden beneath it, some tried to solve this in an aggressive manner like Dilara Hanım, some in a friendly way, some with mockery, some with denigration and some with deep discussions, but none of them reached a satisfactory conclusion.

There were those who said, "His arrogance was so great that in the face of it, not only other people but he himself was made to seem unimportant," there were those who said, "He'd never lost anything, so he lived with the luxury of not knowing that losing was a possibility," there were those who said, "For some reason as a child he rejected life from the start with a great and helpless anger," but no one was satisfied with their own explanation. Nizam didn't hear most of these things, he just smiled at what he did hear, as if he didn't even want to learn the reason he aroused so much curiosity in people.

As for Dilara Hanım, one day soon after Nizam had moved into the mansion she said to her daughter Dilevser, "You see a person's true face when they really, desperately want something . . . In order to get to know Nizam you'll have to wait until he wants something . . . If he ever wants anything I'll be suspicious of that too." Then, with a smile that had a touch of both shrewdness and femininity and that Dilevser had rarely witnessed before, she added, "Likeable rascal."

That night Nizam made everyone laugh a great deal with the stories he told at the table and the imitations he did, for perhaps the first time since Ragıp Bey left and she realized she wasn't going to receive an answer to her letters, Dilara Hanım laughed heartily and forgot, even if momentarily, the realities that caused her such anguish.

The next morning when Nizam set out to visit his older sister, he left behind three people who accepted that he brought warmth and cheer to the mansion and wanted him to return as soon as possible, but the whole way he thought only about his sister.

The streets of Nişantaşı were quiet, there were none of the crowds that smelled of death that he'd seen near the harbor, it was as if the important people who lived in this quiet part of the city had noticed the coming disaster before other districts of the city and closed themselves in, it was as if the mansions nestled in their broad gardens were peeved with the world and had cut their relations with it, most of them had only a few shutters open, the rest of the shutters were closed, the gardens were completely empty, one or two roses were visible in the rose beds, challenging the approaching winter, seeing one or two flowers in those enormous rose gardens heightened the sense that the area had been abandoned.

The trees had long since surrendered their leaves to the winds and gone bare, in a few gardens he saw round, orange Trabzon persimmons hanging from the ends of bare branches,

he sensed something anguished in the juxtaposition of the suc-
culent, appetizing fruit and the weak and helpless nakedness of
the trees. Perhaps because of the smell of death he'd smelled
and the sick soldiers he'd seen as soon as he arrived in the harbor, everything he saw reminded Nizam of death. As long as he
lived in Istanbul he would never be free of this feeling, this city
would make a place for itself in his soul together with this feeling of death.

When he reached Rukiye's waterfront mansion on the
launch that had been waiting for him in Beşiktaş, he thought
of one of Verlaine's verses that began with "the violins of
autumn," deep within him there was a shudder of death that
made itself felt like a chirping bird that had hidden itself in the
forest but whose song was heard constantly.

The moment he stepped onto the quay, Rukiye came rushing out of the waterfront mansion, she ran towards her brother,
not minding that the scarf she'd thrown over her head got
caught by the wind and slid off her hair; they embraced each
other, and remained in this embrace for a long time without
speaking.

Finally Nizam shook his older sister gently by the shoulders
and said, "If we keep standing here without moving they're
going to think we've frozen to death."

Rukiye took a deep breath, as if to say "ah."

"Sometimes I get the feeling I'm never going to see you
again," she said, "I've missed you so much."

Then she took his hand and started walking.

"Come on, walk, show them you're not dead."

They passed hand-in-hand through the well-tended garden
that implied the presence of a fastidious home owner who
could not tolerate nature's disorderliness; among privets all cut
to the same height, carefully pruned trees, rose bushes each
planted in their own heap, sweet williams, chrysanthemums,
cherry, peach, and apricot trees that, though they had lost their

leaves, seemed to possess a strange pride due to the order with which they had been aligned, and went in through the large door of the waterfront mansion. They passed under heavy crystal chandeliers and climbed broad steps covered with carpets to a living room with a bay window that extended out over the sea like a captain's bridge, the wealth and taste that was immediately apparent from the way the furniture had been chosen and placed was so familiar to Nizam that it awoke in him the feeling that he'd seen this house before.

"Your house is very nice," he said.

Then he stopped and added,

"It looks a bit like Mihrişah Sultan's house."

"Is that so," said Rukiye, "I hadn't noticed . . . But you're right, yes, when you say it, there really is a similarity . . . How is she?"

"She's as she always is, just a little older and a little grumpier . . . In my opinion she hates old age, it makes her angry to see realities she can't overcome."

They sat in the bay window over the sea on a sofa covered with Indian silk under a Polish tapestry that hung on the wall.

"Are you hungry?" asked Rukiye, "have you had breakfast?"

"I'm not hungry. But I'll have a coffee."

They were sitting side by side, Rukiye had taken her brother's hand. She was studying his face carefully.

"You're getting more and more handsome . . . So what happened, why did Mihrişah Sultan send you into exile here at a time like this?"

Nizam laughed.

"Didn't she write to tell you the reason?"

"She wrote that it would benefit you to spend some time away before you made enemies of everyone in Paris, but she didn't say how you were going to make enemies of everyone in Paris."

"You know how she loves to exaggerate."

"So perhaps everyone in Paris is an exaggeration, what percentage of the people in Paris?"

Nizam made a face like a small child and shrugged his shoulders.

"You didn't get yourself into serious trouble, did you?"

"No, Rukiye dear, I didn't get myself into serious trouble nor any trouble at all . . . Tell me, how are you, are you happy with your life here, how is your health?"

"I'm well, Nizam, I'm happy. In fact I'm so well that sometimes it frightens me, sometimes I wake in the middle of the night and pray, I implore God, if you're going to take my happiness away from me one day, please don't make me so happy, fortune is bestowing gifts upon me that I couldn't bear to lose, but I don't know why, I just get frightened sometimes . . . When I'm very frightened I go to my father the Sheikh. He's another blessing that fortune has bestowed on me . . . Now you've come, everyone I love is here."

Rukiye suddenly began to cry. Nizam hastily took his older sister's hand.

"What's the matter?"

"I'm crying from happiness, it's not something to worry about . . . I've been very tearful lately, I cry about everything."

Nizam looked at Rukiye carefully. He knew that his older sister seldom cried, that she didn't lose her nerve even in the most difficult of times, that she always believed she could handle anything.

"You've put on a little weight," he said.

Rukiye let out a laugh, her voice turned into a whisper as if the was telling a secret.

"I'm pregnant."

Nizam looked straight at his sister without revealing any sign of emotion, he was like a man sitting alone in an empty room, his mind had been drained of every kind of emotion and thought, his connection to the world had diminished, the expression on his face became vague, as if he was about to nod off to sleep; no one else could have understood what he was feeling, they might think perhaps he hadn't heard what Rukiye had said when she whispered and that there were other things on his mind. But there was a mental and emotional bond, a mutual understanding, that transcended all words, and the seeds of which seemed to have planted the day Nizam was born.

Rukiye reached out and took Nizam's hand.

"Oh stupid . . ."

For this young man, who seemed to have used his entire capacity to love with his love for one person, whose soul was darkened by a selfish indulgence at the worry that she might come to love someone else more than she loved him, no other sound, no other sentence, could have brightened his soul so quickly and cause his genial, childish smile to reappear on his face.

"When are you due?"

"There's a long way to go."

"Have you told mother?"

"Not yet."

"Are you going to tell anyone else?"

"I'm going to tell my father the Sheikh, but I want to tell him in person . . . I was waiting until I was certain."

"Do you think mother will be pleased?"

"I don't know."

"Let's see if she's pleased about becoming a grandmother."

They were talking about Mehpare Hanım with the secret sense of having been orphaned, the anger, insightfulness, mockery, tenderness, strange maturity and shared destiny seen in the children of ethereal women; how strange it was that in the misty confusion of their memories, amidst everything in that darkness that they wanted to forget, the brightest thing they saw was their mother's beauty, when they spoke of this beauty there was a pride reflected in their voices that they weren't aware of, even when they were speaking of memories that illustrated her selfishness it was as if this beauty earned her forgiveness for what she'd done.

There was something lacking in the children, perhaps there were many things lacking; in order for mothers to be able to make a place for their children they have to give up some part of their lives, they place their children in an area that has been cleaned of their souls and their feelings, she never gave them the chance to shelter there with the warmth of their bodies and their love; in this relationship it was always the children who gave things up, made sacrifices and bore hardships, in spite of this they didn't complain, partly because their upbringing caused them to see it as impolite to complain, instead they had fun mocking her in their own manner.

Now when the two of them spoke about their mother they felt a secret shame, not because of what was lacking in their childhood but because they were aware that they were uncomfortable with their mother getting older and losing her beauty, they'd substituted their mother's beauty for the tenderness that existed in other children's lives, and they realized that it was going to be difficult to countenance losing this.

Nizam asked the unavoidable question.

"Is mother getting old?

"No . . . She's as she's always been, when I say as she's always been, as if it's not old age itself, but as if the shadow of old age has fallen on her face . . . Or at least that's how I see it . . . But no, she hasn't grown old, she's still as beautiful as ever, she's still the most beautiful woman in the city."

"Mother's beauty always amazed me."

"Me too . . ."

Rukiye looked at Nizam's face.

"How strange, you inherited mother's beauty but I didn't."

"So who did you inherit your beauty from then?"

"Nobody, because I'm not beautiful . . . Thank God I didn't inherit anything from my mother, but I inherited father's wisdom."

"My father's?"

Rukiye laughed at her stepbrother's confusion, for a moment he'd thought they were talking about Hikmet Bey and had said "my father?" with an almost condescending expression.

"My father, I'm talking about my father the Sheikh."

"Ah, I get it . . ."

"Hikmet Bey is wise too. He's a strong person."

Rukiye looked at Nizam, who wasn't saying anything.

"You don't forgive him for shooting himself, do you?"

"I don't know, I've never thought about it . . . Anyway, let's talk about you . . . Are you excited about being a mother? You're going to be a mother, I'm having trouble believing this, do you know that? We're multiplying . . ."

Later he told Osman, "perhaps for the first time that day I concealed an emotion, a thought, from my sister, there were going to be a few more of us, but it was as if it occurred to me that I would be diminished a bit more . . ."

Nizam hadn't told her, but Rukiye was able to intuit her brother's feelings, she realized that he felt a sadness he was embarrassed to even admit. She didn't let go of his hand the whole time they were talking, but both of them felt that something had changed, on top of that, while this change made Rukiye happy, it worried Nizam.

A pale shadow fell on the loving relationship that had begun the day Nizam was born, and that they held so dear.

They both hoped silently that this shadow would one day disappear of its own accord.

4

Whenthe German intelligence ship SMS Loreley snaked past Topkapı Palace, the sun was rising above Çamlıca, illuminating the dark green wooded hilltops with a light that here and there turned a pinkish purple.

As this white sailing ship, which roamed the Mediterranean gathering intelligence and that looked more like a private yacht that a ship of the fleet, approached Leander's Tower, two motor launches headed out from the shore. Memduh Pasha, the Guardian of Istanbul and his aide Major Nevres Bey were going together to greet the overthrown Sultan.

Abdulhamid, who for three years had been living in exile in the Alatini mansion in Salonica, had been hastily evacuated from the mansion when the Greek army cut the Salonica-Istanbul road. On the request of the Ottoman government, he had been brought to Istanbul on this ship that the German Kaiser had set aside for himself.

Among those who gathered on the deck of the ship to welcome Memduh Pasha and Major Nevres Bey with the German captain was Major Rasim, who throughout the years of Abdulhamid's exile had been commander of the military unit assigned to guard him.

Major Nevres Bey and Major Rasim Bey looked at each other with hatred, as they greeted each other they complied scrupulously with military decorum, but if it had been possible either one of them could have killed the other on the spot, because they knew this, both of them were on guard to counter any unexpected move, neither of them took their hands away from the handles of their guns.

They felt a far greater enmity towards each other than either felt towards the Bulgarians and the Greeks with whom they were now at war. Major Rasim Bey was a member of the Committee for Union and Progress that had overthrown Abdulhamid, and Major Nevres Bey was a leading officer of a military faction known as Halaskar Zabitan. This faction supported the Freedom and Accord Party, the Committee's rival. In both the army and in politics, both groups were engaged in a desperate struggle to seize power.

In those days the Accord supporters were more powerful, there were pashas in power who were sympathetic to them, with the confidence this gave him, Major Nevres Bey was behaving with a superior air, as if he was the real pasha.

Memduh Pasha asked,

"Where is his majesty the dethroned monarch?"

This was the former sultan Abdulhamid's official title, this was how the "deposed ruler" referred to himself.

"They await you in the living room," said Rasim Bey.

Memduh Pasha took out a tortoiseshell tube that was wide at one end and narrow at the other, he put the thin end to his ear and asked again, "where did you say they were?"

"He's waiting for you in the living room, Pasha."

Holding on to his ear-trumpet, Memduh Pasha turned to Nevres Bey and asked, "where did he say?," and Nevres Bey approached the pipe and shouted into the wide end, "he's down below, commander, he's waiting for you."

"Oh, good . . . Show me the way, then, we mustn't keep his majesty the dethroned monarch waiting."

Abdulhamid was sitting in an armchair in a corner of the living room, dressed as always in a grey frock coat and a dark-colored fez he'd had brought from Austria. On his lap was one of the cats he'd brought into exile with him, a cat with soft white fur that looked like a ball of silk thread. He was uneasy, he didn't know what awaited him in Istanbul, as always his uneasiness was concealed behind his politeness. After Memduh Pasha had greeted the deposed Sultan with great respect, he told him that Beylerbey Palace had been prepared for him.

Abdulhamid frowned and objected.

"Noo, I can't live in Beylerbey Palace, I have rheumatism. It's very damp there. Let my brother be approached immediately, have the harem section of the Çırağan Palace prepared for me."

There was a strange silence.

The Çırağan Palace had burned down, but because the deposed sultan hadn't been allowed any newspapers during his time in exile he had no idea that his grandparents' palace had burned.

Nevres Bey spoke before Memduh Pasha.

'While all of your majesty the dethroned monarch's desires are sacred to us, unfortunately the Çırağan Palace burned down, at the moment it's not inhabitable. Also, the preparations for Beylerbey have been completed, in order to move someplace else now, the Sultan would have to be consulted and it would take quite some time for him to issue a new imperial decree, for your highness to wait at sea during this period would create an untoward impression. For now we are honored to welcome you to Beylerbey."

Abdulhamid objected again, and while they were talking the ship arrived in front of Beylerbey Palace, in the end, perhaps because he was afraid of the gossip that this argument would lead to or perhaps, as someone accustomed to being waited for, it would be too difficult for him to wait in the middle of the sea for an order from the palace, the deposed sultan said "Fine."

The two wings of the huge palace door that faced the sea

suddenly opened, on the quay and in the palace gardens, officers were issuing commands in loud voices, soldiers ran here and there, pressing their rifles to their bodies.

Abdulhamid, two imperial consorts who were the mothers of his children, his youngest son Abid Efendi, and his white cat boarded Memduh Pasha's launch and went ashore. The launch went back to the ship to get the women from the treasury, the overseers of the female servants, and other staff.

Abdulhamid had aged during the years he'd spent at the Alatini mansion in Salonica, indeed his body seemed to have collapsed into itself, but now he seemed to have become younger and more energetic, indeed he seemed taller. The extreme respect shown to him by Memduh Pasha and Major Nevres Bey had alleviated his uneasiness; a combination of factors, the Committee members who had overthrown him being driven out of power, the presence in the government of pashas who sympathized with the Accord supporters and being welcomed in Istanbul with such respect after three years in exile had given him new hope. Hope had suddenly made the aging sultan younger, had straightened his back and quickened his step.

While his things were being moved, the deposed sultan wandered around the palace where he would spend the last portion of his life, issuing orders to everyone about where and how everything should be placed, taking measures against the possibility of any kind of raid by having himself and his consorts installed in the rooms that were most difficult to reach. The first order of business was to have all the doors to the stairs leading to the upper floors locked.

After passing through wide halls decorated with gilding and gold leaf and hung with enormous paintings by Aivazovsky and entering the Arabesque Hall, Abdulhamid suddenly stopped in terror, after staring at the magnificent chair for a long time he suddenly shouted, almost in fear.

"Remove this chair at once . . . Immediately, immediately . . ."

As everyone looked at him in surprise, he stamped his feet and continued shouting.

"Put it somewhere no one ever goes. And under no circumstances is anyone to sit in it."

They immediately ran and lifted the chair and put it behind the stairs in the *selamlık* hall.

Abdulhamid's Istanbul adventure began with these screams echoing off the palace walls.

A week after he moved into the palace, when Major Rasim Bey was visiting his old friend Hikmet Bey, he laughed as he told the story.

"I was curious so I had it looked into," he said, "It seems that Abdulhamid's uncle Sultan Abdülaziz, who was killed, used to sit in that chair . . . I don't know, did he sense that the chair was unlucky, or was he terrified because he remembered what had happened to his uncle and he started shouting as if he'd seen the devil."

"How did our former sultan behave after he was deposed and sent into exile," asked Hikmet Bey.

"He's a difficult man to describe, my friend, on the one hand he's a polite man, but I think it's a fake and condescending politeness, he says the same things to everyone. 'You've pleased me very much,' but it's such an unaffected falseness that it's become a part of his nature, so I can't really call it falseness . . . I saw him when he was in exile, when he had no power, I don't know what he was like when he was on the throne, but it seems to me as if in some respects he was the same . . . For instance he often likes to seem as if he's the injured party and say, 'Oh, what I've suffered,' sometimes his eyes fill with tears when he talks about the children he lost . . . He complains about the conditions . . . He sees being deposed as a great injustice, but he'll never get into an argument about his brother on the throne or about the Committee, I think that as someone who's been in power he knows how dangerous this can be. If the subject comes up he just says that he has no demands or complaints."

Rasim Bey paused and laughed.

"He's very interested in the art of medicine, he's always prepared to recommend medicines to everyone, do you know that every morning he prepares a list of what foods are to be cooked that day and sends it to the cook. And he'll talk about the benefits of each of the foods he's chosen. He had long conversations with the doctor . . . On the one hand you see a sick old man, but on the other hand you see a man who ruled an empire for thirty-three years, how can I put it, you can feel the power that's in his very bones . . . Our medic once said that he was 'A tortoise with a dragon concealed deep within' . . . But he doesn't give himself away easily, you can't say he's that kind of man. For instance he's fearful, yes, he's always thinking he's going to be killed, but I happened to have been present when he thought he was facing what he feared, he didn't show any sign of fear, at times like that he asks questions, he tries to understand."

"How is his conversation?"

"Well he really loves to chat, he goes on and on, but he's not boring . . . If you ask whether it's entertaining, well, it's not entertaining but he gets you to listen to him. I've never heard him make a witty remark, nor can I say I've ever heard him laugh at a witty remark, if you want to know the truth, in three and a half years I never saw him laugh. Perhaps he laughs in the harem with the ladies, but I doubt if he laughs there either . . . It's as if he doesn't know how to laugh."

Hikmet Bey was truly surprised.

"He doesn't know how to laugh?"

"It really seems as if he doesn't, my friend, that's what I tend to think."

"You've described a pitiful old man."

"The person I've seen is like that, he isn't ruthless the way he was on the throne, he has no chance to be ruthless now . . ."

"I get the feeling that you're not as angry at him as you used to be, I don't know, I could be wrong . . ."

Rasim Bey stopped and thought.

"When you said that just now . . . Do you know what I suddenly realized, my friend, for years I haven't weighed my feelings about this man, I was so sure I was very angry with him . . . But when you said that . . . I don't like him, it's not possible to like him, but I suppose you're right, I don't carry the same anger I used to . . . Look, I'm confused now . . . What games people's feelings play, they change without you even knowing, you don't even sense it . . . I never saw him when he was on the throne, we knew about his cruelty and tyranny, the way he censored the press, the letters of denunciation people had to write, the spies, we knew about the young lieutenants who were sent into exile in the middle of nowhere, it was impossible not to be angry. Anyone who didn't rebel wasn't a human for me, I still feel the same way . . . But when you meet a man like that after he's lost power, at first you approach with the anger you think will never abate, then day by day he turns into a sick, grumpy, helpless old man . . . You're right, my friend, my old anger is gone . . . Indeed perhaps I even feel sorry for him . . . For instance now I don't feel the hatred for him that I feel for the Halaskar Zabitan and that dog Nevres who boarded the ship so pompously."

Just then a footman came in, Hikmet Bey tried to let him know he was annoyed by asking "What is it?" and the footman, with that strange intuition seen in those whose lives and futures are dependent on other people's decisions, sensed that his master was annoyed, and said in a voice intended to appease Hikmet Bey:

"Dilevser Hanım ordered me to light a fire in the fireplace, sir, her ladyship said that the weather is getting cool."

"Go ahead and light it," said Hikmet Bey with a smile.

Every time, the tenderness shown to him by this young woman who was young enough to be his daughter, this scrupulous care, the way she tried not to show herself as she moved around him and tried to protect him; this feminine, almost maternal concern he hadn't received from his mother or his first wife, touched the same point somewhere within him that he couldn't name, causing him to feel greater tenderness for his young wife than she felt for him.

The unique love of the one who is to be protected making an effort to protect, the maturity that love creates in a young person, the effect that this brought about in Hikmet Bey's soul, the least known of the varieties of love that people experience, a love that has its source in tenderness and that is nourished by tenderness and affection is made greater every time. Every time he experienced this emotion he thought of the Persian folk song he'd liked so much when he was young, "Both my remedy and my affliction," the little lady he was willing to give his life to protect was trying to protect him. She was both the protector and the protected.

"I've also experienced the most savage, torrid, and bitter loves," he said to Osman once, "though people look down on tenderness, I realized that this too is a kind of love, and you can be sure that tenderness possesses power enough to create its own passion, its own fire. Especially if it comes from a place you never hoped it would come from."

A wind that Osman described as "irritable" was shaking the falling evening and rattling the shutters, the dry, thick-veined leaves that had accumulated on the ground were swept up by the wind and plastered against the windows. The flames of the fire that the footman had lit in the fireplace grew as they moved to each of the logs in turn.

Hikmet Bey looked at his friend who used to secretly translate French brochures and send them to him when they were working together as clerks at the palace, it had been a long time since they'd seen each other, but their friendship, the brotherly closeness that came from having embraced the risk of death together, continued. Major Rasim Bey was still a keen Committee member, he preferred to ignore the despotic acts his brothers in arms had committed during the brief period they'd been able to seize power.

"You were talking about the Halaskar Zabitan," said Hikmet Bey.

Rasim Bey was staring at the fireplace, lost in thought, when he heard Hikmet Bey's voice he said "Yes" and pulled himself together.

"You're not going to believe this Hikmet Bey, but the officers at the front are split, I know the hatred they feel for each other firsthand, it's stronger than the hatred that's felt for the enemy. These Accord officers hang prayers on the walls of their offices, they have prayer rugs on the floor, they stop fighting in order to pray. There's a place for everything, brother, you don't need weapons at the Kaaba or prayer rugs at the front . . . They've forgotten about soldiering, they're only concerned about politics and religion. And they're cowards, my friend, I think this is what makes me the angriest, they pray so much, but when it comes time to go to the front they drag their feet. Whenever there's a dangerous mission the commanders look around for a Committee officer, and rightly so . . . Look, you can say what you want about Committee members but you can't question their courage, I've never in my life seen a Committee member who would hesitate for a moment to go to his death for the nation. If I did, I would shoot him myself."

In a soft tone, making an effort not to be offensive, Hikmet Bey said,

"Rasim Bey, don't take offense, but I've come to think that the Committee isn't the answer . . . I believe that you have to test people with power and money . . . . Yes, by God,

Committee members are courageous people, I've never seen a coward among them, but during their brief period in power they didn't give me any sense of security. Being in power drove them mad, they became greedy for money, they were cruel and despotic . . . So, if you ask me whether the Accordists are better, no, they're the same, we've seen what they're like too . . ."

Hikmet Bey leaned towards Rasim Bey as if he were telling him a secret.

"The real issue, Rasim Bey, is that none of them are any good. We've seen both of them, they're both just as bad and they're going to get worse, in the end one of them is going to seize power, then God pity this nation. Right now neither of them are very powerful, perhaps this is for the best but it's not going to stay that way, we both know that. What's going to happen if one side seizes power completely?"

"You know that the Committee's intentions are sincere, are any of us on the wrong path, yes there are, but we'll weed them out . . ."

"I no longer have any confidence. Sometimes this nation seems cursed to me, it's been subjected to affliction, pain and tyranny, I don't know why and I haven't come across anyone who does but this way . . . It won't be easy to get rid of corruption and tyranny in this nation."

"Don't be so pessimistic, my friend . . . What do we have left if we lose hope?"

Hikmet Bey nodded sadly.

"Nothing is left, Rasim Bey, nothing at all. There's nothing left anyway . . . I squandered my youth on a dream . . . It's very difficult to say this, to think this, but it's the truth. It's the reality of these lands, how many more generations are going to be squandered and lost . . ."

"So, what are we going to do?" asked Rasim Bey in an offended tone.

"I don't know about you, my friend, but I'm going to take

Voltaire's advice and keep busy with my garden, soil, flowers, and family life bring me a modicum of tranquility. If not for them I don't know what I'd do . . . I'm a minority in my own country, Rasim Bey, I know how few people think the way I do, the masses are divided in two, they want to seize power as soon as possible and start plundering."

Rasim Bey suddenly laughed.

"Since our youth I've thought that you had a tendency towards anarchism . . . The madness of being the sultan's physician's son and joining a secret organization that opposes the sultan, pardon the expression, I mean it in a good sense, I sensed that you were not willing to fit into any mold."

Hikmet Bey smiled as well.

"I don't want there to be a mold, Rasim Bey, I suppose that's the greatest difference between me and the two sides. They're in pursuit of a mold. They think that there's a mold into which they can pour people and shape them, I don't argue about which mold is better, I'm against there being any molds . . . We started out talking about liberty, look where we've come, the choice we've been presented is to choose one of two molds. Tell me, for the love of God, is this liberty, preferring one mold to the other? I don't want to have any part of that kind of liberty."

They talked a bit about the war, the news they were getting wasn't good, the government was concealing what was really going on but the army was on the brink of defeat, both of them were genuinely distressed by this, they were deeply wounded; this defeat created in them the same emotion that military defeats create in all men, they were seized by the feeling that they'd lost their manhood. The magnitude of the anger they felt about the reasons for losing the war lay as much in this sense of humiliation as it had to do with their patriotism.

Despite Hikmet Bey's insistence, Rasim Bey didn't stay for dinner.

"You should have stayed," said Hikmet Bey, "The French journalist Monsieur Stephane Lausanne is coming, he's just been out near Lüleburgaz, we would have received fresh news."

"I should go," said Rasim Bey, "The wife will be waiting."

As they were parting, Hikmet Bey looked carefully into his old friend Rasim Bey's eyes, he wanted to see if there was a shadow of resentment there because of what they'd been talking about.

Rasim Bey surprised him by laughing, he'd understood what Hikmet Bey was looking for in his eyes.

"Why are you looking at me that way, Hikmet Bey, are you looking for a sign that I've taken offense? Is something like that possible between us? I listened respectfully to your honesty, what else could you possibly see in me except brotherly friendship?"

Contrary to custom, Hikmet Bey embraced his old friend tightly.

"Come again, Rasim Bey," he said, "Old friends are the best medicine for someone who's been wounded by his own dreams the way I have."

5

A hopeless soul seeks everywhere for the happiness it has lost and believes will never be found again, for him everything carries the opportunity for consolation, the potential to be a source of hope. Those people's searches, which they try to keep others from sensing, those who fall on a crumb of hope that others might not pay attention to with the greediness of the hungry in the hope of being filled, is perhaps the most pitiful thing one can encounter; because as they do this they're aware of their own helplessness and powerlessness, they know that they attack the crumb that others turn their backs on and belittle.

For someone like that, war was a possibility for happiness far beyond a "crumb," indeed for someone like Ragıp Bey who loved his profession and loved fighting, it was a promise of a great victory that would eliminate all hopelessness and cause all defeats to be forgotten. When the almost insane degree of courage he'd possessed since birth was combined with his desire for victory, his unit became perhaps the most audacious and aggressive unit in the entire war.

A day earlier, Ragıp Bey's unit had first stopped an assault by a Bulgarian platoon, and then, on Ragıp Bey's command of, "By God, move forward my lions," they began chasing the enemy. Ragıp Bey ran in front of the soldiers who had fixed their bayonets, moving quickly through stream beds and the courtyards of abandoned mills as they pursued the Bulgarian soldiers. Ragıp Bey's courage exhilarated the soldiers who knew him very well, they saw the chance to open a new path through the Bulgarian lines, which in that area possessed loose discipline, for the units coming behind them.

Just then a messenger arrived with an order to retreat, at first Ragıp Bey didn't understand the order, then when he realized what the messenger had said he grabbed him by the throat. It occurred to him for a moment to ignore the order, but if there was no one coming behind them, it didn't make sense to advance and put the men in danger. Despite Ragıp Bey's desire to fight and his need for victory, the only thing Ragıp Bey could do was to put the men into danger without achieving any results, and the men knew this.

He chewed his moustache and said, "We're retreating. God damn them."

When they returned to their positions he tried to find out where the order had come from, but he wasn't successful, it wasn't clear who had issued the order. It was a strange war anyway, sometimes one order came from the battalion and another from the division, commanders weren't aware of the orders other commanders were issuing.

When he entered the shack that was being used as headquarters, he told the sergeant to "bring me the cognac from my kit bag." After his years in Syria he'd made it a habit to put cognac with sulphates in his kit bag as a remedy for malaria, and even if there was no malaria, the cognac helped soothe these kinds of fits of anger.

As Ragıp Bey grumbled angrily to himself and chewed his moustache, the fighting had stopped, this war had a rhythm that Ragıp Bey had never encountered before, skirmishes began and then stopped suddenly, sometimes the silence lasted for days, then the artillery bombardment would suddenly start again. In those first days of the war, it was as if neither side had an aim, as if they were just trying to provoke each other and make each other angry.

As Ragıp Bey was irritably smoking a cigarette outside the shack, a messenger came with a brief message for him.

Ragıp, I'm in Edirne. Let's meet tomorrow morning at the headquarters in the fire station.

Cevat

Ragıp Bey was surprised by this message, he didn't understand why his brother, who worked at the Ministry of War, had come to Edirne, "Have they transferred him to Edirne too?" he wondered, then he decided that he would find out tomorrow. The officers conformed to the strangeness of the war, and most of them spent their off-duty hours in Edirne and returned to the front when the fighting started.

That night he walked around the trenches until dawn broke, he spoke to the men, looked at the dark plain and the silent Bulgarian positions, and as he held on to his fur cap to keep it from being blown away by the wind, he asked the veteran sergeant who was walking one step behind him, "What kind of war is this, sergeant, what do you say?"

For years they'd moved together from one front line to another, they'd been in and out of various battles and skirmishes, they'd seen each other's courage, they respected each other, within their superior-subordinate relationship they'd become brothers in arms, they'd developed a trust, they'd saved each other's lives a number of times. The sergeant knew that even at the most difficult times Ragıp Bey would pull his men out of danger, if it was necessary to fight he would fight to the death, and if it was necessary to stop he would stop and chew his moustache; Ragıp Bey knew that the sergeant would obey every order without a moment's hesitation, that he would carry out his duties even at the cost of his own life.

"Buffoonery, commander," said the sergeant. "If we went on the offensive we could break these Bulgarians, we can't find a pasha who has the heart to order us to go on the offensive. We go, and they pull us back. They've destroyed the men's morale, the time will come when they order an attack and we won't find any men capable of attacking. If the pashas are afraid, won't the men be afraid too?"

Ragıp Bey didn't answer him. He just smiled secretly in the darkness.

When he got up in the morning after a night of waking frequently from nightmares, he put his assistant in command and said, "I'm going to Edirne, I'll be back in the evening."

Edirne was packed with people. Tens of thousands of people had fled there from the Bulgarians. In squares, vacant lots and by the side of the road they'd erected tents made from sheets next to broken-down hay carts filled with furniture. Inside these tents, made from sheets that had ripped when the wind thinned them and that had been roughly patched with pieces of cloth of different colors, there were muddy carpets and cushions whose stuffing was coming out through holes; with tousled, dusty hair that hadn't been washed for days or perhaps even weeks, yellow faces, haggard and hopeless eyes, they shivered inside these makeshift tents that didn't succeed in keeping out the sharp cold. They wore whatever they could find in order to keep warm. There was a sharp smell of coal from the braziers that were burning between the tents. The women were waiting for the men to find and bring back something to cook on these braziers. Some of them were holding their children in their arms on the broken paving stones of the sidewalk and trying to comfort them, watching passersby as if they were waiting for someone to hand them a piece of bread. They were hungry. The men were wandering through the streets of the city like a wild herd, trying to find work, a piece of bread, something to eat, spending their days in packed coffee houses because they couldn't bring themselves to return empty handed to their wives and children.

An anguished murmur could be heard throughout the city.

When Ragıp Bey had pushed his way through the crowd and reached the headquarters, he saw his older brother, he was wearing his coat over his shoulders, waiting for him with a long face. His face lit up when he saw him in the distance.

The two brothers embraced warmly.

"How are you, Ragıp?"

"Thanks brother, I'm fine. We're fighting, that's all . . ."

"Come on. Let's find ourselves a place to sit down, have a coffee, chat a little."

As they made their way through the crowd trying not to lose each other, they looked for a place to sit, all of the coffee houses were filled with unemployed male refugees.

As they were passing the Rumeli Gazino, Cevat Bey said, "Let's go in here," they'd thought that at that hour the place would be empty but the place was completely packed and it stank of sweat and cigarette smoke. They found an empty table in the back, sat down and ordered two coffees.

"I hope nothing's wrong, brother, what are you doing in Edirne? They say that Committee members in the General Staff are being sent to the front lines, did you get banished here too?"

"What you say is true, but they haven't banished me yet. They sent me here with a committee to inspect the Lüleburgaz line and write a report about it in case Edirne falls, we're returning to Istanbul in the evening . . . What's the situation here, Ragıp?"

"Brother, never in my life have I seen a war like this, it's so scandalous I can't even describe it, first of all the men are hungry, the mess wagons don't come. Of course this undermines morale a great deal, perhaps the men wouldn't mind the hunger when they were in battle, but when they see that there's no order their confidence is shaken. We receive contradictory orders . . . Just when we're pursuing the enemy they tell us to retreat, we don't know who's telling us this or why. They say that the pashas are fighting among themselves . . . They say that in the Western army, a corps commander pulled a gun on a colonel, the fight between the Accord and the Committee has divided the army."

Cevat Bey made a distressed face.

"The situation is worse than you think, Ragıp," he said.

"What are you saying, brother, how could it be any worse than I think?"

Cevat Bey sighed, it was clear that he was hesitant to say what he was going to say.

"We've lost the war, Ragıp."

"How can you say we've lost before it's even begun? We're still here, the army is here, there's been no retreat yet . . . Why are you saying this?"

"Ragıp, Edirne could be besieged at any moment . . ."

"What are you saying, brother? Is that possible? Ever since I went to military high school we've been preparing for war in the Balkans, all of our teachers told us that this war was coming, all of our classes had to do with how this war would be fought, all of the officers were worried they'd miss this war, that it would start when they were on a mission somewhere else. How could we lose after so much preparation? We're not behind in numbers either . . . Of course we have a bit of a problem with weapons and munitions but it's temporary, we're still in the early stages, I think it will get straightened out."

"Istanbul is worse than Edirne, Ragıp . . . We didn't lose the war in Edirne, we lost it in Istanbul."

He stopped and took a sip of his coffee.

"You say we've always been preparing for war in the Balkans, what you're saying is true too, but . . ."

Ragıp Bey waited for his older brother to continue.

Cevat Bey continued in a very low voice.

"Even the plans for war in the Balkans are missing, they couldn't find the plans in the General Staff Headquarters . . . As you know, İzzet Pasha, the Commander of the

General Staff, got tired of our Enver's rebukes and asked to be reassigned to Yemen. Hadi Pasha replaced him . . . Now they can't find the plans, Ahmet İzzet Pasha is no longer around, they can't ask him . . . So, another plan could be drawn up, but Hadi Pasha decided that the war was lost before it even began. Before the war Hadi Pasha and your army commander Abdullah Pasha briefed the cabinet. Abdullah Pasha said that the army was in shambles, that it couldn't even stand up to the Bulgarians, let alone all of the Balkan nations . . . He said that if we could stop the Bulgarians at Çatalca he would regard it as a great success. And İzzet Pasha said that we hadn't been able to send even the smallest amount of provisions to Edirne, that because of problems with the regulations the supply chain wasn't functioning properly, I wasn't even able to get uniforms made for the men."

"What are you saying, brother, the barns in the villages are full of provisions, why can't they bring provisions to Edirne?"

"The barns may be full of provisions, but there's no government and no army to transport them to Edirne. Pertev Pasha, the second in command at the General staff, had a fight with Hadi Pasha in front of everyone. Pertev Pasha said we should attack and Hadi Pasha rebuked him. Then Pertev Pasha handed in his letter of resignation."

"What does the Minister of war Nazım Pasha have to say about what's going on?"

"He's a complete fool . . . When the parade officers were entering Sofia before the war he told them to have ceremonial uniforms made . . . The other officers, yes, they're daunted, but this fool has no idea what's going on. Only just now does he realize what's happened to us, if in fact he realizes."

Just then they heard the sound of shouting outside, people had gathered and were looking at the sky. Cevat Bey and Ragıp Bey went outside as well, when they looked up at the sky they saw an airplane flying over Edirne.

"Is that airplane ours?" asked Cevat Bey.

Before Cevat Bey even finished asking this question, bundles of white paper began to fall from the airplane.

"It's Bulgarian," said Ragıp Bey. "If it was ours they wouldn't be throwing paper out like this."

They took one of the papers that came fluttering down through the air. It was a notice that began, "Oh Muslims," it said that they had no problem with the people, that they were at war with the Ottoman government.

When they went back inside they ran into a young telegraph officer who had served under Ragıp Bey once, the young telegraph officer immediately snapped to attention and saluted.

Ragıp Bey acknowledged his salute, asked "how are you, son," then took him by the arm and said, "Come, you're a telegraph officer, telegraph officers hear everything, what's going on, what's the current situation?"

"The Kirkkilise area is very confused, commander . . . The Bulgarians attacked, we scattered them, later there were some skirmishes but then for some reason İbrahim Pasha gave the order to retreat . . . Our forces started pulling back . . . This morning the Istanbul command sent a telegram, they said a new attack was not possible . . . Now the pashas are trying to figure out what to do there."

"Alright, son," said Ragıp Bey, "You can get going."

Then he turned to Cevat Bey and asked, "what do you say, brother?"

"We've lost the war, Ragıp," said Cevat Bey again, "I told you, we lost the Balkan War in Istanbul, there's not much the soldiers here can do."

Ragıp Bey stared chewing his moustache again.

"When are you going back to Istanbul?"

"We're going to set out within an hour."

"I'll walk with you as far as headquarters, then I'm going

back to the front. I'm very troubled. I need to be with the men . . . Whatever kind of war this is."

As they were taking leave of each other in front of headquarters, Cevat Bey said, "I have something to ask of you."

"Of course, brother, whatever you say."

Cevat Bey bit his lip as if he didn't know how to say what he wanted to say, then began speaking.

"I know you, you're very brave, you're audacious, you disregard danger in order to perform your duty. That's as it should be . . . But this war doesn't even resemble a war . . . Of course do your duty, whatever it might be . . . What I ask is that you don't perform your duty with a courage the situation doesn't merit . . . I don't want to lose you because of the idiocy of these useless pashas."

Ragıp Bey was surprised, he hadn't been expecting this from his older brother, he didn't know what to say.

"Whatever my duty is, that's what I'll do, brother, we're soldiers, you can appreciate that more than I do."

At first Cevat Bey frowned, he was embarrassed, and because he was embarrassed he became annoyed.

There was a strong bond of love between the two brothers, even though from time to time they had differences of opinion this didn't damage their relationship, but because they'd had a military education they generally spoke not as two brothers but as two soldiers, they always maintained a distance, they didn't show their love, they believed that a brotherly warmth would be inconsistent with their profession.

"I'm not telling you not to do your duty, you know me, I would never say that, we both swore that we would give our lives for the nation if necessary, I would rather see you die than see you break your oath. I know that you would think the same of me."

Cevat Bey swallowed, then he grabbed Ragıp Bey's arm, perhaps for the first time he departed from their accustomed behavior.

"Ragıp, don't do more than what's necessary, that's what I ask of you. If it's necessary to die, then die, but if it isn't, protect yourself. Promise me this. Swear on your mother's life, if it's not necessary, and you're the one who can best appreciate this, don't show unnecessary courage . . . One person's courage isn't enough to make up for these pashas' idiocy. Everyone fighting here is in danger because of their idiocy, don't make that danger greater."

Ragıp Bey understood that his older brother was genuinely worried, that he was angry at the pashas, that he didn't want to lose his brother for nothing and that he'd been willing to be embarrassed in order to say this.

"Don't worry, brother," he said, "I understand what you said. I'll be careful."

The two brothers bade each other farewell and parted.

Ragıp Bey hurried back to the front, the officers were waiting for him,

"We've received an order, we're moving towards Kirkkilise. They're sending a reserve unit to replace us here."

"When are they ordering us to move?"

"Within two hours."

"Start making preparations immediately."

"We've already begun, commander."

Two hours later Ragıp Bey's unit left Edirne and headed for Kirkkilise, where the skirmishes had intensified.

They were the last unit to leave Edirne, two days later Edirne, and the 30 thousand soldiers in the city, fell under siege, they resisted to the end with a rarely matched valor in military history's last fortress battle.

After a fast-paced march, Ragıp Bey's unit reached Kirkkilise in the middle of the night.

He didn't know that he was going to experience the most terrible night in his military career.

6

As always, when she passed through the *tekke* gate and entered the courtyard where the deep green of the tall cypresses and their dark shadows reigned, she felt as if she was leaving this realm, this world, and accepting the secrets of another realm. The silence, the deep peace that became larger when it was combined with the purplish shade of the cypress trees, drew one gently in and cut one off from the world, as if it was erasing all of the traces that connected one to the past; in was like a moment of birth, every time Rukiye crossed the threshold of this gate she was seized by the feeling that she was being reborn.

The dim courtyard was empty.

Sheikh Efendi greeted Rukiye in front of the *zikr* room.

As always he was dressed completely in black, the skirts of his long cloak reached his heels, the black, broadcloth hood looked like part of his long, glossy hair.

He held his daughter's hands and looked at Rukiye's face.

"Did you bring good news?"

Because of the traits shaped by her nature and the style in which her step-grandmother Mihrişah Sultan had raised her, Rukiye was a coolheaded, confident woman who was strong enough to make decisions on her own, she was not easily influenced, she had the capacity to see solutions to the problems she encountered before everyone else, and she possessed a decisiveness that got her into action immediately. She didn't have the striking, seductive beauty that her mother and step-grandmother had, but people who encountered her frankness, her character that never allowed her to stray from the path she knew was right, and her bright intelligence quickly fell under her sway. In these respects she had more of a resemblance to her father Shiekh Efendi.

Without realizing it she found other people a bit feeble, she was quick to see their weakness, the disdain that she concealed beneath a distant politeness kept people from coming too close to her.

There were only three exceptions in her life, there were three men she set apart from all other people. The great love she'd felt for her brother Nizam from the day he was born, a love that was tolerant of every kind of weakness and that always strove to protect him; the passionate love she felt for her husband Tevfik Bey, a love that brought out all of her femininity and that made her a real woman; as for her father Sheikh Efendi, she was bound to him by the way he made her feel weak and the elation of surrendering to that weakness.

When her father asked "did you bring good news" in his deep, calm voice as if he already knew the news she was bringing, she allowed herself to be swept away by the soft vortex of time made up of the shadows of the cypress trees and became once again a little girl in her maroon abiya. She abandoned herself to her weakness with the happiness of those who weary of their own strength and let themselves go when they're with someone they can trust. It was as if one door after another had opened within her and all of her emotions had been transported to the last closed room in the uttermost depths.

She started to cry. She didn't know why she was crying, but at that moment she wasn't curious about why.

Sheikh Efendi gently took his daughter's head and rested it against his shoulder. Father and daughter remained standing like that for some time in the shaded and silent garden, then in a somewhat bashful and pampered voice she said,

"I'm going to have a child."

"May God destine it to have a fortunate life, my daughter, I'm very pleased."

Later Rukiye said to Osman, "do you know that shadows have a smell? Shadows have a smell, cypress trees have one smell when they're in the sun and another when they're in shade, I think the fragrance in that *tekke* courtyard came from the shade, it's strange, it's difficult to describe, but that fragrance never leaves a person's memory . . . It was a sharp, somber, bitter green smell with thick brown veins . . . A smell that made one feel death and life at the same time . . . In fact there were many times when I thought that everything there, all of the trees, flowers, shadows, that unique fragrance, were bestowed on the *tekke* in order to complete my father the Sheikh's existence."

The courtyard really did have a smell of its own, a smell that reminded those who entered that they were in another realm and that cut them off from everything else.

Added to this smell was the smell of laurel, which seemed to come from Sheikh Efendi's skin.

Rukiye's head seemed to be spinning from excitement, enthusiasm, the shadows and the smell, Sheikh Efendi said, "Come, let's got inside, it's cool out here, you mustn't get cold."

They went in and sat on a sofa covered with carpet, they brought Rukiye honey sherbet.

"How is your husband?" asked Sheikh Efendi.

"He's well, he kisses your hands."

Sheikh Efendi, who received news from every part of the empire and who knew everything, said,

"Your husband has a very hazardous job," he said. "If we think about what's going to happen and what could happen . . . I fear that harm might come to him. They're fighting for power like ferocious herds, but nobody is in power. Under these conditions, having a position like that in the Grand Vizier's office looks to me like cause for concern . . . Perhaps, I'm saying, if he were to resign, if you were to get out of the country for a while, you're accustomed to Paris, Mihrişah Sultan is there as well, you could give birth to your child there, then come back later when things calm down."

Rukiye was surprised to hear Sheikh Efendi, who always wanted her to be near him, tell her to "get out of the country for a while" . . . That evening when she told her husband, who was an official at the Grand Vizier's office, Tevfik Bey laughed.

"That's the way fathers are, Rukiye dear, whether they're sheikhs or porters . . . they're always a bit worried . . . What could happen to me, I'm an official there, I'm not involved in politics, and anyway what would happen if I was? The problem won't get as far as a clerk in the Grand Vizier's office, don't worry at all, my dear wife."

It embarrassed her to be worried in front of her husband, she didn't insist any further, later when she remembered that day she would sigh deeply and say, "Oh, oh, it all happened because of me, my father warned me, he told me, I should have listened to him, I should have insisted, it was because of my pride, I didn't insist because I was embarrassed to look like a worried woman who didn't know anything . . . My pride cost a life and caused a disaster."

After expressing his worry about her husband, Sheikh Efendi asked questions about his daughter's health. At one point he smiled.

"I've seen many pregnancies and witnessed many births, but I panic every time, especially because you're my oldest child, I didn't know at that time, when your mother was giving birth to you I was so frightened . . . Every birth is a miracle, my daughter. Every birth is yet another proof of God's existence. Every pregnant woman carries a part of our Lord, each time, each of you brings the good news of the creator."

The he stopped and thought for a moment.

"That means you're going to be a mother . . . God willing, your child will be fortunate, may God destine a fortunate life."

Rukiye looked at her father, she'd spent her youth hating him, then one day she'd come to face him, to belittle him, to hurt him, to take the pain she'd experienced out on him, and she'd left him feeling admiration, love, and the delight of having found her father. She'd never seen such a simple, pure and genuine power, he had disciples throughout the empire, even sultans paid homage to him, he stood like a mountain, he wasn't affected by his own power, by the veneration he was shown, or the hatred that some secretly felt towards him, he only wanted to please the Lord he believed in, he lived as if he was in his presence at every moment, he tried not to make his creator ashamed.

Once Rukiye said to Osman, "I've never been able to decide whether it was great humility or great pride for him not to recognize any power but God, not to bow before anyone else, to fear no one else, to pay attention to no one else's commands." It was as if not recognizing any power but God made Sheikh Efendi a part of that power. One summer day months earlier when father and daughter were walking in the *tekke* garden amidst the cool smells of the Golden Horn it was as if Sheikh Efendi sensed his daughter's thoughts.

"Humanity was created with weaknesses," he said, "None of us are different from anyone else with regards to weakness, what is it that makes us different, what strengthens us, what protects us from weakness, it's our faith, my daughter, the faith we feel in our creator, the confidence, the surrender. You need to know this well, the degree to which you accept your powerlessness in the face of that magnificent power is the degree to which you will be powerful in this realm. I feel sorry for those who don't accept their powerlessness, no one was created with enough power to rise on his own above the weaknesses that his nature possesses, to say that I'm powerful is in fact to say that I'm helpless, it means I have no friend to protect me from myself, I have no defender, no one who loves me, no one I love. Those who don't bow before the lord bow before humanity. However much you bow before the Lord, you will stand tall before humanity."

He fell quite for a moment, looked at the willow trees whose branches bent down towards the sea, he sighed, it happened like this every time he spoke this way, he thought of his great sin, his great shame, the sensual love he'd felt and couldn't suppress when he first saw and was smitten by that woman of such exceptional beauty; he thought the great love he felt for "that woman" was a weakness, he couldn't forgive himself for allowing his soul, which he was supposed to surrender entirely to the Lord, to become so entangled and to suffer because of the influence of a woman.

"Never look down on the weaknesses that are part of a person's nature, my daughter, you must know humanity's greatest test is within, against oneself. Your enemy is yourself . . . No one else. Be careful not to underestimate your enemy, you carry it within, within your soul, within your flesh, when someone comes against you, you see them, you know them, you can be prepared, you can take precautions, but how are you going to see what comes from deep within you, how are you going to take precautions, by the time you notice it, it's far too late, it has already taken you over . . . You must shelter in the Lord not from others but from yourself, you must say, Lord I have taken shelter in you, save me from myself."

He pointed to a wooden bench beneath a cypress tree and said, "Come, let's sit here." Then he continued.

"I never fear anyone as much as I fear myself, what can they do to me, there's nothing to fear in death, the dungeon or poverty, in this transient life you live whatever you're going to live, none of it can make you ashamed. People can only be shamed by themselves. There's no one who can shame you before the Lord except yourself. When one day we reach the hereafter and are in his presence, on that judgement day who else but you is going to hang your head in shame, who else's actions are going to make me feel ashamed . . . I'm not just afraid of being ashamed, my daughter, I'm afraid of being shamed before the Lord, I'm afraid of not being able to carry the flesh he gave me in a manner worthy of him."

As always happened, at one point in his talk Sheikh Efendi became pensive, as if he was talking to himself, when he was in this mood his talks became more effective.

"Mankind is full of contradictions, whatever kind of feeling you have within, the opposite also exists. People are always confused, why is the humanity that God created so full of evil . . . There's nothing to be confused about, raise your head and look around at nature, all of the greenery, look at all of the animals, look at the heavens, the mountains, the plains, the streams, the oceans, in all of this magnificent variety that God almighty created, humanity is the only one that was granted intelligence. Why would humanity feel the need for intelligence that an animal has no need for, why did out Lord give people intelligence? You don't find contradictions in animals, their desires are simple, the means of satisfaction are clear, it has no room for preference. Why should it feel the need for intelligence? It has no choice, but it cannot take the created world one step further than it was as it was created . . . If it has no need for choice it has no need for intelligence, if it has no intelligence the world can't go beyond what it was when it was created, whatever my Lord created would remain as it was . . . My Lord created animals but didn't add anything of himself, he created humanity and gave it a part of himself, and I created you, he said you create as well . . . Intelligence is the capacity to choose, my daughter, in order to have this capacity there must be possibilities, contradictions. Contradiction is the reason for and the price of intelligence. The choice we invariably have to make between good and evil is the reason for and the price of intelligence."

He bowed his head.

"We can't always make the right choice. Not because of a lack of intelligence, my daughter, but because of the strength of our weaknesses. And this is what makes us feel ashamed . . . When a person can't find the strength to overcome a weakness, he always feels ashamed. He's ashamed before his Lord, he's ashamed of himself . . . For someone who is self-aware, there is no punishment greater than shame in the realm of this world."

As she remembered this talk he had given her once, Rukiye was brought back to the present by the sound of her father's voice.

"Drink your sherbet, my daughter," he said, "you suddenly became so pensive."

"I'm sorry, sir, I was lost in thought, when you spoke of a fortunate child I remembered something you said once . . ."

Without saying anything, Sheikh Efendi reached out and stroked his daughter's hair.

"Have you told your mother?"

When he asked this she saw the smile on his face, she realized he was imaging Mehpare Hanım's reaction when she learned that she was a "grandmother." It was as if there was a revenge in that smile, as if there was a delight that this woman whose beauty had left him in love and ashamed was getting older . . . When she looked again to make sure, that smile was gone.

"No sir, I haven't told her yet, I'm going to go to my mother after I leave you. I'm afraid she's not going to be as pleased by the news as you are."

"Is that possible, my daughter? Don't think that, she's going to be very pleased as well."

"I don't know, I just can't think of my mother as a grandmother, or rather I can't imagine her being able to think about it . . . As you know, my mother is very proud of her beauty, being a grandmother will be like a foretaste of old age, and she hates aging."

Sheikh Efendi walked his daughter as far as the *tekke* gate, when she looked at her father one last time before getting into the carriage, Rukiye could have sworn that behind his usual sorrowful expression there was a roguish smile dancing on his face like little spots of sunlight.

From the *tekke* in Unkapanı to her mother's mansion in Şişli they passed military units that were having difficulty walking, patients lying in courtyards, and the smell of caustic lime and sickness. From time to time she parted the curtain and looked out of the speeding carriage, and each time she felt pain and distress in her heart. The thought of bringing a child into the world at a time like this worried her as much as having to give her mother the news. The further they went from the *tekke*, the more the confidence her father had given her diminished.

Mehpare Hanım was very beautiful as always, it seemed as if the skin in the corner of her eyes had become thinner but there were no visible wrinkles yet, all that could be seen was a transparent thinness that announced that wrinkles would now soon appear, or rather it could be sensed. Rukiye thought that those wrinkles would not do anything to diminish her beauty.

She was wearing a dark blue dress that came down to her ankles and she'd tied her hair up in a bun. Over the dress, near her elbow, she wore a single gold bracelet, about the thickness of a finger, with a diamond set into it.

While she was still kissing Rukiye she said, "I hope it's good news, I've been curious ever since I received your message that you were going to give me some important news."

"Let me catch my breath, mother, I'm going to tell you, after all that's what I came here to do."

Mehpare Hanım was impatient.

"Tell me while you're catching you breath, don't leave me in suspense."

"I'm pregnant."

Rukiye saw the cloud she'd been expecting pass across her mother's face.

"Isn't it a bit early, Rukiye?"

"You were younger than me when you gave birth to me, mother."

"Yes, that's true . . . But still, my daughter, should one get pregnant in the middle of a war? Look at the state of this country."

"If we wait until this country gets straightened out, no woman will ever give birth, the Ottoman Empire will have no future generations."

"Whatever . . . You know best. I'm very pleased, my daughter."

She put her arm through Rukiye's.

"Come, I've had them prepare tea for you in the greenhouse, it'll be chilly outside now."

"It really is chilly."

There were purple and white orchids in a corner of the large greenhouse full of dwarf lemon and tangerine trees.

"Oh, are you growing orchids, mother, and in Istanbul at that . . . You always like to take on difficult things."

"Constantine brought them, I'm not growing them, Rukiye, how could I grow them, the gardener takes care of them, I like them, you know that I've always loved orchids."

Rukiye couldn't contain her surprise, and she asked a question that she sensed she shouldn't ask even as she was asking it.

"Are you still seeing each other, I didn't know that."

A faint flush of pink passed across Mehpare Hanım's face.

"He dropped by when he came to Istanbul at the beginning of the summer. Then he went back to Salonica . . ."

Suddenly she rushed to change the subject.

"I had them make some of those jelly rolls you like, you can have some with your tea."

When they sat at a table by the large glass panes of the greenhouse that looked out onto a large garden, Mehpare Hanım became maternal.

"So tell me . . . When are you due?"

"According to my calculations I'll give birth sometime around the middle of March."

"Are you going to give birth at home?"

"No, I'm going to give birth at the Şişli Etfal Hospital. Tevfik found a German doctor, I'll be under his care."

"Good for Tevfik, that's the right thing to do. Doing it at home with a midwife and so forth is dangerous . . . In this age people are still using midwives. Does your father know?"

"I came here from the *tekke*, I've told him."

"Hmm . . . So you went to see him first."

Rukiye had been expecting this reaction and already had her response ready.

"Getting back to the other side is difficult from Unkapanı, so I went there first and then came to you, mother."

"How is Sheikh Efendi? Is he at least happy with his Lord in that shady garden?"

"He seemed well . . . As always."

"He's as anguished as always. Never in my life have I seen as anguished a man as him, it's as if he committed a sin by being born . . . Anyway, it's none of my business anymore, let his wife think about it."

That sharp timbre in her voice, so reminiscent of a wire saw, never went away, thought Rukiye, her anger never abated. She'd transmitted that anger to Rukiye when she was a child without saying anything, the little girl was angry at her father without even knowing why she was angry, indeed she'd hated her father, for many years she'd carried the heavy load of a child who hates her father. Now she was angry at her mother for filling her childhood with hatred, but she was trying to forget this, now that she'd made peace with her father she didn't want to continue her life with a new anger.

If she were to tell Mehpare Hanım that she'd hated her father as a child, she knew her mother would say, "I didn't say anything to you," she really hadn't, but she had no need for words in order to sway someone's feelings, a glance, a sigh, a sharp swivel of her head was enough for her to shape the feelings of whoever she was with.

It was true, while she was alive Mehpare Hanım never complained about Sheikh Efendi to anyone, she never said anything bad about him, but once she said to Osman, "He was unfair to me, he always talked about what was fair but he was unfair to me, he knew he was being unfair, he made unjust accusations, he was afraid of the love he felt for me so he accused me of being unfaithful to him, I never forgave him, ever . . . I'm not angry at him because he divorced me, it was much better that way, later on I found the happiness I could never have found with him, but he didn't protect me, the man who feels sorry for a sick dog that passes in front of the gate never felt sorry for me, he never pitied me."

Knowing that this would make her angry, Osman had said, "That's what you say, but he always watched you, always protected you, he never left you in a difficult position, he even gave you the house you lived in, he made it possible for you to live a wealthy, prosperous life." Mehpare Hanım shrugged her shoulders and said, "He wasn't trying to protect me, he was trying to protect his own conscience, he comforted himself by thinking that he was paying the price for his unfairness." Then with that fragile swaying of the dead, so reminiscent of a spring wind, she smiled and said, "He never found happiness after me, he always missed me, this made him suffer a great deal, this was the price he paid. No woman ever replaced me."

They brought the tea and the hot jelly rolls sprinkled with powdered sugar on a silver tray. "Eat, Rukiye," said Mehpare Hanım, "you're eating for two now, you have to eat more than usual."

The jelly rolls were like a secret that constituted the closest, warmest and most sincere relationship between mother and daughter, these jelly rolls were not made in any of the homes of this extended family, these hot jelly rolls sprinkled with powdered sugar and filled with sour-cherry jam used to be sold in the patisseries in the district of Fatih where Mehpare Hanım grew up, they were the most secret pleasure for this woman who had an almost obscene gluttony and who ate the most select foods in the best restaurants of Europe with a lustful zest. When Rukiye was little, Mehpare Hanım would have these jelly rolls made, they would eat them together, even though they never spoke of it, it was as if they had agreed never to speak to anyone else about these jelly rolls. The only thing Rukiye remembered about motherly love was these jelly rolls, and eating them together in silence, occasionally smiling at each other. These moments remained in the little girl's mind as memories of happiness, these jelly roll rituals were the rare moments when Mehpare Hanım became a "mother" and her daughter saw her as a mother.

When Rukiye bit into a jelly roll she said, "I really do love these," Mehpare Hanım also bit into a jelly roll and smiled at her daughter. For a moment Rukiye thought her mother was going to hug her, but Mehpare Hanım preferred to remain content with that conspiratorial smile.

After they'd eaten their jelly rolls in silence, Mehpare Hanım said,

"Does Hikmet Bey know that you're expecting a child?"

"I told Nizam, but I don't know, did he tell Hikmet Bey? You know that Nizam is reticent, he may not have told him."

"So you told Nizam as well, it seems that I come last."

"He came to visit me, that's when I told him."

Mehpare Hanım looked at her pensively for a moment, then asked a question that surprised her a great deal.

"Was he upset?"

It would never have occurred to Rukiye that her mother would guess that Nizam would be upset, that she knew her son that well, her mother's intuition had caught her by surprise.

"Why would he be upset?"

Without seeing the need to offer an explanation, Mehpare Hanım gave a little smile that belittled her daughter's condescension and repeated her question.

"Was he upset?"

Rukiye answered in an almost irritable tone.

"I don't know."

Mehpare Hanım continued with the same smile.

"I'm sure he was upset, he thinks you're his mother, I don't think he ever saw me as a mother, in fact he calls me mother, but there's something that tells me he doesn't really believe I'm his mother."

"I don't think so, he loves you very much."

Mehpare Hanım didn't even feel it necessary to discuss the matter further, she just nodded her head as if she was certain of what she'd said.

"I suppose he does."

Perhaps for the first time in years, Rukiye looked at her mother carefully, she was suddenly surprised that this selfish woman who was not at all interested in the world, in people, who wasn't concerned with anyone except herself, who wasn't even capable of showing her children love, could be this aware of the truth, for whatever reason she suddenly felt a great love and tenderness for her mother.

"How are you mother? You never talk about yourself."

"There's nothing to talk about, Rukiye. For the most part I'm home, I play the piano, I read books, I make sure the house is running smoothly, sometimes I wander around in the garden, if some pal drops by from time to time I have tea with them. I'm getting myself ready for old age now."

Of all of the words she uttered, the only ones that rang in Rukiye's ears were "if some pal drops by from time to time," her mother had no "pals," she never had, she remembered the words "Constantine dropped by."

The love and tenderness she'd felt for her mother was suddenly lost, "I'm never going to forgive her," she thought, "I'll never forget the way she left Hikmet Bey and ran away. May God forgive me, because I can't forgive her."

"I'm feeling a bit tired," said Rukiye, "With your permission I'll get going. I'll come visit you again sometime."

Mehpare Hanım looked carefully at her daughter's face, whatever it was she saw there, she didn't insist.

"That's fine Rukiye, let's tell them to get the carriage ready."

When her mother said yes like that without insisting, Rukiye thought she'd hurt her feelings, she suddenly felt sorry, her feelings about Mehpare Hanım never demonstrated any stable order, they ebbed and flowed like the tides of the sea on a moonlit summer night.

"Are you all right?"

"I'm fine, Rukiye."

Suddenly Rukiye realized that Mehpare had accepted that her children didn't love her, that she would never reproach them for this, she wasn't going to try to get them to love her; she concealed whatever sorrow this created beneath the thick shell of her selfishness, adding it to the multitude of feelings she never showed.

They looked at each other, both of them could sense what the other was thinking, Mehpare Hanım took Rukiye's hand and said, "Don't be upset," she didn't explain why she said this and Rukiye didn't act as if she expected an explanation.

When she turned and looked out the back window of the

carriage, she saw that her mother was still in the doorway, watching the carriage drive off.

In her long, dark blue dress she had a celestial beauty and elegance.

Rukiye had told Nizam that she "might drop by" but she truly felt very tired, she told the driver to go to the pier.

Before she got into the launch that was waiting for her, she sent a note with the carriage driver saying she was "tired."

A strong north wind was blowing from the Black Sea, she could feel the wind on her face.

She realized that because she was pregnant, no one was going to find fault with her, she could do anything she wanted now, she wasn't obliged to give anyone any explanation.

Suddenly she was very pleased.

She put her hand on her belly, "I'm going to have a child," she murmured, "I'm pregnant."

7

Monsieur Stephan Lausanne, a reporter for *Le Matin* who had come from Paris especially to observe the war, was paying his second visit that week to Hikmet Bey's mansion. With his boundless energy, insatiable curiosity and his passion for his profession, Monsieur Lausanne spent his days in pursuit of news, going from Yeşilköy to Sirkeci, from the office of Noradinkyan Efendi the Foreign Minister to the French Embassy, from the Headquarters of the General Staff to the French warship Gambetta that was anchored in the Bosphorus, then in the evening he sent whatever news the "censors" allowed him to send to his newspaper from the Galatasaray post office.

There was no news for him to find at Hikmet Bey's mansion, but there was someone there who seemed to interest him more than news: Dilara Hanım.

Hikmet Bey had been introduced to Monsieur Lausanne by an old friend from the days when he worked as a clerk at the palace, Hikmet Bey had been interested by his detailed knowledge about the war, by the way he could speak fearlessly about what he knew because he was not an Ottoman citizen, and the poignant stories with which he livened his talk, so he invited him to dinner.

Dilara Hanım's presence at that dinner had exhilarated Lausanne, he poured out all his intelligence, talent and experience with a hasty ineptitude that wouldn't have been expected of him. The ladies concealed their smiles and bent their heads to their plates, Hikmet Bey and Nizam looked at each other.

The only guest who behaved as if she didn't understand what was going on was Dilara Hanım, she made it felt that she enjoyed this overly rich conversation, and she also provoked the French journalist with her little gibes.

Dilara Hanım was not a woman of striking beauty, but with her brilliant intelligence, her mocking manner, her deep knowledge, and her sharp political attitudes she soon had the men she met under her sway. Those who didn't know her and didn't realize that this freedom that seemed so inviting had its source in a healthy confidence, she had a surprisingly easy manner. She didn't hesitate to clash with men who wanted to show off, she always made her adversary back down, those who truly possessed the intelligence they thought they did would elegantly accept defeat, those who weren't intelligent enough to do so became the target of insulting mockery.

Her beauty became apparent when you noticed her intelligence, men would see the luster of her luxuriant hair, the broad forehead that looked like a layer of ivory, her shapely lips and her large eyes in the light of her intelligence, with her every word, her intelligence made her more beautiful like a magical elixir sprayed on her skin.

For men she was a large chateau with a broad garden from whose courtyards the sound of music could be heard, they enter the garden easily, without any hesitation, they're confident that because they were able to get into the garden they can also get into the chateau, they would come as far as the walls and see that the chateau had no door. This was a chateau that had no door, only secret passages, Dilara Hanım only opened these passages for those who possessed a powerful enough intelligence to surprise her, and these were very few, or for those like Ragıp Bey who possessed an almost fatal courage.

Sometimes these secret passages were opened for reasons that no one knew and an ordinary person was allowed to enter, those men would leave within a few days and be forgotten, and for the rest of their lives they would curse their desire to explore that chateau. Perhaps even Dilara Hanım herself couldn't have explained why she chose which man for these small and unimportant adventures, these choices were determined more by Dilara Hanım's mood of the moment than by the man's qualities. When she wearied of her own strength or of her loneliness, ordinariness was a consolation.

After his first visit, Monsieur Lausanne, with that strange initiative particular to journalists that leads them to believe they can do anything, managed to get Hikmet Bey to invite him a second time.

On his second visit, feeling the need to conceal his interest in Dilara Hanım with politeness, he came with a French lady whose husband, who had worked at the consulate, had died and who had remained in Istanbul rather than return to Paris.

She was a small, calm lady who laughed politely at jokes and didn't draw much attention to herself, no one saw in her anything worthy of attention, but Nizam, with his eerie animal instincts, caught the scent of something strange about Madame Cheriz that he couldn't put into words. Later he couldn't explain how he had sensed this, "I don't know," he said, "I may have sensed it from the way, at dinner, she looked around at everyone without raising her head."

As for Dilevser, she told Osman that, "life always frightened me. Sometimes I saw life as a monster who had hostile plans, you don't even know what it is, a minor coincidence, sometimes a word, sometimes a glance, life drags you into an adventure so different from anything you'd guessed . . ."

That evening Monsieur Lausanne had more self-control, he was talking about what he'd seen of the war.

"Thousands of soldiers are coming from Anatolia every day. They muster them in Yeşilköy and send them to the front . . . Yesterday I went to Yeşilköy, Napoleon said that mud was the fifth weapon, he should have come and seen the mud here. The roads are frightful, the carriage got stuck in the mud four times . . . I spoke with the soldiers there. Their morale is good, there was a private from Ankara, his daily wage was three *kuruş*, I asked him what he'd left behind that he missed most, he said musicians. 'We're going to get the Bulgarian girls in Sofia to dance.' I suppose he liked to dance . . . There are soldiers of all ages. I got the sense that they'd brought whomever they could find, but I don't know if that's true . . . I can also say that they keep that multitude of men under tight discipline."

At one point he talked about how much he admired Hagia Sophia.

"When I went there the soldiers had taken off their shoes and were washing their feet in the fountain in front of Hagia Sophia. Why were they washing their feet there?"

Hikmet Bey smiled politely.

"They were performing their ablutions. Moslems wash themselves before worship."

"Hm . . . The interior is very beautiful. Of course they've plastered over some of the frescoes, but they've maintained Hagia Sophia very well . . . They had straw mats spread on the floor. A soldier was reading the Koran aloud, it was very moving. Anyway, Istanbul is a very impressive city, a very beautiful city. I've never seen such a beautiful city."

Monsieur Lausanne liked the Ottomans, the hospitality and friendliness he'd been shown played a part in this, everyone he'd wanted to talk to had agreed, they'd spoken with him, they'd seen him as someone who could send a message to France and told him what they thought.

"I saw the Foreign Minister Noradinkyan Efendi, he said we've done everything we could to achieve peace, but if the other side wants war, what can we do, please tell your citizens that we want peace. I also saw the Minister of War Nazım Pasha, I didn't know this, but he had a military education at

Saint Cyr, he's a large, fat man, he talks as if he's grumbling, he said, 'Tell my friends in the French army who know me, tell them to support us, we deserve that support.' As far as I understand he's in favor of going on the offensive immediately, he said that if there's a right thing to do, it's to advance. He also said that courage is very important."

At that time none of them knew that this "very important" courage was not to be found in the Ottoman army at the front.

Monsieur Lausanne's strong nationalism became evident when the conversation turned to French cannons, he admired the French cannons in a manner not often seen among journalists, "French cannons will show just how powerful they are in this war, the Ottoman army had bought French cannons, but they were still in the armory on the Black Sea, the ships carrying the shells hadn't arrived yet . . . However, these cannons could change the course of the war."

In a mocking tone Dilara Hanım said,

"Your fascination with cannons makes it clear you're a child of Napoleon . . . I would have expected you to be more fascinated by pens. I hope you don't write your articles as if you were firing a cannon."

As he was reaching for his wine glass to conceal the flush on his face, Lausanne said,

"I want the Ottomans to have the upper hand. These cannons could have been very important for them."

To change the subject, Hikmet Bey said,

"There's not much news about the war in the newspapers."

"That's because of the censorship," said Lausanne, "they don't just censor your journalists, they censor my news as well . . . There's a tall, irritable censor at the telegraph office, when he comes across a sentence he doesn't like he says, 'It wouldn't be pleasant to write this' and draws a line through it."

He took a sip of wine and then continued.

"He said the same thing yesterday about a sentence I wrote

referring to the cholera epidemic in the city, 'It wouldn't be pleasant to write this.'"

There was a silence at the table, this was a reality they tried to forget, to keep the city that was writhing in pain and death from reaching out and catching them and drawing them into the same painful writhing they'd hidden behind the walls of their homes, but hadn't been able to eliminate their fear of sickness completely, they knew that the reality was there, waiting not far away like a crafty hunter. When they had to go somewhere they saw the moaning patients lying in vacant lots and the tumbrels loaded with dead bodies that had caustic lime sprinkled on them.

"I spoke to the pharmacist and had a lot of chlorine brought, I wash everything in chlorine and water," said Dilevser, "and we get our meat from the French Embassy's butcher."

As the people at the table spoke about cholera and about what had to be done, Nizam noticed that Madame Cheriz wasn't as interested in the subject as everyone else, she was playing with her napkin and staring silently ahead. Nizam didn't really care about the issue either, he was so sure he wouldn't be infected with a sickness as wretched as cholera that talking about it seemed meaningless to him.

He leaned towards Madame Cheriz, who was sitting next to him.

"How long have you been in Istanbul?"

"It's been seven years, we came because of my husband's job. After he died I didn't go back, I stayed here."

Without saying anything he remained leaning towards the woman slightly, he knew that silence was the most wonderful way to get people to talk. And his silence really was more effective in getting Madame Cheriz to talk than anything he could have said.

"My husband died in such a meaningless way that death has lost its gravity for me."

Nizam didn't say anything, he just gave her a questioning look.

The woman continued.

"One morning on the hill in front of the embassy, a hay wagon slid, I still don't know why. Claude was run over the moment he stepped out of the embassy, we died under that hay wagon."

Madame Cheriz immediately corrected her sentence, "He died, that is."

Nizam asked in genuine surprise,

"You didn't return to France?"

He couldn't understand why anyone would remain in Istanbul when they had the opportunity to return to Paris.

The woman laughed when she saw the childish look of surprise on Nizam's face.

"I suppose I like Istanbul more than you do."

"I suppose . . ."

"It's very beautiful here, this is a mysterious city. There's always a surprise here, even the streets are like that, you enter a narrow, muddy street, you turn a sharp bend, and there you see a magnificent mansion . . ."

Nizam poured the woman a bit more wine.

"*Merci* . . . To tell the truth I don't have such a wonderful life waiting for me in France, there are some vineyards in the south that belong to my family, we make wine, if I went back I was going to have to go there, my family would have been upset if I stayed in Paris, but when I stayed in Istanbul out of respect for Claude's death they were understanding about it."

"So what do you do in Istanbul, how do you pass the day? In this city there isn't even a proper restaurant a woman can go to, there are no cafes, there's no theater, there are no concerts, there's nothing. Those that do exist are for men only . . ."

"Yes," said Madame Cheriz, "There really isn't."

She picked up her wine glass but didn't drink, she just held it as if she was thinking about something, she looked at Nizam.

"I usually spend my days at home, I have friends from the embassy here, sometimes I meet them, occasionally in the evening I play games."

Nizam was suddenly alert.

"Card games," said Madame Cheriz.

"Gambler," thought Nizam.

"Are there places in Istanbul where you can go and play cards?"

This time the mockery on the woman's face was clear to see.

"Monsieur Nizam, you really don't know this city at all, this city has everything . . . I'll have to show you around Istanbul a bit."

"Please, Madame," said Nizam, "It's clear you know Istanbul better than I do."

Nizam said this in a slightly mocking tone, as if he was having fun with her, but time would show him that this city, with its soft hilltops covered in dark green woods, beautiful palaces, gardens full of flowers, domed mosques, steepled churches, that was born each morning like a miracle with its minarets emerging from the fog, had hidden sides whose darkness was surprisingly deep and impressive, that an entirely different kind of life was lived there.

The door that invited him into this darkness opened for him at an unexpected moment at the dinner table in his father's house, when he turned and looked at Madame Cheriz he saw nothing but an innocent smile. The woman had the innocence of a true sinner on her face, she never thought that what she was doing was bad, it didn't even occur to her.

Later when Nizam was talking about those days with Osman, he said with an unexpected maturity, "true sinners don't know about sin, after all this is what makes them different from others, the others commit sin knowingly and are always anxious, true sinners don't feel the slightest uneasiness."

"Fine," said Madame Cheriz, "I'm going tomorrow

evening, Come along, you can decide for yourself whether or not you were right to belittle Istanbul."

They didn't speak again for the rest of the evening.

They'd already talked about what they really had to talk about, they didn't want to spoil the effect of that conversation with any further idle chatter.

When they returned to the conversation at the table, Dilara Hanım was speaking.

"I would like to have taken part in a war," she was saying, "if you ask me, I would like to die on a battlefield. To be blown apart by an artillery shell at the moment when you've forgotten death because of the authenticity and closeness of the danger of death, when all you want is to kill and survive, one of the most beautiful deaths. In fact I've always wondered, when a person is that close to death does he have time to think about dying? It doesn't seem so to me . . ."

She suddenly became pensive.

"I'd like to have asked someone who has been to war," she said.

She'd remembered Ragıp Bey, and that he was at the front.

Monsieur Lausanne, who without realizing it had found this talk a bit self-indulgent, became irritated.

"I think you're romanticizing war too much, Madame," he said, "there's also being wounded, being crippled, being taken prisoner, hunger, sickness. A constant fear, the terrible noise of the artillery, machinegun bullets whistling over your head, facing cavalry charges . . . You're not considering all of that."

Dilara Hanım replied in a sharp tone.

"You think about that, Monsieur, thinking about those things is not for me."

"If you'd seen war you wouldn't speak like that."

"Have you seen war?"

"I have, Madame."

"What did you feel?"

"Terror . . . Terror in the full sense of the word. I don't think it's possible to feel anything else. Think about tens of thousands of people who want to kill each other attacking each other, Madame, these are people, when the war is over they walk the streets with other people, but there all they want is to kill. They blow each other to pieces. They sever arms, legs, and heads. The more they kill the more pleased they are . . . It's very frightful to see people in this state, Madame."

"I admit that you describe it very forcefully, Monsieur."

"If I'm receiving a compliment like this from you I owe it to war, I can also be in favor of war."

Nizam said with an aggressive smile,

"You were very quick to turn pro war, Monsieur."

Monsieur Lausanne was not one to quail and retreat from such a mocking assault.

"You must admit that I have a far more beautiful reason to become pro war than any war supporter in the world."

Dilara Hanım looked at Monsieur Lausanne, but at that moment she was thinking about something Ragıp Bey had once told her about war.

"A soldier," Ragıp Bey had said, "fights because he's made a promise . . . You've made a promise to protect and you'll do whatever is necessary to keep that promise . . . You die, you kill . . ."

Then he'd stroked Dilara Hanım's hair.

"If I go to war again I'll think of you . . . that I'm protecting you."

Then he grinned with masculine pride.

"Look, that's bad news for our enemies."

Dilara Hanım suddenly missed Ragıp Bey, she thought about how he was at the front, how he was in danger, that he could die, these thoughts increased her yearning, she hadn't received any answer to her letters, she wondered if he thought of her, then she saw a strange vision, she imagined that she suddenly appeared before Ragıp Bey in the trenches at night and asked him gently,

"Do you think of me, Ragıp?"

Monsieur Lausanne said, "you're lost in thought, Madame," and Dilara Hanım said, "Yes, I was thinking about what you said."

Then she continued.

"Now I'd like to go to the front to see what you described for myself."

"Once you see it you won't want to see it again."

"So how do soldiers go into battle again and again? They don't just see it, they experience it for themselves, each time they experience the same fear of death, the same desire to kill but they don't give up."

"There's a simple answer to that."

"What is it?"

"They're soldiers . . ."

"So?"

"They're different from us. They start teaching them to kill while they're still children, and they like to kill, after a time it becomes a habit, indeed even a desire . . . I've met a lot of officers who were saddened because they didn't go to war."

Dilevser suddenly sighed in a manner everyone could hear.

"This war," she said, she paused briefly and then continued, "this war isn't just taking place on the front lines, it infects every part of life, it takes everyone's soul prisoner. Everyone talks about the war, everyone wants to defeat the enemy, we want people we've never met or seen to die . . . We don't talk about literature, art or music anymore, if it wasn't for the war Monsieur Lausanne would be telling us about the latest books to have come out in Paris. We would have talked about writers, we would have enjoyed some minor gossip about literary salons, we would have talked about the latest plays . . . Sometimes it seems to me as if our souls are drying out, war doesn't just kill, it dries people out like trees. War is humanity's autumn . . . The season when we dry out, when we begin to dry out before dying."

There was silence at the table.

"You're right, Dilevser," said Hikmet Bey, "The twentieth century has started out strangely . . . This century has none of the blessings of the nineteenth century, those writers and poets have given way to soldiers. I'm afraid it's going to continue to be like that for some time. It seems as if this century is going to be too fond of death . . ."

That night after everyone left there was heavy rain accompanied by a strong wind, the howling wandered through the house, through the attics and corridors, making the lonely even lonelier, the windows shuddered from the wind and the rain, a groaning sound rose from the trees that were shedding their leaves.

Dilara Hanım was lying with her legs pulled up to her stomach, she was listening to the wind shake the house and the violent blows of the mixture of wind and rain on the windows. It was as if she'd absorbed the howling outside into herself, that howling wasn't just in her mind, she could feel it in every part of her body. There was a growing, fiery anguish and yearning within her like a pile of gunpowder that didn't explode but crackled constantly, she could feel it taking hold of her.

She hadn't received a single paragraph in reply from Ragıp Bey, even though she knew now that she wouldn't write another letter, for some reason she wanted to write, to send him the sentence that wounded her even more as it echoed within her, "I miss you . . ." The sound of the wind seemed to be augmenting her own voice, she'd even thought of persuading Monsieur Lausanne and going to the front the next day, she knew that in exchange she was willing to give Lausanne what he wanted. In order to see Ragıp Bey, in order to appear before him one night in those cold wet trenches that extended like dark corridors and ask him, "Do you miss me, Ragıp?" she was willing to do everything that Ragıp Bey would never forgive, she was willing to do anything; a vortex quickened by the rain was drawing her in, constricting her soul, creating in her a feeling that she wouldn't bear it and crumble to pieces.

She got up, wrapped herself in the shawl on the armchair and looked outside from a corner of the window, it was pitch black, the weak glow of one of the night lights that had been left on downstairs was reflected into the garden through a window, in that pale, trembling light that seemed as if it could disappear at any moment she could see the raindrops that had been swept up by the wind, she focused her eyes on those raindrops, she watched as if she was waiting to see something more than the raindrops.

Fragmentary daydreams were passing through her mind, again and again she imagined her meeting with Ragıp Bey in the trenches, she kept asking the same question, "Do you miss me Ragıp?" in her daydreams there was no answer, she just saw herself asking the question, "Do you miss me Ragıp?" then she saw Ragıp Bey appear in the rain and knock on the door, this was also a fragment of a daydream, that was all there was to it, he appeared in the rain and knocked on the door.

In her daydreams there was no moment of reunion, no embrace, they didn't speak to each other, even her daydreams did not yet dare to do this, there was just one moment when she would meet him, that was what she wanted, to meet, to see him, to know that he was alive.

At one point she caught herself moaning, "My God, my God," she was saying, there were no other words than that, that was all, just a pleading moan, "My God, my God," she didn't say what she was moaning for, what she was pleading for, she was moaning like an invalid.

She also knew that experiencing all of this pain, yearning and aguish in loneliness like a sickness was her own choice, one part of her mind had become dark and cloudy like the rainy night outside, but another part of her mind was bright and clear, she saw the truth, she knew . . . The truth and desperation that the clear side saw increased the anguish of the dark side, there was no consolation, no solution, no hope that the light side could offer.

Later she said to Osman, "No, I never said that all of this was someone else's fault, I didn't blame anyone, I was the reason for what I experienced, I always knew this, I was fond of my little freedoms, in fact compared to what I suffered they seem so meaningless, but I can get up in the middle of the night, have the fire lit, and take a bath, or I can get up early one morning and go drink tea in Eyüp Sultan, if Ragıp was here would he prevent me from doing these things, no, but he would ask questions, I suppose I gave up all of my happiness because I can't bear being asked questions, for such a small, unimportant reason . . . So many times I've asked myself why I did it, and I always saw the frightful truth, I always knew, there's no plausible reason, that's just the way it is, that's how I am, there were times when I had regrets, let me say it in a more sincere way, I always regretted what I did, but I knew this, in spite of everything, in spite of seeing it as a great and absurd mistake, I would do the same thing today, each time I would experience the same results, that's the way I am, may God curse me for being that way but that's the way I am."

In the morning the rain had died down.

Towards noon, two different messengers brought two different messages to two different houses.

The note that Monsieur Lausanne had sent to Dilara Hanım arrived with a bouquet of chrysanthemums, it was clear he hadn't been able to find any other flowers in this city at war.

The note read, "From your admirer, who for you is prepared to consent even to war."

The messenger who came to Hikmet Bey's residence brought a note for Nizam.

The note from Madame Cheriz was brief.

"If you want to come this evening be at my house at eight."

8

For days the palace chamberlain had been running here and there complaining, every day he had fierce arguments with men in flat-heeled shoes, felt jackets and baggy trousers, the kind of men not often seen around there, who came to the gates of Beylerbey Palace.

In the end Mayor Rasim Bey noticed this strange activity.

One day he stopped the man in the palace garden.

"What's going on, your excellency, you seem in a panic these days? You're getting quite a lot of visitors too."

The man sighed and shook his head.

"I'm looking for a silver Leghorn chicken. I've found a black one, a grey one, and a red one, but there are no silver ones, there's no one left I haven't sent word to, nobody can find one . . . Every day our master asks about the chickens."

"So, what are you going to do?"

"I'm going to jump into the sea."

The man said this in such a way that Rasim Bey didn't know if he was serious or if he was just complaining, he watched the man rush off as if he was worried about him.

Abdulhamid had had large bird cages built in the back garden of the palace, he'd had many breeds of chickens and roosters brought, as with every subject, he had a surprising amount of knowledge about poultry, Rasim Bey somehow couldn't grasp how he had accumulated and remembered so much information.

One day when they ran into each other by the chicken

coops, he treated Rasim Bey to a long and fiery diatribe about leghorn chickens.

"Now, no chicken in the world lays as many eggs as these, the most valuable are the silver ones, but our idiots haven't been able to find one, they can't even find a single chicken in this vast empire . . . anyone who can't find a chicken isn't going to be able to find anything else."

He fell quiet, he remembered who he was talking to, the situation he was in and that anything he said could be dangerous.

"Anyway," he continued, "These are in fact Italian chickens, the Italians developed this breed at the beginning of the last century, but in order to develop it they had to give it to the Americans, the whole world sells to the Americans . . . You know a person can't help thinking, why couldn't our people think of something like this, isn't that so, they could have made money, there would have been work for the peasants. But they expect the Ottoman state to do everything, that's what they're accustomed to, that's what we accustomed them to."

As he was saying these things he was sprinkling feed for the chickens, there was such a tender, affectionate expression on his face, he'd named some of the chickens, he called them by name, he praised and congratulated some of them for laying so many eggs, in the same way that he used to reward officials and pashas.

"This freckled one here," he said, pointing out one of the chickens to Rasim Bey, "It's the wisdom of God, this chicken always lays double-yoked eggs, in the morning I drink only its eggs, I would advise you to drink eggs in the morning too, it's good for the body, it strengthens it. And honey . . . you must never neglect that. Now I've had fruit molasses brought in, because it's so damp here the walls are always cold, you have to speed up the blood circulation, molasses is very good for this."

After giving instructions about the chicken feed to the men

who took care of the coop he said to Rasim Bey, "Come, let's have some coffee."

They went together to the large hall that overlooked the Bosphorus, next to the armchair in which Abdulhamid always sat were the newspapers he read from start to finish every morning. The lead-colored autumn sky was reflected in the Bosphorus, the sea was the same color as the sky, Yıldız Palace, where the "deposed caliph" used to reside, was visible on the hilltop on the other side.

As they were drinking their coffee, Abdulhamid began with "I still don't understand."

"How did the Bulgarians and the Greeks make common cause? Their churches hate each other. We never allowed them to reach any agreement, whenever there was a situation we needed to worry about, I would call the patriarchs of the two churches in separately. Now how did they make common cause? Oh, the ineptitude . . . When you're governing a state you have to be vigilant all the time, you have to discern your enemy's move before he makes it so you can act before he does . . . I said enemy, but you have to keep an eye on your friends too, today's friend is tomorrow's enemy."

Abdulhamid believed that he had governed the state better than anyone and that he would always be able to govern better than anyone, he always wanted to tell people this, because he was forbidden to see anyone from outside the palace, he told whoever he could, sometimes to his doctors, sometimes the officers, even the overseers from the treasury.

"The Bulgarian, Serbian, and Greek diplomats are very new at their jobs, compared to them we have some very clever and experienced men. We should send one of the experienced pashas to Europe immediately, and he should make contacts in the political centers. Some advantages must be promised to the British. At the same time we have to enter secret negotiations with the Serbians, the Greeks, and the Romanians. We have to upset the present alliance among our enemies . . . There's nothing easier than suddenly creating conflict between the Greeks and the Bulgarians. After the Bulgarians and the Greeks split, the slightest threat will lead the Romanians to change their minds about war."

He took a cigarette from the box on the table next to him and lit it.

It was clear that he was seriously trying to find solutions to these problems, as if he was governing the country again, when he spoke he talked as if he felt he was on the throne again.

"Then there are two issues. One of them is the cabinet issue. As far as I know, a pigheaded man such as Nazım Pasha is impossible, he can't work with Kamil Pasha. Today we're in fact in a state of war, but we have to engage in politics too, I see Nazım Pasha's situation as hopeless."

He inhaled from his cigarette and looked at the Bosphorus, but it was clear he didn't see what he was looking at, his mind was very busy.

"The second is the issue of the commanders. I know all of the commanders who are serving today. None of them are powerful enough to fight and succeed in today's unfortunate situation. We need more powerful and more experienced men at the head of our army. Muhtar Pasha, Ethem Pasha . . . They're very competent."

He lit another cigarette.

"What's the situation at the front? I can't find anything out from the newspapers, that's not a good sign."

"I don't have any detailed information, sir, but as far as I've heard from my friends, the news from the Kirkkilise area is not good."

Abdulhamid asked Rasim Bey a surprising question.

"Isn't the third army corps under the command of Muhtar Pasha there?"

"Yes sir, Muhtar Pasha's corps is there."

"By God, Muhtar Pasha is up to the task. He left the Naval Headquarters here to go to the front . . . And he was willing to serve under Abdullah Pasha's command. This is a great sacrifice for the nation, I appreciate it. It should have been just the opposite, Muhtar Pasha should have been in command of the army . . . For something bad to happen to Muhtar Pasha's corps would require something very strange to happen . . . I wonder what happened? You can't learn anything here. I try to find out everything from the news in the papers."

Abdulhamid had guessed correctly, something "very strange" was happening in Kirkkilise, a military disaster was occurring that would shame the entire empire and no one knew the reason for it.

"There's still no one who knows what happened," Ragıp Bey said to Osman in an irritable tone, it was clear that even death hadn't been enough to assuage his anger, "how could we have experienced a military disaster that no one knows the reason for, it remains a mystery."

The regiment to which Ragıp Bey was attached arrived in Kirkkilise towards evening, the men settled into the positions they'd been shown, Ragıp Bey was informed of the area he would be defending, he made a duty roster with the junior officers, inspected each of the trenches and assured himself that everything had been done properly.

During the changing of the guard he received information from an officer.

For the past four days units from Muhtar Pasha's corps had skirmished several times with Bulgarian units but the Bulgarians had not been allowed to advance, the units were defending their positions in a systematic manner.

There were three divisions of thirty thousand men attached to the corps and they had not suffered heavy casualties, military reports showed the death toll to be one hundred.

Muhtar Pasha inspected the forward lines in the afternoon,

after he was certain that everything was under control he went back to headquarters.

When darkness fell a sharp frost began.

There was a deep silence, all that could be heard was the occasional sentry sounding off.

The town had fallen asleep.

Until ten o'clock at night there was no sign of the great disaster that was to come, there were no enemy units visible, the corps had not suffered large losses, the trenches had been inspected, the men were armed.

The rumors about what transpired that night were different, according to the official records, cavalry units attached to the Bulgarian Third Army began a breakout attempt on the right flank at ten o'clock.

"That's not how it happened," said Ragıp Bey, "We suffered that disaster because of Rıza Pasha's poor judgement."

According to what the officers said among themselves, Rıza Pasha, who was in command of one of the three divisions, decided to attempt a sortie without informing anyone and put two of his battalions into action.

The night was very dark, the enlisted men were not accustomed to fighting at night.

Just then a storm broke out.

The two battalions started moving through the storm by different routes.

Meanwhile Ragıp Bey, in his tent, had lit candles on each corner of the little table that had been left to him by his previous commander, he was examining a map, trying to memorize the hills, stream beds, and valleys in the area, his wood stove was about to go out, he wrapped his coat around him tightly.

The sergeant came in with a bowl

"You haven't eaten since morning, commander, I brought you some soup."

"Forget the soup, find me some tea."

"Have your soup, I'll bring you some tea right away . . . Let me throw some wood in this stove, the fire is dying out, it's struggling for its life."

"Don't worry about the stove right now, go see if you can find some tea."

"Whatever you say, commander."

Ragıp Bey knew that somehow or other the sergeant would find some tea and bring it, he also knew that despite his having said "don't worry" he would bring wood and get the fire going. Whenever the sergeant believed that something would be good for Ragıp Bey, Ragıp Bey could not prevent him from doing it . . . "He'd give his life for his men, when he was trying to rescue me he took four bullets but he still came and pulled me out of hell itself," he would say to the men about Ragıp Bey, it was clear from the tone of his voice that he found something praiseworthy in being rescued by him.

When he had a spoonful of soup he realized how hungry he was, the thick soup burned his throat, it warmed him, he bit into the hardtack the sergeant had brought with the soup. After having been so hungry, the soup made him feel better.

As he was finishing the soup, the sergeant arrived with tea, every time he came in and went out a sharp frost filled the tent. After he put down the tea he went out, then came back with his arms full of wood, he blew on the fire and placed the wood in the stove.

The stove started to crackle.

Ragıp Bey had lit his cigarette, he was drinking his tea, the stove had warmed the tent. Ragıp Bey smiled and said something he'd learned from the sergeant.

"We live like dogs but we enjoy life more than the pashas do, isn't that so sergeant?"

"Damn right, commander . . . Do you have any more orders for me?"

"No . . . go on and go to bed."

"Aye aye, sir."

Ragıp Bey finished his cigarette, one of the candles had gone out, he extinguished the others, then lay down on the narrow cot next to the table, it was too narrow for his shoulders, and pulled his greatcoat over him.

The tent was shaking in the wind.

"God damn it," he said and pulled his coat over his head, this unending pain he was suffering because of Dilara Hanım was driving him mad, this was no longer an emotional pain, it was a physical ache, somewhere in his body it ached constantly, he couldn't even figure out where it was. Sometimes he forgot the ache, but when he noticed it again he realized it hadn't passed, that it had always been there and that he just hadn't noticed it.

He clenched his teeth and was about to fall asleep when he suddenly felt a shaking like an earthquake. The noise, like that of a herd of bulls charging, was getting louder. He could hear the sound of weapons.

"What's going on?" he asked as he jumped out of bed, when he left the tent he saw groups of soldiers fleeing in disorder. "The cowards are running away," he thought as he drew his pistol, on every side there were soldiers running away from the trenches.

Just then when a lightning bolt tore through the darkness, and in that deadly whiteness that smelled of ozone Ragıp Bey could see more clearly the horror they were experiencing. The sharp illumination remained suspended in the air for a moment, he saw tens of thousands of soldiers across the plain all trampling and crushing each other, rolling in the mud, everyone cursing and running madly in different directions, stepping on those rolling in the mud with their combat boots, flinging their weapons into the mud as they ran. When the lightening flash ended, Ragıp Bey continued to see the running men as if this scene was still illuminated, the scene had remained suspended in his mind.

Just as, in great anger, he pointed his gun at a soldier and moved to block him, the sergeant grabbed him by the arm and said, "Commander, we can't stop them, they're like horses fleeing a burning barn, it's as if they've gone mad, a little further along they pushed Muhtar Pasha aside and rushed past him, let them run, when they calm down a little in the rear we'll muster them again. Even the officers are fleeing. Let me find our horses and we'll follow the men."

"Why are those cowards running?"

"They say there's a Bulgarian offensive."

"Where are the Bulgarians? There's not a single enemy soldier in sight . . . I don't hear any gunfire, there were a few shots but then it stopped."

He stood completely alone in front of the tent, tens of thousands of soldiers were running towards the plains in the dark as if they were out of their minds, they ran without even knowing where they were going.

Just then he saw one of Mahmut Muhtar Pasha's aides run by with a tea set. He grabbed him by the arm and stopped him.

"What's going on, lieutenant?"

"I don't know, the army's fleeing."

"Why are they fleeing?"

"They say there's a Bulgarian offensive."

"Where are the Bulgarian soldiers?"

"I don't know, commander."

"Where's Mahmut Muhtar Pasha?"

"He rode in front of the men to stop them but they almost knocked his horse over . . . He said that if they didn't follow him he would go alone, but no one listened to him, it's as if the men have gone mad with fear."

Ragıp Bey looked at the porcelain tea service the lieutenant was holding.

"What's this?"

"It's the pasha's tea set."

"Why are you carrying it."

"The pasha likes to drink tea from these cups."

Ragıp Bey let go of the officer's arm and said, "get out of here, damn you."

As he chewed his moustache and thought about what to do, the sergeant arrived with two spare horses and said, "Let's get going, commander, there's no one else but us left, the whole army is gone."

"What happened?"

"They say that Rıza Pasha attempted a night attack, two divisions mistook each other for the enemy in the dark and began skirmishing, when the men heard the gunfire in the dark they thought the Bulgarians were attacking the trenches and they started fleeing."

"Where are they going?"

"I don't know, commander, there's word they're going to the station, that there's a train in the station and that they're going to take it to Istanbul."

"Man, how is an enormous corps going to fit in one train?"

"I don't know, commander, don't look for logic, no one's thinking logically."

They set out in the rain, the horses' legs were sinking into the mud, when they climbed small hills the horses' hooves occasionally slipped, way in the distance one or two faint lights were visible, they guessed that this was the station.

The rain began to quicken.

Suddenly they heard a gunshot a hundred yards in front of them, in the dark, the flame that came out of the barrel glowed with red sparks, when they looked carefully they saw that a soldier had shot an officer on horseback, he pulled the officer down and leapt onto the horse.

As the soldier sped away, Ragıp Bey said to the sergeant, "Shoot that lowlife, be quick, we'll lose him in the dark."

The sergeant stood in his stirrups, put his rifle to his shoulder and fired, they saw the horse in the near distance rear and neigh, and the soldier who'd been riding it fall into the mud.

As they made their way towards the station they came across the bodies of soldiers on the ground, looking like shadows in their grey coats, as they fled they'd shot each other for a horse, a piece of bread, a weapon, or a coat.

"My God, what happened to the great Ottoman army?" asked Ragıp Bey, "How did this disaster happen?"

"Fear, commander . . . I suppose they feared having their throats cut in the trenches . . . Morale was already bad, all it took was for someone to shout that the Bulgarians were coming."

When they reached the station they didn't find the crowds they'd been expecting, the men had been afraid to come to the station and had fled straight towards the mountains.

A group of staff officers were arguing with the station master, almost all of them were speaking at once, one of Muhtar Pasha's staff officers was shouting, "Get that train moving, we have to go to Babaeski to get help."

"I can't get it moving, commander," the station master was saying, "there's an ammunition train coming in the other direction, there's only one track, they'll crash."

The officer pulled his gun and pushed the station master into a corner, put the gun to the head of the engineman who was standing next to them and said, "Get the train moving at once."

The staff officers all got into the locomotive, the train started to groan into motion, in the end Ragıp Bey heard the engineman say, "We're going to crash, gentlemen."

"Get going," said Ragıp Bey to the sergeant, "let's head towards Lüleburgaz, maybe in the daylight we can round up some of the men."

They started moving parallel to the train tracks, in the dark the rails glistened in the rain.

They didn't get too far.

The ground and the sky shook, with a great crash, flames opened like a giant flower in the night, the sky became bright red, as the trains crashed the sound of their heavy metal bodies grinding together mixed with the sound of screams, wagons toppled over one after another, shaking the ground as the rolled.

They galloped their horses, and when they arrived at the flames they saw that the two trains had toppled over, the munitions in the train that had been coming from the other directions, the cannon balls and artillery shells, had been scattered and buried in the mud, with each explosion of the ammunition that remained in the train, yellow flames the color of gunpowder shot out.

They immediately got off their horses and ran.

There was nothing they could do, it wasn't even possible to approach the burning, glowing heaps of metal, an oily smell of iron spread from the burning trains.

Ragıp Bey squatted in the mud and held his head between his hands.

"Where are the commanders?" he asked as if he was complaining, "If we could find them . . ."

"Everyone's gone, commander, the army has dispersed, if God helps them the men might gather together near Babaeski."

People who'd come from nearby were trying to help the wounded. They lined up burned bodies in the mud, they were blackened, their eyes had popped from the heat, bones had melted, they'd lost their form, when they touched the mud, smoke and the smell of flesh rose into the air.

They got underway again, keeping an eye on their surroundings as they went, constantly scanning the darkness for anyone who might shoot them for their horses. The shadows were still running, in the rain the plain smelled of dirty people and cloth.

They reached Babaeski towards morning.

Some of the soldiers had come here, some hadn't stopped here but had continued to flee further to the rear.

Ragıp Bey asked about Muhtar Pasha and received the answer that, "They say the pasha has gone to Lüleburgaz." They continued on towards Lüleburgaz.

When the Bulgarian army entered Kırkkilise at dawn from four directions, they were met by empty trenches, abandoned headquarters, forsaken cannons that had been placed in position and piles of shells next to the cannons.

Ninety thousand men had fled without firing a single shot at the enemy.

They considered pursuing the Ottoman army but they couldn't catch up to them, the events were described as follows in the historical records, "The Ottoman infantry fled faster than the Bulgarian cavalry could advance."

In the Third Corps headquarters, all of the documents and plans remained as they had been.

The only thing missing was the tea set the aide had carried away.

9

N izam rang Madame Cheriz's doorbell at exactly eight o'clock, he saw that the woman had been waiting by the door and that she was ready to go out. Even though he'd arrived on time, he sensed that Madame Cheriz was tense and irritable, as if he was late.

"Come on, let's go," said the woman, "if you're hungry there'll be food there."

The woman's rudeness surprised Nizam, he'd been raised in an environment in which certain rules of politeness were always observed no matter what the conditions, and he'd been surrounded by people who always observed these rules. He came from a circle that believed no matter what the degree of your wishes, wants, anger, or fear, it must be expressed without breaking these rules of civility, even though he didn't care about any rule, he complied with etiquette, this was like a part of him, this had been well established in his soul and in his mind since childhood. In his world there were even rules about how to be rude, this was perhaps the first time he was encountering such naked rudeness.

In the carriage they sat with quite a distance between them, the woman didn't speak at all, her face was a bit tense, it was very clear that her mind was preoccupied. Nizam was accustomed to experiencing a certain male-female vibration, no matter who the woman was, when he was with a woman he always created a secret space that belonged to them alone, he always felt the sensation of being drawn like iron filings to a magnet, this feeling of being drawn did not have to achieve any result or have any aim and did not need to be accompanied by any emotion, it had to do with them feeling that they were a man and a woman. Nizam did not create this feeling voluntarily or with any particular goal, he'd been born with this strange talent, when women were around him he could feel their bodies, he emitted a current that constantly reminded them of their bodies. He was very expert in recognizing the response that came from women, when he received a powerful response he would pursue that woman no matter what the conditions were, there was no need to give this response in words or with a look, a smile, or a stance, Nizam would sense it.

There was no space like this between him and Madame Cheriz, the woman didn't pay any attention to him, he wondered why she had invited him, for a moment a suspicion passed through his mind, but when he remembered that this was someone who had been introduced to him by Monsieur Lausanne the suspicion faded.

He retreated into his corner, asked "May I?" lit a cigarette and cracked the window. A wet cold filled the carriage, they heard the sticky sound of the horses moving quickly through the mud, the faint light from the lamps hung from poles that were placed at long intervals only illuminated the bottoms of the poles, the darkness around them was deepening.

Remembering Paris, Nizam said,

"What a gloomy city, how dark it is."

After raising her head and glancing out the window as if she wasn't even aware what city they were in, Madame Cheriz said, "Yes," then drifted off in her thoughts again.

After they'd left the outskirts of the city behind they entered a pitch dark forest, from the speed at which the carriage driver was going it was clear that he knew the road well, as they approached, a growing light became apparent in the darkness, then they reached a pebble road lined on both sides with giant torches, in the light of these torches the trees had changed color, they'd taken on a reddish bronze color.

Nizam remembered a mansion he'd been to in the Bois de Boulogne, but that wasn't a gambling den, it was a completely different kind of place, he turned to the woman and asked, "Is this a gambling den?" the woman said "Yes" in a cold tone and then asked, "Why do you ask?" "It reminds me of a place I saw in Paris but that wasn't a gambling den." As he said this he looked at the woman's face, he would know from her reaction to what he'd said whether or not she knew the place, there was no change of expression on the woman's face.

Nizam smiled at what he was remembering, after passing between the torches with the friend who'd brought him they entered the mansion, they'd seen very elegant couples sitting in a large hall, there was a fire burning in the large fireplace, at first Nizam hadn't realized that everyone was wearing masks.

After taking the drinks the waiter brought, his friend had said, "Take a look upstairs if you want, it's very nice up there too."

A footman standing at the bottom of the stairs handed him a mask.

Nizam climbed the stairs somewhat anxiously and went into a large room through a heavy velvet curtain. It was quite dark inside and at first all he could see was shadows, it was only after he heard the moans and screams that he realized that everyone was completely naked in that darkness.

As he thought of this strange and exciting memory, the carriage had pulled up in front of the mansion illuminated by torches. Broad marble stairs led up to the wide door, on either side of the door stood men of African descent wearing frock coats and purple fezzes.

They went in quickly, across from them was a double staircase, wide rooms could be seen on either side of the large foyer, the doors to the rooms were open.

Madame Cheris led the way and entered the room on the right, there were large leather armchairs, a fireplace with logs crackling in it, a long table, a large tiled stove, and a grand piano in the corner. A wide variety of food was arranged on the table, and a woman in a bitter green gown that left her shoulders bare and whose hair was tied up in a bun was sitting at the piano and playing, Nizam's sensitive ears immediately noticed a delicate mastery he hadn't expected to hear there, the woman was playing a piece by Liszt without adding any emotion but with a very bright spirit and with a technique that was sparkling enough to attract attention. Nizam noticed that no one was paying attention to the piano, they were talking among themselves, some of them seemed tired and others seemed tense and irritable. Later on he would realize that the tired-looking people were the ones who were taking a break from the game and the tense-looking people hadn't started playing yet.

Madame Cheriz knew everyone there, she greeted everyone and asked questions about the game upstairs, she got some information then said "Come" to Nizam.

As Nizam followed Madame Cheriz he kept thinking about the woman who was playing the piano, he was very surprised to encounter someone who played the piano like that at a gambling den, it had aroused his curiosity.

"Who's the woman playing the piano?" he asked.

"I think she's Russian," said Madame Cheriz.

"She plays very well."

Madame Cheriz said, "Is that so? I never paid any attention."

They climbed stairs that had been covered by thick carpets, the upper floor was quiet, the doors between the rooms were open, you could pass from one room to the other, it smelled of cigarette smoke and perfume, there were large chandeliers hanging from the ceiling, hundreds of candles had been lit, green baize tables had been placed side by side, the men and women sitting at the tables were elegantly dressed, they held their cards and didn't look at anyone except the other players, all that could be heard were the players' brief statements, "Pass, two cards, ten more gold coins" and the soft clicking of the chips.

After looking the room over very carefully, Madame Cheriz decided on a table, "I'm going to sit there," she said, "find a table for yourself, I'll see you later."

Nizam started wandering around the rooms, in one room a woman with white hair at a table with two other people asked him, "Monsieur, are you going to play? We're short one player."

"Sure," said Nizam.

He sat at the table. They started playing.

A while later a heavy numbness started to spread through his mind, his bonds to the world were breaking, all the lights of his attention were going out one by one like shops in a bazaar that was closing, all of his thoughts were collapsing into a darkness and only one place remained illuminated, all he saw was the table and the cards.

This was the state he liked the most, when he only saw, heard and thought about what he was doing at that moment. It was as if he carried on his life only to experience moments like that, and he could only reach this state when he was with a woman or when he was gambling.

He'd tried smoking opium in Paris, but opium hadn't produced the effect he wanted, he didn't want to lose control, to intoxicate himself, or weaken his capacity to think in any manner; he only derived pleasure from being busy with one thing, without thinking about or taking interest in anything else, experiencing the trance of having the brightness of his mind focused on a single point.

His true desire was to experience those sparkling moments

when he cut his relationship to the people with whom he had not formed a bond and whom he regarded as strangers no matter how close he pretended to be, and when he forgot the life he didn't enjoy very much. He was in pursuit of that magnificent stretch of time when his attention was concentrated on a single target without any distraction, when every particle of his being vibrated with a strong excitement.

Now he was looking at the cards he was holding, trying to guess what cards the other players had, reaching conclusions from their body language and their voices, lying as he wished and bluffing, keeping back a sound card until the last minute by playing a hesitant game and then confusing his opponent with a large raise.

He didn't know how long he played, he saw that he'd won twenty gold coins and then, as always, he got bored.

If he could, he would have liked to spend the rest of his life at a gambling table or making love in bed, but there always came a point when he suddenly became fed up and bored. He hadn't been able to find a solution for this.

He excused himself and stood up, he put the coins in his pocket, but the sound they made and their weight made him uncomfortable, he put his hand in his pocket and held the coins tightly as he wandered around the rooms, at one point he saw Madame Cheriz from a distance, her face was tense, her eyes had become smaller and her lips had become thinner.

As he wandered from room to room he came out by the stairs, a young man in an elegant frock coat was talking to a middle aged man with long sideburns and a moustache who was clearly a manager there; the young man had a pleading manner, but the manager seemed to be taking a rude and condescending attitude. Nizam suddenly became irritated, as if someone had been rude to him, he got caught up in a feeling that was difficult to understand, as if some man had been disrespectful to him, and he got angry.

He went over to them.

"Excuse me," he said, "May I ask what the problem is?"

As the manager tried to get rid of Nizam by saying "It's nothing important, sir," the young man said with a very innocent sincerity, "My money is finished, but they won't extend me any credit, even though I've been coming here for years."

"Ha," said Nizam, then he took the twenty gold coins he'd won out of his pocket. "If you allow me, I can give you a loan," he said and handed them to the young man, the manager, with the arrogant complicity that those in a good situation have when faced with someone in a bad situation, was trying to signal to Nizam not to do this.

The young man took the money without any embarrassment or haste, "What's your name?" he asked, "How will I pay you back?"

"I'm going to have a drink and listen to the piano downstairs," said Nizam, "I think the lady I came with is going to continue playing for some time, if you win while I'm here you can pay me, if you lose we'll accept our common misfortune and forget it."

The young man smiled, there was no gratitude in his manner, it was clear that Nizam's gesture had amused him.

"Here goes," he said, "let's see what effect generosity has on destiny."

As he walked towards the room he turned around and said, "Don't you dare leave without learning the outcome, we're going to put destiny to the test, it would be a shame if you left without seeing the outcome of this momentous matter."

Nizam went downstairs, there were only a few people in the room on the lower floor, everyone else had gone upstairs and got caught up in the game, the woman at the piano was playing a Chopin nocturne with the same unemotional interpretation and bright spirit, Nizam sensed that someone who could play like this could if she wanted give the piece the emotion it deserved, he thought that she was secretly insulting everyone there and life itself, that she had an angry contempt. He knew this kind of elegant insult well and always felt an admiration for it.

He got himself a glass of wine.

He walked slowly over to the piano and leaned on it, then looked at the woman's face. The woman didn't raise her head from the keys, she just glanced briefly at the man who was leaning on the piano then looked back at the keys.

There was almost no makeup on her face, her thick eyebrows grew thinner towards the ends, her cheekbones protruded slightly, she had a large, hooked nose and thin lips, and one could see a strange, disturbing expression in her eyes that Nizam couldn't put a name to right away, later he said to Osman, "she looked at people as if she was looking at a dead body, her first glance was unsettling."

"To play this piece with so little feeling amounts to an insult to the listeners," he said to the woman.

Again the woman looked up without saying anything, then looked down again. It was impossible to say what she was thinking or what she was feeling, "She was like a green box whose contents you couldn't see" Nizam said to Osman later.

When the woman didn't respond, Nizam decided it would be rude to press her, so he walked away from the piano, sat in a leather armchair nearby, and began drinking his wine.

He wasn't in the habit of remaining curious about anything for long, he would become interested in a person or event that caught his attention, he would remain interested only as long as there were developments that nourished his attention. The woman's lack of response had dispelled his interest, he was just sitting there, drinking his drink and not thinking about anything, there were times when his mind emptied out like this, he'd become cut off from events and from people, including himself, he allowed himself to sink into a void with a sense of lightness.

He had closed his eyes and was on the point of falling asleep.

Suddenly the sound of the piano stopped.

For a moment he couldn't decide whether to open his eyes or to fall asleep, he could have done either with the same ease. Like the route of a gigantic ship being determined by a rudder much too small for it, there are in a person's fate, in the direction he will take and the adventures he will experience, little incidents that at first glance seem unimportant, these little incidents can alter the course of a life's fate like the turning of a rudder; a waiter dropped a crystal glass on the floor, half of the glass hit the stone and half hit the carpet, it didn't make much sound but that sound caused Nizam to open his eyes.

The pianist was standing by herself smoking a cigarette at one of the windows that reflected a red darkness. It was as if she wasn't looking at anything, and there was no expression on her face. Her face was like a void that pulled one in, it wasn't her expression but her expressionlessness that attracted Nizam.

He got up slowly and went over to the woman with that childish self-indulgence that made him believe he could do anything.

"What's your name?" he asked.

Without realizing it, he was speaking French. And the woman replied in flawless French, she had a very faint, almost unnoticeable Russian accent, this accent added a tart flavor to her voice, like the plum jam Nizam used to spread on his croissants when he was a child.

"Why do you ask?"

"I was curious."

"Why are you curious?"

"I don't know, perhaps I'm curious about encountering someone who plays the piano so well in a place like this."

"There's nothing about me for you to be curious about."

"Madame, do you think it's impolite of me to talk to you?"

"Do you talk to everyone like this?"

"Everyone who attracts my interest, yes . . . Please don't see it as rudeness; if that's what you think, I apologize."

The woman put out her cigarette.

"I have to play the piano."

Nizam realized that the woman really didn't want to talk, that she preferred to remain alone, despite being so self-indulgent, he knew where to stand.

"As you wish, madam," he said, "I apologize again."

He went back to his seat, the woman had embarrassed him, he remembered the woman's question, "Do you talk to everyone like this?" If she hadn't been a pianist, would he have been as comfortable speaking to her? He probably would have talked to her anyway, he wasn't one to pay much attention to boundaries that prevented him from doing what he wanted, perhaps he would have been more careful, perhaps he would have come up with a different opening, perhaps he would have been more delicate, he felt distressed. He erased everything that had happened from his mind, he was able to do this, perhaps this capacity was the result of comfortably being able to look down on people and on his own life.

He closed his eyes again.

He must have slept a bit, he was woken by a voice saying, "Hah, I've found you," the young man to whom he'd given twenty gold coins upstairs was standing by his armchair.

"Destiny does not leave generosity unrewarded, that's what we've learned tonight."

Nizam was still dazed by sleep and didn't fully understand him.

The young man took two bags of gold from his pocket.

"We won . . . here's your twenty gold, we made two hundred gold in profit, since we're partners here's your hundred gold."

Nizam took the twenty gold coins.

"I don't want the rest," he said, "that belongs to you, you won it. I have no claim to that."

"Please, if it wasn't for you I couldn't have won. That idiot wasn't going to lend me any money. How rude and savage these unimportant people become when they suddenly feel they can be important."

"*Merci*," said Nizam, "I won't take what rightfully belongs to you."

The young man didn't insist further, not because he was stingy or because he was pleased he'd won money, but because he didn't care about money.

"In that case," he said, "be my guest tomorrow, at least grant me that, don't allow your generosity to crush me."

"Fine," said Nizam.

They agreed to meet the following day at the gambling den.

A grey light appeared in the windows, the red of the torches paled, the crowd upstairs was noisily coming down, the quiet had ended with morning.

Madame Cheriz came into the room, looked around for Nizam, waved from a distance when she saw him and then went over to him.

"Let's get going," she said, "it's morning."

Her voice was relaxed, her attitude had softened.

As they were leaving the room, Nizam turned and looked back, the pianist was standing in front of the window again, he saw that the woman was looking at him, the woman saw that he was looking at her, when she saw that he was looking at her she immediately lowered her eyes.

That was enough for Nizam, small signals determined his feelings and his life, he understood that the strange conversation hadn't finished there.

When they went out into the cool of the morning, even the short trip to the carriage made them shiver, they got into the carriage and followed the train of other carriages that passed between the torches and the trees that were now taking on a lavender color, Madame Cheriz sat a little closer to Nizam.

"Morning is breaking," she said, "I've always loved this hour of the morning."

"Did you have fun?" asked Nizam

He'd asked this because it seemed inappropriate to ask, "Did you win?" or "Did you lose?"

"Yes. It was a good night. You brought me luck. I won forty gold. There was a pasha from the palace, he lost a lot of money but he didn't mind . . . The pashas here are very rich."

Nizam didn't answer, people's wealth didn't interest him, he thought everyone was rich, everyone he knew was rich, no one spoke about money, despite the great excitement of gambling, for Nizam the only boring aspect of it was playing for money, it added a cheapness to a great entertainment.

As if he was talking to himself, he said, "Russian roulette is good, it's good that the Russians came up with that game."

"The Russians are crazy," said Madame Cheriz, "you can die playing that came, you gamble with your life."

"It's better . . . At least it's better than money, it's more real."

Madame Cheriz laughed.

"You're crazy too, but that's normal at this hour of the morning . . . It's impossible to be clever when the sun is rising, I think it was a magical effect like that."

She was as cheerful and full of energy as if she'd just got up, the lines on her face had softened, she wore a happy expression.

"She likes to win," thought Nizam.

When they reached her house, Madame Cheriz said in a polite tone, "I don't think you ate anything all night, come in and I'll have a nice meal prepared for you. I'll have the carriage driver bring a note to your home so they don't worry about you."

"Alright," said Nizam.

He never made even the slightest effort to change the course of life, he went with the flow; making an effort and trying to change the course of events bored him, letting himself go seemed more fun to him, and he generally had fun.

Madame Cheriz really made up for her lack of hospitality at the beginning of the night and revealed all her talents by having a sumptuous meal prepared, and as she ate with an almost gluttonous appetite she warbled like a cheerful goldfinch, talking about her childhood, their vineyards, having wine and bread for breakfast during harvest time, about her siblings, about her oldest brother's grumpiness. From what she said, it was clear that Madame Cheriz' family possessed more land and wealth than Nizam had guessed.

As they were drinking their coffee after the meal she asked, "Are you tired?"

"A little."

"We didn't sleep all night, of course it's normal to be tired . . . Come, rest a little."

They went upstairs together, when they arrived in front of a door Madame Cheris took Nizam's hand, she said "Let's not bother making up a bed at this hour," and opened the door.

They went into the bedroom.

Nizam undressed calmly as if this was the right thing to do after all, at the same time he watched Madame Cheriz undress.

In bed he was truly surprised, she was not the calm woman he'd seen at dinner at his father's house, nor the rude and ill-tempered woman in the carriage on the way to the gambling den, nor the warbling goldfinch she'd been at breakfast.

All of those women were gone, and in their place emerged a completely different woman, she was full of lust, everything about her made it clear that she adored making love.

Before falling asleep, Madame Cheriz brought her mouth so close to Nizam's ear that he could feel the heat of her breath and said, "At that place you went to in the Bois de Boulogne, did they wear masks?"

Before falling asleep Nizam thought "Life is fun," he remembered that.

10

C evat Bey was startled by the bell, he said "Damn" and answered the telephone, somehow he couldn't get used to this new contraption, he was surprised every time it rang. He put the earpiece to his ear and brought the tube-shaped microphone to his mouth.

"Who is it?"

"Cevat Bey?"

"Yes . . ."

"This is Talat, Cevat Bey."

"How are you Talat Bey, what can I do for you?"

"Can you drop by the center in the evening, there's a pressing matter we need to discuss."

"Of course."

Towards evening, as it was getting dark, he left the Ministry of War and walked to Cağaloğlu by way of the Grand Bazaar. The Grand Bazaar was crowded, the smell of the steam rising from the clothes of the people who'd been in the rain mixed with the smells of the cloth that had been arranged on the shelves, kebab, tobacco smoke and the smell of crowds of people. The buzzing of the crowd echoed off the thick walls of the bazaar, sometimes one could hear the clicking of the tongs the coffee man held as he brought tea to a shopkeeper on a brass tray.

"It's as if there's no war," grumbled Cevat Bey angrily amid the noise of the crowd, but for those people it really was as if there was no war, the newspapers didn't offer any real news about the war, it would difficult to guess about one of the greatest defeats in military history, every item of news was twisted and hidden from sight. Cevat Bey got angry at those newspapers and called them "villainous," but six months earlier these "villains" had been directed by Cevat Bey's friends' "orders," concealing the news they wanted concealed and twisting the truth in the manner they wanted it twisted.

Cevat Bey emerged from the Grand Bazaar grumbling, passed in front of the Nuruosmaniye mosque and reached Cağaloğu square, then turned onto Bab-ı Ali hill, it was drizzling, the weather was cold, he raised the collar of his greatcoat.

He passed the Iranian Embassy and reached the mansion where the Committee for Union and Progress had its general headquarters, the mansion's garden was deserted, there weren't many men inside, "just six months ago this mansion was completely packed," thought Cevat Bey, at that time a government under the control of the Committee had been in power, people sought solutions for every problem at that mansion, later Cevat Bey said to Osman, "in six months that mansion turned into a spring that had run dry."

Talat Bey was waiting for him and greeted him excitedly.

"Come in, Cevat Bey, how are you?"

"Thank you Talat Bey, except for the anxiety and anguish about the war, everything's fine."

Talat Bey sat at his desk, after playing with his pen and thinking for a moment, he spoke.

"You follow the situation in this country more closely than I do, Cevat Bey, the Balkan nations have driven the great Ottoman army as far as Lüleburgaz, a corps of ninety thousand men fled in one night without firing a single shot. This is all happening because of this government's incompetence, cowardice and lack of foresight."

He examined his pen carefully, as if that pen was going to tell him what to say, he frowned.

"It's come to this, Cevat Bey."

Cevat Bey didn't say anything and waited for him to continue, he realized he was going to say something momentous.

"We have to overthrow this government, it's impossible for these men to save the Ottoman Empire . . . But we need someone the people know and trust. Our friends met with İzzet Pasha but he was hesitant, he said it wasn't the time. Whenever the time is . . . Could there be a more appropriate time than the present? The army is dispersed and in retreat, the empire is being trampled underfoot, the soldiers are fleeing . . ."

He played with his pen a little more.

"What I ask of you is to take two more friends and go to Mahmut Şevket Pasha. Tell him that we're going to overthrow the government and that we want him to be grand vizier. Convince him."

Cevat Bey was surprised.

"Will the pasha accept this, Talat Bey? Just four months ago we removed him from the position of Minister of War, would he forget that? Would he trust us again?"

Talat Bey laughed his fatherly laugh, he was the most intelligent and most dangerous of the Committee leaders, unlike the others he managed to conceal his ruthlessness beneath this fatherly manner, he had the ability to convince people when he talked to them. He wouldn't reveal his real thoughts and feelings, but he was good of weighing the mood of whoever he was talking to.

"The pasha enjoyed having power," he said, "he knows he wasn't successful as Minister of War, he'll be willing because it means he can both clear his name and have power again."

Even though Cevat Bey knew the question would be disrespectful he couldn't hold himself back.

"Are you certain, Talat Bey? The pasha is an angry man, let's not do the wrong thing."

"I'm certain, Cevat Bey. Besides, he likes you, he trusts you.

And we're offering him the prime ministry, we're not telling him to become a butler for the bathhouse owners . . . No one else but us is going to offer this to him, who would give the prime ministry to the pasha? We need him, but he needs us too."

"Yes sir," said Cevat Bey, "if you think it's the right thing to do I'll go with Ali Rıza Bey and another friend, we'll sound him out."

"That would be great, Cevat Bey . . . Don't forget that this is a matter of national importance. It's now up to us to save the army's honor and the empire's future. You're going to be carrying out an essential and historical mission."

Cevat Bey said, "Certainly sir" and left, but he wasn't quite at ease . . . He was deeply attached to the Committee for Union and Progress, he believed they were the only ones who could save the Ottoman Empire and the army, if a military coup was necessary he wouldn't hesitate for a moment to put his life on the line, but he wasn't quite sure if he could convince the pasha.

He had other worries he hadn't told Talat Pasha about.

After the pasha entered Istanbul at the head of the Movement Army and put down the March 31st uprising and Abdulhamid was forced to abdicate, the pasha, as Minister of War, became the most important and powerful man in the empire. As Minister of War, he recognized neither laws nor regulations.

When more than one million in gold was found in Abdulhamid's palace he paid no attention to the law or to the objections of the treasury ministry and added this money to the Ministry of War's budget, he'd constantly disparaged the government and the grand vizier, he hadn't even attended cabinet meetings, he threatened Parliament to get them to pay the money he wanted for the army, he's said, "Give it, gentlemen, give it, we're going to re-establish the imperial army."

In his time they engaged in corruption, the Committee simply took the money, his military decisions and investments turned out to be wrong, when the opposition raised its voice about this they arrested all of them and put them in the military prison, they set up special courts to try them.

They arrested so many men that there weren't enough courts to try them, and there was no room in the prisons because of a surge in ordinary crime.

On top of this Mahmut Şevket Pasha invented a "new order," ordinary criminals were no longer tried, they were sent to prisons to be bastinadoed, they were beaten and then released. Meanwhile those who had been arrested for their opposition were beaten in prison and subjected to torture.

Then Ahmet Samim Bey, a writer for the *Sada-yı Millet* newspaper that opposed the Committee, was shot and killed in broad daylight in Bahçekapı.

This pressure caused the opposition to grumble even more, a faction called "Halaskar Zabitan" was established in the military to oppose the Committee.

The Committee thought that Mahmut Şevket Pasha's ministry of war was becoming a liability for them, Talat Bey, who had just told Cevat Bey to "offer the pasha the prime ministry," had made a plan six months ago to topple the pasha.

The pasha was a very unyielding man and he had no intention of giving up power, if they tried to remove him from his position they could all end up being arrested.

Talat Bey was going to strike him at his weakest point, he cooked up the plan to overthrow the man who was ruling the Ottoman Empire on his own with Hacı Adil Bey, the craftiest man in the Committee after himself.

In accordance with this plan Hacı Adil Bey, who at the time was Minister of the Interior, and Seyit Bey, representative for İzmir and head of the Committee's Parliamentary Group, would visit the pasha together "about an urgent issue."

First they praised the pasha at length, like all dictators the pasha loved praise, this was one of his greatest weaknesses.

Once the pasha had been well softened, Hacı Adil Bey got down to the actual matter at hand.

"Unfortunately, pasha, we've received some very bad news," he began.

"What is it, Adil Bey?"

"Pasha, you know that we all have great respect for you, we all know how worthy you are and that you saved the empire, we tell this to everyone, but the opposition is going too far and targeting you, you know . . . Now we've heard they're preparing unthinkable and unimaginable perfidy. They claim that Chief Quartermaster İsmail Hakkı Pasha misrepresented some of his acquisitions for the army and embezzled the money. They say they have records. Now they've met among themselves and have reached a decision, they're going to call you into Parliament for questioning as İsmail Hakkı Pasha's superior."

Mahmut Şevket Pasha's face went completely white, he was frowning and his jawbone was moving so much it looked as if it would come off. They knew he had the power to have them arrested at any moment, but despite this Hacı Adil Bey continued.

"Of course we know that all of this is a lie, but our friends say that the Pasha shouldn't be questioned in Parliament about such ugly matters, that it would be deeply offensive for us and for the Pasha to be subjected to this treatment, they all deplore this, they say they kiss the Pasha's hands and that he should resign rather fall into this ignominy."

When Hacı Adil Bey finished speaking there was silence.

İsmail Hakkı Bey's corruption was being talked about throughout the empire, he was stealing openly without even trying to conceal it, he was amassing a huge fortune, but this had nothing to do with Mahmut Şevket Pasha. He wasn't the one who was protecting İsmail Hakkı Pasha. Enver Bey, the

Quartermaster General and the Committee's military leader, was leading a secret organization loyal to him within the military, this was why he was being protected by Enver Bey and his thievery was being ignored.

Until then the Pasha had been accused of being dictatorial, of using unnecessary violence, and of silencing the Committee's opponents, but his name had never been associated with this kind of disgrace, he had never been stained by "larceny." He hadn't seen any harm in being accused of beating, killing, and silencing the opposition but he had been shaken by the mention of "theft and corruption."

With an unexpected naivete he said,

"Fine, since our friends see this as the appropriate thing for me to do, I'll resign."

That evening he'd gone to his house in Üsküdar early. The Committee greeted this with delight, the "success" was celebrated at the general headquarters and they waited for the pasha to resign.

That night there was no news of resignation, "I suppose he'll do it tomorrow," they thought, but at that time Talat Bey thought of another issue, "What if the Sultan doesn't accept this resignation?" he said. In the middle of the night they woke the Chief Palace Clerk Uşakkizade Halit Ziya Bey and called him in, they told him that because of the Chief Quartermaster's corruption, Mahmut Şevket Pasha was being called to Parliament for questioning and they would "put him through the wringer," that in order to prevent this the Pasha had resigned, and that he absolutely had to convince the Sultan to accept this resignation, otherwise there would be very bad consequences, they threatened him obliquely.

Mahmut Şevket Pasha resigned the following day, and contrary to what the Committee had thought, Sultan Reşad feared the Pasha and had never liked him, and had been delighted to accept his resignation.

The Committee didn't get the results it wanted from this trap, a week after the Pasha resigned, the entire cabinet resigned, they were replaced by what was called the "Great Cabinet," which was made up of elderly pashas and former grand viziers who formed a new government, all of the Committee members were pushed out of the government. The Committee fell into its own trap and allowed the power they'd held to be snatched from them.

Now, four months after all of this, Cevat Bey was going to go to the Pasha and say, "Be our leader, we're going to over-throw the government."

Despite all of his worries, it was not in his nature to hesitate to undertake a mission "in the name of the party," the following morning he called Mahmut Şevket Pasha, said that he would like to come and have a meeting with him and asked for an appointment, when the Pasha said, "You're welcome to come this evening," he picked up Ali Rıza Bey and they took a row-boat across to Üsküdar.

Cevat Bey was one of the officers who really liked the Pasha, he'd always admired his successes in artillery, his efforts to reform the army, the way he'd always protected the Committee, the way he never hesitated to use violence against the "lowly" opposition, and in fact he hadn't approved of the way he'd been led into a trap. The Pasha liked him, he appre-ciated him.

Even though the Pasha was aware of the games the Committee had played with him, he greeted them cordially, he smiled when Cevat Bey said, "Pasha, your presence is missed."

After they spoke for a time about the progress of the war and the disasters that had been suffered, Cevat Bey got down to the matter at hand.

"Pasha, there's a matter I want to bring up with you . . . As you know, the war is proceeding disastrously, this govern-ment can't conduct the war properly, they'll save their skins by selling out the Ottoman Empire and submitting to a humiliating agreement. We're not willing to accept this, no patriot could accept this."

Cevat Bey raised his head and looked at the Pasha's face, he was listening attentively.

"Pasha, we've reached a decision, we're going to overthrow the government . . . If we succeed we would like you to join us, your presence will give us added strength and power."

He stopped speaking and waited for an answer.

The Pasha spoke very slowly.

"The future is dark, but if measures are taken the situation can be remedied. If the army's leadership and management is immediately placed in competent hands, if the opposition officers are disciplined, if the enlisted men are given confidence, it may be possible to emerge from this disaster."

The pasha paused again, it was clear that he was weighing what he was going to say.

"Fine, I'll join you . . . However, I will assume the position of grand vizier, and Hacı Adil Bey and Talat Bey will not serve in any cabinet I form . . . If these conditions are acceptable to you we can work together."

"Of course, Pasha," said Cevat Bey, "Your wish is our command. However you wish . . . By participating in this movement you will be saving the empire, you will go down in history."

They left the Pasha's house in delight to bring the good news to Talat Bey, who was waiting for them, they hurried down to Üsküdar and found a *caique*. As the *caique* bobbed on the choppy sea, the only sound that could be heard was the "huh" sound the oarsman made as he pulled the oars.

Ali Rıza Bey said in a tone that the oarsman couldn't hear,

"Cevat, we've just decided to change the course of history, are you aware of that? We're going to tear this government down, we'll show those scoundrels. This time we have a better idea of what we're doing, we'll never again allow anyone to divide the nation."

"Yes," said Cevat Bey.

They both knew that in order for the coup to succeed, the Ottoman Empire had to lose the war, the reality that had distressed them two days earlier was now a cause for hope.

These two officers who were so eager to reach the far shore to tell their friends the "good news" didn't know that the "poisonous good news" they carried would bring down an empire, destroy their own futures and bring grief to the life of a young woman named Rukiye who was laughing and eating dinner with her husband in a waterfront mansion that they'd just passed, they were enjoying their cigarettes as they tried to protect themselves from the wind.

They'd set in motion what would be perhaps the most bizarre military coup in history.

Later Cevat Bey said in a philosophical manner that Osman would never have expected of him, "Sometimes destiny chooses the people who are to sow its seeds with an ironical fastidiousness, it makes you happily do something that will bring about your own downfall, you don't even have a clue."

11

T hat morning as Monsieur Lausanne was on his way to the Karaköy Post Office to send Dilara Hanım a telegram, he saw a row of rowboats loaded with coffins move away from the shore towards Üsküdar one after the other. The rowboats loaded with coffins wrapped in green flags bobbed up and down on the waves like a chain of death.

He asked a man standing nearby what these rowboats were.

"Corpses," said the man, "the corpses of soldiers who don't want to be buried in Europe, who want to have their eternal rest in Asia, on Muslim soil . . . They're taking them to the far shore to be buried."

Lausanne didn't quite understand what the man said but he didn't want to ask too many questions, he was going to say, "There are Muslim cemeteries in the European part of Istanbul, aren't they Muslim soil?" but he changed his mind.

He went to the post office and sent Dilara Hanım a brief telegram.

"The foreign minister has invited me to dinner this evening. Matters that interest you will be discussed. If you should wish to attend, it would be a great pleasure and honor for me to accompany you."

Dilara Hanım, who informed him that she would be "pleased to come," was in a strange mood in those days, the war made her worried and anxious about Ragıp Bey, and this anxiety increased her yearning in a painful manner.

There was nothing strange about either her anxiety or her

yearning, but she had an unusual way of coping with it, with a strength of will seldom seen in people experiencing this kind of yearning, she concealed her feelings about Ragıp Bey from herself, from her own consciousness, she tried to bury them somewhere in her soul and cover them up, and for the most part she was successful. The yearning never abated, it was always there, sometimes it manifested itself as a sudden pain that seemed to rip through her, sometimes as an unbearable anguish, but this did not affect the flow of daily life that Dilara Hanım insisted on maintaining.

She rejected the idea of being a recluse or a lonely woman who spent her life with her daughter and son-in-law so violently that this denial and her yearning were constantly clashing, apart from momentary victories, the yearning usually had to accept defeat and retreat. The denial was more suited to Dilara Hanım's personality, ideas and habits, in any event the yearning behaved in a hostile manner to her, as if it was a stranger, or as if it belonged to someone else, in this war that was raging within her she sided with denial, she supported it.

Unavoidably, this created a sense of partition within her, it wearied her to constantly struggle to bury one of her emotions deep within her; this weariness led her not to give up on life but to cling to life more violently.

Sometimes she blamed Ragıp Bey for being the cause of all this and got angry at him, but at other times she thought that he was right, her weakest moments were the moments when she accepted that Ragıp Bey was right, at those times she wasn't able to prevent the yearning from taking her over, all of her resistance was broken, she blamed herself. "Why," she asked, "why did I behave that way?" These questions inevitably paved the way for the unending questions, "Why am I like this, why do I harm myself, why do I obstruct my own happiness?" She didn't want to find the answer to these questions, she was afraid, because at those times she felt that if she questioned herself a bit more she might come face to face with her own truths. She already knew what those truths were, but every time she faced them they caused her pain and wore her out, and it didn't produce any outcome, nothing changed, that's why she avoided it if at all possible.

When she remembered one of those moments she said to Osman, "People's relationship with themselves is like their relationship with death, they know the truth but they don't accept the truth, they prefer to forget the truth."

She stopped and then continued, "Because they can't live with that truth. Is it possible to live feeling death at every moment, knowing that it's coming, it's approaching, that it's inevitable? You have to forget that truth and bury it deep in your consciousness, the truth about yourself is like that too, you feel it, indeed you know it, but no one can live with that truth . . . No one can bear to know the whole truth about themselves. We have to forget ourselves, trick ourselves, we have to see ourselves as someone we've made up in our minds."

Her face suddenly fell, "I hate picking myself apart, because of Ragıp I had to think about things like that, I'll never forgive that," she said angrily.

She hadn't changed her lifestyle when she was with Ragıp Bey, and she didn't change it after Ragıp Bey left, after her husband died she had distanced herself from the crowds; this was a vague, twilight area that was observed by no one, the entirety of which no one saw, Dilara Hanım's own life was like a private garden in which she lived as she pleased without showing anyone and without asking anyone. Those who were given permission to enter the garden only saw part of it but they couldn't explore all of it.

The fortune her husband had left her had helped develop this garden's thick walls, "Wealth shields you," she said once to Osman, "money is good for buying your liberty, if you ask me it's not much good for anything else."

After Ragıp Bey left, this twilight area, which she saw as the most precious part of her existence, which she defended with an almost mad passion and had hidden from everyone, began to seem like her enemy, "I couldn't bring liberty and happiness together," she said to Osman, "What use is liberty that doesn't bring happiness? It's such a simple question, but only idiots think there are simple answers to simple questions. They don't realize that sometimes it's impossible to find an answer to a simple question. Yes, when there's no happiness, liberty is rendered meaningless, but is happiness that destroys liberty of any use, there's that question too." She paused, she thought, she allowed her frail and transparent body that came from the world of the dead to ripple in the wind, then continued, "perhaps I didn't want happiness," she said, "liberty is uneasy and vague, it doesn't give a person any sense of security, it keeps its door open to all dangers, yes, that's how it is, happiness requires you to close some doors within yourself, I was never able to close those doors, in my opinion I'm attached to liberty in an unhealthy way, I'm fond of that ambiguity and danger . . . That's why I could never reach happiness, no that's not completely true, there were times when I did reach it, I was happy with Ragıp, I'd closed the doors, but he wanted me to close all my doors. He never understood that this was impossible for me . . . Yet I still liked happiness, perhaps even more than I liked my liberty . . . But I could never digest the idea of giving up my liberty . . . This contradiction, this peculiarity in my nature determined my entire fate . . . Everyone has some kind of madness, well this is mine, believing that happiness and liberty can't coexist."

In these days full of contradictions. of internal reckoning and of emotional uprisings that she tried to put down, Monsieur Lasusanne was struggling to get into her twilight garden as an insistent guest, and in a sense he was succeeding too.

He was a very well-informed and entertaining man, like

most journalists he had a lot of stories to tell, a lot of experience, because of his profession he wasn't intimidated by obstacles, if he was stopped he would find another way around, he had a likeable predacity, he thought he had a right to ask and do anything, he had a self-indulgence that was decorated with intelligence. His responsibility in his work, his success in breaking news and his fame made him trustworthy.

He had the means to bring Dilara Hanım to the places where the people who knew most about the war were to be found. Because of Ragıp Bey, the war was slowly becoming a passion for Dilara Hanım, and he was perhaps the only person who could satisfy her desire to obtain the latest news.

Without realizing it, he was entering Dilara Hanım's life on a path that had been cleared by Ragıp Bey, he was exploring that twilight area because he had the means to ease her worries and anxieties about Ragıp Bey. But to say that this was all there was would be unfair to Monsieur Lausanne, his presence and his conversation affected Dilara Hanım, he was succeeding in establishing a place for himself on the shore of that vast area of Dilara Hanım's soul that Ragıp Bey overspread.

Dilara Hanım was aware of the situation, and it both pleased her and made her uneasy. She couldn't quite grasp why she was uneasy, but the pleasure that seeing Monsieur Lausanne created in her had something saddening about it, after Ragıp she didn't want any man to create a stirring of emotion within her, but she didn't reject any joy that helped obscure the ache that Ragıp Bey had created. As Osman also said, she was full of "contradictions."

That evening they went together to the dinner at Foreign Minister Noradinyan Efendi's house. The guests who came to the mansion in Taksim had to wait some time for their host. Noradinkyan Efendi arrived with a yellowed face and apologized for being late.

"Unfortunately we're living through one of the most difficult times in our history," he said, "our army is retreating towards Lüleburgaz. This shouldn't have happened, our European friends shouldn't have left us alone, they know how much we've struggled for peace but the Balkan states wanted war."

To get clearer information Lausanne asked,

"What is the Ottoman army's current situation?"

The Foreign Minister was inviting foreign diplomats and journalists to develop a pro-Ottoman campaign in the eyes of both governments and peoples to force Europe to help. If he concealed the truth he wouldn't be able to request this help, but if he told the truth he would be announcing the Ottoman Empire's helplessness to the entire world.

"As you already know, the Bulgarians have taken Kırkkilise, there have been local skirmishes as our army retreats to the Lüleburgaz line. At Lüleburgaz our units will be reorganized and will give the enemy the answer they require . . . But it's in Europe's hands to make sure that too many people don't die in this war, by putting pressure on the Balkan nations that wanted and started this war they could force them to end the war. From the beginning of this war we have shown the entire world that we want peace and that our intentions are good . . . However, the world has remained deaf to this."

Then, evidently thinking that he should threaten as well, he continued.

"The Ottoman Empire is not an empire that can be overthrown by four Balkan nations, the world couldn't contend with the death of the Ottoman Empire, the order and stability of the entire world would be shattered."

This was met with complete silence. No one answered. It was clear that just as Noradinkyan Effendi hadn't found the assistance he sought in official meetings, he wasn't going to find it in these private gatherings either.

The German Ambassador suddenly said in a deep voice,

"If the Ottoman foot soldiers had anything to eat this war wouldn't have turned out this way."

Monsieur Lausanne's nationalism tended to raise its head especially when he was faced with Germans.

"If food hasn't reached the soldiers, whose responsibility is that, Monsieur Ambassador? The quartermaster corps . . . If the quartermaster corps is at fault so is the army it's part of . . . If we consider the German generals in the army, then it's clear that these are German mistakes."

The Foreign Minister intervened before the Ambassador could answer, the last thing he wanted was for this gathering to become a German-French duel and for the guests to argue among themselves.

"At the moment we're not in a position to look for who is at fault," he said, "that will be for later, of course our army will take the required steps to achieve the required results. Our mission at the moment is to bring about peace. By explaining this situation to your governments you can convince them that they can help in achieving this peace."

Again he received no answer.

At dinner Dilara Hanım was seated next to the foreign minister, she took the opportunity, leaned towards the minister and asked the question she was most curious about.

"Have there been many fatalities among the men?"

Noradinkyan Efendi made a face.

"I don't know how to answer that question, should I say thankfully or should I say unfortunately . . ."

It was clear the foreign minister was very distraught, he seemed wearied by the truths he knew.

"We haven't had too many losses, indeed we've had very few losses. We lost almost no men when we left Kirkkilise to the Bulgarians. We had some casualties, but they were more because of some unpleasant incidents that occurred during the retreat."

"Have there been many casualties among the officers?"

Noradinkyan Effendi suddenly leaned back and looked at Dilara Hanım with suspicion, he didn't understand why was she asking so many questions, why she was interested in these kinds of details.

When Dilara Hanım saw the expression on the minister's face, she felt the need to offer an explanation.

"I have a close friend at the front . . . I haven't heard from him in a long time."

Noradinkyan Efendi sensed the woman's sorrow,

"What's his rank?"

"I don't know, I suppose he's a colonel . . . Or something like that."

"As far as I know we haven't lost any officers of that rank. You can rest assured . . . At the moment we're not losing men, all we're losing is the empire's territory and pride."

No one would have guessed that someone could be this delighted by news of a war being lost, but Dilara Hanım had rarely in her life been this delighted. For her the person she missed was much more precious than an empire, "Patriotism," she'd said to Osman, "what an absurd word, it's one of the names men invented for their own death games, I wouldn't have traded Ragıp for the entire Ottoman Empire . . . And do you want me to tell you something, every woman who had someone she loved at the front thought the same as I did, anyone who didn't couldn't be called a woman, in fact I don't think they could be called human beings, but because men have a different conception of humanity, they keep talking about the necessity of death, that we need to be pleased by these deaths . . . They say it brings a person honor, I say men are idiots, for a sane person, what could be more precious than the life of someone you love?"

"But," said Osman, "you said once that you wanted to die in battle."

"Is that so, I don't remember, but is it the same thing, can you equate your own death with the death of someone you love? What a strange comparison . . . If I were to choose a way to die, yes, it could be, I might prefer to die in battle, but who would prefer the way someone they love dies, this is something you can only say about yourself."

She was happy that evening, the men were having serious discussions about what tactics should be used in this war and about Europe's position towards the war, but Dilara Hanım wasn't listening to any of it, the interest she'd had in the war had vanished, no topic interested her more than the delight she felt.

The dark weight on her soul of always being anxious, of worrying, of waiting for bad news, had been lifted from her; when she received the heartening news that evening, Dilara Hanım realized that the anxiety had penetrated every particle of her soul, the most secluded corners of her consciousness, her happiest memories and all of her dreams about the future. Suddenly she saw the light of the candles in the crystal chandeliers reflected in the gold-leafed mirrors, the Chinese vase on the walnut console in the corner, the brocaded fringes of the curtains, people's faces, the different lines on those faces, only a blind person who had suddenly regained their sight could have been this surprised, Dilara Hanım realized with great amazement that she hadn't seen any of these things until that moment.

"I wonder what I saw when I looked before," she said to Osman, "what had I seen before for those images to amaze me so much. I don't remember anything about what I saw before that moment. In my mind there's only what I saw at that moment."

When she turned her head to the right she saw that Monsieur Lausanne was looking at her, "He's handsome," she thought, Ragıp Bey would probably have preferred to have died than for her to have experienced that moment, but he hadn't died, and Dilara Hanım's delight about this had made it possible for her to notice that Lausanne was handsome. She smiled at Lausanne, the French journalist had never seen Dilara Hanım smile at him that way, there was a powerful femininity in that smile, it had a cheerful coquettishness, there was a delight not often seen in Dilara Hanım.

Ragıp Bey, who at the time didn't know what had happened and what would happen because he hadn't died, was trying to make his way from Kirkkilise to Babaeski, accompanied by the gnawing, animal-like jealousy he'd already been carrying for a long time, to find his unit and the division it was attached to. In the unending rain, the plains that stretched as far as the eye could see looked like a monster that was preparing to swallow everything like a swelling swamp of mud. In those piles of mud, among the cannons, discarded rifles, hay wagons, villagers fleeing the enemy, he came across some hungry, unshaven, sunken-eyed soldiers.

He came across four soldiers who were kneeling at the foot of a tree looking at a book they were holding.

"What are you doing?" he asked.

"We're lost, commander, we're trying to figure out which direction to go."

"How are you going to figure that out?"

The soldier held up the book and showed it to Ragıp Bey.

"We decided to look at the Holy Koran, it will show us the way."

Ragıp Bey chewed his moustache and said, "Good God," he was fighting with soldiers who tried to find their way with the Koran rather than a map.

"You should have read that book before you fled rather than after," he grumbled, "follow me."

With Ragıp Bey and the sergeant in the lead on horseback and the soldiers struggling through the mud on foot behind them, hungry and thirsty, they reached Babaeski. There was no one there either.

When he came across a villager he asked, "Where's the army?" The man said, "They're pulling back to Lüleburgaz."

"Do you have a little food you can give us?"

"No," said the man, "They looted it all before they left, not that there was enough for all of them, it was gone in no time."

They got under way again towards Lüleburgaz, on the plain they saw groups of two or three silhouettes, some of the soldiers were trying to desert and get home and some of them were trying to find the army, but none of them could figure out which direction to go, they were stumbling through the mud in a disorderly manner in fear of the enemy coming up behind them.

Ragıp Bey was completely fed up, "I suppose the army is going to muster in Lüleburgaz," he said, "God damn it, we won't be able to hold out in Lüleburgaz, we should have mustered on the banks of the Ergene, these idiots are going in the wrong direction, don't these high and mighty pashas ever look at a map, what use are the staff officers?"

Ragıp Bey didn't know it at the time, but he wasn't the only one who thought this way, the Minister of War Nazım Pasha, who before the war had strutted about saying "We're going to Sofia," had, after the Kirkkilise fiasco, set out for the front with a group of staff officers including Cevat Bey with the intention of "setting everything straight within a few days."

When they set out, an optimism that radiated from the minister's large torso reigned on the train, this was not the type of optimism that is infused in those around him by a real leader who sees chances and possibilities others do not. On the contrary, it was the misplaced, hollow hope of those who do not see the truth.

The young staff officers could better see and evaluate what was happening, but those who had received a good military education were falling into step with the minister because they wanted to hope that these pashas who spoke so loudly and confidently knew something they didn't know. And of course there were also the obligations of military life, they had to adapt their moods to the moods of their commanders.

This optimism lasted as far as Sinekli Station.

When they stopped in front of the small, yellow station with dirty whitewash they saw that the platform was full of wounded and refugees, and they were passed by trains full of dead and wounded soldiers heading to Istanbul.

The pasha and his entourage got off the train and went to the telegraph office to get in touch with the command headquarters of the Second Army, which was supposed to be in Lüleburgaz. The Second Army had retreated without informing anyone and had moved its headquarters to Çorlu.

Meanwhile one of the Istanbul bound trains had stopped at the station, a division commander on the train came to the telegraph office to see the Minister of War.

The minister asked in an angry voice,

"Where are you going?"

"To Istanbul, commander."

"Where is your division?"

"I lost them at Kirkkilise, commander, they scattered in all directions, I'm going to Istanbul to get new orders."

The minister rose to his feet, his voice made the entire station tremble.

"You're fleeing, coward, you've abandoned your army and your division and you're running away, I'm going to have you courtmarshalled immediately, you'll pay the price for your cowardice."

These were empty words, there was no court there, nor was there sufficient military order to arrest that division commander and confine him.

The minister returned to the telegraph and to his communication with the Second Army headquarters.

He was trying to figure out where the soldiers, corps and

divisions were, he learned that the First, Second and Fourths Corps had piled up in Lüleburgaz and were trying to reorganize themselves there.

"Advance to the banks of the Ergene river immediately and dig in, face the enemy there," he commanded.

The answer he received was disheartening.

"It's not possible to move the men to the Ergene, morale is very low, the army is in disarray, our only chance is to dig in and face the enemy here."

Another telegram arrived from Yaver Pasha, one of the corps commanders.

"All of the men including me are hungry, we can't find anything to eat in Lüleburgaz. We're faced with the necessity of fighting a war with starving soldiers."

And the minister wasn't able to insist, the news he received and the misery he saw had destroyed his resilience and hope, the corps commanders weren't listening to his orders, he was listening to the corps commanders.

An army that was in disarray, without order or discipline, whose commanders had lost their units, that couldn't supply provisions, that couldn't establish communication, that had lost belief, was going to have to face the enemy on a front that stretched twenty-five miles.

Nazım Pasha gathered together his staff officers and returned to Istanbul.

He too had realized that disaster was unavoidable.

12

The war was approaching Istanbul like a dragon spewing flames, but the city still wasn't quite aware of this, the newspapers concealed the truth from the people with incomprehensible news, indeed in newspaper articles people were encountering claims that the army's victory was at hand.

Without informing anyone, indeed without even informing himself, Hikmet Bey had withdrawn from the world, he lived within a reclusiveness into which from time to time he consented to allow a few people he liked, in the boundless lands of the love he felt for Dilevser, the prickly worry he felt for his son, the dim and anguished recollections of a memory that was trying to forget the past and the ghosts of lost hopes that had accepted they no longer had a future, as had long been his custom he read the newspapers every morning, he tried to understand what was really happening in the war, trying to seize clues from the structures of sentences and the choice of words.

Only great events like war could form a bridge between life in the mansion and the outside world, could establish a relationship, arouse curiosity, he made an instinctive effort to hold on to this interest, struggled not to be completely cut off from the world, he carried a secret fear that if he cut himself completely he would suddenly grow old.

He had a peaceful life that was nourished by Dilevser's tenderness, but the passions that in his youth had exploded like a torchlit parade with love, rebellion and his rising expectations had not completely died, they had just faded from hopelessness; his inner life was something like autumn, the old trees still stood but they had shed their leaves, were they dead or would they become green again with the first sunny rain, even Hikmet Bey didn't know, "There is no passion without hope," he'd said to Osman, "your passions require hope in order to live. When hope appears those passions are resurrected."

He was thinking about old age, "You become old the moment you stop having dreams," he'd said to Osman, "the greatest indicator of youth is the capacity to have dreams, as long as you have dreams, as long as you have the strength to carry a dream, you needn't fear old age . . . But old age . . . Old age means not having the strength to dream, with every dream that ends, that is consumed, that fades into the distance as you draw closer to death, when the dreams are finished you're dead, if your body still draws breath even though the dreams have ended they call you old, and when the breathing stops too, they bury you."

If it hadn't been for Dilevser he might have been willing to accept old age, he would have waited for death with dreams that no longer breathed and a body that did, but his young wife's presence kept alive his desire to have dreams and to hang on to life, he thought that to give up on this would be unfair to her. It was partly for this reason that he kept his interest in the war fresh as he would have when he was younger.

"It's impossible to get information about the war from these newspapers," he said, "they give so little news about the war, I don't even know where the army is right now."

With the nonchalance and merciless frankness that always upset his father, Nizam said:

"That means your side is losing the war, that's why they present the news like that."

Unlike his father, Nizam didn't take any interest in the war, it was of no importance to him whatsoever whether the Ottoman Empire or the other nations won or lost the war, he wasn't interested in nations or in people, for him, anything that didn't directly affect his life wasn't worth paying attention to.

The pianist he'd seen at the gambling den was much more interesting to him than the war, a conversation he'd had with her, a word the woman had uttered, seeing that she was watching him when he left the gambling den, was much more significant that the emptying out of Kirkkilise and the Ottoman army fleeing. Life was a mirror in which he watched himself, he could not bear watching an event that didn't reflect him, he always sought his own reflection, his own existence.

Hikmet Bey had been annoyed by the words "your side."

"It's our side, Nizam, not my side, this is your country too."

"I'm sorry father, but I don't feel that way, I'm sure you wouldn't want me to lie . . . But I feel no connection to this place."

"Where do you feel a connection to?"

"Nowhere . . . Is it necessary for me to have a connection to some place? Why? Why should force myself to try to establish an inauthentic connection to people? I like Paris more than Istanbul, but I don't care in the least who's governing Paris unless they try to close the restaurants . . . Who governs Istanbul or who should govern it is not a matter of interest to me . . . Of course if there was someone who was going to clean up the piles of mud, illuminate the city better and open good restaurants and cheerful cafes it would be good . . . I'm sure you can agree that it's not the Ottomans who are going to do this, they haven't done it for centuries, they won't do it now. If you want the truth I don't think they'll be able to do it in the coming centuries . . . And weren't you the one who was saying that this country has no aesthetic, that there are no aesthetic values."

"If our only significant values were aesthetic we would have to live in museums, Nizam . . . There are other kinds of connections between people."

"What are they, father? The past? How could I have a

common past with this country? I didn't grow up here, and what if I had, everyone's life is different, isn't that so, do my life and my desires resemble these people's? Language? French is my language . . . Religion? I'm not religious . . . Dreams for the future? How could these people and I have common dreams for the future? They don't want the kind of country I want . . . Literature? Ottoman literature, when we have French, English, German, and Russian litera-ture? Music? What music? Is it music when the players sit next to each other and all play the same notes? I see that this truth upsets you, but I don't feel any connection to this place. I don't feel it with any place . . . The people who walk the streets are very important to you, I know that you placed your life in danger for their sake, but to tell the truth I don't under-stand why you did it. I myself wouldn't lift a finger for these people. What makes them more important than my own life? Which of their values would I give up my life for, would I take part in their wars for, would make their future significant for me? People are pathetic, insignificant creatures, they have no great value that can be taken seriously."

Hikmet Bey didn't conceal that this had angered him.

"Are you the only one who's significant, Nizam?"

"To me, yes . . . for them no . . . But anyway I'm not telling them to find me important, I'm not asking them to come with me and form a bond, I'm saying let them live their lives and let me live mine."

Nizam suddenly laughed as if he didn't even take what he was saying seriously.

"My agreement with the world is this, you live your life and I'll live mine . . . Don't expect me to participate in any of your wars."

"One day you might need that world. You live in that world. You talk like a fish that's denigrating the sea it lives in, if that sea should recede you won't be able to breathe."

"It won't recede . . . It wouldn't recede if you told it to . . . If it receded it wouldn't be the sea."

Dilevser, who was listening to the conversation and growing anxious that Hikmet Bey might become irritated, or worse, might be saddened, thought that it was necessary to intervene.

"Everyone has their own understanding of life, yours is this way, Nizam's is that way . . . He's not very wrong either, he's still very young, don't you always say that young people are more devoted to their independence and freedom? Well he's devoted to his own independence, I think he wants to establish his independence without forming a bond with anyone."

The two men suddenly looked at Dilevser, they realized she was anxious.

"I'm worried about Nizam," said Hikmet Bey, "if he builds such a thick wall around himself he'll be very lonely in the future, he won't have any close friends, any pals, any country . . . These other people that Nizam belittles are shelters for each other, harbors to shelter in during difficult times. A ship without a port is to be pitied . . . Where is it going to go? What place will it yearn for?"

Nizam had lost interest in the argument, he smiled again.

"Accept me as a pirate," he said, "they don't have harbors either. Just let me wander through life as a pirate, it's more fun that way, you can accept that too."

Hikmet Bey was going to say, "They hang pirates," but he didn't, even though his son had made him angry he didn't want to frighten or sadden him. He felt he needed to be protected, but, as he said to Osman, "his egotism always saddened me, but his loneliness always frightened me, he didn't have anyone around him to prevent him from getting hurt, he didn't know how badly life can hurt you, he was always like a small child, he never learned to grow up, or rather he couldn't manage . . . He remained a small child . . . Egoists never grow up. They always remain children. In my opinion, egoism is remaining a child . . . Never helping anyone but always thinking that there are people who are obliged to help him."

Nizam didn't understand why his father became annoyed, why he worried, why he wanted him to take an interest in the war and in other people, nor did he struggle to understand, he wasn't interested in what anyone thought, including his father. Whatever they thought, he was certain they would love him, he believed he deserved to be loved, he never questioned why he should be loved, he just believed this, his instincts told him not to delve into this, whenever he asked "why," all of his confidence vanished, and he didn't want this at all.

Dilara Hanım, who watched Nizam more carefully than anyone, and who figured him out better and more quickly than anyone, said, "That likeable boy wanted the whole world to love him without him having to love anyone, if the whole world loved him but there was one person who didn't love him, or who he thought didn't love him, he would pursue that person . . . Anyway that's why the disaster occurred . . ."

Osman was surprised by the indifference with which Dilara Hanım said this, "Didn't you like Nizam at all?" he asked, and Dilara Hanım said, "He made me laugh a lot, but I suppose I didn't like him, I don't like people who want everyone to love them, I find them greedy. People like that don't know the value of love, they greedily want more, they want it from everyone. They're arrogant, but at the same time they demand love like beggars from everyone they see . . . Who likes arrogant beggars? Not me, anyway."

Osman was surprised that Dilara Hanım spoke in such a harsh and hostile manner, he suddenly wondered about the reason for this secret anger and looked at her with suspicion, but he hesitated to ask the question that came to mind. In any event, the dead can't conceal their secrets for very long, what one wouldn't tell him, another would, or yet another would say something in such a way that a truth that had been concealed as a secret was suddenly illuminated.

As for Nizam, he wasn't even aware of any of this, he was thinking about the cold and silent Russian woman at the gambling den, he wondered how she was able to play the piano like that, why she'd been so unresponsive to him, why she looked at people as if they were dead, why her eyes were so empty, the mark on her face, her life.

Even if that young gambler hadn't invited him he would have gone to the gambling den that night, there was a riddle there that interested him and all of his attention had now gathered at that point, he was going to solve it, he was going to show the woman and himself that she wasn't going to be able to resist his charm.

He dressed with greater care than usual, he examined himself in the mirror for a long time, instead of wearing his coat he threw over his shoulders the thick, dark blue broadcloth cape that he used to wear on Paris evenings, he took the sword cane his father had used in his youth; he felt bewitched, he was excited, he knew that he was alive. No matter how boring he found the entirety of life, people, crowds, events and wars, the only point within that life that had succeeded in attracting Nizam's attention was so exciting and attractive.

As the carriage passed along deserted streets that the pale street lamps made even more pitiful, through darkness that smelled of mud, past silent mansion gardens and cemeteries with leaning tombstones, Nizam wasn't even looking outside, he'd closed himself in like a flower that had closed its petals, he was filled with his own being and with his desires.

When they turned onto the torch-lined road he felt a slight shiver, in the flames of the torches the trees swayed like bronze shadows, the mansion in the distance shone like a giant firefly, calling to people.

At first a burning sensation rose from his lungs to his

throat, he squeezed the leather strap on the corner of the window, then an icy cold covered his entire mind and numbed
him, for a brief period of time, every type of feeling disappeared in the darkness behind a heavy shutter. He was accustomed to his mind's maneuvers, its games, these waves of hot
and cold, he didn't panic, he knew that he was preparing to
experience some very strange, very exciting things, and that he
was going to create all of those events himself without any con-
tribution from anyone else. He had no need for people or for
life, life was already within him, what he experienced was just
a reflection in the milieu of his own mind. Life was interesting
as long as it reflected the games his mind played, according to
Nizam there was no need for any other creature in this nonsense they called life.

He felt a tingling as he walked towards the room from
which the sound of the piano was coming, the tingling vanished the moment he entered the room, his mind's games
stopped, he calmed down, by the time he experienced an event
his mind had finished its preparations, he had regained his
arrogance and his confidence.

There were a few people in the room, they were sitting in
the leather armchairs, Nizam didn't even pay any attention to
them, right away he looked towards the corner where the
piano stood, the woman was playing the piano in the same
green gown as she'd worn the night before, as if everything was
the same as the night before, he heard the same extraordinary
and surprising notes produced by that unemotional and magnificent technique. Nizam was very surprised that the woman
was wearing the same gown she'd worn the night before, this
was perhaps the first time in his life he'd seen a woman wear
the same dress two nights in a row. The woman's stance, playing, hair and dress were the same as the night before, she
looked as if she'd never left the place, as if she'd continued to
sit in the same place and play the piano.

Nizam walked slowly over to the woman and leaned on the piano, the woman just glanced up at him as she had the night before, once again her eyes were empty, there was no meaning in them, she continued playing as if Nizam hadn't come. For a moment Nizam felt that there was a note that was slightly off, but it had happened so quickly that he couldn't be sure whether or not it had happened.

He went and sat in one of the leather armchairs and started watching the woman, he was trying to figure out what it was about the woman that attracted him, she wasn't very beautiful, she wasn't coquettish, she wasn't interested, she possessed no feminine warmth, she didn't exhibit a strong rejection, she just acted as if she had no interest in life or in people. Nizam didn't admit it to himself openly, but somewhere in the back of his consciousness he accepted that he wanted to prove to the woman that he didn't deserve this lack of interest, and he relaxed. This was also among Nizam's capabilities, he could see a truth and at the same time he could ignore it, as if his mind squinted its eyes as it looked at the truth it wanted to understand, it saw that it was there, but closed its eyes before it grasped the details.

Nizam waited calmly waited for the woman to take a break from playing the piano and go smoke a cigarette over by the window. He wasn't impatient, he had a vast silence within him.

The piano stopped.

Once again the woman went and got a glass of wine, then went over to the window and lit a cigarette, as she did so she didn't pay any attention to her surroundings.

Nizam went over to the woman.

The woman raised her head and looked, then lowered it again.

"May I learn your name?" asked Nizam.

Compared to the previous night, his tone was more respectful and careful, the woman had taught him quickly that he couldn't behave with his usual ease.

"Why do you want to know?"

"I'm curious."

"Why are you curious?"

Nizam lit a cigarette and laughed.

"Is there a password?" he asked, "last night you used the same words. Is there a password? I'll say the password and the gates of the castle will suddenly open up and I'll learn you name? Is that it?"

The woman put out her cigarette.

"I have to play the piano."

Everything was the same as it had been the night before, as if the woman only lived one day, every day she repeated the same day and waited for it to end.

Nizam was either genuinely annoyed or he wanted to provoke the woman.

"When you play the piano can you manage to play with feeling, or is that no longer possible for you?"

The woman turned and looked at Nizam, for a moment he thought she was going to say something, but without saying anything more the woman went and sat at the piano and began playing with the same unemotional yet superb technique. Despite the woman's lack of response, he sensed he had touched her somewhere, he didn't know what he had touched or what kind of effect it had aroused, but he sensed that he had managed to pass behind the woman's empty eyes.

As he made his way back to his armchair, he saw the middle-aged manager from the night before coming towards him with an obsequious grin.

"You misunderstood me last night," the man said.

Without realizing it, Nizam looked at the man the same way the woman looked at other people, as if he was looking at a dead person.

The man thought Nizam didn't remember him.

"Remember you gave Kamil Bey a loan," he said, "because we wouldn't extend him any credit."

"Yes."

"Kamil Bey is a valued customer of ours, we meant no disrespect whatever, if it had been within my power I would certainly have extended him credit . . . But we're forbidden to extend him credit, we can't do it."

Once again Nizam looked at the man without saying anything. The man felt obliged to continue.

"Kamil Bey is Necip Osman Pasha's son, his brother works as a clerk at the palace. He comes from a very distinguished family but his family has forbidden us to extend credit to him, if we don't obey their wishes they can have this place closed down within an hour. Otherwise I would certainly wanted to help Kamil Bey . . ."

Nizam found it embarrassing to talk to this man about Kamil Bey, despite the man's unctuousness and the greasy smile on his face, there was a condescending, pitying tone in his voice when he spoke of Kamil Bey, and Nizam couldn't stand this.

Without drawing it out, he said, "Fine," turned his back and went and sat in the chair he'd been sitting in, for a moment the man didn't know what to do, then realizing there was nothing left to say, he sighed and left.

Nizam watched the pianist, he was looking at details he hadn't noticed the night before, she had broad, round shoulders that shone when she moved in the light, her green gown was growing thin from being cleaned and brushed every day, she was wearing ankle shoes with low, thick heels, the kind of shoes ballerinas wear, "A good type of shoe," thought Nizam, "but they're worn out."

Everybody has their mysteries, but you don't often encounter someone who is a complete mystery, until that day he'd never met a woman who wouldn't even tell him her name and who rejected any kind of relationship from the very start. Neither a joke nor a taunt could break the woman's cold silence.

As he was thinking these things he heard Kamil Bey's cheerful voice say, "ah, here you are."

Nizam stood and asked, "how are you?"

"*Merci*, I'm fine, tonight I lost the money I won on account of you yesterday, my father's generosity doesn't have as powerful an influence on destiny as yours did. Perhaps it's because his generosity isn't as sincere and genuine as yours, but I don't know about that part."

"If you want I can give you another loan."

"No, thank you. There are limits to taking advantage of politeness, even though I'm not known to be careful about limits, there are still limits that I respect."

Kamil Bey stopped and thought, then smiled and continued.

"Still, I shouldn't boast about the matter of limits, gamblers like me can lack sensitivity regarding limits."

He straightened his fez and said, "Come on, let's go."

"Let's not put my will power to the test again here tonight, I'm not always successful in passing these tests."

Nizam hesitated, in fact he didn't want to go anywhere, what he really wanted was to stay there and watch that woman and try to talk to her.

Kamil Bey, who sensed that he wasn't enthusiastic, glanced at Nizam and saw that he was staring at the pianist.

"Ha," he said, "Anya has attracted your interest. She won't talk to anyone, a lot of men have tried but they all gave up."

"But she's spoken to you . . ."

"Nooo . . . How did you arrive at that opinion?"

"You know her name . . . She refused to tell me."

Kamil Bey laughed his cheerful and carefree laugh.

"It cost me ten gold . . . I lent ten gold to Lütfullah Bey, the man who refused to give me a loan last night, and he told me the woman's name . . . But that's all, he doesn't know any more than that either, if he did he would have told me because he knew I would have given him more money. Perhaps the owner Monsieur Gavril knows, but he doesn't see anyone, I know that he comes here every morning after the customers have gone to go over the accounts, then he has breakfast and leaves. He's another mystery . . . All I know is that he has a glass of milk and a slice of bread for breakfast. He must be a skinny man."

"She won't speak to anyone?"

"Who, Anya?"

"Yes . . ."

"She won't talk to anyone, if you ask her name she'll ask you why you want to know, that's all."

"Weren't you ever curious?"

"How could I not be curious, my dear man, I told you I paid ten gold just to learn her name. No words could be as attractive as this woman's silence. The woman either knows this or she really doesn't want to talk to anyone, she won't talk . . . But she plays the piano very beautifully."

"She plays without any feeling . . ."

"How can Anya play with feeling when she doesn't have any feelings?"

"I wouldn't be so sure about that . . . I'm sure that one day she's not going to be able to stand it anymore and play in a completely different way, even if people tolerate it, the piano is not going to be able tolerate someone who plays that way . . ."

"Maybe she plays differently at home."

"Where does she live?"

Kamil Bey stopped and looked at him carefully.

"You're more interested in Anya than I guessed. If you'll excuse my disrespect, my friendly advice is to stay away from silence. It will draw you in . . . It's worse than gambling. If you take one step towards that silence it will draw you ten steps further in. You won't ever get out. Every man here has circled around Anya, they all saw the danger and stepped back . . . It's strange, but I think their passion for gambling saved them, because of their passion for gambling they weren't seized by another passion . . . But as far as I can see you don't have that kind of passion . . . You're more vulnerable to the danger than any of us."

Nizam didn't answer, he'd heard what Kamil Bey had said but he wasn't frightened of passion, he knew from experience that it wouldn't work its way into him, that after a time it would lose its power.

Kamil Bey took his silence as a sign of touchiness.

"I hope I haven't offended you, that you don't think I was being disrespectful. I just wanted to give you a friendly warning . . . I wouldn't want you to spend your life here the way I do, even if for a different reason, I wouldn't recommend it. I owe you a debt of friendship, the money part doesn't matter, what you did was very obliging, I'm not someone who wouldn't appreciate that. That's why I just wanted to warn you . . . If you felt I was being disrespectful, I apologize."

"No, no, it's nothing like that, please. I know you meant well, I was just thinking about what you said, that's all . . . Come on, let's go. I don't imagine you want to spend the whole night talking about Anya . . . Where are we going?"

"Let that be my mystery. You'll see when we get there. By the way, the lady I saw you with yesterday is upstairs, she's playing, if you want to go say hello . . ."

"I don't think that at the moment she's going to have much interest in me. Let's go . . . Let's go solve your mystery."

The two young men went out into the flame-lit garden, the torches all around them evoked the sense of being in the middle of a fire.

They got into Nizam's carriage, Kamil Bey told his driver to follow behind.

"Fire has an appeal," said Kamil Bey, "In my opinion, these torches are the main reason this gambling den is so popular . . . Monsieur Gavril knows what he's doing."

"Have you been coming here for a long time?"

"Since it opened . . . I suppose you've noticed that I'm a gambler," said Kamil with his open and cheerful smile.

Nizam smiled as well.

"I noticed."

"I wake in the morning with the desire to gamble, in the daytime I go to one or two places in the city, and in the evening I come here, in spite of Lütfullah Bey's impudence."

"Lütfullah Bey?"

"He's the one you saw last night, the man who wouldn't lend me any money, he's the manager. He's a good man, in fact, he'll do anything if you give him money . . . But my father scared these people, he's forbidden them to lend me money."

"Don't they realize that this could put you in a bad position? Someone like Lütfullah Bey could refuse you . . ."

"In fact they're right," said Kamil Bey frankly, "I can get carried away, my father could find out the next day that the mansion he likes so much belongs to someone else. They're setting a limit on me that I can't set on myself, if you can't set your own limits you're condemned to other people's limits, my good man, and you have to accept it . . . In one sense I'm happy about it, I feel more secure . . . I can't stop gambling, when I play I get carried away, the outcome is better for all of us when someone looks out for me. Of course it's not easy for them either, they're ashamed to have to tell people not to give their son money, but there's no other way."

Nizam looked at Kamil Bey's face, it was a radiant face, in a strange way it gave one a sense of trust, his unaffectedness and sincerity could be seen on his face. Even when he was anguished his face didn't grow dark, the lightness of accepting life as it is, with all its evils, hardships and sicknesses, was reflected in all of the lines of his face.

"They tell me to stop gambling . . . If it was possible I'd like to stop, I've been struggling with myself for a long time to quit . . . But it doesn't work. It's a disease, like tuberculosis or pneumonia, and there's no medication for it. I think it's fatal . . . After I accepted this truth at least I was able to give up feeling bad about it. I'm going to carry on this way until I either get better or I die . . . But I wouldn't recommend it to you. Not because I think gambling is bad, if you ask me there's nothing more fun and exciting in the world, but sometimes the outcomes can be embarrassing. You could end up having to bicker with someone like Lütfullah Bey. I see this as a side effect of the disease. Worse than the sickness itself . . . One good thing is that I'm struggling to control myself. When I'm almost out of money I start telling myself that I have to go, I've trained myself, I'm usually able to walk away, though sometimes I can't . . . Then it's bad."

"Has it been a long time since this began?"

"Four years or so . . . I was working at the Foreign Ministry, my father is an anglophile, he sent me to Oxford, I studied law, I was a good student, I know it's hard to believe, but I was, when I returned I started at the Ministry . . . At this point in the story a woman always appears . . . Mine appeared as well. She was a beautiful woman, charming . . . Instead of falling in love with the woman I fell in love with gambling. She's the one who brought me to a gambling den for the first time . . . That means I'd waited my entire life for the moment I saw a gambling den, it was love at first sight for me, I saw those tables, the green baize, the cards, I tasted the excitement of the game . . . Then suddenly I became a completely different person. Since that day I don't think about anything else, I'm not interested in anything else. I have some income from my mother, my father gives me an allowance, but they take measures to make sure I don't exceed that . . . Because every month I lose all of the money. In a consistent manner . . . I'd never managed to be this consistent in my life. Every month I give the same amount of money to the gambling den, in return they give me an excitement nothing else can give me. It's an honest exchange."

He spoke like clean water pouring from a clear spring, with an almost childish innocence he wanted to reveal all of his sins and weaknesses. Despite his childish candor to someone he'd just met, there was the sound of wounded maturity in the way he took secret revenge on himself by presenting himself in a sense as completely naked. He saw gambling as a serious disease, one sensed that he was trying to apologize to everyone for catching this disease, but he did this in such a nonchalant and cheerful way that rather than pity, you felt affection and trust.

They'd left the torch-lined road behind, Kamil Bey leaned out the window and said something to the driver, then came back in and leaned back.

"I've talked too much," he said, "it happens sometimes, I think I generally respond this way to a friendly attitude . . . There's not a lot of friendship in gambling dens, as you can imagine, everyone plays as if they've been poisoned by their own greed, they almost never pay any attention to anyone else . . . What do you do, as far as I can see you're not that fascinated by gambling . . . "

"Nooo, I like gambling, like you I find it exciting, I think the difference for me to a degree is that I suddenly get bored. I don't have your passion, for anything . . . I mean I can't say that I'm not envious either."

Kamil Bey was surprised.

"You're envious of my being a gambler? This is the first time I've heard this, my dear man, everyone pities me, they try to counsel me . . . It wouldn't be a lie if I said I never met anyone like you, what is it that you envy?"

"Your passion, having a bond that doesn't break . . ."

Then he added with a laugh, "your consistency."

"Don't you have any passion, something you're passionately addicted to, a person, a game, an event?"

Nizam remembered the conversation he'd had with his father that morning.

"No I don't think so . . . I have no addiction, no passion."

Kamil Bey leaned way back, lit a cigarette, and looked at Nizam as if he was amused.

"Then, my good man, you must be addicted to passion itself."

"Perhaps . . . I don't know, I don't think about this kind of thing much, I know that I don't have any passion, sometimes this gives me a great sense of freedom, but sometimes . . ."

Kamil Bey waited for Nizam to continue, and when he realized he wasn't, he asked:

"Sometimes what?"

"I don't know," said Nizam, shrugging his shoulders, "sometimes I don't know what it is."

"I envy you too," Kamil Bey said cheerfully, "but I don't think we're going to find anyone else who envies our situations."

Just then the carriage shuddered as it turned onto a dark, cobblestones street, a little later at the end of the street they stopped in front of a mansion whose shutters were all closed, and from which no light could be seen.

Kamil Bey looked out the window and said, "We're here."

Not in any hurry to get out, he said,

"There's nothing like this place anywhere in the world, ladies work in this house. This isn't a figure of speech, real ladies, some of them are wives of government officials, they generally come during the day . . . Sometimes they come at night when their husbands are out of town, last year a treasury inspector met the wife of a luminary here, they became a ballad for all of Istanbul, I'm not joking, they really made the incident into a ballad, you still hear it from time to time."

They got out of the carriage together.

Kamil Bey banged the iron knocker on the carved wooden door a couple of times, a small hatch in the door opened, a black face appeared, the hatch closed and the door opened.

The stone-paved vestibule they entered was dim, there was a thick curtain hanging at the end of the vestibule, a large man of African descent greeted Kamil Bey without smiling but with great respect and opened the curtain for them.

They were greeted by a dark redness that looked as if candlelight had evaporated and filled the air, the velvet sofas in the hall, the curtains, indeed even the walls were red, the gilded fringes of the curtains shone yellow amidst all that red, in a corner a woman was pensively playing an oud, she was singing softly in a nasal tone, the women were elegant and beautiful, indeed there was one, with curly dark hair, arched eyebrows, a Greek nose, full, heart-shaped lips, and a long white neck who sat like a goddess in that redness. The room smelled of candles, fire and violets. In a corner was the largest tiled stove Nizam had seen in his life, inlaid with green and pink.

Nizam didn't conceal his surprise.

"What a strange city Istanbul is, by day the muddy streets are filled with soldiers who have cholera, by night it's like the nights of ancient Rome . . ."

"Istanbul doesn't reveal itself easily, my good man, in Paris or London you can't find the entertainment that exists here. The only condition here is to not be seen . . . That's why everything bright and beautiful is hidden, you have to search in order to find it."

Nizam looked at the dark woman.

"She's a beautiful woman," he said.

"Evangeliki . . . They say she's the daughter of a Greek ship

owner, she ended up here after her father went bank-
rupt . . . That's what they say, God alone knows how true it
is . . . She could be the daughter of a Jew from Balat. Here it's
not quite possible to distinguish the truth from the lies, I
wouldn't recommend even trying to do so, you'll get caught in
a vortex . . . But since you like her, let's invite Evangeliki."

As they were talking among themselves, an older woman, in
a plum-colored gown and with her white hair tied up in a bun,
came over to them.

"Welcome, Kamil Bey," she said, "I had your room upstairs
prepared as you ordered, which of the ladies do you like?"

"The gentleman wanted Evangeliki, and send me Şadiye if
she's free."

"What do you mean, of course she's free, you go on up, the
ladies will join you shortly."

The butler who'd opened the door for them led the way,
they climbed the stairs, the butler opened the door to a room,
the walls were lilac colored, the sofa in the corner was covered
with a purple cloth, in the middle, on the floor, white porcelain
plates of appetizers had been arranged on a copper tray.

Nizam made a face.

"Eating on the floor?"

"We're going to have to put up with it," said Kamil Bey
cheerfully, "tables haven't arrived here yet, I suppose they continue to do this because it's easier to gather up and hide if
there's any kind of raid."

Kamil Bey sat at the tray with one leg under him and the
other leg bent in front of him, there was a laughable air of inexperience in the way he was sitting, but Nizam, who was still
standing and couldn't quite figure out what to do, was even
funnier.

"Can you manage to sit the way I have?"

"I don't think I can manage . . . And people look so strange
when they sit like this."

Kamil Bey laughed, he never seemed to lose his cheerfulness.

"You look strange standing there like that too, my good man . . . Anyway, I won't insist, to tell the truth I'm uncomfortable sitting this way, you sit on the sofa, I'll tell them to bring a coffee table and put the tray on that."

Kamil Bey stood, as they were standing there in the middle of the room, the door opened and Evangeliki came in, accompanied by a sandy-haired, pretty-faced woman of about the same height but with a little more flesh on her bones, Nizam guessed she was Şadiye.

When Şadiye saw them standing there like that she asked, "What the devil are you doing? Why are you standing, why don't you sit down?"

"We can't quite manage to sit on the floor, Şadiye, could you please ask them to put the tray on a coffee table, then we can sit on the sofa."

Nizam noticed that Kamil Bey had said "we" so as not to embarrass him, and he was pleased by this.

"Of course," said Şadiye.

She opened the door and called to someone, a little later they brought a coffee table and placed the tray on it and everyone sat on the sofa.

"What would you like to drink?" asked Şadiye.

Kamil Bey turned to Nizam and asked the same question, "What would you like to drink?"

"Do they have wine, I wonder."

Kamil Bey made a face.

"I don't think they'll have wine here, if we ask they'll send a man to go get some, but I doubt if it would be drinkable . . . Will *rakı* or brandy do?"

"*Rakı* will be fine."

Şadiye was teasing Kamil Bey.

"You haven't come here for a long time, somehow I can't

compete with playing cards, you always find them more attractive than me."

From the way the woman spoke, it was clear there was some kind of closeness between them.

"Well I'm here now, Şadiye."

With coquettish emphasis, Şadiye said,

"Once in a blue moon. Do I deserve this?"

Raki was poured, they started drinking and eating, the food was delicious enough to surprise Nizam.

He could feel Evangeliki's warmth and smell her scent, it was the same violet scent he'd smelled when he entered the room downstairs, she sat very close to Nizam, the round indentation of her waist was touching Nizam's elbow, she acted as if she wasn't aware of this. Both women behaved in a demure manner, there was no forwardness, none of the crassness that would have made Nizam uneasy, or rather Şadiye was talking, and despite the coquettishness of her tone she didn't adopt a discomfiting manner.

Evangeliki turned to Nizam and said, "You don't talk much." She had a faint Greek accent.

"Are you shy, or is it that you just don't like me?"

"Neither, it's just that I don't know what we could talk about."

"What do you do?"

"I don't do anything, I only arrived here recently."

"Where were you?"

"Paris."

"Ah," said Evangeliki with a deep sigh, "Paris is the city I most want to go to . . . Is it as beautiful as they say? They say it's always brightly lit."

"It's more beautiful than they say."

"Of course you met some very beautiful women there."

"There are very beautiful women there of course, but it would be very difficult to find one as beautiful as you."

Evangeliki's answer surprised Nizam.

"You're very gracious."

"Where are you from?" asked Nizam.

"I'm from Salonica, I came here as a child . . . A little more *rakı?*"

Nizam realized that the woman didn't want to talk about herself and didn't persist.

They talked about Paris, London, Istanbul, food, drink, gambling, Evangeliki nestled closer and closer to him.

Şadiye said, "Shall we retire to our rooms? We have things we need to talk about one on one."

Evangeliki took Nizam by the hand, they left the room and went to another room, the walls had been painted lavender, there was a purple cloth on the bed like the one they'd seen in the other room. There was a small tiled stove in the corner, it warmed the room.

The woman undressed herself first, she had a body that could be called perfect, that hadn't been worn out by the life she lived, Nizam looked her over from head to toe, her firm skin possessed a smooth light, her soft curves evoked a sense of feminine warmth and healthy vivacity. Evangeliki took Nizam's clothes off unhurriedly . . . Nizam didn't say anything about what she was doing, he was curious about what she was going to do, the numbness in his mind had begun when they got into bed, the woman pressed her entire body against his, as if she wanted him to feel her warmth, her softness, her femininity, Nizam didn't see anything anymore, he only felt. There was nothing but that vivacious warmth, that smooth softness, everything else had disappeared.

Every time Nizam made love he was seized by a physical adoration, his entire body fell in love with the woman, he would caress her passionately, then caresses wouldn't be enough for that fire within him, that love couldn't be satisfied by touch alone, his body would become savage, as if he wanted to tear the woman to pieces and make her part of his body. He felt his passion violently.

As they made love Evangeliki whispered, "whatever you want, whatever you want, let's see if the women in Paris are any better . . ."

They stopped when the cold grey light of morning began to seep through the curtains, Nizam suddenly got up and began dressing.

"Are you leaving?"

"Yes."

"You weren't pleased?"

"On the contrary, Evangeliki, I was very pleased, there are really very few women like you."

"Will you come again?"

"Should I?"

"Come . . . If you can't, send for me and I'll come."

"I'll come. But now I have to go, I'm late."

He dressed and went downstairs, the white-haired woman was sitting alone in the room, it was as if the night had only just begun for her, there was no sign of weariness on her face.

Nizam looked at the woman, undecided about whether or not he was supposed to give her money, the woman understood and said, "You're Kamil Bey's guest, sir, you're welcome any time."

Nizam rushed out and told the carriage driver to get out of there quickly.

It was just beginning to grow light as they raced down the empty streets, as they turned onto the torch-lined road the servants were extinguishing the torches, the front of the mansion was empty, all the carriages were gone.

The carriage stopped in front of the gambling den, Nizam hurried out of the carriage, ran into the gambling den, there was no sound from the piano, the mansion was silent, he went to the room on the side, the lid of the piano had been closed, he scanned the room, Anya was by the window, smoking a cigarette.

When Nizam started walking towards her, he saw surprise in her eyes for the first time.

He went and stood next to the woman.

"What's your name?"

"Why are you asking?"

"Because I was curious about whether you would tell me your name when there was no one else around, when the two of us were alone here in the light of early morning."

"Is that why you came?"

"Yes, Anya, that's why I came."

"You've learned my name."

"I have . . . But I was curious about whether or not you would tell me your name . . . What's your name, Anya?"

Anya looked at Nizam, she looked into his eyes and saw what no one else had ever seen, had ever been able to see, the glow of a madness that was burning itself, destroying itself. This didn't frighten her, it might have frightened someone else but it didn't frighten her, on the contrary something akin to cheerfulness appeared for the first time in those empty eyes.

"You're mad."

"Yes, Anya . . . What's your name?"

Anya took a puff from her cigarette, blew the smoke towards the ceiling, turned to look at Nizam, she looked at him for a long time, then slowly, almost tenderly, she said,

"My name is Anya . . ."

13

All day Captain Neşet Bey, with his large eyes and large moustache, went to visit to units of the officers he knew, he kept repeating almost exactly the same words with great dismay and anger, "Thrace is a breadbasket, the harvest is in, the warehouses are full of grain, how is it, brother, that the soldiers here are hungry and have no provisions? If you put a thief in charge of the Quartermaster Corps, of course he and his gang are going to be too busy with thievery and extortion to bother with supplying provisions . . . The men here remain hungry and miserable . . . Those bastards have left us defenseless against the Bulgarians . . . We've lost face, they've rendered our honor worthless, God damn them, God damn them."

As darkness was falling, the sergeant came to give Ragıp Bey the news.

"Captain Neşet shot himself just a little while ago."

Ragıp Bey bit his lip and just said, "He was a dignified man," during the past week the same thing had occurred to him several times, he thought it would be the best way to be freed of all this anguish and shame, but then he pictured Cevat Bey saying, "Don't put your life in danger, promise me," and he decided that it would be dishonorable to break the promise he'd made his older brother.

"Is there any of my cognac left, sergeant?"

"I can find some, commander."

"Bring it."

He climbed a knoll to the right that looked over the

Karaağaç Forests, stood perfectly erect as if he was challenging the enemy, life, fate, and "those bastards" and drank a little cognac from the flat flask.

Like all of the other officers, he couldn't understand why the army had been left hungry and why no provisions were being supplied, as Neşet Bey had said, "Thrace is a breadbasket," why were the men being left hungry in a place like this, as he said to Osman, "politics and thievery ruined the army."

The army that had fled Kırkkilise, which would later be renamed Kırklareli, without firing a shot had moved to the Lüleburgaz line and was being reorganized there, a large number of the soldiers who had fled had rejoined their units. The right flank of the front would be defended by the corps under the command of Mahmut Muhtar Pasha, the center by the corps under the command of Şevket Turgut Pasha and the left flank by the corps under the command of Abuk Ahmat Pasha, while the army commander Abdulla Pasha had established his headquarters in Sakız Köyü.

At the request of Muhtar Pasha, who was acquainted with Ragıp Bey, he had been assigned to the Third Corps under his command in Kırkkilise.

The Ottoman army had dug in along a twenty-five-mile front, but no communication was possible among the corps or between the corps and the army commander, no one knew what anyone else was doing.

There wasn't a single road that could be said to be "paved" on this vast plain cut by deep valleys, villages deep in the valleys, consisting of a few houses of mudbrick and straw, had been abandoned, the unceasing rain had turned the plain into a swamp. There was an ocean of wet and sticky mud as far as the eye could see.

Mahmut Muhtar Pasha, one of the best and most courageous commanders in the army, had brought all of the cannons together and had placed the artillery forces under Ragıp Bey's command. Ragıp Bey lined the cannons up and adjusted their angles, had the shells placed in shelters covered with tarpaulin, he'd had large planks placed side by side over the mud and had the ammunition crates placed on them.

As Muhtar Pasha was inspecting the front, when he came to the artillery forces he looked at the placement of the cannons and asked, "Are you ready Ragıp?" "We're ready Pasha." "Make them regret that they came." "We'll make them regret it Pasha." Muhtar Pasha, with that proud stance that suited him so well, smiled, "You will Ragıp," he said, "I know you, God willing we'll get our revenge for Kırkkilise."

On the 26th of October, the infantry of the Bulgarian Third Army, under the command of General Radkto Dimitriev, reached the banks of Karaağaç Stream, which ran along the side of the Karaağaç Forests, the mud was slowing their advance as well.

The Bulgarians began their first attack the following day, but Ragıp Bey's artillerymen scattered them and truly made them regret it. General Dimitriev retreated. He waited for the rest of his army.

On the 29th of October the other units of the Bulgarian army arrived, they spread out along the length of the Karaağaç trenches, the following day the Bulgarian First Army under the command of General Kohtichev positioned themselves on the right flank.

Both armies were prepared for war.

Nearly three hundred thousand people were lined up facing each other on a muddy plain, waiting for the hour when they would move into action to kill one another.

That night was very cold, it rained unceasingly, there was a firm, sharp darkness, there was constant noise from both sides, the smells of rain, human sweat, animals, greasy bullets, and steel mixed together. Nobody could sleep. The restless movement of hundreds of thousands of people in corridors that had been dug into the ground, the swishing of wet uniforms, spread across the entire plain. Everyone there knew that some of them were going to die in the morning, and that they could be among those who were killed.

Ragıp Bey went to all of the positions, inspected the cannons, the shells, and the artillery teams, and reassured himself that nothing was lacking and that no mistakes had been made.

Towards midnight he sat on an artillery shell under a tarpaulin that had been placed over the shells.

A soldier began reading the Koran aloud, Ragıp Bey listened to him, when the soldier paused between verses there where whispers of "amen."

"We're going into battle tomorrow, sergeant," he said.

"We're going into battle, commander."

"We could die," said Ragıp Bey with a laugh.

"If God ordains us to die, commander."

Ragıp Bey felt a jubilation within him, exploding again and again, striking his chest, his lungs, his nasal passage as it tried to get out, he felt elated by the prospect of going into battle, restoring his honor, getting revenge and most importantly by the possibility that he might die. Very few people wanted to die as sincerely as Ragıp Bey did, he'd decided that as long as he was alive he would never be free from the anguish that had now become part of him and from the yearning he was ashamed to feel, without even informing himself he had been entreating fate to allow him to die for a reason that had nothing to do with him, and now he was facing this possibility. Death was a deep silence that would quiet all of the voices within him, he yearned for that silence.

A thought that suddenly occurred to him alarmed him and made him shudder.

"Sergeant," he said.

"Yes, commander."

"Sergeant, there are three letters in my breast pocket, if

anything happens to me, take those letters and burn them without showing them to anyone."

"Yes, sir."

Ragıp Bey relaxed. The soldier had stopped reading the Koran.

A thick darkness was trembling with rain, a thick vapor was rising from the men into the darkness.

"I wish it would start," he thought to himself, in fact everyone wanted it to start as soon as possible. "In war," he'd said to Osman, "the most difficult thing for a soldier is waiting for the fighting to begin, when you're fighting you don't think about anything, you just fight, you move according to your instincts, but when you're waiting you think, you envision what could happen, in times like that it's necessary to keep the men's morale fresh."

"Sergeant, shall we frighten these Bulgarians?"

"Let's frighten them, commander."

"Belt out a folk song towards the mountains, make it a song that all of the men can join in."

He sensed that the sergeant was smiling in the dark.

He began suddenly in a deep voice.

The brave stand firm the cowardly flee
There's roaring and rumbling all around
The king of kings opens the council
The council will roar and rumble

It was as if the whole valley suddenly fell quiet, this was a sound no one had been expecting, as the sergeant sang, one or two voices from the artillery emplacements joined in, then all of the men began singing in unison.

The brave stand firm the cowardly flee
There's roaring and rumbling all around

When the song finished there were enthusiastic shouts from the trenches.

Ragıp Bey thought, "We're ready. If only I had a cigarette."

In the middle of a rainy night, sitting on one artillery shell and leaning his back on another, waiting for the battle to begin, the cloudy thoughts and trembling dreams of a mind that was half asleep appeared and disappeared in fragments, "We could have been happy," he thought, "but she didn't want that," "perhaps I'll be killed by an artillery shell, that would be the best," "we could have been happy," "we were happy at one time," "one morning she wept," "we could have been happy," "death would be the most auspicious," "the artillerymen are ready."

The words, "We could have been happy" kept inserting themselves among all of his other thoughts and dreams, he experienced all of the disappointment and regret of a person who had found happiness and then lost it, he kept asking himself why this happiness had been broken, he wanted to understand, "Why had two people who could have been happy not been able to be happy?" He was seeking the answer to this question, he couldn't find it, without realizing it he was muttering, "We could have been happy."

"We could have been happy . . ."

The first shell ripped through the darkness, which was beginning to be illuminated by a silvery mist that was drifting down from the hilltops, with a sharp whistle, it exploded in front of the trenches, sending out a shower of shrapnel that looked like red sparks. The shells were coming in through the rain with sharp and frightening whispers, the were exploding in the trenches, screams of "Oh, mother!" could be heard, Ragıp Bey gave all of the batteries the order to fire.

There were shouts of "Load, ready, fire!" "Load, ready, fire!"

They were spotting the flashes from the cannons on the other side through binoculars and making adjustments, shouts of "Fifteen degrees up, twenty degrees to the right!"

"Load, ready, fire!" mixed with the screams of those who had been hit.

With each shell that fell there was a rain of mud and blood, there was no end to the screams, yells, shouts and orders, it was raining fiercely, the artillerymen were carrying shells to the cannons, loading them and firing according to the system that had been devised earlier.

Hours and hours and hours passed, neither the rain nor the artillery fire abated, the men were loading the cannons with mechanical movements, waiting for the order and firing, loading another shell, waiting for the order and firing; they were all covered in mud and blood, the frightful cracking of the explosions had made all the men drunk, in that hellish cacophony they'd forgotten everything.

Ragıp Bey saw a howitzer shell land in a nearby trench and blow a team of five people to pieces, their arms, legs, heads, feet, chunks of their flesh, and their bones scattered with the shrapnel, they remained suspended in the rain for a moment and then fell into the mud.

No one paid any attention, death had lost its reality, now on the battlefield neither death nor life was real, hundreds and thousands of people were under the sway of a different situation, a different mood, a different mode of existence that no one could name and that was beyond life and death, they no longer thought about dying or killing, all they wanted was to carry more shells, to fire more shots. People had become parts of their cannons or rifles, they had no emotions, they consisted of steel, iron, and gunpowder.

As the rain increased, the mud became deeper, when the gun carriages recoiled after each shot, their wheels sank a little deeper into the mud, red pools of blood mixed with the dirt and changed the color of the mud, a cloud of gun smoke had formed above the plain, making the rain increasingly grey, the sky smelled of burning gunpowder, this smell overlay all other smells.

They fired cannons at each other for two days, without eating, sleeping, stopping, or thinking, the ground shook with the explosions, the ground under their feet was shaking, all of them were completely wet, they were wet from the rain and their own sweat, as they moved, steam that smelled of blood and gunpowder rose from them.

There were no medics or doctors around, the dead were immediately carried to the rear and left there, the wounded were pulled into a corner. Dead bodies with pierced brains, gouged eyes, lungs that had been torn apart and severed arms and legs were accumulating into a small hill, blood was seeping from the bodies into the mud, rain was filling the hollows in these punctured, shattered dead bodies.

For forty-eight hours neither army moved a millimeter, they just fired their canons to get the other side to retreat.

Ragıp Bey's artillery men fired constantly, but they didn't know the situations of the other units in the corps nor in the other corps, they weren't getting any news from anywhere.

At the time they weren't aware that preparations were being made for a disaster that would affect the entire army. They were to learn about what happened later.

On the night of the 30th of October, Bulgarian units across from the left flank that was under the command of Abuk Ahmet Pasha ceased firing, there was a sudden quiet, the commanders and the men thought that the Bulgarians were pausing until morning.

The men hadn't slept for two days, they wrapped themselves in their greatcoats and fell into a deep sleep in their muddy trenches.

Towards midnight, Bulgarian infantry began crawling through the mud and advancing silently, night and the rain concealed them, the men were in a deep sleep, the infantry stopped when they were three hundred yards from the Ottoman positions.

The Bulgarian units suddenly lit the acetylene-powered

projectors they had with them, the Ottoman positions were illuminated as if by daylight, the Ottoman soldiers couldn't see the Bulgarians in the blinding light of the projectors but the Bulgarians could see even the smallest details, by daylight they'd identified their targets and adjusted their cannons.

In the steel white of that sharp acetylene light, they suddenly began their bombardment, the men were caught unprepared, they couldn't see, they couldn't take aim, they were being torn apart by shells, they helplessly lay in the mud in their trenches and tried to hide.

The left flank of the front collapsed under this assault, in the middle of the night a Bulgarian division attacked the trenches in the district of Türkbükü and took control of them, they remained there until morning, and in the morning the Bulgarian artillery moved to the Türkbükü positions.

That morning the Ottoman lines were breached, six thousand Bulgarian soldiers and thirty cannons flowed through the breach and moved to the rear of the Ottomans.

The Bulgarian command staff had sensed the weakness of the left flank and began firing all of their howitzers, Abuk Pasha's men hadn't responded because they weren't as well prepared as Mahmut Muhtar Pasha's corps, they'd used up all of their artillery shells.

The left flank couldn't withstand this assault, towards noon on the 31st of October the Ottoman Army's left flank began to retreat in a disorderly manner.

Dilara Hanım learned about how the disaster had developed and about the strange twist of fortune sooner and in more detail than Ragıp Bey. Monsieur Lausanne's English colleague Mr. Berthold, a correspondent for the *Daily Telegraph*, had witnessed this disaster in person, and later had spoken of it to his colleagues and written about it to his newspaper.

Mr. Berthold, an intrepid man, had gone first to Lüleburgaz by carriage, from there, with a local guide, he'd gone on horseback to Sakız Köyü where Abdullah Pasha had established his headquarters.

Fate loves to play games and do strange things, the question of how one of the greatest disasters in military history would have unfolded had Mr. Berthold not gone to Sakız Köyü remains unanswerable.

Mr. Berthold found Abdullah Pasha sitting completely still in a thatched house that smelled of straw, the Pasha's face was completely white, there were rings under his eyes, he had difficulty speaking, he couldn't move.

He hadn't eaten for four days.

His aides were boiling the corncobs they'd found in the garden and trying to render them edible, after they'd been softened a bit they tried to eat the cobs. Abdullah Pasha was holding a cob too, from time to time he brought it to his mouth and forced himself to bite into it.

He wasn't receiving any news from the front, he had no information about what the army under his command was doing, there was no telephone or telegraph in the headquarters, he'd tried to send a few couriers but they came back when their horses got stuck in the mud, from the crumbs of information he got from soldiers and villagers he encountered he guessed that Mahmut Muhtar Pasha's corps was fighting with superb courage and that the left flank was retreating.

Mr. Berthold gave the canned meat, chocolate, hard tack and biscuits in his bag to Abdullah Pasha's aide. They opened the cans by tearing them apart with their knives and ate the contents with their hands.

As he ate, blood returned to Abdullah Pasha's face, he regained his color and gathered his strength, then gave the order to "get my horse ready."

He got on his horse and set out with his aides to the army's left flank, after they'd gone a few miles they came across the first of those who were fleeing, he realized that he'd guessed correctly and that the left flank was retreating.

If the Pasha hadn't encountered Mr. Berthold, if he hadn't eaten the food he gave him, if he hadn't gathered his strength and set out, if he hadn't come across the fleeing soldiers, would he have given the same order, no one knew the answer, but the Pasha had set out and had encountered the fleeing soldiers. When he saw the fleeing soldiers he immediately panicked, thinking that if the left flank had been breached he wasn't going to be able to protect the positions of the center and the right flank, he sent the order for Şevket Turgut Pasha and Mahmut Muhtar Pasha to retreat in an orderly fashion.

When they received the order to retreat, Şevket Turgut Pasha had stopped the Bulgarians and was preparing a counterattack, and Mahmut Muhtar Pasha had the Bulgarians pinned down in the mud.

They were hungry, they were sleepless, but holding the enemy off and not being driven back had strengthened everyone's morale, their enthusiasm enabled them to ignore their hunger.

While Şevket Turgut Pasha was preparing an assault he had to grumblingly accept the order to retreat, he gave the order for the corps to retreat.

An hour or two later Abdullah Pasha realized that the order he'd given had been a mistake and changed his mind, he sent an order to Şevket Turgut Pasha to return to their positions immediately and to continue engaging the enemy, but it was much too late.

With the order to "retreat," morale immediately plummeted, thousands of soldiers, like sleepwalkers who'd been woken, suddenly realized they were hungry and sleepless and were seized by a terrible fear. They refused to return to their positions and started running away.

Mahmut Muhtar Pasha, now alone on the front line, was also obliged to "give the order to retreat." The order to retreat had the same effect on his corps.

An army that would have attacked if given the order to "attack" became like animals fleeing a forest fire when given the order to "retreat"; they fled without caring about anything.

When Ragıp Bey received "the order to retreat" he didn't understand at first what the messenger was saying, his face turned a deep red, his veins bulged, his chest heaved violently.

"I have shells, I have men, why the hell should I retreat, you miserable creature," he shouted, but there was nothing the messenger could do.

Before giving the order to the men he said to the sergeant, "Take a few men and bring me the artillery mules," the sergeant came back a little later and said, "They've taken the mules." "Who took them?" "I don't know, commander, it might have been the quartermaster corps, they're hungry, perhaps they'll butcher them." "How could they butcher the artillery mules, what's going to happen to the cannons?" The sergeant stared straight ahead and didn't say anything.

All of the soldiers pulled together to get the cannons out of the mud but they couldn't, the wheels were halfway buried in the mud.

"Load the cannons," said Ragıp Bey.

They loaded shells into all of the cannons, "Now fill the barrels of the cannons with mud," they packed the cannons with mud, the put fuses in all of them, then they retreated twenty paces.

"Fire!"

As he watched the fuses crackle as they burned, the sergeant said, "I hope to God the rain doesn't put them out," and Ragıp Bey said, "if they go out I'll go and fire them one by one myself."

The fuses reached the cannons without going out, with a terrifying explosion all of the cannons were lifted half a yard into the air as if they were rearing, all of their barrels became bright red, split, and fell apart.

In a slow voice, the sergeant said, "The enemy is getting closer, commander."

"Alright, we're retreating in an orderly manner, no one is going to be separated from the unit, I'll shoot anyone who tries to leave."

"There aren't that many of us left," said the sergeant.

"How many are we?"

"Fewer than thirty . . ."

Ragıp Bey looked at the little hill of bodies to the rear, he looked at those young people who had been torn apart, it was only now that he could grasp that they were dead, he'd forgotten the idea of death.

"What are we going to do with our martyrs?" he asked the sergeant.

"The enemy is approaching, commander, all we can do is leave them to God's mercy."

"We can't even bury our dead," said Ragıp Bey, "God damn us."

They were the only unit to take the trouble to destroy their cannons, the other units fled and left their cannons as they were. The mud was now up to their knees, each step they took was like sinking into a swamp, it was only with great difficulty that they could lift their feet.

"If we move at this speed, the enemy cavalry will hunt us down," said the sergeant slowly to Ragıp Bey.

"Don't panic, horses can't move through this mud, they're tired too. They won't come after us."

As they walked they came across cannons, ammunition crates, rifles and dead soldiers in the mud, it was raining ceaselessly, it was cold, hunger was not just gnawing at their stomachs, it was gnawing at their lungs.

The plain was covered by a hundred thousand people trying to flee through the mud without knowing which way to go, they looked like black ants in the rain.

Sometime later they came across miserable crowds of refugees, they were trying to drag their ox carts through the

202 · AHMET ALTAN

mud, they wanted to save whatever possessions they'd been able to take from their homes, the wheels of the ox carts were squeaking, they could hear the moaning of wounded men who'd been abandoned in the mud.

As Ragıp Bey had guessed, the Bulgarians didn't come in pursuit of them.

The miserable army moved towards Istanbul with the refugees, fleeing in terror even though there was no one pursuing them.

The following day an official notice concerning the battle of Lüleburgaz was published in the newspapers.

"Chance plays an important role in war, and while the aim of every front line is victory this is not always possible. A nation that has accepted war must accept the outcome with great calm and steadfastness. Therefore it is not right to either take unnecessary pride in the results achieved or to be seized by grief and panic at seeming lack of success. For instance in the war that is being waged, Ottoman soldiers conducted a successful defense in the vicinity of Schodra and Yanya, but in order to conduct a more successful defense the Eastern Army has been temporarily moved to Çatalca. Of course everything possible will be done to defend the nation."

That was all.

Thousands of people died, thousands of hungry soldiers fled, and the only thing people were able to learn about this battle in which a wrong order led to a military disaster were the confused words of this brief notice.

The state hadn't managed to feed its army, to fight and defend territory, but as always it had managed to deceive its own people.

The truth only appeared in the foreign newspapers.

Monsieur Lausanne filled Dilara Hanım in on the details that had not been written about.

14

Nothing can stand in the way of an anxious woman's worries; Dilara Hanım was one of the few people in that vast empire who followed the war most closely, who learned almost all of the details in the shortest time. Sometimes she learned more quickly than the Commander of the General Staff.

Monsieur Lausanne spent his days visiting embassies and ministries, sometimes he went as far as he could on the Lüleburgaz road, sometimes he spoke to correspondent friends who had managed to reach the front, but every day he came and told Dilara Hanım everything he had been able to learn about developments in the war, the positions of the Ottoman and Bulgarian armies and skirmishes and their outcomes.

In a strange way, her worries about Ragıp Bey had turned learning about the progress of the war into an unhealthy passion, there was no logical reason, but she believed deeply that as long as she observed the war closely, nothing bad would happen to Ragıp Bey. If Monsieur Lausanne was a little late she would panic, she was seized by the worry that bad news would come.

Monsieur Lausanne was like a secondary road she had to take to get to the main road, the more she wanted to reach the main road, the more reason she had to take the secondary road, there was an inevitable closeness developing between them, after he gave her information about the war, they talked about life and about people, Lausanne told her small items of gossip, sometimes they went together to embassy receptions. Lausanne was aware that the war increased the closeness between them, he began gathering information more for Dilara Hanım than for his newspaper. He was trying to ascertain whether this strange curiosity was due to the concern she felt for someone at the front or if this was her way of expressing an interest in him, sometimes he decided it was one and sometimes he decided it was the other, but he was never certain. Once he thought about asking, but for some reason he didn't.

When he brought good news, when the fighting had paused, he noticed that Dilara Hanım was clearly relieved, and also that her interest in him increased, he tried to find good news, but he never told Dilara Hanım a lie, his professional ethics and his honor would not permit that.

When Dilara Hanım was alone at night, she thought, and tried to understand her emotions, "Love," she said to Osman, "seems to be like any emotion blown up to monstrous proportions in an unhealthy manner, I can't make out which emotion this is, it could be tenderness, it could be jealousy, it could be worry, but somehow this emotion, I don't know how, grows and thickens and turns into love, for instance when the affection I felt for Ragıp was combined with worry, it grew, it became unbearable." She stopped, remained silent for a time, then added, "Of course when your body is sick like that it's vulnerable to every kind of influence, you don't know what's going to happen to you, sometimes because you're in love with a man, perhaps simply for this reason, you become close to another man."

One evening in the first days of November, as Lausanne and Dilara Hanım were drinking their coffee and listening to the howling of the wind, he said, "The wounded are arriving from the front, all of the hospitals are full. Tomorrow I'm going to go see the wounded and talk to them about the war. Would you like to come?"

"Of course, I very much want to."

"Seeing war wounded might not be as easy as you think it is, I have to caution you about this. You might see some very horrible wounds. You might not be able to bear it . . ."

"You have no idea what I can bear, Monsieur Lausanne, we're definitely going together tomorrow."

"As you wish, I'll pick you up on my way in the morning."

That night Dilara Hanım hardly slept at all, she was imagining encountering Ragıp Bey among the wounded; he was lightly wounded, he was walking with a cane or his arm was in a sling . . . then she saw his lacerated face wrapped in bandages, in her mind she was talking to him, consoling him, she was explaining to him, she was pleading with him.

She also imagined Ragıp Bey saying he was "sorry," it was as if should he say this, should he be able to say this, a miracle would occur and everything would be straightened out, but at the same time she felt that if Ragıp Bey did say this he would be transformed into a completely different man before her eyes, perhaps into a man she didn't love. Dilara Hanım had fallen in love with his stern, unshakable, inflexible side, even if there were weaknesses and failings in his soul he never allowed them to seep out, never allowed anyone to see them. Dilara Hanım wanted to see them, but she herself didn't quite know whether she wanted to see these weaknesses in order to be united with him or in order to be free of him.

"Men like Ragıp wear a person out," she'd said to Osman, "yes, you fall in love, but that menacing power, that inflexibility, his refusal to surrender, the way he stands there in that dark, sturdy castle without revealing what's inside, it exhausts you . . . Love needs weakness too . . . It dies if it's nourished on nothing but strength . . . But people like Ragıp establish their love on strength alone, perhaps that's why it neither dies nor lives, it seeps into your life like a ghost, hurling you from one regret to another."

As they rattled along the wet cobblestones towards the French Hospital on the far side of Pera, she could feel the cold outside in her flesh, she was shivering slightly with little shudders, she regretted her decision, she wasn't ready to meet him, she wasn't ready to see him wounded, to meet him in the company of another man and perhaps for this reason to lose him forever. She was certain she would see Ragıp Bey in the hospital they were going to, while she thought during the night she'd made herself believe her thoughts and dreams. Now she was huddling exhausted in a corner, shivering from cold, from tiredness, and from her frightening fantasies.

"You're shivering," said Lausanne tenderly.

With a laugh, Dilara Hanım gave him the answer that André Chénier had given on the way to the guillotine when a friend had said, "you're trembling."

"Not from fear, from the cold."

"Oh, Dilara Hanım, oh you . . ." said Monsieur Lausanne, then stopped.

Later, when Osman gave her a mocking look, Dilara Hanım said in an irritated tone, "yes, I'm like Ragıp, so what?"

In the early hours of the morning the hospital, with its white tiled walls, smelled of Lysol and soft soap, nuns wearing thick white aprons with the straps tied crosswise over their long, dark blue robes, starched coifs, black socks and black flat-heeled shoes hurried along without making a sound, tending to the wounded lined up in stretchers in the corridors and on the beds arranged side by side in the wards. The hospital was quiet, all that could be heard was an occasional moan from one of the wounded.

Because Lausanne had made an appointment beforehand, they were greeted by the chief physician, who said, "Let me bring you to the officers' ward." Dilara Hanım's inner trembling continued, she believed that if Ragıp Bey was in that ward she would know it the moment she entered, they passed through glass doors, they turned and walked, but somehow they didn't reach the ward. The tiles on the walls were becoming whiter, they were growing, moving, they swirled around Dilara Hanım like a snowstorm, making her dizzy, her stomach heaved slightly.

The chief physician was telling Lausanne something about the new cartridges.

"The gunpowder makes the cartridges so hot that they're disinfected, when they enter the body they don't bring any bacteria with them . . . Besides, today all bullets are made from steel, they're very different from the old bullets. In fact steel causes less harm, because they don't change shape before they hit, they don't bring fragments of cloth into the wound with them, therefore if a bullet goes clean through you and if there are no significant complications, if you don't die within three hours you have a ninety-five percent chance of recovering within a week."

The chief physician pushed open yet another glass door and they entered a ward, there were ten or fifteen beds arranged at regular intervals, Dilara Hanım scanned the entire ward quickly, Ragıp Bey wasn't there, she was certain of this, she didn't know how she was certain, a great sense of relief spread through her, she was seized by a feeling that she'd been sick and had suddenly recovered.

In a nearby bed was an officer whose face had been lacerated, the bullet had entered his mouth and lodged in his palate, next to him was a wounded man whose face was twisted in pain, a howitzer shell had shattered his shoulder, a little further away they could see one of the wounded smoking a cigarette and reading a newspaper, the chief physician explained his situation, "the bullet entered his back and exited from his arm, as I was just saying, because it was steel it didn't do too much damage, he'll be able to go back to the front in a couple of weeks if he wants to."

The wounded who could speak all gave the same answer to the question they were asked.

"Where were you wounded?"

"In Lüleburgaz."

All of them had been shot on the same day, on that frightful 31st of October.

At the far end of the ward were three seriously wounded officers, folding screens had been placed around their beds, these screens were like a sign of death, very few of the wounded who had a screen placed around their bed got out of there alive.

"These men were hit by howitzer shells," said the chief physician, "when the shrapnel enters the body, it doesn't pierce it and exit, it spreads through the body and tears apart everything in its path."

By the time they left the hospital she had seen with her own eyes what war was like and what it was she worried could happen to Ragıp Bey; she remembered Ragıp Bey's scars, remembered when he'd said "A soldier lives on the edge of death, Dilara, we love the place where life and death touch, that's where we breath, where we grew up, where we were raised, we don't even know if anywhere else exists, we walk towards death, sometimes we cross the line and die and sometimes we come back, then we walk back towards death, this is what a soldier's life is." "Have you seen much death," she'd asked, and Ragıp Bey had said, "a lot" in an indifferent tone, "it's not something to blow out of proportion, a piece of iron the size of the tip of your finger is enough to kill a person."

When Ragıp Bey had laughed and said, "and you know that when we die we go straight to heaven, if the enemy goes straight there too, that means we'll be fighting on the other side too," his sarcasm was almost visible.

She remembered how once when she'd asked, "aren't you ever afraid," she'd seen him recoil, she'd seen how afraid this man who feared nothing was of fear itself, in panic he'd said, "God forbid, what kind of nonsense is that . . . fear finishes you, you stop being human, those men are entrusted to me, how can I protect those boys, how can I give them orders, forget about that Dilara, how could I embrace you if I was frightened."

She felt as if a part of her now belonged to Ragıp Bey and was living like an independent being; as Dilara Hanım was living her life, talking to people, being pleased, being saddened, the part of her that belonged to Ragıp Bey was living a different life with different emotions, that area was like a rebellious city that had declared its independence, it was disordered, confused, the lights were dim and there was a lot of activity, even Dilara Hanım herself couldn't intervene there. "Oh, Ragıp, you've torn me to pieces," she murmured.

They'd swept the hospital garden, the dead leaves had been piled in a corner, the trees had shed all of their leaves, a drizzle was falling, the pebbles with which the pathways were paved glistened white.

As Dilara Hanım was breathing in clean air after the smell of Lysol inside, she went over to Lausanne, who was saying goodbye to the chief physician and thanking him.

"You look a little pale," he said, "were you shaken?"

"Yes, it upset me to see those people like that . . ."

"I shouldn't have brought you, I guessed that you would be upset,"

"What do you mean," said Dilara Hanım, "while those people are living like that am I going to be afraid and stay away and so forth, I'm upset, yes, but I'm glad I came here, I'm not the kind of person whose frightened of and avoids being upset, I don't even like people like that . . . If that officer isn't afraid of getting a bullet in the face I won't be hesitant to see him."

"If you'd been a man you would have been a general," said Lausanne, half in admiration and half mockingly.

Dilara Hanım looked at him.

"If I'd been a man," she said, "I would have been a man."

"Sometimes I don't understand you."

"Don't worry about it, Monsieur Lausanne, sometimes I don't understand myself either."

She wanted to take Ragıp Bey's face between her hands and say, "Ragıp," no other words came to mind, she just wanted to look at his face and repeat his name; at that moment this was all she wished for.

Monsieur Lausanne sensed that at the moment Dilara Hanım wasn't interested in him, that she'd closed herself off, "Let me drop you off at home," he said, "and I'll try to gather news about what's going on. I'm going to Bab-I Ali, Kamil Pasha has formed a new cabinet, I want to see what the atmosphere is like there. If you wish I can come my after I've written and sent my news, after all you're my most careful reader, indeed you're my editor."

"I'll definitely be expecting you," said Dilara Hanım, "Don't eat before you come, I'll have dinner prepared."

The cabinet that had been formed by Grand Vizier Ahmet Muhtar Pasha, father of Mahmut Muhtar Pasha who had assumed command of the corps on the left flank of the line defending Lüleburgaz, had resigned following the military disaster, and seventy-five-year-old Kamil Pasha had been chosen as grand vizier.

Tevfik Bey, a clerk at the Grand Vizier's office who hadn't taken his father-in-law Sheikh Efendi's warning seriously, was distressed as he boarded the launch that came to pick him up in the mornings, he smiled and waved at Rukiye, after he waved he would lose himself in deep thought, in the evenings he came home late, tired and worn out.

"No government can last in this country, Rukiye," he'd said to his pregnant wife, "it's been barely four months since Ahmet Muhtar Pasha formed his government, and he was obliged to resign . . . Poor Kamil Pasha took on this enormous burden at the age of seventy-five, but, Rukiye, even at that age he's still very capable, he works halfway through the night."

"I know, Tevfik," said Rukiye, "he's working, my husband is working too, I only see you at breakfast in the morning, and you're always in a hurry . . ."

"The situation is bad, my dear Rukiye, the army has suffered a major defeat, I've been thinking about it for days, what will we do if, God forbid, Istanbul should fall . . . I don't know what your father the Sheikh thinks with respect to this, but I wonder, might he consider taking you and bringing you somewhere in the interior of Anatolia for a time?"

"Are you mad, would my father leave the *tekke,* he'll just say that it's God's will and resign himself to his fate."

"God's will doesn't seem to be quite in our favor these days, he might not think about himself, but when it comes to you . . ."

"Why aren't we going to Paris to stay with Mihrişah Sultan, she's closer to me than my mother, for some time she's been insisting in her letters that we come."

"I can't leave my job at this time, Rukiye, it would be unseemly, the enemy is marching on Istanbul, a seventy-five-year-old man is working halfway through the night, the other day he gathered all of the ambassadors and told them to inform their governments that he would never consider withdrawing from Istanbul, that if the Bulgarians came they would find him there . . . How could I leave under these circumstances?"

"Is the enemy going to enter Istanbul?"

"I don't know . . . Today Kamil Pasha is going to meet the minister of war and the commanders of the front, but it doesn't seem as if there's much hope."

"Am I going to give birth to our child in a city that's under foreign occupation?"

"God forbid . . . If it comes down to it I'll send you to Paris."

"I won't go without you.:

Tevfik Bey fell quiet, he thought about what to say, he knew how decisive and stubborn Rukiye was.

"My dear Rukiye, let's speak of this again in a few days when the situation becomes a little clearer, perhaps we can consult Sheikh Efendi . . ."

"My father the Sheikh wants you to leave as well, I told you, indeed the day we talked he seemed more worried about you than about me."

These two young people speaking about their future didn't know that the greatest danger facing them wasn't a Bulgarian occupation but that it was right next to them. The doors within that darkness called the future open onto such different places, such unknown paths, such unimaginable forms, that sometimes what you feared is your salvation, and what you awaited delightedly and thought was your salvation turns out to be a disaster.

Rukiye didn't know it yet but she was going to experience that disaster, later, in the rebellion that she created within the terrible anguish she experienced, she said to Sheikh Efendi, "How could people laugh as they walk along the edge of that cliff before the monster-filled darkness called the future, what they call life is unconsciousness, life is a blindness that doesn't see reality, in any event if we opened our consciousness and our eyes we wouldn't have the courage to live . . . It's that kind of contradiction, you can only live because you don't see the realities that you wouldn't be able to live with if you saw them . . . If it wasn't for my baby I wouldn't have wanted to live through that. My suicide wouldn't have been because of my pain, it would have been because I couldn't stand being subjected to this insult, this denigration, this blindness and unconsciousness."

Sheikh Efendi held his daughter's hands.

"If we knew, we wouldn't have been able to live through it, you're right my daughter, that's why our Lord conceals the future from us, that's why he doesn't show us. So should we complain about this blindness, or unconsciousness as you refer to it, no, my daughter, we should walk through this darkness knowing and trusting that there is a power prepared to hold us, that is watching after us and protecting us."

Rukiye, as she did when she was angry, prefaced her response with "Sheikh Efendi."

"Am I going to surrender myself to this Lord who brought these disasters upon me, am I going to trust him, what did I do to him, in what way did I harm him, what great sin was I punished for, who did we hurt for him to give us this punishment? Are you advising me to suffer this pain, bow my head, accept and not rebel? Do you realize how much you're asking for?"

"My child," said Sheikh Efendi in a tender voice, "my daughter, my dear Rukiye, life doesn't consist only of this world, this world is a roadside inn where we stay as guests, are we going to complain about the inn and give up our journey? Don't give up, my daughter . . . We don't always know the reasons for what happens in this inn, we have to carry on our journey towards benefaction, demonstrating resignation and acceptance, we have to continue walking with the belief that there's a reason . . . There's no power on this globe that can console you, that can ease your pain, there's no such guest in this inn, the power that will give you strength, the power that will lead you through this darkness is the power that brought you on this journey . . ."

"Am I to expect the one who gave me this pain to console me, is the one who opened the wound going to heal it, is the one who gave me this misery going to offer a remedy? Does your Lord see that I deserve to be left in need of consolation and then offer me consolation? What kind of protection is this,

Sheikh Efendi? You say this world is an inn, did I decide to come to this inn, isn't it the power you say holds me by the hand that brought me here and left me here? My life, my past and my future are all dark now, I'm not expecting any light, any illumination, any consolation. Don't expect any gratitude from me after what I've seen and experienced. You talk about believing, about trusting . . . To believe in the existence of your lord, to believe in this fate you call a journey would make me an enemy of the power that created this fate. You shouldn't want me to believe, wanting me to believe amounts to nothing more than wanting my enmity, don't you see this, don't you understand this? Are you just as incapable of understanding as you are of offering consolation? Did your Lord also forbid understanding in this inn?"

"I understand," said Sheikh Efendi in an anguished tone, responding to his daughter's disrespect in a tolerant manner, "I understand, my daughter . . . I see that immense pain, I'm aware that you see what happened to you as a great injustice. How could I not understand, my daughter? I'm also aware of my own helplessness and powerlessness. I'm just telling you where you can find the consolation and peace that I am unable to give you . . . You're asking whether the one who gave you the pain is going to give you the remedy. Yes, my daughter, the one who gave you the pain is going to give you the remedy. Only he who possesses the power to give you that pain has the power to give you the cure for that pain. Who else is there who can offer you a cure, there's no one . . . Your rebellion won't take anything away from my Lord, anything, my daughter, he knows everything about his creatures' attitudes, he understands, in any event that's why he sent us here, to this world, to see those attitudes. But think, my daughter, about what you'll lose by not believing, by rebelling and remaining alone in the darkness with your helplessness, how are you going to carry this pain alone? Your rebellion saddens me, yes, but not because of the wrong you've done my Lord, if you're my daughter, you're his daughter too, every one of his creatures is his child, he took you out of his own heart and created you, he brought you into existence out of nothing, he understands you much better than I do, he sees much more than I see, he'll understand the reasons for your disrespect, and I hope he'll forgive you as well . . . But how can you, my daughter, live with this rebellion, this loneliness, this anguish without Him, how can you walk through this darkness, how can you find your way? Believe, my daughter, believe, my dear, believe my dear Rukiye, the one who gave you the pain will give you the cure."

"Why did he do this, father, please tell me . . . please tell me that."

"I don't know, my daughter, not everything is clear to us in this world, everything has a reason, even if we don't know it or see it, there's a reason. This is how I believed, I took shelter in him, I had faith that there was no shelter other than him, that we have no other protector than him, that's how I found my way in the darkness, my daughter . . . I'm not underestimating your loss, your pain, I'm saying you can find consolation in him for great agonies such as this. I'm telling you not to turn away from him . . ."

She didn't know whether it was his words, his voice, his tenderness, or his love that was more effective, but in those terrible days it did Rukiye good to talk to her father in the *tekke*, perhaps it was the only thing that did her good, that gave her a modicum of consolation, that eased her anguish slightly. In those days she stayed at the *tekke*, proclaiming her rebellion against God among those who believed in God's power. Her rebellion gained meaning among those who said we must not rebel.

That November morning they did not yet know what was going to occur, what was going to happen to them.

Tevfik Bey boarded the launch that had come to get him,

bobbed up and down on the increasingly swollen waves until he reached Eminönü, from there he went by carriage up to the Prime Ministry.

A day earlier Kamil Pasha had sent a telegram to the army that was fleeing Lüleburgaz to ask if they could succeed in holding the Bulgarians off at Çatala for five or six days, he was hoping that in this period of time he would be able to find a solution by appealing to foreign capitals, but the telegram he received from Minister of War Nazım Pasha didn't give him much cause for hope.

"The army is still in the process of retreating. Meanwhile many cannons have been lost. The degree of the possibility of holding on at Çatalca is dependent on the degree to which we can bring cannons, weapons, ammunition and men when we get there. The degree of morale in the army is also of great consequence. At the moment we can't know how all of these things will be."

The following day Nazım Pasha sent another telegram informing him that, "whatever happens" a truce had to be arranged by diplomatic means.

While the Minister of War wanted a truce to be arranged with foreign help as soon as possible, the Minister of Foreign Affairs informed him that his contacts with the great powers had brought about no results.

"We're between a rock and a hard place, Tevfik Bey my son," said the grand vizier, "the situation is worse than I thought, together we've managed to kill the empire, they transferred me to the prime ministry and made me the official in charge of the funeral . . . Now I want you, please, to write a letter to each of the pashas currently serving, indeed to all of the retired pashas as well, inviting them to attend a meeting immediately. Let's see, we'll listen to the pashas, let's find out what their recommendations are."

He'd written to all of the pashas and invited them, and all

of them except Mahmut Şevket Pasha had informed him that they would attend.

When Tevfik Bey arrived at Bab-ı Ali, the pashas had already begun trickling in, all of them had the extreme seriousness of old men who are considered important, they were talking among themselves, occasionally sounding angry.

Şevki Bey, an official in the prime ministry, looked at the pashas and said to Tevfuk Bey, "It looks like they're going to read a eulogy," Tevfik Bey thought to himself, "I'm going to tell that to Rukiye in the evening," then he rolled his eyes at Şevki Bey to quiet him, but Şevki Bey, with the mercilessness particular to the young, continued, "what can I do, my dear man, it looks just like a funeral procession."

After thanking them for coming, Kamil Pasha gave them a frank assessment of the situation and said he wanted to hear their recommendations, "I will put these recommendations in writing and send them to the minister," he said.

After the aging pashas discussed matters at length all day, they arrived at a conclusion that would lift Kamil Pasha's morale slightly, they'd decided that the army could form a new line at Çatalca and resist.

First of all, they were opposed to the Minister of War's calls for an armistice to be arranged, "Making a peace under these conditions is a threat to the future of the state," they said.

According to the pashas, 120 thousand men would be placed at the Çatalca line, even if 20 thousand of them were not fit to fight, they would still have 100 thousand men. They were going to send a 65-thousand-man force from Anatolia.

"Assuming that the retreating army has a hundred cannons, and if we consider the 140 cannons and howitzers that are going to be sent from Istanbul, we have sufficient fire power to conduct a defense, during the course of the war the Bulgarian army has also suffered casualties and been weakened.

According to this plan, by holding out at Çatalca they could gain time for political undertakings," they said.

They added one last recommendation to these recommendations.

"As many as a hundred turbaned hodjas and members of the *ulema* will be sent to the army from Istanbul, they can provide sermons and counsel."

When Şevki Bey heard this he nudged Tevfik Bey and said, "that, my good man, is how we say only God can help us in Turkish."

Kamil Pasha was a little more hopeful, "the situation might not be as bad as we thought, Tevfik Bey my son," he said after the meeting, "now pass these recommendations on to the Minister and inform him that I await his answer."

A telegram that arrived the following day from the Minister of War stated that "the situation is as bad as the grand vizier thinks."

"The forces in the army that is retreating to the Çatalca line number not 120 thousand men but 40-50 thousand. None of the 140 cannons and howitzers that they say will be sent from Istanbul have arrived at the front. The old howitzers that we have in hand are of no military value. The retreating army lost many artillery officers. If the 65 thousand men they plan to gather in Anatolia and send to Istanbul have no military training, they will undoubtedly have a deleterious effect on an army whose moral has already collapsed.

The situation into which the army has now fallen has less to do with the result of defeat than with the collapse of morale for a variety of reasons. In the past two or three days we have had cases of dysentery and other suspicious diseases. These sicknesses will worsen the army's already miserable state.

As for the enemy, with the help of the Greek fleet they can land additional forces at Bolayır and Gallipoli. In summary, the outcome of any fighting at Çatalca is in doubt. For this reason, it is clearly necessary for the government to undertake what we have already suggested in writing."

When he read this response, Kamil Pasha frowned and sighed.

"Apparently we need to send the *ulema* not to raise the morale of the men but that of the commanders . . . Please call Minister of Foreign Affairs Noradikyan Efendi, let's talk to him yet again about what he might be able to do . . . Our army is finished, the commanders were finished before the army was. Before the war Nazım Pasha was talking with a swagger, he was talking about going to Sofia, but when he gets close to the front it's a different story."

It was clear that the grand vizier was angry, and that he'd been left in an impossible position.

They wanted him to govern an empire whose army couldn't even gain him four days to seek peace.

And in the answer he'd received there had been mention of "suspicious diseases."

"I fear that the cholera in Istanbul has spread to the front," said Kamil Pasha, "how are we going to prevent the spread of an epidemic among soldiers who are living side by side in the trenches? We don't even know if we have medicine. Tevfik Bey, if you could call in the guardian of Istanbul for me, we'll talk to him about measures we can take against a possible occupation, make sure the public doesn't get crushed underfoot . . . Good God, look at what I'm being made to go through at my age."

15

It was almost impossible to understand Nizam, his emotions were like a stream that flowed around and over rocks, changing form and color; you could follow it, but then it would disappear under a rock, after that even Nizam didn't follow it. In any event he didn't take the trouble to follow and understand his feelings. He preferred to be a creature that consisted only of its actions, and was without thoughts or feelings, even his own feelings bored and tired him. What he wanted was not to understand anything, he wanted to do whatever he felt like doing without having any barriers placed in front of him, without any prohibitions or questions, without caring whom he hurt or whom he saddened.

He went to the gambling den every evening, no one including himself knew why. He wasn't curious about Anya's mystery, if she sat down and told him, he would grow bored of listening after a point.

What was drawing him there wasn't curiosity.

He wanted to see a meaning, a connection, an admiration in the empty eyes through which Anya looked at the world, his desire for her to realize that he was different from other people had become almost an obsession, he could follow his emotions this far, but why he wanted this, why a woman had become an obsession for him simply because of the look in her eyes, why this had become a matter of life or death for him, remained a mystery.

He liked the torches on the road, he liked the atmosphere,

the lighting and the excitement of the gambling den, first he'd go into the room where Anya was playing the piano, he'd lean on the piano and say, "How are you Anya," Anya would say "*Merci*," that was all, and continue playing, then Nizam would go upstairs and gamble.

People would wait for him to come.

When he came, people would gather around and watch him because he played like a madman, he would raise his bets, bluff with a pair of sevens, place piles of gold on the table, when he won he won big, when he lost he lost big, no one including himself knew when he was going to stop playing, he would just stop the moment he got bored, without caring if he was winning or losing, at that moment he would gather up his gold if he was winning, if he was losing he would just shrug his shoulders and walk away.

The strange thing was that this behavior quickly earned him a great deal of respect in the gambling den, "Nizam Bey, the grandson of Abdulhamid's physician Reşit Pasha," they would say, if he was a little late they would worry that he wasn't coming, when he arrived it was as if the gambling den had become brighter and more fun for everyone, when he left, everyone else wanted to leave as well.

When he arrived he always went and asked Anya how she was, but when he left he did so without bidding her farewell, Anya never knew whether or not he'd left, from time to time she would glance around the room to try to figure out if he was there.

After the gambling den he always went to Evangeliki, there, too, as at the gambling den, he'd turned everything upside down, he didn't want elaborate meals, musicians and singers, he'd just take the woman by her wrist and take her to the room, the first time he took Evangeliki by the wrist she sensed what it was he wanted.

Each night the woman repeated what she'd said on the first night, "Whatever you want . . ."

Nizam wanted everything that a woman's body had to offer, he included every part of Evangeliki, everything from her hair to her shapely feet, every atom of her, in his love-making, in a surprising manner he didn't behave egotistically, he managed to derive pleasure from the woman's pleasure. He didn't treat the woman's body as if it was the body of a prostitute, he made it possible for her being to be part of the love-making, and he had the mastery and experience to be able to do this. He just didn't want his emotions in the bed, he didn't like emotions.

When they were making love he spoke French, in between he would speak Turkish, he made Evangeliki laugh without trying to, her laughter could be heard outside. They'd grown accustomed to the screams as well, he would shout in French, "*l'animal, l'animal,*" at first they thought he was mistreating her but then they understood the situation and got used to it.

As at the gambling den, his presence made the place brighter and more fun, when he arrived it was as if the house became wider and taller. As he left he teased the women he saw in the room, he always kissed the madam, and he paid more money than anyone else.

Every time, the other women would gather around Evangeliki, curious to learn what they'd done, but she didn't really tell them anything, she worried that the other women might try to seduce Nizam, all she said was, "He's crazy."

Even though Nizam had made no such demand, Evangeliki no longer went with any other men, she waited for Nizam to come, she wanted to be free when he came, she feared that if she was with someone else Nizam might choose one of the other girls.

Wherever he went, everything happened the way he wanted it to happen, he didn't even have to say anything, he didn't ask for anything, but people tried to please him, he'd inherited this trait from his mother Mehpare Hanım, like his mother he could make people do what he wanted without them even realizing it.

Some nights he and Kamil Bey went together to the house in Fatih, Kamil Bey would have a table prepared for him, sometimes he called Şadiye and sometimes one of the other girls, in the beginning he would ask Nizam if "he cared to join" him, but then he realized that this annoyed Nizam.

When they were leaving together one morning as it was growing light, he'd asked, "Don't you get tired of always being with the same woman, even though you say you get bored easily?"

"It's true that I get bored, but even I don't know when I'm going to get bored."

"As far as I understand everything becomes a ritual until you realize that you're bored, like some kind of obsession . . ."

In a manner that made it clear that he found talking about subjects like this boring, he said,

"I suppose so."

"One day you told me that you envied me because I had a passion, to tell the truth I envy you too, you derive pleasure from every kind of passion but you never get caught up in it, this is a great talent, my good man, I wish I could be like that, I wish I could enjoy things as much as you do and be able to drop them as easily as you do . . . An enviable situation."

Nizam laughed.

"I didn't think either of us was in any way enviable," he said, "we're nothing more than two playboys spending other people's money. And there isn't even any inheritance to speak of."

"Sometimes you can be very merciless about yourself."

"I'm just telling the truth."

"Sometimes telling the truth is merciless. I don't avoid telling the truth, perhaps I do so too often, but in what you just said, how should I put it, I can't find the right word, it sounds almost as if you had a secret hostility towards yourself."

"I don't think so," said Nizam.

Later on one of the dead, Osman couldn't remember which one it had been, had said, "Nizam was a boring man when he was with other men, he got bored of men, and he would become a boring person for them, his intelligence and his attractiveness only came out when he was with women, what brought out his intelligence was his desire to impress, I don't know what men remember about him, those who remember what he said, who remember his witticisms, are generally woman."

Although friendships with men generally bored him, he wasn't bored by his friendship with Kamil Bey; his candor, the sincerity that was so surprising to encounter in a gambler, the childish way in which he put himself down, the clarity that came from the way he put nearly all of the truths into words, he had an authenticity that Nizam truly envied. He gave one a sense of trust, all of his thoughts and feelings were out in the open, he was open to everyone, he didn't hide from anyone, on the contrary he wanted to reveal his sicknesses and weaknesses as much as possible. He did this not to be pitied or to seem tragic, on the contrary he did it to make people laugh, as if he was amusing himself.

They were almost exactly the same age, but Kamil Bey wasn't treated with the same respect as Nizam was at the gambling den, people were more deferential to Nizam, of course no one was rude to Kamil Bey, but no one greeted him with the same respect as they greeted Nizam. Even aging pashas and palace clerks wanted to talk to Nizam, even if only in passing, as for the women, when they weren't caught up in gambling they enjoyed being around Nizam. Once Kamil Bey had said, "If you hear the sound of women laughing anywhere in the gambling den, you can be sure Nizam is there."

Anya had learned this too, she knew that when there was laughter Nizam would be at the center of it, but not once did she attempt to join this laughter, as always she played the piano, from time to time she would stop and have a glass of wine and a cigarette, then she would go back to the piano and continue to play with her wonderful technique and extraordinary lack of feeling. The only difference from before was that when she was smoking her cigarette she would raise her head and glance around the room as if she was looking for something.

Like everything extraordinary that's repeated often, after a time Nizam's presence became ordinary, he became an accustomed part of the gambling den and "the Madam's house" and he repeated the same rituals again and again; he would come and great Anya, he would gamble like a madman and surprise everyone, he would laugh with the women in the gambling den, he would go to the Madam's house, he would take Evangeliki upstairs, then in the morning he would return home.

One day this routine current was broken by a small scene that no one else might have noticed, when Nizam arrived at the gambling den and went to the room he saw Kamil Bey standing by the piano, Anya wasn't looking at him, she was playing the piano, and Kamil was listening without talking.

Nizam just hesitated, moved his head back a little, squinted his eyes and looked, then changed his mind about going into the room and went straight upstairs, sat at a table and began playing poker as usual, there was no change in his manner or in the way he played, he just smoked more cigarettes than usual. "I don't remember what I felt at the time," he'd said to Osman, and it's possible that he didn't remember.

People's memories remind them of what they don't want to remember in order to protect them, they can behave in a hostile manner for the sake of protection, but Nizam's memory would take what Nizam didn't like and it would be lost among the underground waters beneath that dark rock, that memory would be lost but the emotions that created them would later emerge again into daylight somewhere else and shape Nizam's behavior. Nizam wouldn't know why he was behaving that way, or rather he would sense why he was behaving that way but he would send this intuition into the same dark waters. His memory and his consciousness were generally bright and gleaming, there were no disturbing, ugly or bad memories, there were no saddening images there, those were all in the darkness, Nizam was unaware of them, then later those darknesses would suddenly take control, and Nizam would do things without knowing why he was doing them.

He left the game earlier than usual, when he went outside the torches were blazing, they were warming the night with a copper light, the tops of the trees had turned a carnelian color, in the wind they swayed like illuminated fans in the darkness of the night.

He went to the Madam's house, he didn't think about anything in the way, his mind was as empty as a desert, in order to erase a single thought and feeling he'd erased all his thoughts and feelings, a heavy silence was falling from his mind to his body like a pile of sand. He happily abandoned himself to this silence.

Everything happened as it always did, he took Evangeliki to the room upstairs, they screamed as they made love, he made her laugh between sessions, then he left the house towards morning.

It was a cold, grey morning, the sunlight that was trying to emerge from behind the hills was being smothered by black clouds, a leaden light whose source was unclear was spreading across the sky, there were heaps of red leaves on the ground.

He told the carriage driver to go to the gambling den.

"Fast," he said.

When they arrived at the gambling den he could sense even from a distance that the mansion was empty, everything was wrapped in a silence that suited the morning cold.

He got out of the carriage almost in a panic.

He'd been calm when he left the gambling den, but now he was hurried and excited, the possibility that Anya was gone gave him a tense and ferocious fear, if it had been possible to keep records of what happened in his mind that night, one would have been able to swear that these were the emotions of two different people, a calm, self-possessed man had been replaced by a hurried, panicked person who was almost trembling with fear.

These quivering emotions continued until he saw Anya by the window, he calmed down the moment he saw her, indeed he was angry at himself for coming there, coming there suddenly seemed very meaningless.

He walked self-confidently towards Anya, she raised her head and looked at him.

He stood right in front of her.

"Play a piece for me, Anya," he said, "but play with your emotions, I want to hear you play like that."

"I can't play like that."

"Please play."

"I can't play like that."

Nizam took Anya by the wrist and sat her at the piano.

"Please play."

Anya sat at the piano, for a moment she looked at the keys, then she turned to Nizam, the emptiness was gone from her eyes, she was looking at him with an almost pleading expression, Nizam was never able to know whether she was looking at him like that out of fear, because of something she remembered, or because she was worried that what she was going to do would set her on a path from which there would be no return. The look in her eyes just remained in his mind, he was never able to erase that image.

"What do you want from me?"

"Please play."

He saw Anya take a deep breath, a reddish grey light was coming in through the windows, the embers in the fireplace crackled from time to time, the entire mansion was silent.

Nizam sat in one of the leather armchairs, he was looking at Anya and waiting.

The sound of the piano surprised him, it was only when he felt this surprise that he realized he'd believed she wouldn't play, when he heard the first notes he said to himself, "Schumann, grand sonata."

Nizam thought that the first notes were too harsh, but then the piece found its balance, it began to flow, sometimes rising and burbling, sometimes becoming lonely and melancholy, he leaned back, listened and looked at Anya.

He could see that she was slowly getting lost in the notes, that she was flowing with the notes, when the notes became faster she swayed her head with the notes, tossing her hair, her fingers were roaming across the keys like independent creatures.

At the transitions, she looked as if she was preparing to jump over an obstacle, she waited a little longer than was accustomed, then she suddenly picked up speed.

She wasn't sitting straight as always, she was bending over the keys, she was almost covering the piano, sometimes her hair touched the keys.

For a moment after she played the last note it was as if she was going to take a bow before the audience, then she stopped, closed the piano lid and laid her head on the piano.

She'd played extraordinarily well, "A virtuoso" thought Nizam to himself.

When she raised her head and looked, Anya could see the admiration on Nizam's face, and Nizam could see the exhaustion on Anya's face, it was as if she had grown older, the lines on her face had deepened, her eyes had become narrower, the roots of her hair were sweaty, there was a thin, transparent curtain of moisture in her eyes.

They both sighed at the same moment, as if they were having difficulty breathing.

Nizam got up from his seat slowly, took Anya by the hand
and said, "Come." Anya took her coat from beside the door,
they went out together, there wasn't a soul to be seen, everyone
had gone, it was as if the mansion had been abandoned, the
silence enveloped them like a stagnant lake. It had grown light,
orange lights seeped through leaden clouds that had become
dark in the center, in the morning light the leafless trees
seemed to have grown older, Nizam's carriage stood there like
a black, fairytale carriage in the pearly grey light.

"Give the carriage driver your address," said Nizam.

Anya didn't object to anything Nizam said, she did everything she was told as if she were in a dream, as if she were
sleeping, it looked as if she'd given up on everything, indeed
even on that cold anguish.

They stopped in front of a stone building in Nişantaşı, they
got out together without saying a word, Anya opened the door,
they went inside, someone had lit the stove, the house was
slightly warm.

The house was better furnished than Nizam had expected,
the furniture was not very expensive but it was elegant, it had
been arranged with delicate taste, but among the ordinary furniture that you could see anywhere there were some surprising
things, Nizam's practiced eye noticed a priceless tapestry hanging on the wall, on the coffee table was an ivory curio inlaid
with diamonds that was clearly the work of a master craftsman,
signs of a past great wealth were sprinkled throughout the
house.

Anya left her coat on the armchair next to the door, there
was a surprised ineptness about them, as if they didn't know
what to do.

They stood facing each other in the middle of the room.

Once again Anya asked, "What do you want?"

Nizam didn't answer.

There was an angry expression on Anya's face, as if she was preparing herself for disappointment, she was staring at Nizam, she was thinking about something.

She slowly raised her hand and took the straps of her gown off her shoulders, the gown and the slip beneath it slid to her feet, they covered her feet, she looked like a mythological creature standing in that green water.

Her body had grown old, her not very large breasts sagged slightly, her white belly was slightly rounded, there were thin lines on her legs, but this body looked more attractive to Nizam than Evangliki's perfect, youthful body, he felt the full piquancy of his desire.

In an almost hostile tone, Anya asked,

"Is this what you want?"

Nizam didn't say anything, he looked at her with an anguished expression, he walked towards Anya very slowly, touched her neck with his finger, then moved his finger downwards, between her breasts, across her belly, when he reached her loins he could feel the shivers running through her body, he kept his finger there for a moment and then moved it away.

"No," he said.

He leaned down, picked the gown up by the straps and dressed Anya.

He kissed her very lightly on the lips.

"Get some sleep, you're very tired . . . We'll see each other tomorrow."

Before going out the door he turned and said, "Thank you very much, you're the best pianist I've ever heard. No one can play the way you do."

16

The Chief Eunuch entered Rasim Bey's office in a panic and said, "His majesty the deposed caliph is asking for you."

When Rasim entered the room, Abdülhamid was sitting drinking coffee by the broad window that looked out over the Bosphorus. The way he drank coffee was almost like a ritual, they would bring him a coffee pot with an ebony handle on a golden tray, on the tray there would be two white cups, with the letters A.H painted on them with special care, that had been made at the Yıldız ceramic factory. Abdülhamid poured coffee into the first cup, drank it, then poured the rest of the coffee into the second clean cup and finished that.

He always drank his coffee without sugar, "sugar ruins the taste of the coffee, anyone who likes coffee drinks it without sugar," he would say. There were some of his special cigarettes on the coffee table in front of him, there was also a dish of tobacco, when he felt like it he would roll a cigarette instead of smoking the ready-made ones, and he did this with surprising skill.

When Rasim Bey came in he was drinking his second cup of coffee, he'd lit a cigarette, "Welcome, sit down," he said, "let them bring some coffee for you, too."

As Rasim Bey was sitting down, Abdülhamid asked in an irritable tone,

"What's happening, Rasim Bey?"

Rasim Bey didn't understand.

"I don't understand what you're asking about, sir."

Abdülhamid pointed outside. The Bosphorus was full of European warships, there was an almost steely grey wall on the surface of the sea. They were communicating with each other with whistles, lights, and flags.

"They're here to protect the personnel in the embassies, sir."

"Are we unable to protect embassies in our own city?"

"The army is retreating to Çatalca, sir, it's not clear whether or not they'll be able to hold on, I suppose they were anxious, and the government allowed their ships to come."

Abdülhamid sighed.

"Is this how low we've sunk? And against the Bulgarians at that . . ."

He lit another cigarette.

"I wonder who appointed Abdullah Pasha commander of the army? I know Abdulla Pasha well, he's one of the ones I trained myself. He was an abandoned child, first I sent him to the palace school, then I sent him to the military school to make a soldier out of him. After he became an officer I sent him to Germany. He returned from Germany a well-trained, polite and gentlemanly officer. I used to like his bearing and his polish. Because he knew a foreign language I put him on the staff of my chief advisor Şakir Pasha. He was quick to grasp his job. Subsequently, after Şakir Pasha's death, he took care of the work in the chancellery than had been left unfinished."

Abdülhamid stopped and sighed.

"I'm saying this because I knew him very well, Abdullah Pasha performed all of his duties very well, but he was never cut out to command an army . . . Because being a commander is very different from being a desk officer."

Abdülhamid looked straight ahead as he spoke, it was clear that he had ideas about all of the pashas.

"They made Egyptian Aziz Pasha commander of a corps,

that man knows nothing about anything except hunting, he doesn't have a clue about soldiering. How could someone like that be appointed corps commander . . ."

Later Rasim Bey told Hikmet Bey, "The man knows the entire army by name, it's almost as if he could even name the sergeants."

He didn't like Abdülhamid, he was against him, but he knew that most of what he said was true, in any event it was clear that it was true from the miserable state the army was in.

"Look, they made Nazım Pasha minister of war in the new cabinet. I wonder if that was the right choice? Doesn't the insistence that he be minister of war amount to accepting he has no responsibility for the miserable situation we're in today? I've known Nazım Pasha for a long time. He's Ali Pasha's son-in-law. When he was still a captain they recommended that he take part in the negotiations concerning the withdrawal from Thessaly and be a member of the council that gathered at Yıldız Palace. I accepted out of respect for Ali Pasha. Apart from being very arrogant in the council, I heard that he was saying some things about me here and there. But I didn't attach any importance to this. Indeed one of the clerks, Recai Bey, was his relative, he asked me several times to 'bring Nazım Pasha onto your staff,' and I didn't let him down. I made him a member of the Commission of Military Inquiry. But the complaints about him began before four days had passed, I had them looked into, all of the complaints had to do with his fractiousness. When I didn't pay any heed to the complaints, Nazım Pasha really went too far. He was drinking, he said whatever came into his head. One day he got drunk in Beyoğlu again, he was in uniform and he was found in a state unseemly for a great lieutenant general. When I heard about this my patience came to an end, I didn't think he deserved to continue to reside in Istanbul so I sent him to Erzerum."

Abdülhamid made a face as he thought.

"So what happened? When constitutional monarchy was proclaimed he came back to Istanbul with all of the other exiles, and he gave himself a political posture . . . As you know, this was fashionable at the time. Even the bums and hoodlums that the Istanbul police had sent into exile here and there were portraying themselves as political victims. And the public was so overexcited that they showed these people great mercy and respect without thinking about who they were or questioning why they had been sent into exile . . . They would lift anyone who said down with Abdülhamid onto their shoulders."

He lit a cigarette.

"Should Nazım Pasha have been minister of war, is he qualified for the position? Would he have been able to rise to this position if I hadn't exiled him to Erzurum and he hadn't returned posing as a political exile? Look, there are foreign ships sitting right outside my window, doesn't it hurt you to see that? In fact I'm not the sultan anymore, but do I have to be sultan for this to hurt me? I would not have allowed this for a single day."

Abdülhamid always liked to point out the new administrations mistakes and to point out that if he was still in power none of these things would have happened.

"For starters, I would have obstructed an alliance between the Greeks and the Bulgarians from the beginning, I prevented that for years. This is what governing a state means, knowing where the threat will come from and dealing with it before it becomes a threat. I governed this nation for years without getting into any wars . . . I wouldn't have made Nazım Pasha minister of war, and I would never have appointed Abdullah Pasha to command the army. If there was going to be a commander of the army it would have to be Mahmut Muhtar Pasha, he's known as an arrogant person, and he is, he's quite haughty, but no one can say anything about his qualities as a soldier or about his courage, then you have to put up with his arrogance . . . . And I appreciate what he's done in this last war. His father was prime minister, he was Minister of the Navy, what did he do, he dropped everything and went to the front. This is what being a soldier is about."

Rasim Bey knew that most of what Abdülhamid said was true, but he couldn't bear the former sultan portraying himself as blameless and the new administration as being wrong about everything, trying not to be disrespectful, he said,

"They say that in the old days, military preparedness was very bad, for years the necessary reforms weren't made . . ."

Abdülhamid suddenly sat up straight.

"Hah, am I the one who's at fault for this? I haven't been on the throne for three and a half years, they didn't even keep me in the city where I was born, they exiled me to Salonica . . . So let's ask, why haven't the necessary reforms been made in three and a half years? When Mahmut Şevket Pasha was minister of war he scared everyone and took millions in gold for the ministry's budget, I'm going to enact reforms, he said, what happened to that gold, why is the army running away in spite of that money? They bought mountain artillery from the French, the war has begun and is almost over and those cannons are still sitting in ships in the Black Sea, they haven't even reached Istanbul. Is this the kind of supply and management that's needed? Where's the planning, the logistics? They say the soldiers are hungry, is anyone asking what the quartermaster general is doing? How can an army be hungry in Thrace, it's not as if you're going on an expedition, you're fighting in your own territory, how can you leave your soldiers hungry? How could a hungry soldier have any kind of morale, any trust in the government or the commanders?"

Rasim Bey listened, surprised at how a man who was imprisoned in a palace on the shores of the Bosphorus knew all of these things, and Abdülhamid, remembering that everything he said would be reported, was suddenly spooked by what he'd said, he worried that any idea they might have about him thinking about reclaiming the throne could put his life in danger. He changed the tone of his voice, pulled in his shoulders and started talking like an old man.

"I'm an old man now, my health is not so robust, look, last night I ate two potato croquettes and a spoonful of squash and syrup, even that upset my stomach, of course my brother appreciates these things better than I do, he'll take the necessary measures, after all he's the caliph, he's the one to decide . . ."

He looked at Rasim Bey.

"I heard that Şevki Bey's wife as ill, I wonder how she is."

One of the palace guards on Rasim Bey's staff, Captain Şevki Bey's wife was ill, he'd asked for leave to go take care of her, and even Abdülhamid knew about it.

"She's better, sir, Şevki Bey will be returning to duty today."

"They still haven't found our Leghorn chickens . . . We're just looking for a chicken, we're not even capable of finding a chicken in the capital of the great Ottoman Empire."

"They found some, sir, they just couldn't find any the color you wanted."

"It's a chicken you're looking for, sir, not a treasure. Why can't it be found? And the lead-colored Leghorn lays the nicest and biggest eggs, if they achieve this great accomplishment and find the chickens, I'll send you some of the eggs, you'll see that you've never eaten anything like them. And I give them special feed, their yolks are bigger than any you've ever seen."

Abdülhamid put out his cigarette.

"Anyhow, I've detained you too long, don't let me keep you from your duties . . ."

Rasim Bey realized that Abdülhamid was disturbed by his own words, that he wanted to be alone to reevaluate them.

"With your permission, sir," he said as he stood.

Just as he was going out the door, Abdülhamid called after him.

"If you hear anything more about the ships, please inform me."

It wasn't just the former sultan who was curious about the ships, the entire population was wondering why those ships had come.

Monsieur Lausanne laughed as he told Dilara Hanim about a rumor he believed the government was behind.

"According to a rumor that's going around among the public, these are ships that the army captured from the Greeks . . . There are people who believe this."

The public soon became accustomed to the ships, the whistle sounds that rose from the ships, the signal lamp communication between the ships and the embassies on the shore, the marines who communicated to each other with flags from the decks of the ships, and the *caiques* going back and forth to the ships, the issue people were talking about was whether or not the army could hold out at Çatalca; everyone from the sultan to the water-seller on the street was talking about this and was curious about this.

The army that had been broken at Lüleburgaz was retreating in disorder towards Istanbul, their only hope before Istanbul was to gather at Çatalca and resist, if they didn't, the Ottoman capital would be occupied.

When Monsieur Lausanne spoke to Colonel Cafer Bey, Chief of the Ministry of War's Intelligence Division, he asked whether or not the Çatalca line would hold.

"They can hold the Bulgarians off at Çatalca for a month," said the colonel.

At that time the army's greatest expectation was to delay the Bulgarians for a time, *Times* correspondent Lionel James and *Daily Telegraph* correspondent My. Berthold, both of whom had been to the front, told Lausanne that "the Bulgarians can get through in forty-eight hours, the army is fleeing the Bulgarians in disarray."

The army truly was fleeing in disarray, hungry and sick, some of the soldiers had fled towards the Marmara and some had fled towards the Black Sea, but the larger part of the army couldn't figure out where to go and were flowing towards Istanbul.

"As those crowds approached Istanbul it began to look like judgment day," Ragıp Bey told Osman, "the refugees' ox carts, women walking barefoot, crying babies, sick people lying in the ox carts, knee deep mud, among the refugees were sick, miserable soldiers who'd been separated from their units, all trying to move through the rain smelling of sickness and sweat."

A tired and sick crowd in tatters dragged itself through the mud like a wounded centipede, as walking became difficult, the belongings in the ox carts were thrown piece by piece into the mud. The pile of mud that was assaulting people and swelling like an animal was being filled with chests, broken wheels, bundles that had lost their shape and color, clothing, consoles and torn boots, later the mud would suddenly swallow all of it.

"What was most surprising was how silent the crowd was," said Ragıp Bey, "there was almost no sound, no one had the strength to speak, all that could be heard was the moaning of the sick and the wounded."

The soldiers were without hope, they were afraid of being caught by the Bulgarians, of being killed or taken prisoner, they were praying to find a slice of bread, they didn't know where to go or where to stop.

Officers who hadn't slept for days, with red eyes that looked like plates of blood and growing purple rings under their eyes, were trying to muster the men together, trying to at least turn this rout into an orderly retreat.

Voices were heard saying, "Get into line or I'll shoot you right here."

Nerves were strained, anger was growing like a creature walking beside the crowd, if they'd had the strength that crowd would have torn one another apart, but no one had the strength to move that much.

Ragıp Bey had managed to keep the surviving men together, they were marching through the mud without getting separated from one another, but they weren't marching in unison, they were so tired they could barely stand, they didn't have the courage to desert, partly out of respect for Ragıp Bey and partly because they didn't know where to go, Ragıp Bey had moved to the head of the unit while the sergeant was taking up the rear.

"How could we have won the war when we had to take measures to keep the men from deserting," he'd said to Osman, "if they didn't desert it's because they had nowhere to go."

Near Çatalca, when the rain was once again becoming more violent, Ragıp Bey saw several men approaching on horseback. The large bay horse in the lead was stumbling through the mud, it was moving slowly because with each step it had to lift its legs out of the mud.

As they approached, Ragıp Bey could make out Muhtar Pasha through the rain, as if to be sure, Muhtar Pasha shouted, "Ragıp"

"Yes, Pasha."

"Ragıp, my son, I'm going to ask you to take on a very important mission, can you do it?"

Ragıp Bey didn't even ask "What is the mission?"

"Yes, Pasha."

"You've managed to keep your men together, good for you, I know you're very tired now, but this is a matter of life and death . . ."

The men were also listening to what the Pasha was saying.

"Pick up your pace now, get in front of this crowd and

reach Çatalca before the others, when I say Çatalca I mean the Terkos-Büyükçekmece line, we have some bunkers there left over from the Russian war, we can muster there and put up a defense, but you have to get in front of the men and not allow them to pass, let the refugees pass but keep the soldiers there, we'll form a line . . . I'm going to round up a few more units now, I'll be right behind you, let's hold on there, Ragıp . . . We'll establish a line."

"Yes, Pasha."

"I trust you."

"Thank you, Pasha."

"O.K., then. May God be with you."

The pasha and the horsemen with him moved off through the mud, parting the crowd, to look for a few more disciplined units to send.

Ragıp Bey turned to his men.

"Did you hear the pasha?"

"We did, commander."

"Are we going to march?"

They answered in feeble voices.

"We're going to march, commander."

Ragıp shouted as loudly as he could.

"Are we going to march?"

This time the answer was more robust.

"We're going to march, commander."

"Men, Muhtar Pasha has entrusted you with a mission to defend the honor of the empire and the future of the Ottoman capital, you're tired, you're hungry, but where we're going there will be shelter and bread . . . We have to hold on a little longer, my brave men . . . Are you going to hold on?"

Sounding as if their morale had been raised by seeing Muhtar Pasha and by the promise of bread and shelter, the men answered,

"We're going to hold on, commander."

"Good for you, my brave men . . . Forward, march . . ."

He turned to the back and called out,

"Sergeant . . ."

"Yes, commander."

"Double time, get the men in step with the 'Pilevne' march."

"Yes sir."

They lined up in the mud, one of those strange military miracles occurred, a straight, strong command, seeing the most senior commander struggling through the mud, Ragıp Bey's decisiveness and the dream of finding bread had suddenly enlivened them with the last strength remaining in their flesh, their bones and their veins, they began to march.

The sergeant was raining commands.

"Heads up, chests out, march in step, let the world see what Muhtar Pasha's soldiers are like . . . One . . . Two . . . One . . . Two . . ."

The crowd looked at this orderly military unit that had suddenly appeared march decisively through the mud, they watched in amazement as they sang the march at the tops of their voices.

They parted the crowd, marching as if they were on a flat road, Ragıp Bey saw that other soldiers were joining the unit and that their numbers were growing, at that moment discipline was giving all of the soldiers hope, they were joining the marching unit on both sides.

From time to time Ragıp Bey shouted, "Faster, today isn't like any other day, you're going to save the honor of the Ottoman Empire . . ."

"Civilians can't understand," he'd said to Osman, "sometimes a march can save lives, sometimes a march can save a nation, a good march can straighten out the men's enthusiasm and morale, it stokes their heroism and pride, we sang marches all the way to Terkos, the men didn't march, the marches marched them."

The line called the "Çatalca line" was in fact some distance beyond Çatalca, it was a twelve-mile line between Büyükçekmece and Lake Terkos, as Muhtar Pasha had said, there were bunkers and artillery emplacements left over from the Russian war, they hoped that if they could establish themselves along that line they could stop the Bulgarian forces. They calculated that the Bulgarian forces coming behind them were also tired, that they wouldn't be able to get their cannons through the mud, that as they distanced themselves from their country they would receive fewer provisions and that as they themselves approached Istanbul they might be able to bring food and bread to the men.

They marched as far as the Terkos line, singing marches and without breaking formation, only once they passed Çatalca one of the soldiers who was singing marches suddenly shouted, "Oh damn!"

The sergeant went over to him.

"Why the hell are you shouting?"

"One of my boots ripped . . . It's full of mud."

"Keep marching, man . . . Are we going to let the Ottoman Empire sink because your foot is cold? Don't slow us down, keep up the pace."

The man laughed and continued singing and marching.

Sometime after Ragıp Bey's unit reached the Terkos line, the other vanguard units that Muhtar Pasha had sent began to arrive, as well as some new units that had set out from Istanbul.

They stopped the soldiers and let the refugees keep going, they got the weary survivors of the Lüleburgaz disaster into line, officers found their men and men found their units, soldiers found one another, the bunkers and artillery placements were cleaned out, they pitched the tents that had been sent from Istanbul in the rear, bread and the first hot food the men had eaten in days was distributed.

The small cannonballs that had come from Istanbul were stowed in the artillery emplacements.

As the Ottoman army was settling in, the Bulgarian army still hadn't arrived, the mud was tiring them, and as the pashas had guessed they really did have to leave their heavy cannons behind in the mud.

When the Bulgarian army arrived and slowly began to take up position two days later, the Ottoman units had already taken cover and were prepared for battle.

Those two days were very difficult for Ragıp Bey, after that wearying march through the mud and dealing with hunger, sickness, deserters, and shattered morale, he spent most of those two days emplacing the mountain artillery that had been brought from Istanbul, distributing tents to his men, ensuring discipline and order in the unit and preparing to go back into battle.

The sergeant found a small shack just to the rear of the artillery emplacements and requisitioned it for Ragıp Bey, they put a cot in it, lit a fire in the fireplace, the walls, blackened by smoke, were of mud brick, and it was thatched with straw, but the shack seemed like a palace to Ragıp Bey, he'd had a good, long sleep, he'd eaten, and there was a teapot on the fire.

The real difficulty emerged after the preparations had been completed, for the third time during this miserable war they were waiting for the fighting to being, waiting was very difficult and heavy for Ragıp Bey; the defeats he'd experienced, the breaking of his pride, the helplessness, the hunger, the lack of trust he saw in the men's eyes were all added to the sense of defeat he carried with him everywhere, the thin scars of the wounds he'd expected would heal with time had been scraped off and the wounds had reopened.

He'd come to the point of almost hating his emotions, his anguish, his loneliness, himself, and his life, he was angry at himself because he felt besieged and imprisoned by his own emotions.

It was perhaps the first time in his life that his manhood had been crushed like this, without realizing it, the personality that had been constructed on that manhood had been shaken to its foundations, removing the reason for its existence.

Dilara Hanim, who for years thought about why they'd lost their happiness and whose fault it had been and who looked at all men trying to understand Ragıp Bey, trying to find clues about Ragıp Bey in their actions, attitudes, and conversation, surprised Monsieur Lausanne with a tirade when one evening he was talking about Oriental women and meanwhile alluded to Oriental men in a somewhat mocking manner.

"Those Westerners who always find Oriental women fascinating and mysterious can't easily understand the emotions of Oriental men they know nothing about, these strange creatures who seem so plain and shallow to them. Perhaps they don't know how fragile this magical power called manhood which constitutes almost the entire life of Oriental men is, how even the slightest damage can destroy all confidence. Manhood fills their entire being, fills their personalities, their emotions, their minds, and the most secret, hidden corners of their souls, and from there it overflows into the world. They live smelling the smell of the manhood that overflows from them, drawing their manhood into their lungs at every moment, wanting to fight all men like animals and to possess all women. They believe that they can defeat all other men and that all women will become unconditionally attached to them. They're blinded by this belief, Monsieur Lausanne."

She paused, took a sip of her tea and continued.

"In order to live, in order to exist, in order to reproduce, to make their presence in the world felt, they feel the need, like wild animals, for a female who will accept their strength unconditionally. That female is the only being who can prove to those men that the false world they've created in their minds is real, that female's betrayal, change of mind, doubt or reluctance can suddenly tear apart this world that men created and believe is real . . . This may seem strange to you, but Oriental men are even prepared to kill their women in order to prove to themselves that their worlds are real. Not from jealousy, love, desire or sorrow but because they have the need to believe that the world they see, smell and taste is real, they threaten the lives of women who ruin that reality, they kill them like animals. They're dependent on women who will tell them that the world they designed in their minds while they smelled their manhood is real and to prove it to them with their attachment. When the woman's attachment is missing, the world ends, life ends. In bed and in every other aspect of life they need to possess in an absolute and inarguable manner, to know they possess, and to see that the woman accepts being possessed."

She paused here for a moment and sighed, then turned to Monsieur Lausanne, who was listening to her in surprise, and said with an anguish whose source he didn't understand,

"If they think they don't possess a woman they'll either kill her or they'll flee."

Then she laughed and added,

"To tell the truth I don't know which is worse for a woman who can love a man like that."

Ragıp Bey was exactly the kind of Oriental man Dilara Hanım was talking about, despite having lived in Germany for years and having internalized a number of Western values, the traces of thousands of years of ancestry had been indelibly chiseled into the walls of his mind and his soul even as he was being born.

He'd loved Dilara Hanım, even if he couldn't admit this to himself, he loved her even though this truth made him angry and even though he struggled to reject it; he'd expected the woman he loved to once again prove the existence and authenticity of the world he'd created in his mind, in which he stood at the center and which expanded with the smell of manhood that overflowed from him, to internalize this world, to enter this world, that's what a woman in love would do, as Dilara Hanım had said, he believed this. According to him, a woman in love would accept being possessed by her man, would want this.

Dilara Hanım hadn't wanted this.

Dilara Hanım had brought down all of his confidence in his world as if she had broken a tent's pole, and now this collapsed confidence enveloped him like thick tent-cloth, leaving him unable to breathe and destroying his desire to live.

He couldn't have killed Dilara Hanım, despite his animalistic manhood, the training he'd received, the life he'd lived, the values he'd accepted, the "manly honor," a different measure of manhood adopted by Oriental men of his level, would never permit harming a woman; in fact it was this dilemma that was destroying him, his soul was like a monster that was half animal and half human, he was neither animal enough to punish Dilara Hanım's reluctance with death nor human enough to accept that this might be another form of love. This dilemma didn't leave him any way out, it suffocated him, it constricted him, it left him no recourse but to wish for his own death.

Despite all of the disasters he somehow hadn't managed to die on the battlefield, he hadn't been cautious, he hadn't hidden, but none of the inauspicious artillery shells that had killed so many young men had hit him.

The pain he experienced, the yearning he felt, was like an insult to his own manhood, pride and existence, the feeling of humiliation was crushing him, leaving him without breath, but even worse, there was another yearning within him that seemed very feminine to him and that wounded him in a different manner; his desire to see Dilara Hanım was turning into an almost physical pain.

Sometimes he took the letters out and held them in his

hand, he looked at them for a long time, he smelled the paper, sometimes he thought about crumpling them up and throwing them into the fire, at those times he anxiously put them in his pocket to hide them from himself. "I'm caught like a mouse in a trap," he would grumble.

Dilara Hanım's face, her laugh, her voice, and some of the things she used to say said were wandering by themselves through the labyrinth of his memory, sometimes they disappeared, sometimes they would emerge at an unexpected time and erase whatever he was experiencing at that moment, he wanted them to go away but at the same time he was afraid that they would go away. These contradictory desires and feelings that he was not at all accustomed to tore apart his confidence in himself, and worse, his respect for himself, he decided that he was powerless and weak; to believe that he possessed traits that he had never tolerated and had always looked down on was for him in a real sense worse than death.

One night he woke abruptly from his sleep and said, "I'm going to burn those letters," at that moment he believed they were poisoning his soul, he quickly took the letters out of his pocket and went over to the almost extinguished fire in the fireplace, but he felt that his fingers were locked, his hands wouldn't obey his orders, he refused to burn the letters on the orders of someone else within him who he didn't know and couldn't see.

Full of self-hatred in that dark shack, he shouted, "God damn you, die already . . . die."

17

As the Çatalca line was preparing for battle, meetings about the coup were gathering pace in Istanbul, the Committee officers were observing the progress of the war, but at the same time they were making plans to free themselves from this "government of traitors."

They were meeting in Vefat Emin Bey's house, they arrived one at a time after darkness had fallen, moving through the narrow streets with their cloaks and coats wrapped around them, their mouths and faces hidden by scarves, they talked about how they were going to overthrow the government in a room with a bay window whose curtains had been closed, drinking the tea that the woman of the house brought them constantly.

Talat Bey said the same thing at every meeting.

"We can't wait too long, this government will finish off the Ottoman Empire with a dishonorable agreement, we mustn't permit this."

They were all impatient to regain the power they'd lost five months earlier, but Talat Bey had other reasons that no one knew about to be precipitate.

Cemal Bey, whose hatred for Talat Bey was reciprocated, told his friends in the party with a laugh,

"Being a soldier has scared the hell out of Talat."

The hatred between these two men, who three months later, together with Enver Bey, would promote themselves to the rank of pasha and become part of the "triumvirate" that would govern the Ottoman Empire, would continue for the rest of their lives, they were going to try a variety of games to destroy each other, but Cemal Bey's words weren't just out of hatred, he was also telling the truth.

It was one of Cemal Bey's favorite stories, whenever he was angry at Talat Bey he would repeat it to whoever he was with.

"As you know, five months ago our Talat was the glorified interior minister of the Ottoman State, of course all ministers have their faults, his fault was that he'd deserted from the army. He managed to avoid his military service until he was thirty-nine years old, he's crafty, he's good at that kind of thing . . . This past month, just before the war, he went to Edirne, I think someone informed on him, the military police detained him for desertion and brought him to the city guardians. They dressed him in a military uniform, put him in a tent, he went deathly pale. He sent telegrams to everyone asking them to get him out of there, Cevat intervened and had a leave permit made up for him, then they went and got him . . . But now he's in deathly fear that at any moment they'll come and take him into the army. He talks big, but when there's a real war he takes a step back. Everyone's son is going and fighting, why are you running away? Look at Muhtar Pasha, his father was grand vizier, he himself was serving as a minister, he left it all and volunteered to go to the front . . . Sometimes I'm about to say it but I stop myself, this is a matter of national importance, let's get this revolution done before there's any discord."

They wanted to carry out the revolt as soon as possible, but they were delaying a bit until Enver Bey, the most determined among them, returned.

At the last meeting Cevat Bey had asked,

"When Is Enver Bey returning, Talat Bey?"

"Our other colleagues have returned from Tripoli, but as

you know, Enver Bey went to Libya to organize the movement there. I sent him word to return at once. He'll be here within a month."

"So what are we going to do?"

"I say we chose our trustworthy friends here, we'll get them assigned to duties by the General Staff, they can go and talk to our officer friends at the front, get them to join this movement, with those officers' help we can march the army to Istanbul, the government won't resist, they'll withdraw, we'll make Mahmut Şevket Pasha grand vizier and form a cabinet, then we'll scatter the Bulgarians, saving the Ottoman Empire and gaining sympathy from the people."

Emin Bey said,

"How are we going to get their transfer orders, won't they suspect?"

Talat Bey turned and looked at Cevat Bey. Cevat Bey said,

"I'll take care of it, I'll get their transfer orders done this week without anyone catching on, the major in charge of that is one of us, it won't be difficult to get it done."

"Let's do it right away."

"I've become a little suspicious of Mahmut Şevket Pasha," said Cemal Bey, "he might change his mind if there's too much delay."

Talat Bey told Cemal Bey what he'd told Cevat Bey earlier.

"The Pasha is fond of power, he won't change his mind easily, but of course he shouldn't be left idle . . . Cevat Bey, are you visiting the Pasha?"

"A few of us go almost every week, I don't think the pasha is going to change his mind either, he's given no indication of that, on the contrary he seems very decisive, he keeps talking about what he's going to do when he comes to power."

"Is it the pasha who's coming to power?"

"That's what he sounds like, I won't lie . . . And we don't say anything."

"We're the ones who are staging the revolt, is he going to take all the power?"

"It seems as if that's the way the pasha thinks . . ."

"We're finished, we're finished . . . But there's nothing we can do about it, we need a dignified pasha like him, anyway let's stage our revolt, let the pasha take charge and see what happens later . . . Everything in its own time."

There was a silence, the Committee members knew more or less what words like this meant and what kind of results they led to, but no one objected. For the Committee, human life was not the most important thing in the world, they'd all accepted this, this had been their political position from the beginning, power had strengthened this position, "for the sake of the nation" it was permissible, indeed necessary, to eliminate every threat to their power . . .

Cevat Bey said to Osman, "they say we were very harsh, we had people assassinated, we killed people, we oppressed the opposition, but they never thought about the conditions under which we came into being, when he first started we were fighting against Abdülhamid's spies and Bulgarian guerillas, then we struggled against the reactionaries, we put down the March 31st uprising, then the Accord and their Halaskar Zabitan faction in the military appeared, then we were overwhelmed by the Balkan War, then finally there was the world war, let someone tell me what we could have done under these circumstances, how could we have established a soft administration, they would have overthrown us, they would have cut off our heads and put them on stakes, in addition, for the love of God, these Ottoman intellectuals who never stood against Abdülhamid's spies are uncomfortable with how repressive we are, when have the Ottoman's ever experienced a time without repression for them to complain about us . . . If you ask why they're always complaining about us, it's because we always represented civilization in these lands, we stood against the reactionaries, the intransigents, and the bigots, we brought modernization, the army and life were modernized during our time, they didn't want modernization, yes, the public didn't want it either, this is a people who for centuries lay down and slept in the mud called the caliphate, ignorant, undeveloped, numbed by religion, what were we to do, how were we going to bring the Ottomans to the level of Europe, those ignorant people even denied science, to them everything was infidel nonsense, they were against any innovation because it was the work of the infidels, they called ignorance piety, what else could we do except be harsh, when we talked about modernity, they talked about religion, about the Koran, they talk about God, how are you going to struggle against that, tell me how you're going to struggle against that, if someone comes and shows God as the guiding principle of all reactionaries, if he lies, how can you have anything to say to him, are we going to fight with God, perish the thought, we silenced the fanatics, there was no other way, there couldn't have been . . ."

The dead who slid through the emptiness of the air with a slight breeze as they wandered through this large and empty mansion generally didn't speak to one another, they said what they wanted to say only to Osman, but Osman knew that they heard one another, he was surprised by how angry they were despite being dead, how restless they were, how much they wanted to show themselves to have been in the right.

Hikmet Bey, who in his youth had joined the ranks of the Committee for Union and Progress to struggle against Abdülhamid, putting his own life and his father's entire existence in danger, never forgave the Committee for what they did later on, "Money and power drove them mad," he said, "I knew most of them in their youth, they were honest people, they set out to save the empire, to end tyranny, to bring about a revolution here like the French Revolution, their intentions were pure and good, but later they came to power much more quickly and easily than they'd guessed. They were confused, they were powerful enough to overthrow a sultan, but they didn't have the capacity or the knowledge to govern a state. This is the greatest danger, to have the power to overthrow but not the power to govern, because when you've overthrown, you believe that you have the right to govern . . . But there's such a great difference between the two . . . We saw this throughout the time the Committee was in power . . . A sultan is the owner of the state, the treasury is his own personal wallet, he doesn't steal from the treasury, he spends the money, sometimes he squanders the money, have you ever heard anyone calling Abdülhamid a thief, no one says that, is he going to steal his own property . . . But the Committee robbed the treasury, and how they robbed, how they stole, how corrupt they were . . . Is there anyone who doesn't know how Quartermaster General İsmail Hakki Pasha robbed the entire army, this thievery came out into the open, the complaints couldn't fit into the filing cabinets, did they do anything, no . . . Why? Because he was Enver's man . . . They all formed their own gangs within the government, they fought with each other, they hated each other, the way Talat plotted against Cemal, even the deaf sultan heard about how he blackmailed and threatened him . . . They say they were modern, they say they were civilized . . . They used talk of civilization to serve their power in exactly the same way that Abdülhamid used religion to serve his power . . . At least Abdülhamid believed, he was religious, but those people didn't even believe what they were saying, in fact they didn't even know what they were saying . . . They thought that civilization was dressing like Westerners and men and women sitting together in *cafés chantants* . . . They didn't even turn and look at the philosophy, industry and art of Western civilization . . . they thought that what they'd seen in the cafes of Salonica was civilization, they saw the effort to turn the entire nation into Salonica as civilization . . . They gave up on that later anyway, they were only interested in preserving their power and stealing money . . . They threw the opposition in prison, tortured them and killed them, without even stopping to listen to what they were saying, to what they were criticizing . . . In their language civilization came to mean murder and robbery . . . Abdülhamid's men would follow people and write denunciations, their men shot people in the head in the middle of the street and then walked away . . . These people made murderers governors . . . Was there a single Committee member who didn't know how they killed the Armenians, how they seized their property and kept it for themselves and became rich . . . They didn't make a mistake, they did it deliberately, they killed in order to rob . . . For five years they burned down the great empire and scattered its ashes into the air . . . I won't ever forgive them, do you know why I won't forgive them, I won't forgive them because they made people miss Abdülhamid's tyranny, they came saying they would tear down that tyranny and then they created a worse tyranny than the one they tore down. I won't forgive them because they made people say that Abdülhamid was better."

Hikmet Bey always felt this anger, he truly never forgave the Committee for stealing from him the excitement of struggling to bring Abdülhamid down, the hope, the dreams he'd had for the future of the nation, but this anger did not lead him to join the ranks of those who opposed the Committee and hid behind a coarse religiosity. He believed that things wouldn't straighten out for many years, he no longer concerned himself with society, as he'd said to Rasim Bey, he'd begun to concern himself with "his garden" and his own life, but there was always something broken within him. Just like the Committee wanting to turn the Ottoman Empire into Salonica, he in fact wanted to turn the Ottoman Empire into Paris, he wasn't aware of it but this was what he wanted, it saddened him to realize that this was in no way possible, that a France wasn't going to emerge from the Ottoman Empire, even though he'd ceased to be interested in politics, he didn't give up on thinking, reading books and struggling to understand why the Ottoman Empire couldn't and wouldn't reach the level of France.

One morning, while Hikmet Bey was talking about these things with Nizam and Dilevser at breakfast, Nizam, with his eyes slightly swollen with morning drowsiness, said with his usual nonchalance,

"Father, why don't you settle in Paris. You spent your entire youth there, my grandmother is there, why do you insist on living in this strange country, in this unlit city, even though it makes you sad?"

Hikmet Bey sighed, he was as annoyed by the question's lack of emotion as he was that it was logical and correct, but he struggled to not let it be sensed that he was annoyed.

"That's a logical question, my son, but there's no logical answer . . . Because feelings have no logic and my choice is based entirely on feelings, yes, we could go settle in Paris, we could be happier there than we are here, but this wouldn't solve my problem. I love this place . . . When I first arrived, this was like a dark pile of garbage after Paris, I wanted to go back, my father wouldn't permit me. Then I started to like this place. The strange thing is that I really liked it . . . I loved it despite all it lacked, despite the filth, the darkness and how primitive society was, but loving is a little bit like that, isn't it, do you only love the perfect and the good? Sometimes you love someone who seems ugly to everyone else, who perhaps is truly ugly, you've seen something hidden beneath the ugliness, you love because what's a secret from others is evident to you, in spite of everything this city has something, something that doesn't exist anywhere else."

As if to remind his father of his mother's beauty and of how much he'd been in love with her, Nizam said,

"I thought you loved beauty, this is the first time I'm hearing that you love ugliness."

As Dilevser waited for her husband to answer this question, she put down the fork she'd been holding and looked at Hikmet Bey.

"That's true, I had a fondness for beauty, like everyone . . . Then later I learned that what's beautiful isn't always valuable and that what's valuable isn't always beautiful. I discovered the difference between what's beautiful to everyone and what's beautiful to you."

"So what is it that you love about this place, about this country, this city, what is this beauty that I haven't seen but you have, father?"

Hikmet Bey didn't know how to answer this, he sensed that he should talk not about what he saw but about what he felt, but he knew that Nizam wasn't going to take the trouble to try to understand these emotions. Nizam's intelligence and attention were almost consciously blind and deaf to the emotions that people belittled.

"It's difficult to explain, my son . . . Perhaps to feel a beauty you have to have struggled for it, or rather to bring out the beauty you sense but can't see requires you to have made an effort . . . There's a bond between me and this city, Paris is very beautiful but it doesn't belong to me, this place belongs to me, this city is mine, whatever they do they can't take this away from me."

Hikmet Bey took a sip of his tea and smiled.

"And I found Dilevser in this city, that alone is reason enough to love it . . ."

Dilevser's face lit up when she heard this, but at the same time an expression of such disbelief and belittlement appeared on Nizam's face that Dilevser was seized by a violent suspicion about the love Hikmet Bey felt for her, or more accurately, the suspicions she already had suddenly grew larger.

Hikmet Bey had seen the expression on Nizam's face, he thought it was very cruel for him to do this in front of Dilevser, when he glanced at Dilevser out of the corner of his eye he saw that the young woman's face had gone pale. He wanted to say something to put Dilevser at ease, that would please her.

"But if Dilevser would like to go, I'll go," he said, "If Dilevser were to say let's go right away, I'd get up now and start getting ready."

"Really, father?"

"Really . . ."

Nizam, not taking heed of how Dilevser had been pummeled by this conversation, flung from one emotion to another, caught between delight and suspicion, Nizam turned to her cheerfully and said,

"Tell him you want to go, tell him so we can go to Paris."

"I want to be with Hikmet Bey, wherever he's happy is the place I want to be. If he loves Istanbul I want to stay in Istanbul too. How could we be happy in a place Hikmet Bey didn't want to be, a place we went to on account of my wishes alone?"

"But there they have new novels, concerts, exhibits, intellectual debates . . . Everything you love is there."

With great sincerity, and knowing that Nizam might mock this sincerity, Dilevser said,

"Everything I love is in this room. I don't want a city, I want a room . . . Perhaps this is what you don't understand."

"Dilevser, you're very modest for someone who lives in a twenty-room mansion."

Hikmet Bey couldn't stand it.

"Why do you make fun of everything, Nizam? I don't think this is such a good habit, my son. And especially to mock sincerity, isn't that a cruel and unfair attitude?"

Nizam shrugged his shoulders.

"I'm not making fun, I'm just talking in a logical manner,

however, please forgive me, but you're not giving logical answers."

Then he began to worry that he'd been rude.

"I didn't say that to hurt you, Dilevser, if I was rude and hurt your feelings I apologize, that's not what I meant."

Dilevser, concealing her hurt feelings and being genuinely tolerant of Nizam, said,

"Don't worry about it, I know that wasn't your intention . . . Now eat your egg before it gets cold."

Even though Nizam, who was full only of his own emotions and was blind to any feelings other people had that weren't about him, had angered him with what he said, Hikmet Bey knew that he was partly right, especially in those days when the city was so sick it was struggling to breathe, cholera was spreading, the streets were full of sick people and a throng of sick refugees was approaching the city step by step.

The city was behaving as if it hadn't noticed this disaster, death had encountered no obstacles and was enveloping the city like an octopus with thousands of slippery arms; death had never been so lively, so active and so visible, as a hostile army was marching on the city gates, cholera had begun consuming the city from within.

Apart from gathering those who had died in the streets every morning, carting them away in tumbrils, dumping them in deep holes and spreading caustic lime other them, it appeared that no measures were being taken, there was no news in the newspapers, even the foreign press was being censored, they were also forbidden to mention cholera. Within a deep silence, cholera was carrying off dozens of people a day.

Monsieur Lausanne had mentioned cholera several times in his dispatches to his newspaper, but those sections of his articles had been erased by the censor.

Lausanne had written about the cholera cases he'd seen in

the city, but in fact he saw the true dimensions of the catastrophe in a place he'd never anticipated or expected.

In order to get an idea of what was going on behind the front lines, he rented one of the automobiles that were appearing in the city at that time and set out for the Belgrade Forrest.

When he passed Büyükdere Valley and reached the edge of the Belgrade Forrest, a military unit was visible in the distance, the way they were marching seemed strange even from that distance, there was a lack of discipline but it didn't seem completely disorderly, it seemed as if the crowd was shivering.

As they approached they saw "human wreckage," they were leaning against each other as they tried to walk, there was no flesh left on their faces, their skin had taken on a greenish color and was clinging to their bones, their eyes were sunken hollows. They weren't walking, they were dragging themselves along.

There was a large crowd approaching from behind them. They were all the same as those in front, the wagons were piled with dead bodies in uniform, there were some who had lain down among the bodies out of weariness.

There were dead bodies by the side of the road. Those they couldn't fit into the wagons were left by the side of the road and in the fields.

A frightful, dirty smell had spread everywhere.

The driver understood what was going on before Lausanne did.

"Sir, they have cholera . . ."

As if he was talking to himself rather than to the driver, Monsieur Lausanne asked,

"Where are they going?"

The driver didn't answer. They looked at the soldiers in terrified silence.

Some of them had stopped walking and were collapsing by the side of the road.

It was there, that day, that Lausanne realized how much the epidemic had spread and that the epidemic had started killing the soldiers before the enemy even arrived.

There, for the first time, he witnessed clearly how this city that was preparing for a coup and a war was being subjugated by death.

18

In his selfishness, having gathered every worry from almost every source he encountered and having built a wall that kept him apart from other people around these worries, Nizam was not someone who worried, he was worried neither about the war nor the sickness that was slowly grinding the city. Indeed the war seemed like completely meaningless nonsense to him, "How could a person have hundreds of thousands, millions of enemies or millions of friends?" he'd asked Osman once, "I can never understand this . . . I never met anyone who could convince me that all Bulgarians are my enemies and all Ottomans are my friends."

If he listened from time to time to what Hikmet Bey had to say about the war, he was thinking of Anya.

It wasn't a manner of thinking that he was accustomed to, Nizam generally only thought about a woman if she made him passionately jealous or if he passionately desired her, otherwise the women he'd known were for him like paintings hung in a gallery, when he came across them as he wandered through the gallery of his memory, he would notice them and then forget them again.

He didn't yearn passionately for Anya, he wasn't passionately jealous and he didn't desire her passionately, but still, thoughts about her would spread through his mind like a fog before he could get hold of them, before he could catch them; he wasn't able to grasp what his thoughts about Anya really were, it was just that he constantly caught himself thinking about Anya, but by the time he did so, the source from which those thoughts had been born was gone, his own mind was playing tricks on him.

Generally in his thoughts there was an image of Anya's cold and insulting expression as she lowered the straps of her dress. He'd never encountered a surrender that completely rejected the other person's being. He'd never seen a woman who could give her body so indifferently, as if she was handing over an old dress, denigrating the other person's desires and believing they wouldn't have the strength to ask for anything more.

Nizam's feelings about Anya had such an unaccustomed color that he was confused, he realized that he felt a tenderness, whereas he didn't usually feel much tenderness for women, pity perhaps but not this kind of tenderness, but this feeling of tenderness would be suddenly cut off by Anya's cold stance, the woman had such an unusual strength, there was a fear and respect mixed in with the tenderness, and these emotions were not emotions that Nizam was accustomed to.

None of these emotions were very strong, but together they formed quite a crowd, and they were mixed.

After that night, Nizam didn't leave the house for two days, he didn't go to the gambling den or to the Madam's house, in the evening he sat at home with Hikmet Bey and Dilevser, he saw how pleased his father was that he was there, he talked to Dilevser about Paris, they played the piano together, Nizam made them laugh with his witticisms and with Istanbul gossip that he'd picked up at the gambling den, secure within the warmth radiated by the large, tiled stove, they listened to the wind outside, and to the rain striking the windows.

For two days he rested his weary body in the warmth of the house, but the real reason he didn't go wasn't because he needed rest, he knew instinctively that disappearing from the scene after that night would make Anya curious, that it would open a breach in that thick barricade she'd erected against people; he was also punishing her because he'd had to think about her, no woman was allowed to make Nizam think about her, any woman who did so she should be punished. Since childhood he'd felt a strange anger towards people he had to think about, whether it was from tenderness, love, or yearning, it annoyed him when his mind was occupied with other people.

There are similarities between fathers and sons that they themselves are not aware of, without realizing it, Nizam was sheltering in the same sanctuary that Hikmet Bey had found in his youth; his mother. They both had extraordinarily beautiful mothers, and when a woman started wandering through their minds, their mother's beauty became a strange haven for them.

During those two days, he went to visit his mother for the first time since he'd arrived, he knew that going so late like this could sadden his mother, could hurt her feelings, but he believed that this kind of hurt healed very quickly; he wounded people with his indifference, then healed them with his smiles and his jokes.

In fact he himself didn't know whether he loved his mother and father, he had been taught that he should love them, he thought that he should love them, but he never forgave either of them. Because his mother had run off with another man, he could forgive neither his mother for leaving nor his father for allowing her to go, the anger he felt deep down at both of them remained. He didn't know if there was a real love beneath the taught, memorized, shallow love on the surface and the anger deep within him, he wasn't curious either, if he didn't see either of them he wouldn't feel a great desire to see them.

When images, thoughts and feelings about Anya began to wander through him, when his mind unexpectedly set aside room for someone other than himself, he wanted with an almost animal instinct to go to his mother and see her unequalled beauty. He sensed that her beauty would make all other women seem pale and insignificant.

Just as he'd surmised, Mehpare Hanım greeted him with an exceptional coldness, she didn't reproach him, she didn't ask him, "Why didn't you come?"

"How are you Nizam?"

"I'm fine, how are you, mother dear?"

"I'm fine, thank you."

"I'm a little late to come visit you."

"I noticed."

"It's difficult to get used to a new city, I thought I'd settle in before coming."

"You did the right thing."

"Are you angry at me?"

"Noo . . . Why would you think that?"

Nizam laughed.

"If you weren't very angry, if you were only a little angry, you would have complained."

"How many times have you seen me complain?"

"I never have . . . You're indifferent, that's why."

"You behave in an indifferent manner and at the same time you expect people to be hurt by this? Mihrişah Sultan has spoiled you even more than I'd supposed."

Nizam realized then that he'd forgotten that his mother was narcissistic enough not to tolerate her son's narcissism, she wasn't going to be able to forgive as quickly and easily as other people did.

He looked carefully at his mother's face, she really was very beautiful, she was still beautiful, still proud, she still believed that she could put any man under her spell if she wanted, there was something in her eyes that was reminiscent of Anya's eyes, it wasn't an emptiness like hers, she didn't look at people as if they were dead, but it was as if there was a transparent curtain in her eyes that separated her from other people, it looked as if it would be very difficult to tear that curtain and move past it.

It was very difficult to understand why and how Nizam's

feelings changed, but the coldness with which he'd been greeted and the inaccessibility he'd seen in his mother's eyes increased his respect if not his love for his mother, he wanted her to love him too, and sensing that this wasn't going to happen as quickly as he wanted strengthened the feeling.

For a moment he wanted to hug his mother, but he knew that she would say "Nizam" in a cold voice and push him away, that she would rebuke him for showing his feelings openly like a "common person," that she would be surprised by this kind of behavior, "can you imagine a family in which a person hugging his mother is made into a problem," he'd said to Osman, "what kind of family is that, they always confused me, but it didn't occur to anyone to confuse this family." Osman thought about saying, "all of this is natural in a family where the son waits so long to visit his mother," but as usual, he changed his mind.

Nizam stood there not knowing what to do.

"Come," said Mehpare Hanım, "let's go inside."

"Mother, aren't we going to make peace?"

"If we were angry with each other we could have made peace, but we're not, so stop talking meaningless nonsense and come have some coffee."

They went into the large, glass greenhouse that looked onto the grass, as they walked Nizam looked at his mother and realized once again that the way she walked, her figure, her grace and her elegance made her a woman unlike most others, she walked through the world with an indifferent looseness, the balance between decisiveness and softness in the way she walked gave her entire body a different harmony, the glossiness of the hair she'd gathered behind her head flowed into the whiteness of her neck, and from there it spread to her surroundings, it seemed as if she was walking in honey-colored light.

"Mother, as always you're very beautiful."

Mehpare Hanım realized from the tone of Nizam's voice

that he'd said this with genuine admiration, but she wasn't affected.

"*Merci*," was all she said.

She wasn't affected by praise concerning her beauty, next to her own admiration for her beauty, other people's admiration wasn't very meaningful, it was as if she believed that other people had a duty to admire her.

Just as with Mihrişah Sultan, next to Mehpare Hanım, the realm of womanhood seemed pale and insignificant, all other women lost their importance.

Anya was erased from Nizam's mind, all images of her faded and disappeared, no matter how angry he might be with her, he fell under the control of his admiration every time; the way she lightly threw back her head, the cold smile on her face, the proud stance that wouldn't even condescend to rebuke, that mysterious light that enveloped her . . . All other people, all troubles, became smaller next to that light.

For a moment he wanted his mother to love him with a true love, he realized he missed feeling as if he was her son; and it wasn't motherly tenderness that he expected, he wanted to be accepted as part of this beauty that that spread out like a cold and illuminated sea, he wanted permission to shelter in these enchanted waters when he got bored with people. At that time no love, no tenderness could give Nizam the confidence that Mehpare Hanım's coldness and beauty did, the love he felt for himself and the admiration he felt for his mother combined, enveloped him and separated him from the world.

"Admiration is more effective than love," Nizam said to Osman once, "you can always find someone to love, but there are so few people on the face of this earth that can be admired . . ."

As they drank their coffee and ate their pastries, Nizam succeeded in making his mother laugh with various imitations, jokes and stories, and this pleased him as if he'd won a great prize.

At one point Mehpare Hanım asked in a serious tone, "have you grown accustomed to Istanbul?"

"I'm growing accustomed."

"Don't get up to too much mischief . . . I don't want to be saddened by you as well."

At one point in the conversation she said, as if she was mentioning something unimportant, "I know you don't love me."

"Who doesn't love you?"

"Rukiye and you . . . You don't love me."

"How can you say something like that, mother, we admire you . . ."

Mehpare Hanım pursed her lips.

"You might admire me . . . But you don't love me . . . Anyway, it's of no great importance . . . What was I saying?"

She carried on with what she's been saying as if she hadn't interrupted herself, as if they'd never had this conversation, Nizam didn't understand whether or not Mehpare Hanım was saddened because her children didn't love her.

At one point, in order to please his mother, Nizam said, "I'm thinking of staying with you for a little while," and Mehpare Hanım replied, "What would you do here with me, you'd get bored."

As he was leaving she kissed Nizam on the cheeks and said, "Istanbul is dangerous, be careful."

Nizam kissed his mother on the cheeks, got into the carriage, then got out again and went over to his mother, who was about to go into the house.

"I do love you, mother," he said.

Mehpare Hanım smiled.

"Good."

Someone else might have left an encounter like this feeling unhappy, but Nizam left feeling very pleased, order had once again been restored to his mind, which he had feared would be unhinged by images of Anya, his mother's magnificent beauty had given him confidence and peace, he was like someone had been given an antidote after being worried he'd been poisoned; that beauty had seemed more impressive and sparkling to him within the distinct coldness that enveloped it. In addition he felt a strange kind of gratitude for this coldness, if his mother had tried to win his love by behaving in a warmer, more tender manner, he knew from previous experience that he would hate her, but Mehpare Hanım had not permitted the warmth and closeness that would have brought out the hatred between mother and son. When Nizam was leaving, he'd been sincere when he said, "I do love you," at that moment he'd really felt love for his mother, he loved that beauty, that coldness, the admiration people felt for her, her indifference, the indifference that gave him so much confidence.

Mehpare Hanım's beauty was like the magical water that Achilles' mother washed him in, when he entered that water Nizam gained a power against all women, that's how he felt. "If I'd loved my mother, or rather if I'd loved her the way everyone loves their mother, she wouldn't have been able to give me that power," he'd told Osman, "it's not a power that love for a mother can give, it's a power that admiration for a mother can give." Osman, opening his eyes with a mocking smile, asked, "And what about Achilles' heel?" and Nizam said, "That's the place she held me, a place devoid of love."

That night when he set out again for the gambling den, he thought that he was free from the effect, which he couldn't fully understand, that Anya had on him, his mother's presence had erased Anya's image.

When they turned onto the torch-lined road, he was surprised to feel that he was excited, it was as if he'd truly believed that his mother had enchanted him against any kind of influence; among the flames, Anya's pale image rose like a mythological giant climbing towards the sky, gaining life as it passed the copper-colored trees, that voice that belittled him as it surrendered kept repeating in his memory, "Is this what you want?"

He was surprised by the excitement he felt, but he didn't panic, on the contrary he liked it, when he was far from Anya he was far from the effect she had on him, as he approached her, being under her influence was appropriate for the excitement he was seeking. The pleasure of the excitement he felt at the thought of Anya, the sight of her, the sound of her voice when he was with her wasn't what made Nizam uneasy, it was thinking about Anya when she was far from him that made him uneasy. It made Nizam angry when people who interested him moved out of their "location," and their presence and image was kept fresh when they weren't there.

The room was quiet as usual, and he gathered his poise and entered. Anya was playing the piano, once again her shoulders were straight and tense as she played. Only her hands and her fingers moved.

He walked very slowly, he was curious about how Anya would look at him when she saw him, he stood next to the piano, Anya looked at him, nothing in her face changed, nothing changed in her eyes either, though sometimes people can see things that are not visible; Nizam could see the reproach and the gratification under Anya's skin and deep in her eyes. They weren't in fact visible but they were there, Nizam could not have explained how he saw them, but he saw them.

He looked at Anya for a brief time, Anya continued playing the piano without looking up, then he left and went upstairs. The tables were all full, he wandered among the tables, he wasn't in a hurry to sit down and play, it wouldn't have mattered to him if he didn't play but when an older man got up from one of the tables they invited Nizam and he sat.

It was one of the nights when he was very lucky, as Kamil Bey used to say, "the cards were flowing," he got one good hand after another, the other players were eager to beat him, this eagerness drew them into the game and they lost.

He didn't remember how long he played, but he suddenly got bored, even though he had a very good card in his hand, he asked a woman who was watching him, "Would you like to play?" then gave her his cards, this wasn't a very common or acceptable thing to do, but they were accustomed to Nizam doing things like this and didn't say anything . . . He gathered up his winnings and left the table, he didn't even count the money he'd won.

He went out in front of the mansion, he couldn't decide what to do, it was still quite some time until morning, it would be boring to sit there and wait, and he didn't really feel like going to Evangeliki. He was smoking a cigarette and thinking about what to do when he suddenly heard a voice, "Thank God you're here."

He turned, it was Kamil Bey, his face was strained, his eyes seemed to stare, "Can you please give me a small loan?" he asked.

There was an almost threatening tone in his voice, this tone irritated Nizam, for a moment he considered not giving him any money, but to withhold money from a desperate man seemed like an unnecessary rudeness.

"How much do you need?"

"How much can you give me?"

Nizam took the money he'd won out of his pocket and handed it over, Kamil Bey took it all without counting it, as he turned and ran towards the stairs he realized he hadn't said thank you so he came back and said, "*merci*, my good man, you're always generous."

He remembered Kamil Bey having said, "Sometimes I can't stop at the limit," it must have been one of the nights he was unable to stop, later he said to Osman. "Not being able to stop is very pitiful, I saw this truth again that night, as someone who doesn't like to stop, I think I was very angry at Kamil Bey for causing me to see this."

In distress, he signaled for the carriage to come, he went to the Madam's house, he took Evangeliki upstairs, he sat on the bed, the woman sat next to him and rested her head on his chest, he stroked her hair and lit a cigarette.

They sat without speaking.

At one point Evangeliki asked, "Are you alright?"

"Yes," said Nizam, "I'm fine."

He left when it was growing light. Ash colored clouds had gathered above the city, the air smelled of smoke and seaweed, it was chilly, he wrapped his cape around him, he got into the carriage unhurriedly, this time he was certain that Anya would wait for him.

When he reached the gambling den, Anya was in the empty room smoking a cigarette, Nizam went over to her and said, "come." They went to Anya's house, where the stove had been lit, they didn't speak on the way or when they went into the house. It was as if they feared that even a single word would demolish something they hadn't identified, whatever this thing was that they were afraid might be demolished appeared to be so fragile that it had to be carried very carefully like a newborn baby, a wrong movement, a wrong word, a wrong glance could have killed the invisible creature between them.

Anya took off her coat and left it on the armchair by the door, she walked ahead and opened a door, there was a fresh light that couldn't get in, that got caught in the heavy cloth of the khaki curtains, the room in which this light was vaguely reflected was dim. He helped Anya undress, he lay her on the bed, then he undressed himself, they nestled together, he could feel the softness and warmth of Anya's slightly worn-out body.

At first Anya was very shy and apprehensive, sometimes she started at Nizam's touch as if she was frightened, sometimes she rested her head on Nizam's chest and stayed that way, Nizam caressed her gently, he gave her little kisses on her neck and her shoulders. Tenderness wasn't an emotion Nizam was accustomed to, indeed in bed tenderness seemed meaningless, but as always he'd left himself to his instincts, an animal intuition made him feel that he had to show tenderness.

Anya had let her hair down, it was thick and soft, it fell over her shoulders towards her breasts, there was a vague smell of flowers that Nizam couldn't identify, Nizam was touching her tenderly, indeed almost compassionately, when Anya suddenly tensed he'd stop, he waited for her to relax again, he stroked her hair.

The first time they made love they were very slow, very calm, they didn't speak at all.

"Are you alright?" asked Nizam.

"Yes."

"We can stop any time you want and I'll go."

"I don't want you to go."

"Fine."

From the way she tensed and started, Nizam realized that it had been a long time since a man had touched Anya's body.

Crossing the barbed, spasm filled barricade created by the mind being constantly awake with the fears accumulated from past wounds, bad memories and painful touches, of always being careful, of always being prepared to flee; the transition to the craving drunkenness of desire, to the willingness to lose oneself fearlessly in the dark, could only be realized though unhurried, unpanicked, soft and tender kisses.

Anya slowly freed herself from her bashfulness and apprehension, there was something strange and legendary in their lovemaking, like a water lily or a beautifully colored bird being transformed into a woman, a creature changing shape, and Nizam could feel the magic that was moving human flesh towards the soul.

This was a way of making love that he'd never known, this was a feeling that he'd never known.

Through his own slowness, tenderness, and soft touches,

Nizam was reaching truths he hadn't known existed; to possess a desire that at any moment could turn into a violent passion with a savage scream, to restrain it, to feel the warmth of the woman who was embracing him apprehensively, caused Nizam, who in bed was accustomed to hearing only the voice of his own flesh, to be able to hear other voices as well; he could taste the innocent desires of the timid body, with its sagging breasts and soft protruding belly, that was holding him.

This innocence had a taste, a taste he'd never known and didn't know how to describe. It was like the taste of the rose petals he would secretly pick and eat in the garden when he was a child.

From time to time Anya murmured a word in Russian, sometimes the tone of her murmuring rose.

They were making love as if they were swimming in a stagnant lake.

Nizam realized that he liked the warmth of the body that was embracing him, he felt that in a very short time he had become accustomed to this warmth that began so innocently and then transformed into a powerful desire that he never wanted to leave, that he wanted to touch constantly.

Nizam realized for the first time that night while he was making love to Anya that a woman's body is a mystery. When the violence that overflowed from his own body was withheld, he realized that every woman can be desired in a different manner, that the warmth of each woman's body aroused a different kind of desire.

Anya was not the most beautiful woman he'd made love to, he'd made love to some very beautiful women, but Anya was the first woman he'd wanted to touch constantly, he wanted to touch that body when it was curled up next to him during breaks in lovemaking, when her hair was spread across the pillow as she lay face down, when she snuggled against him, to make love to her again with unquenchable desire, to embrace that body, to lose himself in that body's warmth.

He never knew why he desired Anya so much, why she was different from other women, why he made love to her in a different manner than he did with other women, why wanting her delighted him so much.

It was through this desire that he discovered the mystery in a woman's body that he hadn't known about, he never solved that mystery, but he learned that there was a mystery.

19

Istanbul woke that morning to the sound of cannon fire.
It was just beginning to grow light, thick black clouds,
soiled by gunpowder and with a steely glow around their
edges, had gathered above the city, the roaring of the
Schneider-Cruesot cannons, the repeated hoarse and frightful
explosions, could be heard all over the city, rising smoke could
be seen in the distance.

People climbed onto roofs and housetops and leaned out
windows to try to figure out what was going on.

The war was only twenty miles from the capital of the
Ottoman Empire, that morning the Bulgarians planned to
breach the Ottoman positions with a violent artillery assault,
then push back the final obstacle and enter Istanbul. The fate
of the Caliph's capital lay in the courage of the soldiers holding the Çatalca line.

As at Lüleburgaz, the Bulgarians went on the offensive at
six thirty, suddenly firing all of their cannons at once, the field
cannons rumbled and the shells falling one after another shook
the ground.

At about six o'clock, while Ragıp Bey was atop the emplacements in Lazarköy that had been placed under his command,
looking out through his binoculars, he noticed a movement in
the Bulgarian army that had been waiting for nine days, shadows were moving around quickly, he said to the sergeant, "let
all of the batteries know, tell them to be on alert, they're up to
something."

The batteries had been set in the emplacements left over from the Russian war, during those nine days the emplacements had been reinforced.

The Creusot cannons had been placed in the rear of the emplacements on the first day, however the cannons didn't have mechanical arms, Ragıp Bey said to the sergeant, "Go and see if you can find our old Krupp cannons' mechanical arms." The sergeant took three men and went all along the front, he found as many old cannons that weren't being used as he could, gathered their mechanical arms and brought them back. With an improvised file and a hammer, Ragıp Bey managed to adapt those mechanical arms so they could be used with the cannons they had, the artillery training he'd received during his years in Germany proved very useful in getting this done.

When the four hundred cannons along the front began firing at once, the Ottoman cannon started firing quickly, the sergeant said, "We don't have many shells, use them sparingly," and Ragıp Bey replied, "Is this a time to be economical you fool, we're going to go at them with all our strength . . ."

The Bulgarians concentrated their artillery fire on the district around the villages of Lazarköy and Kastanya that was being defended by Muhtar Pasha's corps, the Ottomans were responding with the same ferocity, they were firing cannon at each other without stopping for a minute, the tents behind the emplacements were being hit, tent fires had begun, they were toppling onto each other as they burned, as the artillerymen fired the cannons, the foot soldiers were putting out the tent fires in the rear.

The emplacement Ragıp Bey was in received a hit, the emplacement shuddered and shook, a stone or two fell, dust flew through the air, but the emplacement endured, "faster," shouted Ragıp Bey, "faster, don't dawdle," the artillery commander's orders were exploding like the cannons.

The government was panicked by this battle just outside their gates, by the sound of the unceasing cannon fire and the Bulgarian army's sudden assault, they didn't know what to do.

After a hurried breakfast, Monsieur Lausanne set out for Foreign Minister Noradikyan Effendi's house in Taksim.

The minister received him right away.

His face was completely yellow, it was apparent that he had serious doubts about whether the army could hold out, and that he didn't trust the army.

"Look at what's happening," he said, "we wanted peace. We asked the victors about conditions for peace . . . They didn't even answer us, this is their answer, they went on the offensive, they continue to shed blood . . . History will judge them for this."

The sound of cannon fire filled the room, the minister's almost sobbing voice was punctuated by these terrifying sounds.

The desperate minister was appealing to the correspondent.

"I wonder if you got in touch with the French government they might prevent the Bulgarians from entering Istanbul in the name of humanity, in the name of general security?"

"Your excellency, I think it's much too late for that . . . Even if I could reach the government through the French ambassador, it would take them a long time to reach a decision."

The minister leaned on his desk, for a moment Monsieur Lausanne thought he was going to collapse.

"In that case," said Noradikyan Efendi, "I have no recourse left but to do my duty."

As the Foreign Minister tried to find a way to stop the Bulgarians through foreign journalists, the battle at the front proceeded violently, even though the Bulgarian army had numerical superiority, this time the conditions were different from those at Kırkkilise and Lüleburgaz, the Bulgarians were moving farther away from their homeland, the Ottoman soldiers had their backs to the capital, they knew they had nowhere to go, they'd taken up their positions, bread was coming from the city, they were low on ammunition but this time the men's morale was higher.

Monsieur Lausanne told Dilara Hanım that, "throughout history it has been difficult to defeat Ottoman soldiers in trench warfare, they have trouble when they attack, but if they go into their trenches it's impossibly difficult to get them out of there and drive them back."

Towards noon the Bulgarian command made their greatest mistake of the war, Third Army Commander General Radko Dimitrief, thinking that the artillery fire had worn out the Ottomans and that the Ottoman soldiers would flee as they had the previous two times, gave the infantry orders to march and sent out two divisions.

The Bulgarian infantry started moving towards the Ottoman emplacements across an open, muddy field.

The Ottoman cannon and machine guns fired on the Bulgarian infantry, the men could neither advance nor retreat, they'd been caught in the open, this time the mud changed color from the Bulgarian soldiers' blood, young Bulgarian men were being torn apart and collapsing before they even had a chance to fire.

Fully ten thousand Bulgarian soldiers lost their lives on the shores of Büyükçekmece Lake that day.

As darkness fell, Ragıp Bey was directing the batteries with his uniform wet with cold sweat, the sergeant said, "We're running out of shells," Ragıp Bey shouted, "they're retreating, they're retreating, keep firing."

In the darkness, a tremendous storm burst, it started raining violently, the dead lying in the mud sank a little more, every time lightning struck it illuminated the soldiers lying in the mud in their bloodied grey uniforms, the bodies moved when the rain struck them violently, they looked as if they were going to get up and walk.

As the lighting, thunder and the violence of the storm extinguished the violence of the battle, both sides were forced to stop, as night fell the battlefield was silent, the only sound was the sticky sound of the rain falling on the mud.

The sergeant said, "The Bulgar can't do anything in this rain, you get some rest, commander. If you continue to go without sleep you'll fall asleep at the front."

Ragıp Bey had found an empty stable with a hayloft in back in a ravine between the emplacements and the soldiers' tents, he'd moved his cot, his table and his maps there, he laughed when the sergeant referred to that stable as "headquarters."

The sergeant had made a fireplace of stones in a corner of the stable and lit a fire in it, a soldier brought a bowl of soup left over from the evening mess wagon and a little stale bread. Ragıp Bey had been drenched by the rain, he took off his jacket and put it next to the fire, he wrapped an army blanket around himself and sat next to the fire, he drank his soup, he ate that stale bread with great appetite, "That bread tasted better than anything you can get at the Tokatliyan restaurant," he said to Osman later.

The sergeant brought tea as well.

"Have you checked on the sentries, don't you dare put your faith in the rain, keep the sentries awake, in a little while I'm going to go take a look around too."

"All of the sentries are in place, commander, don't worry, their morale is high, none of them will leave their positions . . . Today we scattered the Bulgarians, I can die in peace, running away was very difficult for me to swallow."

The sergeant's reminder of how they'd fled made Ragıp Bey angry.

"Stop talking nonsense and go check on the sentries . . ."

The rain was striking the roof of the wooden stable, it was as if thousands of nails were being pounded into the roof, there was a monotonous rattling sound as water dripped from the roof and ran down the walls, the entire stable was rattling, his weariness and the monotonous sound made Ragıp Bey sleepy, he lay on the field bed's tarpaulin, which widened towards the floor, to get fifteen minute's sleep.

In the dream he had during the short time he slept, Dilara Hanım was leaning over him, her face wasn't visible and he could only see her hair, Dilara Hanım was saying "Ragıp" as if she wanted to wake him, he felt pleased to hear her voice but somehow he couldn't wake up, he couldn't open his eyes, he couldn't answer her.

Suddenly the stable was shaken by a terrifying roar, Ragıp Bey's bed was knocked over, he leapt to his feet, a Bulgarian field cannon shell had hit the hayloft in the rear, the hay had caught fire immediately, it didn't take long for the wooden partition to catch fire, by the time Ragıp Bey pulled himself together the flames had started to spread into the stable, he immediately rushed outside, the rain had subsided a bit.

Soldiers had come running and were watching the stable burn, Ragıp Bey suddenly realized he'd left his jacket inside, the sergeant tried to stop him as he ran towards the stable but he quickly knocked the sergeant to the ground and dove into the flames, he grabbed the jacket, which had started burning at the edges, and ran outside, then he beat the jacket against the ground to put out the flames. Immediately he put his hand in the pocket, the letters were there.

"Commander, you could have died," said the sergeant.

"I left my jacket inside, you idiot, should I have let it burn?"

The sergeant didn't understand this answer at all, so he chose to curse the Bulgarian artilleryman.

"He's a pimp who sells the wife he bought at the market, is he drunk, what's the point of firing your cannon you whoremaster, are you going to win the war with one cannot shot?"

With a cheerful laugh that surprised the sergeant even

more, Ragıp Bey said, "Our headquarters has burned down, sergeant, what are we going to do now?"

"I don't know," said the sergeant in distress, "we can settle in one of the emplacements, it's not so great, but until we find another headquarters . . ."

Until the stable burned and collapsed it had been raining lightly, but the rain suddenly became violent again, what was left of the stable turned into pitch black smoke, the smell of wood spread across the entire front.

"Come on, let's go check on the sentries," said Ragıp Bey.

He felt a joy within him, it was as if he'd really seen Dilara Hanım, the honor of that day's victory didn't attempt to silence this joy, he allowed it to wander freely through his mind so that it could play with the images in the darkness of his memory.

Meanwhile Monsieur Lausanne was telling Dilara Hanım the latest developments, in any event he came to the mansion every evening now, they ate dinner together and he told her everything he'd learned, including what he hadn't been able to send to his newspaper. "You're my best reader," he would say, "I don't think anyone in France follows what I write as carefully as you do."

The war had turned into a passion for Dilara Hanım, it seemed to her as if it would be very unlucky if she missed even the smallest detail, as if Ragıp Bey would be shot and killed, what the letters were for Ragıp Bey, news about the war was for Dilara Hanım, "it's difficult to find a love that was rejected so violently and dragged along so stubbornly," Dilara Hanım told to Osman, then with that mocking smile she added, "I don't know if you can call this love, but to tell the truth I can't find another name for it."

She asked Monsieur Lausanne about everything, she wanted to learn every last detail, which units of the Bulgarian army attacked, which units advanced, what did the Ottoman army do, where were the artillerymen, what was the situation in the emplacements at Çatalca . . . Once Monsieur Lausanne said,

"If you'd been a spy you would have been very successful, you get all of the information I have out of me bit by bit."

"It doesn't seem as if you would be very guarded about giving information to lady spies, *mon cher*," said Dilara Hanım.

It was difficult to describe the relationship between them, perhaps it could have been described as a tense friendship into which some very delicate sexual jokes had been mixed, Monsieur Lausanne didn't express his feelings openly, but he didn't go to any lengths to conceal them either. It was clear that Dilara Hanım was pleased by Monsieur Lausanne's company, but even Dilara Hanım couldn't figure out where the limits were. The love she felt for Ragıp Bey and the feelings she had for Lausanne had become inextricably intertwined, the day she stopped loving Ragıp Bey would be the day she stopped seeing Lausanne, she was certain of this. If the love she felt for Ragıp Bey was compared to a tower, what she felt for Lausanne was that tower's shadow, as the tower grew, the shadow lengthened.

Monsieur Lausanne told her first about his conversation with the Foreign Minister.

"The minister looked devastated," he said, "I think he no longer has any hope left, he believes the Bulgarians are going to enter Istanbul."

"Do you think they can?"

"I don't know, Dilara Hanım, but during the fighting today they encountered a resistance they hadn't anticipated, indeed I can say that even the Ottomans were surprised by this . . . According to the news coming from the front, the Bulgarians suffered heavy losses."

"How did it happen like this, when even the foreign minister had lost hope . . . How did this miracle occur?"

"I suppose the Bulgarians overestimated their strength and

had too much self-confidence, and they underestimated the Ottoman army . . . Look, for days I've been reading what my colleagues at the Bulgarian front have been writing for the French newspapers, the Bulgarian generals told these correspondents almost every detail of their planned attack. All that Ottoman intelligence had to do to learn the Bulgarian General Staff's plans was to read the French newspapers . . . And on top of that they attacked in exactly the way they said they would."

However it was that she'd learned, Dilara Hanım knew that Ragıp Bey was serving in Muhtar Pasha's corps, for this reason her attention was focused especially on Muhtar Pasha.

"What did Muhtar Pasha's corps do?"

Even though Monsieur Lausanne didn't know the reason, he'd realized for quite some time that Dilara Hanım was deeply interested in Muhtar Pasha, indeed he'd even had suspicions about whether there was a relationship between Dilara Hanım and the pasha.

"Your hero Muhtar Pasha . . . Since the beginning of the war the most intense fighting has been between his corps and the Bulgarians."

At this point there was a tone of pride Monsieur Lausanne's voice that he couldn't conceal.

"Muhtar Pasha was trained in France and has a high degree of military knowledge, he's also a very courageous man. He's been very successful in the use of artillery. He can always stop the Bulgarians. They say the Bulgarians lost thousands of men in today's fighting."

Dilara Hanim was being careful not to allow her voice to change, she wasn't aware that she was squeezing her napkin.

"Did the Ottomans suffer losses?"

"Very few compared to the Bulgarians . . . I stopped by the General Staff Headquarters on my way here, a colonel there told me that Muhtar Pasha's artillery positions were hit by nearly two thousand artillery shells, but because the men were in the old emplacements they only lost two men."

"Two men?"

"Yes, only two privates."

Dilara Hanım couldn't prevent herself from taking a deep breath.

"This means that the Bulgarians are not going to win this war, isn't that so?"

"To tell the truth I've begun to think that, but the foreign ambassadors don't."

"Why?"

"I don't know, but they're preparing to land troops."

Dilara Hanım asked in amazement, as if she didn't believe what she'd heard,

"Where are they going to land them?"

"In Istanbul . . . To protect their embassies and their staff."

"What does the government say about this?"

"It seems they agreed, tonight all of the diplomats met at the Austrian Embassy, they're discussing how and when to bring the troops."

"But you said our army stopped the Bulgarians and that they suffered heavy casualties . . ."

"Yes, but it seems that the embassies still want to be certain."

"But the situation at the front is good . . . Isn't that so?"

"The situation is good, commander," said Lausanne with a laugh.

Then, trying to conceal his anguish behind a mocking smile, he said,

"I don't want this war to end at all."

"Why?"

"Because I feel that when the war ends I will no longer have any value or importance in your eyes . . ."

Dilara Hanım gave Monsieur Lausanne a light slap on his hand.

"You'll always be a very valued friend for me, conditions won't change that, neither the war dragging on nor the war ending . . ."

Lausanne's sensitive ears separated the word "friend" and set it apart from all the other words, he felt a slight tension within, but he grasped that he wasn't going to get more than this that night, that any further insistence might create a situation that was embarrassing for both of them.

"Still, if the war lasted a little longer it would be good," he said, "it's a selfish thought but unfortunately that's how I feel."

Dilara Hanım didn't answer, she couldn't figure out how to answer, instead, with a feminine smile that suited her very well, she changed the subject.

She didn't want to lose Lausanne, but she didn't want to carry the relationship beyond what it was now; the reason she didn't want to lose him wasn't that she saw him solely as a source of information, he was valuable to her because she could learn what was happening at the front, but Monsieur Lausanne had entered her life as "the man who brought news from the front," but had slowly gained an importance of his own, his company was an important consolation for Dilara Hanım, his conversation and his jokes masked her desperation and her loneliness, he helped Dilara Hanım not to see the realities she didn't want to see.

Towards morning on that night when the entire city was curious about what was going to happen, Muhtar Pasha went to inspect the front before day had even broken, when he came to Ragıp Bey's unit he asked, "What's your situation, Ragıp?" "Thank you commander." "Do you have any casualties?" "No, commander," "How is your store of ammunition?" "Towards evening we were running low, but we spent all night restocking it," "You're prepared, you mean?" "Yes commander" "They're going to attack in the morning." "We're ready, commander," "I don't want them to advance a single step." "They won't advance, commander." "God be with you Ragıp." "Thank you, commander."

Half an hour after Muhtar Pasha left, when a faint light was appearing behind the hills, a messenger arrived.

"Muhtar Pasha commands that a squadron of men join him immediately," he said.

Ragıp Bey immediately set out with a squadron and made his way behind the trenches to where the other battalion's positions were and joined Muhtar Pasha. The Pasha was very annoyed. The battalion commander was standing at attention in front of him with his head bowed and his face bright red.

"How could you not be aware," Muhtar Pasha was saying, "The Bulgarians took three positions in the night, the men retreated without you being aware of it . . . Are you a commander, are you an officer, or are you a scarecrow, what the hell are you? And we entrust you with a battalion."

The battalion commander stood there without saying anything, he knew that he deserved this reprimand.

"I'm taking over command of the battalion, we're not going to wait at all, we're going to get into action right away . . . Are you here, Ragıp?"

"Yes, commander."

"We're going to take those positions back before the day gets warm. You keep our left flank secure."

"Yes, sir."

They began an operation that had rarely been seen in war before, a corps commander took personal command of a battalion and went on the offensive against two positions between the ravines.

Machine gun fire began to come from the positions the Bulgarians had taken, Muhtar Pasha was leading on horseback when he was shot and fell off his horse, "Keep going!" he shouted, "Keep going, don't stop, take those positions!" It was as if the pasha being shot had sharpened the officers and the men, they advanced, returning fire against a hail of machine-gun bullets.

The Bulgarian unit was surprised by the Ottoman soldiers' sudden assault, they knew that no one was going to come to support them, they fired as they retreated, within twenty minutes they'd retaken the two positions.

Muhtar Pasha was immediately carried to the rear of the front, he wasn't badly wounded. Ragıp Bey returned to his own unit.

Just as he was entering the emplacement, the Bulgarian artillery began firing.

They bombarded each other with artillery fire until noon like two maddened street fighters, after noon the firing slowed down and towards evening it stopped, the Bulgarians really hadn't been able to advance a single step, on the contrary the resistance they'd encountered had sapped their courage and their confidence.

As for the Ottoman ranks, there was a sense of holiday joy.

"We lost out bravest pasha, but we won the battle," they were saying.

The following day French newspapers printed a speech by Third Army Chief of Staff Colonel Rostov.

"Dysentery is ravaging the army . . . Our numbers are steadily decreasing . . . However within a few days we will once again go on the offensive."

This was the last statement about the Bulgarian "offensive," they didn't attack again. Their strength had been consumed.

The men's courage and confidence had been refreshed, they'd managed to stop the enemy twenty miles from Istanbul. The capital of over three hundred years had escaped occupation.

Now at the front they would have to contend with a much more dangerous and deadly enemy.

20

Rasim Bey hadn't even begun his breakfast when he was informed that Abdülhamid "requested his presence," he hurriedly finished his tea and went at once to the large hall overlooking the Bosphorus.

Abdülhamid was pacing in the hall with his hands clasped behind his back, his head bent and his chin touching his chest, he was murmuring something to himself. When he saw Rasim Bey he asked almost angrily,

"What's going on, Rasim Bey?"

Rasim Bey looked at the Bosphorus flowing outside the window, launches were approaching the ships, bringing soldiers to the shore, then returning to pick up more soldiers, the sea was full of launches, the large European warships were sending each other flag signals.

"They're landing troops, sir."

"Who's landing troops?"

"The Europeans."

In an admonishing tone, as if Rasim Bey was responsible for this, he asked,

"They're landing foreign troops in my capital?"

Then, feeling that he had to amend what he'd said, he repeated the same question in a different way.

"Are they landing foreign troops in the Ottoman capital?"

Abdülhamid, who was generally very careful about what he said, he was particularly careful not to say anything that might give the impression he was thinking about returning to power or that he was still angry at those who had overthrown him, had not been able to control his anger.

"Was it for this that they overthrew me? What does it mean for foreign troops to land in the Ottoman capital, this is the Caliph's city, foreign soldiers shouldn't even step foot here . . . I wonder what my brother has to say about this."

"They can't land troops without the permission of his highness the sultan and the government, I'm sure that you can appreciate this as well, sir . . ."

"For what purpose are they landing troops?"

"To protect the embassies . . ."

"Who are they going to protect them from?"

"The Bulgarians, presumably, they fear a Bulgarian occupation."

"I heard that we stopped the Bulgarians at Çatalca."

Rasim Bey couldn't quite figure out where Abdülhamid got his news, there were still sounds of cannon fire coming from Çatalca, even though it had lessened, but the former sultan had even learned that the Bulgarians had been stopped . . .

"They say we stopped them, sir, but the foreigners still wanted to take precautions."

"Good God," said Abdülhamid, "Good God . . . What a bitter day for a caliph, they're landing troops in the capital. And on the eve of the blessed Feast of the Sacrifice. I suppose they're going to sacrifice the Ottoman Empire. What kind of holiday is this going to be? How could they allow this, I can't comprehend it, they should have stood against this to the end, no foreign troops have set foot in this city since the time of Mehmet the Conqueror . . . The army is fighting at Çatalca, but foreign troops are landing in Tophane . . . Oh, Rasim Bey, what is this government doing, Kamil Pasha is an experienced man, how could he agree to this, I don't understand, a state can't allow something like this. It's not as if this is an ordinary state, look at the condition the great Ottoman Empire has been reduced to . . ."

Rasim Bey realized that Abdülhamid was truly saddened and angered, he was as angry as if someone had entered his harem, he'd been dethroned, but he still saw himself as the ruler of an empire.

As they were talking, they heard the sounds of a military band playing on the French warship Gambetta.

"What's this now?"

Rasim Bey listed to what the band was paying and said, "The French national anthem."

When the anthem finished they started playing another.

"So, what's this?"

Rasim Bey didn't know why he had to explain all of these things as if he was some miserable butler who had to answer to his master, it irritated him that this man he'd never liked and had always seen as an enemy was speaking to him as if he was calling him to account, but he was surprised at the way he was defending the state, later he told Hikmet Bey, "We never upheld they state the way he did, we never embraced the state the way he did."

"I think they're playing all of the national anthems of the soldiers who are being landed on the shore."

The band on the Gambetta played nine national anthems in a row.

Each time one anthem stopped and another began, Abdülhamid counted in a harsh voice that sounded like the cracking of a whip.

"Nine countries landed troops, is that correct, Rasim Bey?"

"It seems so, sir."

"I wonder who these nine countries are that are powerful enough to land troops in the Ottoman capital . . . Nine countries, hah . . ."

He paused for a moment and frowned.

"I don't know if you noticed," he said, "but they didn't play our national anthem."

Then with that mocking smile he seldom showed to anyone outside his own family, he said,

"I suppose it wasn't necessary because we didn't land any troops in our own capital."

After that the expression on his face changed, and with his usual polite smile he said,

"I'm tiring you early in the morning, Rasim Bey, but this hurt me so much that I couldn't contain myself . . . Anyway, don't let me keep you from your duties."

Just as Rasim Bey was going out the door, Abdülhamid called after him.

"They said my brothers sent me gifts for the holiday."

"Yes, sir. His majesty the sultan sent a Hereke carpet, the heir apparent sent a basket . . . I'll have them brought to you at once, sir."

An expression appeared on Abdülhamid's face the like of which Rasim Bey would never have believed he would see on a sultan's face, it was a young, tough expression of the kind you would see in a gangster from Tophane.

The carpet the sultan had sent was immediately laid out in one of the large halls, the silk bundle that Prince Vahdettin had sent was opened in the guards' room in the presence of the chief eunuch, it contained a basket. The basket was filled with round, transparent, honey-colored candies.

When the basket was opened, a lovely smell the like of which the officers had never encountered spread through the room, one of the officers couldn't contain himself and said, "I suppose this is what heaven smells like."

Rasim Bey asked, "What are these?"

"Ordinary candy," said the chief eunuch, "They're made in Enderun before the holidays, they're sent to the sultan and the princes . . . The heir apparent sent them to his brother as a gift."

"What about that wonderful smell?"

"They add musk and ambergris, that's what you smell."

The chief eunuch took one of the candies, divided it into three and gave the pieces to three officers, "Please, eat them, you won't be able to say you've never eaten the sultan's candies," then he took the basket and left, and the heavenly smell followed him like a mist.

Rasim Bey said to Hikmet Bey, "It's impossible for us to understand the Ottomans, brother, the man was overthrown, there's a twenty-four-hour guard on him so he won't get up to any mischief, but the heir apparent sends his brother candies as a holiday gift . . . but what candy . . . We ate those candies, we couldn't control ourselves . . . We realized that damned chief eunuch was having fun with us . . . They're sending this to a seventy-year-old man . . . And he knows what's coming, he was smiling because his brother had sent him a gift . . . The Ottoman family is a completely different world, brother, a completely different world."

Monsieur Lausanne, who had gone out that day to see what was happening in the city, encountered a scene he hadn't expected, the city was very calm, people were looking at the foreign soldiers indifferently. The foreigners had divided the city up. The French units had settled into Saint Benoit Lycée and were guarding the Ottoman Bank in Karaköy, the Germans established a headquarters in front of Foreign Minister Noradikyan Efendi's house in Taksim, the English were in Beyoğlu, the Russians had taken control of the Galata Quay, indeed they'd placed two squadrons in front of the Ottoman Parliament, the Austrians were next to the Germans, the Italians and the Dutch were wandering around randomly.

Monsieur Lausanne was almost annoyed by how indifferent people were to foreign troops landing in the city, later he said to Dilara Hanım, "I can't understand how people can remain so apathetic about foreign troops entering their city so casually, to tell the truth I was surprised by how relaxed they were."

He experienced the real surprise the following day when he was speaking to Foreign Minister Noradikyan Efendi.

The minister, who two days earlier had been a wreck as he was waiting for help from the Europeans, had pulled himself together when the Bulgarians were stopped and had changed completely.

"We stopped the Bulgarians all along the line, they'll never take Çatalca."

"Presumably negotiations will begin soon . . . What kind of concessions are the Ottomans considering making?"

Noradikyan Efendi laughed as if he was amused.

"What concessions . . . We're not going to give up an inch of territory, we have no intention of abandoning anyplace in Thrace, Macedonia, or Albania."

"But the Bulgarians are still at Çatalca, they're occupying Thrace, the Greeks have taken over the whole region."

The Foreign Minister was very sure of himself.

"We'll take it all back," he said.

That evening Lausanne said to Dilara Hanım,

"The war has stopped but it hasn't ended, I don't know when but it's bound to begin again . . . The Ottomans want to take back the territory they lost."

"When do you think it will begin?"

"I don't think it will begin right away, both sides are worn out, but the Ottomans want to take revenge, that much is clear."

Dilara Hanım was worried about the war starting again; she was worn out by fear and worry, later she told Osman, "I believed that if anything happened to Ragıp I would be certain to hear about it, that's what my feelings said, but my mind knew that those emotions weren't real, who was going to tell me if Ragıp died, how was I going to hear about it, of the thousands of dead, how was his name going to reach me, my mind was wearing me out in those days."

During those days, when her mind was shining light on those frightening truths for which she could find no solution, Dilara Hanım preferred to abandon herself to the tumultuous darkness of her emotions, to dive into the vague corridors of illusion and to create consoling fantasies out of the shadows and dim figures she found there, as she said to Osman, "This eased me, I felt the need for some consolation and peace, even if it wasn't real."

"Of course there are dangers to be encountered when a woman whose mind is tired of clashing with reality turns to the shadowy side of her emotions," she added later, "you can think that emotions that don't exist are real and end up doing the wrong thing."

Suddenly she sighed and said, "There are times when women are weak," at the time Osman didn't quite understand why she'd said this, but he grasped that Dilara Hanım's hadn't finished settling accounts with herself. He couldn't figure out whether this settling of accounts had to do with Monsieur Lausanne or with Nizam, whose comments about Dilara Hanım were angry enough to arouse suspicion. But he was certain that in the twilight of her emotions Dilara Hanım had turned onto a path that she later regretted.

Monsieur Lausanne said, "I'm going to the grand vizier's office tomorrow, I'll get more detailed information about the war there."

"You'll tell me, won't you?"

"Ah, Dilara Hanım, everyone thinks I'm gathering information for my newspaper, but I'm actually working for you," said Monsieur Lausanne with a laugh.

Then he suddenly became serious.

"Why are you so interested in the war?"

"Is it possible not to be interested?"

Monsieur Lausanne didn't pay attention to this evasive answer, partly because of the wine and partly due to his anguish, and with an almost childish curiosity, he asked the question he'd long wanted to ask and the answer to which he in fact knew better than anyone.

"There's someone at the front, isn't there Dilara Hanım?"

"Yes."

"Lucky man."

"Because he could die?"

"No."

Monsieur Lausanne didn't say another word, he knew that it would be inappropriate to drag this conversation on, he regretted having asked this question, he hadn't asked it in order to learn the answer but with the thought that it might bring to life a spark of hope, after that answer he wanted to leave as soon as possible and be alone. His somber face, which when he was cheerful shone with a jocular light that made him look younger, now looked like a wax mask, he was trying to keep a smile that was costing him too much effort.

When, after drinking his coffee in silence, he said, "I'd better be going," Dilara Hanım was afraid he wouldn't come again.

"You're coming tomorrow, aren't you?"

As French men are taught to do when they're still children, Monsieur Lausanne had distanced himself and had retreated behind barriers of politeness, but he had been raised well enough to know that retreating behind such a cold politeness could display an unattractive weakness.

"Of course, Dilara Hanım," he said, "I'll come whenever you wish me to,"

Then he couldn't contain himself, and the pain he felt emerged as mockery.

"I'm fully aware of my position as postman."

"You're not a postman for me, Stephan."

Dilara Hanım was addressing Monsieur Lausanne by his first name for the first time, she reached out and touched Lausanne's hand.

"The truth doesn't always fit into a single answer . . . This is a painful lesson we all learn."

An emotion that a man thinks is unshakable, a pain that seems like a castle built on rock, can be changed by one word from a woman into a clear and endless joy like a summer sky, indeed the way in which this word is uttered, the tone of her voice, is like magic, and a man's attachment to a woman who can bring about this magic is like the admiration a primitive person feels for a sorcerer; it had the same effect on Lausanne, with the way in which she'd uttered a single sentence, indeed with only the word "Stephan," Dilara Hanım had completely transformed all of his emotions, the pain that a moment before he'd thought couldn't change or be brought down had suddenly been shattered and he was surrounded by cheerfulness. In order to maintain his dignity, this man who had observed and recorded wars, deaths, collapses and betrayals, closed his eyes for a moment to conceal the emotions that were swelling and changing like waves crashing against a breakwater and sending out arcs of round drops.

A number of answers occurred to him but he didn't have the courage to put any of them into words, he found them all either idiotic, childish or inappropriate.

"May I have another coffee," he said, "I've never had coffee as good as the coffee in this house."

"Of course," said Dilara Hanım, "I'll make it for you myself."

The following afternoon when he went to the Grand Vizier's office, he found Tevfik Bey and Nazif Bey laughing in their office, this had become a common scene in recent times.

Monsieur Lausanne realized at once that there had been a new development.

"I think there's good news."

"You can smell news, my dear Monsieur Lausanne," said Nazif Bey.

"If it's possible, Nazif Bey, may I have the news now?"

The two young officials looked at each other, when the Bulgarians had been stopped at Çatalca, the Grand Vizier Kamil Pasha had said, "It's not clear whether or not we can hold out if they were to go on the offensive again, at the moment the Bulgarians' morale is low too, they're even more weary than we are, it's just the right time, let's meet with the Russians and propose negotiations with the Bulgarians."

Rather than having an official meeting, Tevfik Bey had dinner with the first secretary of the Russian Embassy, he'd told him that Kamil Bey wondered whether or not the Russians might bring the Bulgarians an offer to negotiate, that the Ottomans were prepared to negotiate if the Russians would act as intermediaries and if the Bulgarians were prepared to negotiate.

And the answer came sooner than they'd supposed, just a little while earlier they'd learned that the Bulgarians had accepted the proposal to negotiate. This way the Ottoman Empire would gain some time to recover.

When Monsieur Lausanne heard this he thought, "Dilara Hanım is going to be very pleased," he even thought about sending her a telegram right away, but then he decided that he would prefer to tell her in person that evening.

As he was sending word of these negotiations to his newspaper from the Beyoğlu telegraph office, the General Staff and the Committee for Union and Progress learned about the developments.

Talat Bey called Cevat Bey and said, "fill everyone in on this news and we'll all meet in the evening."

When they met, Talat Bey took the floor.

"Friends, the Ottoman Empire has lost all of Thrace, Greece and Albania, now they're preparing to enter humiliating negotiations. The people are angry. I think that it's necessary to get into action at once to prevent these negotiations and to appease the public's anger."

Emin Bey said,

"You're right, Talat Bey, but how are we going to get into action, what are we going to do, how are we going to overthrow the government, shouldn't we be making a plan and getting the necessary forces ready?"

"We can make a plan right away with the party affiliated officers in Istanbul."

Ziya Gökalp Bey, one of the Committee's ideologues, asked: "When is the negotiation conference being held?"

"They say it will be held within three weeks, they'll meet in the middle of December."

"I wonder if we should wait for the results of these negotiations to make a decision?" said Ziya Gökalp Bey, "Perhaps the government will resign of its own accord because of the harshness of the conditions of the treaty."

"How would the government's resignation help us, it will just be replaced by a similar government, the important issue is not this government relinquishing power, the important issue is us seizing power."

Someone at the meeting asked,

"When is Enver Bey coming?"

Enver Bey's arrival was important to all of them because he was the most intrepid, enterprising and courageous of them.

Cevat Bey said, "He's been granted leave, he'll be here by the end of the month, he'll join his unit at the front right away."

"Then let's not rush things, we'll wait for Enver Bey to come and we'll see what the results of the negotiations are . . . The public will be even angrier when they learn the conditions of the treaty."

They decided to wait until Enver Bey arrived.

No one was yet aware that these meetings at Emin Bey's house were paving a road that would completely change history.

21

I n a city besieged by war, sickness and misery, Nizam and
Anya were living as if on an island surrounded by a vast
expanse, it was as if life was flowing somewhere far away
and out of view.

In that period Nizam had lost not only his passions, but his
capacity to be passionately attached to anything even temporarily, while he was waiting for Anya he gambled to pass the
time, but he didn't put himself into the game, he didn't enjoy
it; his feelings about Anya were the same, he liked to make love
to her, he was fond of the softness and worn-out warmth of her
body, but if she were to suddenly disappear from his life he
didn't think he possessed a powerful enough desire to go in
search of that body.

He went to see Anya every day, he brought her home, he
stayed with her until noon and then he went home. What he
felt was not a deep affection or love, there was no power or
depth to frighten him, it was more superficial, shallower, what
he felt was an emotion like a plant that had grown quickly but
didn't have sound roots, like a habit, it wasn't a passion that
came from within, what he felt for Anya was like a loosely
woven net, it gave the impression that it could be escaped easily, but without even realizing it, Nizam was unhesitatingly
wrapping it around himself.

Sometimes he made Anya laugh, but it was weary and reluc-
tant laughter, Nizam realized that she didn't want to laugh,
that the laughter didn't work its way into her, it was as if she

quickly regretted her laughter and tried to erase it. It was as if Anya's mind was always somewhere else, somewhere far away, in the past, among the things she'd lost; Nizam couldn't bring her to the present, even when he touched her, when he embraced her, when she let out those little Russian screams, there was a wide and invisible period of time between them, Nizam couldn't get past this time.

Their conversation was disjointed, like a ship stuck in the ice, trying to move but not making any headway.

Once Nizam said,

"This trinket is very valuable, if you sold it you could live the rest of your life without being in need of anything."

"I don't need a lot of money," said Anya, "What I earn is enough for me."

It was as if it wasn't just money that she didn't need, it was as if she didn't need anything, not even to live, as if she was distant from everything.

Once Nizam asked, "Why are you with me?"

"I don't know," said Anya.

She didn't tell him anything about herself.

Once, for the sake of conversation, Nizam asked her "Where are you from?" and she said, "I don't want to talk about the past."

But one night she'd said, "This is as much as I can give you, Nizam, I can't give you anything more, because I don't have anything more . . . This is all I am, I'm nothing more than this body you see."

Nizam had laughed and said, "That's good too, it's a very nice body."

Anya just said, "Hmm," as if there was something about her body that she knew but Nizam didn't, for a moment Nizam expected her to say, "You should have seen my body when I was younger," but Anya didn't say anything.

When Nizam occasionally asked her to play the piano she

would say, "I play all night, I'm tired," she never played the piano at home.

Sometimes she looked at Nizam for a long time, he would say, "What is it?" and she would say, "It's nothing."

One rainy morning, when the leaden light was trying to seep into the room through the curtains, Anya suddenly said.

"You're going to get tired of me."

"No I won't."

"You will, everyone gets tired of someone like this."

"I won't."

"If you're not going to get tired of me are you going to fall in love?"

Nizam sensed that she was waiting attentively for an answer to this question that she'd asked as if it was of no importance, there was a painful silence, as if they were walking on broken glass.

"No, I won't fall in love either."

"No, because you can't."

They didn't say anything else, if this conversation could be said to have been "about feelings," it was the only conversation they ever had about feelings.

Anya had blocked all access to her emotions like a town that had blocked all roads leading into it, her emotions couldn't be reached from outside and no sign of her emotions seeped out, no matter how much you circled around her you couldn't see anything.

Someone else might have tried to press Anya to talk about her feelings and about her past, would have tried different ways to learn about this woman, but Nizam didn't do any of these things. It seemed very natural to him for Anya to conceal her emotions and her past, his lack of curiosity about people protected him in this relationship, he just wanted Anya to surrender herself to him in such a way that she would be willing to tell him everything, if one day Anya became willing to tell him, Nizam would very probably listen to what she said and immediately forget it, or at least that's how he felt at the time.

There were days when he felt tired and thought about not going to see Anya, indeed there were times when he decided, "I'm not going to go" but later found himself getting ready, he didn't find this odd, either, since he didn't see a great difference between going and not going, it didn't surprise him that he was going despite having decided not to go.

They continued to see each other with an obstinacy that they weren't aware of, didn't understand and hadn't noticed, they didn't mention their feelings, perhaps they themselves didn't know what their emotions were, they'd concealed those emotions from themselves somewhere deep and inaccessible in their consciousness. They carried on their existence like those weird-looking creatures that live at the bottom of the ocean, without ever emerging into the sunlight, in those dark waters that light never reached, and there they grew. When one day those emotions rose from the darkness and emerged into the light of consciousness, their souls would be tangled by an apocalyptic terror. They didn't recognize the danger of two people who touched each other so much concealing their emotions in this way, of their inner worlds remaining so stagnant, of darkness occupying more space than light.

They didn't ask each other questions, they didn't talk about their childhoods as all people in love do, they didn't talk about their memories, they didn't say anything that would stir hope, they didn't have shared dreams, in the morning when the sun was shining they snuggled together in a warm, dim room, making love with a surprising tenderness. They got past Anya's sudden contractions, which didn't pass easily, with merciful kisses, and they didn't find any of this strange. They'd accepted that on any given morning they could see each other for the last time and lose each other, every morning was a surprise for them, this

surprise was the only movement on the surface of their stagna-
tion, the vague joy that this surprise created.

They thought it would always be like this, but one morning
a stranger stepped foot on "their island."

Towards the middle of December, when Nizam arrived at
the deserted gambling den in the black and orange tinged
morning twilight, as an indecisive snow had begun to sprinkle
and the snowflakes were swaying and slowly melting as they
rose from the heat of the torches, he saw a short man dressed
in black waiting by the wide door.

The face beneath the red fez looked like a turnip that had
just been pulled out of the ground, it was covered in scars and
stains, the movement of the pupils of his squinted eyes could
be seen from a distance, even though he was completely
motionless, there was a strange and comical energy radiating
from his little body that made one think that he could somer-
sault into the hall, leap about, and do cartwheels.

Nizam guessed that this was the gambling den's owner
Monsieur Gavril, who he'd never seen before, and he suddenly
felt an unexpected fear and worry, his stomach seemed to
move upwards towards his lungs, he thought he was going to
give him bad news about Anya.

As he walked quickly towards the man, the man suddenly
smiled, his face, his bearing and his appearance changed completely, the light of a mature, trustworthy and affectionate man
radiated from his face, his smile looked like the smile of someone who was philosophical and good, someone who had seen
a great deal and suffered much pain, in the light of that smile
appeared the shadow of an anguish that been there for a long
time and that had perhaps even been forgotten.

"Monsieur Nizam, I presume," said the man as he extended
his hand.

Nizam shook his hand reluctantly.

"Yes."

"In any event, no one but you would come at this hour . . ."

Nizam wasn't listening to the man, he was glancing around, looking for Anya to be sure that nothing had happened to her. Monsieur Gavril, who could intuit the panic in Nizam's eyes, said,

"Anya is fine, she's smoking a cigarette inside . . . I've heard you mentioned so much that I wanted to meet you."

Nizam was bored, it seemed meaningless to him to make friends with this strange-looking man at the entrance to an empty gambling den at this hour of the morning. He could watch the conversation between the two of them as if he was someone else, and he found them ridiculous. Sometimes in unaccustomed situations like this, Nizam could suddenly observe the whole scene as if he was a stranger, he could step outside of everything and see himself and his surroundings, it would all happen within a misty frame before his slightly misted eyes, he would watch the movements, listen to the conversation, everything he said sounded like something a stranger was saying; at that moment he was bored as he watched this old man who looked like a puppet talk, he wanted it to end as soon as possible.

"Good . . ."

As they were talking he saw Anya come out of the room and walk towards them, he realized that she knew the man had been waiting for him, she was walking calmly and somewhat reluctantly.

"It's morning, I thought we might have breakfast together," said Monsieur Gavril.

"We don't want to impose on you" said Nizam.

Anya intervened.

"We can have a tea if you like."

Nizam suddenly looked at the two of them in suspicion, there was no apparent reason for either the invitation or its acceptance, the owner of the gambling den, whom no one ever sees, suddenly appears, he invites them to breakfast, and Anya, who never talks to anyone, says that they accept the invitation.

Without realizing it he was squeezing the handle of his cane, to feel the security of having a weapon when encountering something that was both boring and unexpected . . . For a moment he thought about saying "I have to go" and leaving, but this would be a very rude thing to do so he reluctantly said, "Fine."

Monsieur Gavril opened a door in the back of the foyer that Nizam had never noticed before, they started down a flight of stone stairs and descended to a large kitchen furnished in wood, there was a long wooden table on which breakfast dishes had been arranged, an older woman whose hips were large enough to surprise a person, they moved like millstones under her large flannel dress as she brought things to the table, a large stove was burning in the middle, a teapot was bubbling on top of it. The kitchen wasn't at all like the upper floors, it was plain and peaceful, the woman, like a mother calling to her children, said, "Come on, where have you been, everything is going to get cold."

Nizam looked at the table, it was clear that this breakfast had taken a long time to prepare.

"I heard that you just have milk and bread for breakfast," he said to Monsieur Gavril,

"I'm still going to have bread and milk, this breakfast is for you."

"You've gone to a lot of trouble."

"It's no problem, I thought you would be hungry by this hour."

Anya and Nizam sat next to each other at the table and Monsieur Gavril sat across from them, he was examining Nizam carefully, as if he was looking for something he already knew was there. Nizam smiled and looked at Monsieur Gavril, these kinds of nonsensical games amused him, in tedious situations he always managed to find some way to amuse himself.

The old woman put a copper bowl of warm milk and a piece of dry bread in front of Monsieur Gavril.

Gavril started dunking the bread into the milk and eating it, Nizam and Anya watched the man eat with surprising appetite. He would swish the bread around in the milk, bring it to his mouth, suck out the milk and then eat the bread, he ate with an appetite that looked as if it could never be satisfied, like a man defiling the chastity of a virgin in an ancient shrine, it was as if he'd forgotten who he was sitting with, Nizam understood why the man always had breakfast alone.

Suddenly he put the bread on the edge of his plate and looked at Nizam.

"They say you're Reşit Pasha's grandson."

Nizam had not expected the man to say something like this.

"I don't understand," he said in surprise.

"They say you're Reşit Pasha's grandson."

"Yes."

Nizam leaned back and laughed.

"I'm also Mihrişah Sultan's grandson, Hikmet Bey and Mehpare Hanım's son, Rukiye Hanım's brother, Tevfik Bey's brother-in-law, Dilevser Hanım's stepson, and let me say it before I forget, I'm Hakkı Pasha's neighbor, he and his family live in the mansion next to us."

Nizam didn't know whether Monsieur Gavril had decided beforehand to give the answer he gave, or whether he said it because he was angered by Nizam's mocking manner, but what Gavril said was something he'd never expected to hear.

"I knew Reşit Pasha."

"You?" he said, unable to conceal his surprise.

This time it was Gavril's turn to lean back and laugh.

"Me," he said.

Nizam looked at Anya, she was pushing a piece of cheese around her plate with her fork as if she wasn't listening to their conversation.

"My grandfather never gambled."

"I don't gamble either."

When Nizam looked at Anya out of the corner of his eyes, he saw her look up, glance at Gavril and then look down again, he hadn't seen her eyes, but he thought she had a resentful expression.

"When did you meet?"

"I think it must have been fifteen or sixteen years ago, the Pasha's mansion in Caddebostan was very beautiful, the garden was unique, you'd be hard put to find something like that even in Petersburg . . . I remember that he was very fond of yellow roses."

"How did you meet, Monsieur Gavril?"

Gavril realized that Nizam believed what he'd said, suddenly he waved his hand as if he'd lost interest in what he'd been talking about.

"It's a long story . . . I'll tell you some other time . . . You haven't eaten anything . . . Safiye Hanım prepared all of this for you . . ."

Nizam looked at Anya, he realized that she wanted to leave.

"We're not very hungry," he said, "If you'll excuse us, we should be off."

Monsieur Gavril saw them to the kitchen door but he didn't come upstairs, he had assumed an air of dignity, of a nobility not often seen in the owners of gambling dens, it was clear that he was not one to show respect to a young man but that he was a man who expected to be shown respect.

They got into the carriage, the torches had begun to go out.

Nizam remained silent, he expected Anya to say something, to offer an explanation, but Anya seemed to be lost in her own thought, she was looking out the window.

"What was that?" he asked in an irritated tone.

"What was what?"

"What just happened."

"I don't know, he wanted to meet you."

"Why?"

"I don't know."

"Where does he know my grandfather from?"

"I don't know."

"Where do you know him from?"

"From a long time ago . . . From Russia."

"Who is this man?"

Anya didn't answer. Nizam asked the question that had been in his mind since he met Monsieur Gavril.

"Is he your father?"

For the first time Nizam saw Anya really, genuinely laugh, without trying to suppress it, or rather without having had time to suppress it.

"No . . ."

"Is he your lover, or was he your lover?"

Anya's voice was icy, it was as cold and sharp as icicles hanging from the eaves of a house, and when he heard it he regretted having asked the question.

"Nizam, that's not a polite question."

"Anya, a little while ago I sat at the breakfast table with the owner of a gambling house whom I'd never met before, only because of you . . . Don't you see that you put me in a rather strange position?"

"Don't do anything you don't want to do . . . If you do, don't blame others."

Nizam fell silent. This conversation had embarrassed him, and he suddenly cut off his relationship with Anya and Monsieur Gavril in his mind, now he was forgetting what had just happened, within an extraordinary silence, he was erasing all of it from his mind with a giant, invisible eraser, he wouldn't remember this incident for a long time, that section of his memory would fall asleep and die like a man lying in the snow.

They didn't speak until they reached Anya's house.

As Anya was getting out of the carriage in front of her house, she said, "I'm a bit tired this morning, we'll see each other later." She closed the door softly behind her.

Nizam didn't go to the gambling den that night, he didn't go for three days after that either, during those three days he had another strange experience, it was as if life was trying to upset his monotony, the gravity that was like a stagnant lake, with sudden waves.

On the third evening Kamil Bey dropped by, he'd done so several times before, Hikmet Bey knew his father from Salonica, but he'd won Hikmet Bey's and Dilevser's hearts with his own amiability, he read Hamlet's "To be or not to be" tirade in a French accent, then he amused them all greatly by speaking French with an English accent, he didn't tell them that he was a gambler, he could entertain the entire household as if he was a troupe of entertainers with amusing incidents within the government and with gossip about Istanbul's wealthy. Kamil Bey tried to forget the damage his "disease" had caused his soul, that he'd been transformed from what he could have been into someone he didn't want to be, that he couldn't find a solution for this, that he couldn't improve behavior that was better described by the English word "needy" than the Turkish word "dependent," with a curtain of amusement created by his mind from the cheerfulness and wittiness that emerged from his nature, and most of the time he did forget it. Nizam had once heard him say, with an anguish he seldom displayed, that his cheerfulness was "the last healthy aspect of a very sick person."

That night he'd dropped by, he'd made Hikmet Bey and Dilevser laugh, then he'd turned to Nizam and said, "where have you been, my good man, I've been worried, come, let's go get some fresh air."

They went outside together, Kamil Bey said, "I'm not going to go to the gambling den today, at least that's my decision at the moment, I lost a lot again last night, on top of that I didn't just lose money, I lost control, let me stop today and see . . . Shall we go to Madam's? We'll eat a nice meal, throw ourselves off the cliff of self-indulgence."

"Sure, let's go," said Nizam.

"The way you're so open to what life has to offer always makes me exceedingly happy."

"Since we don't have anything to offer life, we might as well accept what life has to offer us."

"Sometimes you're so merciless to yourself."

"Reality is merciless, not me," said Nizam with a laugh, "I'm just reality's interpreter . . ."

On the way he asked, "What's going on at the gambling den?" in the hope of getting news about Anya, and Kamil Bey said, "It's as it always is."

At one point Nizam asked, "Have you ever met Monsieur Gavril?"

"No, as far as I know, no one has ever met him, no one has ever seen him. Sometimes I wonder if he really exists. He's such a legend . . . A mythological presence . . . The god of the gambling den . . . The one holding a deck of cards, son of Hades, god of hell, and Klothos, the Goddess of Fate, who weaves the threads of life, nephew of Pithos, the goddess of seduction . . ."

"You mean nothing is known about him except that he's the son of Hades . . ."

"So much is said about him that it's more accurate to say nothing is known. It's been said that he was the Tsar's doctor, that he fled because he was involved in a murder, it's also said that he's an Armenian prince, that he's a master jeweler who was Fabergé's apprentice, that he's a smuggler, that he's an unrivaled horse trainer . . . There are countless stories about him. I don't know who makes them up, but he's one of the favorite subjects for people taking a break from gambling."

Nizam was having fun.

"How tall is he?"

"There are people who say he's a dwarf and there are people who say he's a giant . . ."

They talked all the way to Madam's house, where they were greeted as they always were, Kamil asked for a table to be prepared, Nizam, contrary to habit, didn't retire to a room with Evangeliki but was willing to drink with him.

It was known that they didn't like sitting on the floor, so the food was arranged on a coffee table, the girls came, they opened the *rakı,* which Nizam was only just becoming accustomed to. Even though Nizam wasn't quite acclimatized to this "Istanbul style," he amused himself with a traveler's curiosity about a place with "exotic food."

As they were eating there was a commotion outside, there was hardly ever any commotion in that house, Şadiye said, "I'll go take a look."

When she returned a little while later her face was completely white.

"Köhnenin Memet is here."

Nizam noticed that Evangeliki's face had gone yellow and that she was biting her lip.

"Who is Köhnenin Memet?" asked Nizam.

"He's one of the Beyoğlu gangsters . . .

"What does this have to do with us?"

Şadiye made a face, looked at him, and said almost in a whisper,

"He wants Evangeliki."

Kamil Bey suddenly stood and said, "What next?" and left the room before Nizam had a chance to say "Stop." Nizam was obliged to take his cane and go after him, at the bottom of the stairs a large man with a pockmarked face was shouting, he had two friends with him.

With an anger that surprised Nizam a great deal, Kamil Bey said, "Why are you shouting, brother?"

"What's it to you if I'm shouting, you blueblood," said the man with a mocking smile, "I want Evangeliki, are you her pimp?"

Köhnenin Memet was one of the remnants of a gang run by Fehim Pasha, one of Abdülhamid's chief detectives, he wouldn't interfere with the more powerful gangsters, he extorted money from small gambling dens and taverns, he regarded the obsequiousness he was shown wherever he went so that he wouldn't cause a scene as a gangster's due. He saw the two "bluebloods" as easy game, and he was making fun of them.

Nizam saw that Kamil Bey was furious and that he was going to cause trouble. It seemed meaningless and laughable to Nizam to have a fight with a gangster at the Madam's house "over a woman." Mihrişah Sultan had raised him in the same style as she'd raised his father, as a "prince," in addition to making sure he learned philosophy, literature, and music, she took great pains to ensure he also learned "manly" sports, she'd made him take classes in everything from Far Eastern stick fighting to boxing, which had very recently become fashionable, and from using a knife to fencing, she'd observed some of the classes herself, "You can be whatever you want," she'd said to Nizam with that sarcastic expression that looked down on the entire world, "but you're not going to be a spineless playboy, I find that the most unbearable kind of person." Once when Nizam was hit very hard and was late getting back onto his feet, she'd said to him, "You have to learn to be a man, if you learn how to be a man, you can handle any problem." Holding his aching arm, Nizam had said, "Or I'll die," he never forgot his grandmother's response, "That's always one way to handle things."

This strict education had served its purpose, Nizam had always had a healthy self-confidence, he'd been involved in a couple of duels, when he was wounded in the shoulder he stayed with a friend to keep his grandmother from learning about the incident. He didn't fear duels, conflicts or fights, he had a strange, unusual courage, it wasn't the kind of courage that saw danger and rushed towards it, it was an indifference that came from his spoiled belief, which had penetrated every fiber of his consciousness, that "nothing will happen to me."

If it had been a nobleman rather than a gangster that he was facing, he would have suggested that they meet somewhere else and "settle the matter," but it seemed "ugly" to him to fight a street tough in Madam's house, Nizam was capable of anything, but he would never do anything he considered "ugly."

Without being concerned about whether they might think he was frightened, he held Kamil Bey's arm and said,

"Let's go, it seems this gentleman is an old friend of Evangeliki . . . We'll come some other time."

Köhnenin Memet laughed.

"Aha, smart boy, you're saying it's not worth getting cut up over a woman, a modern young man, bravo . . . Now get out of here."

Kamil Bey freed his arm from Nizam's grasp.

"Evangeliki Hanım is with us, you come some other time."

The women were watching in fear, the Madam said, "Kamil Bey, Nizam Bey is right, Memet Bey is an old customer of ours, let's not have any unpleasantness, you can come another time, we'll more than make it up to you."

Kamil Bey made a face and said, "So, you're saying that a modern young man will just abandon a woman," that was when he realized that Kamil Bey was drunk and that he was angry at him.

Köhnenin Memet suddenly shoved Kamil Bey.

"Don't drag this out, kid, now get the hell out of here before I make mincemeat out of both of you."

When Nizam saw Kamil Bey reach towards his waist he pushed him aside with his left arm and stepped between them.

He looked at Köhnenin Memet's face, he saw every detail,

his tensed lips, his yellow teeth, his largeish ears, his long, scraggly beard, the pointed nose that looked as if it was made of wax, all of the doors of his attention closed, all of the lights in his mind went out, now all he saw was the man's face and his threatening grin.

In a very calm voice he said,

"Leave."

"What are you saying, kid?"

Everyone was surprised, no one said anything.

Nizam repeated in the same calm voice,

"Leave."

When Könenin Mehmet said, "What are you saying, rich boy?" and reached under his arm to attack, Nizam pulled the thin, steel sword from his cane and put it to his throat. He slowly pushed him to the wall.

"Do you know what will happen if I feel like it? Your windpipe will be pierced, the air in your lungs will come out through that hole, your lungs will crumple up like a paper bag, your blood will stop flowing, you'll struggle to breathe but you won't be able to . . . Should I push a little harder?"

When he pushed the sword a little harder, a thin stream of blood appeared on the man's neck.

His friends looked as if they were going to make a move, but Kamil Bey pulled out the gun Nizam hadn't known he carried and pointed it at them.

"Your neck is bleeding," said Nizam.

The man seemed more terrified by Nizam's expression, by his fixed stare, by what he said and by the calmness of his voice than by the sword itself.

"A thin, red stream . . . Do you want to see it, should I bring you to a mirror?"

At that moment Nizam felt an excitement he'd never known before, he felt a pleasure he'd never known ripple through his entire soul. That he had control over someone's life, that he could kill him, finish him, made him feel as if he was the master of fate.

"Actually you should see it, your own blood . . . They say it has a hot, salty taste, have you ever tasted it? I've never tasted it, but it should be tasted . . ."

He put the tip of the sword between the man's lips.

"Taste it," he said, "but be careful not to slice your tongue . . ."

Everyone in the room was petrified, they wouldn't have been this frightened if there had been a fight, indeed even a murder, but they were frightened by Nizam's voice, his words, this attitude they'd never seen or heard of, the way he stared fixedly at the man, the way he enjoyed making the man bleed, the impression he gave that he wouldn't think twice about killing the man, the way it was impossible to guess what he was going to do, they were as terrified as if they were watching a sorcerer turn a handsome prince into an animal.

For a moment it seemed as if Evangeliki was going to make a move towards Nizam to stop him, but Nizam raised his left hand to stop her, the woman didn't dare make a move.

"If you like I can cut open your stomach, your stomach will fill with your own blood, it will be very painful, you'll writhe in agony . . . Would you like that? You'll have an unforgettable experience, the only problem is that you won't be able to tell anyone . . ."

He put the sword to the man's throat again.

"It seems as if you don't want Evangeliki any more . . . Or do you want her?"

He pushed the sword a little harder.

"You have to answer me . . . Didn't they teach you that it's very rude not to answer a question? Can't you speak? Nod or shake your head then. Do you want her?"

Nizam saw the man's pupils grow larger, his nostrils flare, his Adam's apple bobbing as he tried to swallow, his face go white, indeed he even saw his beard grow, he was looking at the man's face as if through a microscope, he didn't see anything else, the man's face was illuminated but everything around it was pitch black and dark.

For a moment he wanted to stick the sword into the man's throat, he felt a great and unsettling desire to do this, at that moment the man's face became pale, the lights came back on around him, the doors of his attention opened again, Nizam saw the room, the women, the men, Kamil Bey, the thin steel sword he was holding, the red stain on Köhnenin Memet's neck.

He suddenly felt bored of the whole thing.

He lowered the sword.

In a jaded tone he said,

"Leave already."

Whether they were frightened by Nizam, by the strange state he was in or by the gun Kamil Bey was holding, the men staggered backwards as if they were drunk and got out of there.

Nizam turned to the Madam.

"I wonder if you might be able to find me a glass of cognac."

"Of course, Nizam Bey," said the woman, she went to another room in back and returned with a bottle of cognac, Evangeliki poured some into a glass and gave it to him.

"Thank you."

After he'd put his sword back in his cane and drunk his cognac very slowly, he turned to Kamil Bey and said,

"Let's go now, if you like."

"As you wish."

As they were leaving the house, Evangeliki pressed herself against him softly and said, "You're going to come back, aren't you? If you don't want to come here, send for me, I'll come."

"Of course," said Nizam with a smile.

In the carriage Kamil Bey said,

"You frightened me, my good man."

"I was trying to frighten the man."

"I think you frightened everyone."

"You had a gun and you were frightened by a sword," said Nizam as if he hadn't understood what Kamil Bey meant.

"I was frightened by the person who was holding the sword."

Nizam leaned back.

"I didn't know you carried a gun."

"All aristocratic gamblers carry guns."

"You mean all of the men at the gambling den are armed?"

"I wouldn't be at all surprised if the women had weapons in their bags."

"Everyone is armed, huh?" said Nizam, "What a country . . ."

The sky was turning grey, after he'd dropped Kamil Bey off at his house, he told the driver that they were going to the gambling den.

He sank into his seat and sighed.

His mind was slowly being buried by piles of sand, it was as silent as a desert as it emptied, all images and incidents were being erased, there wasn't even the smallest trace left of that "ugly" incident, he had only one emotion in that desert, the pleasure he'd felt as he pressed the sword to the man's throat, the desire to stick the sword further in; sometime later he would forget the incident that had brought about this pleasure, he would remember only the pleasure itself.

He'd never felt anything like that before, even during duels he'd never felt the desire to kill, he'd only found the situation "entertaining," he didn't know why he'd suddenly changed like that, why a feeling like that had abruptly risen up from within him; the man's rudeness, his threatening manner, his failure to follow the rules of etiquette and his arrogance may have had a part in why Nizam had come so close to possibly killing another person for the first time. A duel was a conflict between equals, governed by rules, when he went up against this man the actual feeling he had was a desire to punish; that desire, and having the power to fulfill that desire, may have created that pleasure, despite the "ugliness" of the scene, the ability to punish someone who deserved it, or who Nizam thought deserved it, had left a deep and unforgettable line of pleasure on the surface of the sand.

"Yes, I liked having the power to punish someone who deserved it," he said to Osman later, "it was something very different from a duel."

They were nearing the gambling den, the shock of the incident and of the emotions he'd experienced had destroyed his anger at Anya, had made it small and unimportant; that's how Nizam felt.

When he arrived at the gambling den, Anya had put on her coat and was getting ready to leave, when she saw Nizam's carriage she stopped and waited in front of the door.

When Nizam saw Anya he opened the door.

Anya got in without saying anything.

They didn't speak.

At home, after they'd gone to bed and made love silently, Anya pressed herself against him and said, "I thought you were never going to come again . . ." but she didn't finish her sentence.

22

Two opposing armies were lying in the mud.

The harsh winds of Thrace and the snow that howled as it fell weren't enough to erase the intensifying smell of the bodies, on the contrary, the wind, the snow, and the earth smelled of death.

A peace treaty full of conditions unfavorable to the Ottoman Empire had been signed, the war had stopped for the time being, but the two armies had encountered a terrifying enemy: cholera.

It was killing more soldiers than the war, on both sides dozens, hundreds, were dying, large graves were being dug in the mud, every morning they gathered the bodies, threw them into the grave, and covered them with caustic lime.

Despite all of the savagery of the war, there was an epic, legendary valor in being shot and killed at the front, but to be covered in filth, consumed and dried up by cholera, to die being wracked by painful convulsions, destroyed not only the dignity of the body but that of the soul as well, denied the dying soldiers the right to a dignified death.

They boiled and chlorinated all the water, but this didn't forestall the epidemic. Their only hope was that the cold and the snow would kill the germs and bring an end to this slaughter.

Ragıp Bey had grown thinner, he was angry, he was worried about the men, he and all of the other officers were struggling to forestall the epidemic, but at the same time, in this mud that smelled of death and where the guns had fallen silent, he struggled to come to terms with himself and with his unending, relentless, and increasingly monstrous yearning. Like a male spider that had been caught in his own web, he was both spinning new webs because it was his habit and nature and struggling to free himself.

The emotions that were exploding inside an iron safe that had been made out of pride didn't blow the safe apart, but the safe couldn't prevent these emotions from triggering each other and setting off a chain of explosions.

Ragıp Bey, whose pride and manhood had almost fused together and become intertwined, believed that to give up his pride would be to give up his manhood, and that pride was constantly swelling, growing, and surging from the jealousy it produced; what had seemed to Dilara Hanım like an oversized pride and conceit was in fact a colossal jealousy that wouldn't allow itself to be expressed as anything but pride.

This pride and jealousy didn't allow the love he truly felt for Dilara Hanım to mature, didn't allow his feelings to gather in their own combs and grow like a beehive; there was none of the tenderness, mercy and warmth that love requires, like a fruit that has grown but hasn't sweetened, it would rot before it matured.

Even though he wasn't openly conscious of this, his instincts sensed it, he felt that he'd constructed his own cell, but he didn't know how he was going to free himself from this. There are few types of imprisonment more desperate than a person who, while wanting to escape, constantly beats himself and ends up moving backwards, Ragıp Bey had become his own guard, it life opened all of the doors in front of him, he wouldn't be able to pass through them.

On those long winter nights, as he listened to the wind whistle through the wooden walls of the shack in which he was staying, watching the snow being blown by the wind in the rectangles of stained light reflected through the windows, he wondered, "Did I exaggerate things?" it occurred to him that he might have made a mistake when he decided that Dilara Hanım didn't want him, at moments like that he began to suspect himself rather than Dilara Hanım, even if only briefly, his love overcame that distasteful rawness, became more mature and he felt a great tenderness, a warm friendship and an unbearable yearning. He remembered Dilara Hanım's smile, the way she said "Ragıp," the way she let her hair down, the way she snuggled against him, the way she looked at him, the way she asked, "Would you like another coffee?" the way she said "Be careful" when they parted. If it had been possible he would have been willing to live within these memories alone, these memories softened the soul that had been hardened by pride and become thick and rough, a smile would appear on his face.

Later, when it occurred to him that she hadn't wanted him enough, when he thought she hadn't loved him enough, he asked "Why didn't she love me?" when he struggled to find the answer to this question, his belief that "she didn't admire me" raised its head, that belief woke his pride, and the whole terrible cycle began again.

Some nights he dreamed about Dilara Hanım, even though she sometimes appeared to him naked, they never made love in these dreams; like every soldier at the front, he had erotic dreams, but it was always other women who appeared in these dreams, he couldn't solve this mystery. When he dreamed about Dilara Hanım he woke missing her terribly, he would be very quiet all day.

After the armistice, they began to grant brief leave to the officers who'd fought in the war, Ragıp Bey arrived in Istanbul at the end of December.

On the first night he had a fire lit for a bath and washed himself for a long time, he had a good meal, he went to bed early between lavender scented sheets and, without having to worry about sudden screams, artillery shells, and the rattle of machine gun fire, he fell into a deep, dark sleep.

The following morning he decided to go visit Sheikh Efendi, he'd missed the Sheikh, he knew that he would be able to give his soul some peace, but beneath that was the hope of seeing a former marine named Hasan Efendi. Hasan Efendi was the most loyal of Sheikh Efendi's disciples, he knew what all of the women in this extended family, and Mehpare Hanım in particular, were up to, no one understood how he knew and where he got his information, but he kept track of even the smallest details of where they went, who they saw, and how their health was, and he passed on the more essential information to Sheikh Efendi. He'd long since decided that Mehpare Hanım, Mihrişah Sultan, and Dilara Hanım were "whores," but he would never have said this to anyone, it was only later, in the broad freedom of death, that he told Osman; when he'd heard Dilara Hanım say "women have difficult times" he'd murmured between clenched teeth that "the whore has a lot of excuses."

Hasan Efendi, with his large, closely shaven head and his huge body, was for Osman perhaps the most entertaining of the dead, "these women have a predilection for unbelievers," he'd said once, "I suppose they resemble each other because they're all loose women." In order not to sadden him, he hadn't told the Sheikh that Mehpare Hanım had seen Constantine before the war, but he had said in passing that Dilara Hanım was seeing "an unbeliever named Lausanne."

He'd told Osman that "Your family is like a gruel made out of honey and tar, molasses made from pitch, some of them were firm believers and some of them had been influenced by unbelievers, look at how this drove you crazy, at how you wander around half naked chatting with the dead, you're suffering for the sins of these people who dressed up as unbelievers."

Hasan Efendi was also an enemy of beauty, "beauty seduces you, it deludes you, it leads to depravity. No one else will tell you this but, I'm telling you. Beauty is satan's invention, anything beautiful is satan's work, if you see something beautiful, stay away, change direction at once, there were a lot of beautiful women in your family, there was a lot of sin, if you ask why, there's no beauty without sin."

Despite all of his rambling talk, Osman liked the sincerity of his tactlessness, the smell of sin in his piety, how he somehow couldn't come to terms with beauty and the thousands of stories he told, and he believed that the Sheikh had loved Hasan Efendi for the same reasons.

At the *tekke* Ragıp Bey found Hasan Efendi first, the two old friends embraced, Hasan Efendi asked him about the war and Ragıp Bey told him the situation, Hasan Efendi cursed those who were "the cause" of the situation, then they talked about what had been going on in the city, it was Hasan Efendi's turn to talk, because he was undecided about whether or not to tell him about what was going on with Dilara Hanım he danced around it, then he finally came out with it, "Dilara Hanım has a French journalist they call Lausanne, they see each other quite frequently, if you ask me the guy is a Frankish spy."

Ragıp Bey's first thought was to prevent what he felt on hearing this from being apparent to others, he struggled with all his strength to keep his face from flushing, to not allow his expression to change, it was when he succeeded at this that he felt the real pain, he felt as if all his internal organs had tensed, crumpled, and shut down, he swallowed, said "hah" in an indifferent manner and changed the subject, but a few minutes later he came back to the subject, "So you're saying the man's a spy."

"That's my opinion . . . If you asked Sheikh Efendi he'd say not to judge anyone hastily, but the man is poking around everywhere, he's always going to the French Embassy, sometimes he mediates between the Ottoman government and the

French government, he goes to the front, he knows more about what's going on at the front than you do . . . He went to visit our wounded at the French hospital, he brought Dilara Hanım with him."

Ragıp Bey swallowed again,

"Did Dilara Hanım know anyone among the wounded?"

"No, how could she know anyone . . . She just visited."

"Good God."

"He pokes around all day, and in the evening he goes to Dilara Hanım's for dinner."

By now Ragıp Bey had given up on struggling to control himself, he was just asking questions.

"Does he stay there?"

"No . . . After dinner he goes back to his hotel."

Ragıp Bey was surprised by his own reaction, but he would have preferred Hasan Efendi to have said "Yes, he stays with her," then both he and Dilara Hanım would have died in his mind, but now he felt as if he'd received a wound that would leave him crippled, he was having difficulty breathing, it was as if a large stone had been placed on his chest, he regretted having visited the *tekke*.

He wanted to get away from there as soon as possible, he felt the need to be alone, to breathe deeply, "I'd better get going," he said, "I suppose Sheikh Efendi is busy today, I'll see him the next time I come." "That wouldn't be right," said Hasan Efendi, "I'll go let him know and we'll see . . ."

He didn't give Ragıp Bey a chance to say anything, he leapt up and rushed off with an agility that wouldn't have been expected from such a large body, Ragıp Bey was breathing deeply and trying to pull himself together like a boxer between rounds, it was as if all circulation of air had been cut off and he'd been left without oxygen, he was struggling to revive his numbed brain and body, he had no strength left, he didn't have the energy to talk, he felt weary and sleepy.

His mind was completely empty, there was a snowy plain, a plain on which nothing moved or shifted, and Hasan Efendi's voice and what he'd said, he wasn't thinking about anything, his flesh ached like an animal that had been shot, the pain had not yet spread to his soul, he didn't know what damage had been done to his mind, what he would feel when he was alone at home, from now on it was going to be difficult, he could see this.

"God damn it," he said, he kept saying the same thing over and over again as if he was moaning, he himself didn't know who he was cursing or why, it was just that saying this lightened the pain a little.

Hasan Efendi came in looking pleased, "Come," he said, "Sheikh Efendi is waiting for you, he was very pleased when he heard you'd come."

They went to the courtyard together, in the false light of the bright snow clouds, the tall cypress trees whose green needles carried a purple shadow seemed to grow larger, their grandeur besieged the entire courtyard. The smell of acorns mixed with the smell of elderberry trees.

Ragıp Bey stopped for a moment, breathed in the clean air, he struggled to wipe off the traces the conversation had left on his face, he knew that Sheikh Efendi would see at a glance what Hasan Efendi had been unable to see, he feared that his weakness would be seen.

Sheikh Efendi greeted Ragıp Bey at the door to the *zikr* room, they looked at each other's faces to read the traces of what had happened since they'd last seen each other, Sheikh Efendi said "welcome" and smiled.

"It's good to be here, your excellency the Sheikh."

"How are you? You must have gone through some difficult times . . ."

"Very difficult times, your excellency. Times that make a soldier ashamed . . . We didn't just lose territory, we lost all of our dignity and honor."

"Don't be so severe, Ragıp Bey, the army defended Çatalca heroically."

"The war began in Edirne, your excellency the Sheikh, and we put up a heroic resistance at Çatalca. Who are we resisting heroically? The Bulgarians . . . The great Ottoman Empire was holding off the Bulgarians. We were holding off the tiny Kingdom of Bulgaria, if I took Bulgaria and threw it into a map of the Ottoman Empire, it would get lost, it would take three days for anyone to find it . . . Even the story of our heroism is abysmal, are we going to console ourselves with that . . ."

"You're angry."

When Ragıp Bey realized that his uncontrolled anger was pushing the boundaries of respect, he was embarrassed, "Excuse me, your excellency," he said, "I suddenly got carried away."

"Don't worry, Ragıp Bey, what happened is not your fault, nor is the pain you suffered or the anger you felt . . . What happened happened, we can't change that, but it saddens me to see you being so harsh with yourself, we know how valiant and heroic you and Muhtar Pasha were, it's not as if there was something you could have done that you didn't do, you did more than you could do. It would be unfair if you were to carry the sins of the vast Ottoman Empire on your own."

The Sheikh looked out the window.

"It looks like it's going to snow . . . Come, if it's not too cold for you we can take a little walk in the garden, we can talk as we walk."

They passed through the purplish shadows of the garden and reached the shore that smelled of seaweed and chrysanthemums, the Golden Horn was swelling in place on its own like a smoke-colored cat.

"Sometimes a multitude of troubles can pile up on top of us," said Sheikh Efendi as if he was answering a question Ragıp Bey had asked. "Anguish is not an army that you can attack and force to retreat by fighting, on the contrary we strengthen our anguish when we fight it. You become angry with yourself, you become your own enemy. Don't become your own enemy for the sake of your anguish, don't persecute yourself. Shelter in a place that's more powerful than anguish . . ."

"There's no place left to take shelter," said Ragıp Bey in a hopeless tone.

After the Sheikh gave Ragıp Bey an offended look, as if he was reproaching him, he said with a mature smile,

"There's always a place for us to take shelter."

If there hadn't been a war, Ragıp Bey might have left the army that day and settled in the *tekke*. He felt this not because the Sheikh's words had led him to suddenly discover religion but because he saw that the Sheikh had known and tasted the anguish that was tearing him apart, that he'd succeeded in living with this anguish without losing his mature calm. He felt the trust that a sick person feels in someone who has had the same illness, the Sheikh knew the stages and tribulations of this sickness, and he knew the cure, this created a feeling in Ragıp Bey similar to the sense of brotherhood felt by people who have suffered the same pain; the deep sorrow and loneliness in his voice was the sanctuary that Ragıp Bey needed at that time. Being with someone who shared a similar pain but was kind enough not to speak of it openly soothed the wounds in his soul, even if only temporarily.

When he left the *tekke* the bright clouds were growing darker, he started walking without thinking about where he was going, he passed a butcher cutting legs of lamb hanging in front of his shop, street barbers, beggars, muddy streets, soup kitchens, elderly houses that leaned against each other to stay on their feet but he didn't see any of them. As he moved away from the *tekke*, Sheikh Efendi's soothing voice grew fainter, as if a spell was being broken, the echo of Hassan Efendi's voice grew louder, he felt his soul drying out, wrinkling and hardening.

Now, as he faced reality, he knew better that none of the

miseries he'd experienced during the war, miseries that had made him suffer and led him into paroxysms of anger, were in fact real misery; at that time he'd still had the hope that he was wrong; despite the anger that was swollen by his jealousy and his pride, there still remained within his soul, which cried that it would never forgive, a hope, which tried to pass the time necessary for his wounds to heal and which on those always cloudy nights waited for the frozen moonlight to emerge again from the clouds, that he could forgive, this was what gave him the strength to carry on in spite of everything.

In the dim, abandoned gap between consciousness and subconsciousness he created fantasies that he struggled to keep from ever being reflected in his conscious mind: when he and Dilara ran into each other one day, Dilara would tell him in a convincing manner that "The truth wasn't what he thought it was," he would create various settings in which he thought that there was in fact nothing to forgive, they would meet on an excursion to Kağıthane, while shopping in Pera, on a spring day in Küçüksu, in his fantasies he would see the initial surprise, the delight, the bashfulness. These were fantasies created by the secret hope in the very depths that was concealed even from its owner.

As he walked alone in the light snow that had begun to fall, down narrow streets where there were fewer and fewer people, his footsteps echoing from the cobblestones, he realized that when he'd designed his future, he'd always placed Dilara at the center of that future in the hope that her presence would make all of his tomorrows better. Now that future was sinking with all of his dreams about Dilara Hanım, Ragıp Bey had no future, life was ending that day, indeed it had already ended. In his thoughts he had rejected the past, destroyed the future together with his dreams, and the thin slice of time that was left to him was full of loneliness, the wounds of broken pride, jealousy and anguish.

All of those vague suspicions now had an identity and a

form, "a French journalist, a spy, a man," was intimate with Dilara Hanım, he was spending time with her, he was laughing with her, he was making love to her. Images of Dilara Hanım rose from the depths of his memory and combined with the Frenchman whose face he'd never seen, she was smiling at the man, she was letting down her hair in his presence, she was moaning beneath the man, after making love she kissed the man's chest. How strange it was that what hurt him most was the image of that last kiss which women give their men to display their proud gratitude when their femininity is satisfied.

Without realizing it, he had established his life on his own manhood and its reflections, now that life was being destroyed by the images entering his mind, it was being torn apart by humiliating defeat just like the empire in which he was serving as an officer. With every act, with every word, with every attitude, he saw that the entity he'd sculpted like a statue was becoming meaningless and vanishing into nothingness.

This feeling was like a person watching his own death, as the soul died, the body helplessly experienced the pain.

Later he said to Osman, "People are afraid of death, what idiocy, if there was no death, they would have lost their last consolation."

He was hungry but he didn't feel like eating, he felt as if he wasn't going to be able to go into an enclosed space, wandering around aimlessly like this seemed meaningless, but he couldn't think of anything else to do. "Sorrowfulness isn't something that suits a man," he said to Osman on another occasion, "it's something for women, but sometimes men feel it too, then they feel bad about feeling bad."

He'd made arrangements to meet his older brother Cevat Bey at Maksut that evening. It was beginning to snow heavily, his condensed breath froze on his moustache. He started climbing towards Beyoğlu, as he approached, the streets were more crowded, the gas streetlamps had been lit, smells of fresh food and anise wafted from restaurant doors, musicians were tuning their instruments as they prepared for the evening.

These were familiar sounds and smells for Ragıp Bey, when, during Abdülhamid's reign, the fight between Fuat Pasha and Fehim Pasha spilled out of the palace and into the streets, he'd had quite a few skirmishes with Fehim Pasha's toughs as one of Fuat Pasha's young officers, Fuat Pasha had ordered him to wander around Beyoğlu almost every night. After he'd shot the gigantic Arab Dilaver İpek, one of Fehim Pasha's "mastiffs," in his home, his name had been mentioned frequently in underground circles, for a long time the story of the fight in which he'd shot Dilaver had been told in coffee houses, cabarets, and taverns.

Ragıp Bey remembered those days and smiled, he never spoke of those days and he didn't like it when people spoke of them in his presence, but those memories always entertained him, the skirmishes and fights in those days of blood and thunder had suited his nature. If he hadn't been passionate about the military and war, if he hadn't had a military education, he might have become one of the senior gangsters of Beyoğlu. Young officers talked among themselves about how he carried a knife in his sleeve even on the battlefield and how he'd shown amazing skill in knife games.

When he went into Maksut's tavern, it smelled of salted fish, anchovies, mussels, and *rakı*, the tavern was still empty, in the front section there were marble-topped tables and in the rear section, which was reached through an open door, there were small, low wooden tables and wooden stools, as always, Maksut, with his stocky body and dirty moustache, was standing smiling among the liter bottles, colored bottles and barrels of all sizes behind a counter that faced the door

When he saw Ragıp Bey he hurried out from behind the counter and rushed over to him,

"Oh Ragıp Bey, what wind blew you here? You haven't stopped by for quite some time."

"How are you Master Maksut? So you remember me . . ."

"Is there anyone who doesn't remember you, Ragıp Bey, they still talk about you around here . . ."

Ragıp Bey laughed, for whatever reason, it pleased him to be remembered.

"Good," he said.

"Are you alone? Where do you want to sit, go to the back if you like, it's quieter there."

"My brother is coming, I'll go to the back, it's better . . . quiet would be better, we haven't seen each other for a long time and we have a lot to talk about."

Maksut seated Ragıp Bey at a table in the back.

"What are you drinking? *Rakı*?"

"*Rakı* of course . . ."

"Shall I open a liter bottle?"

"Go ahead and open one, why not . . . We might as well drink tonight."

"What do you want to go with it? Shall I have them make quail kebab?"

"Bring whatever you want, Maksut . . . And bring my *rakı* so I can slowly get started."

With the *rakı* Maksut brought liver, anchovies, stuffed mussels, barrel sardines, and white cheese, Ragıp Bey filled his first glass, he poured water into his *rakı* and watched it turn white, then took a long drink. He felt the warmth of the *rakı* first in his nasal passage and then in his stomach, then the warmth spread through his entire body.

Cevat Bey arrived as he was finishing his first glass. As they embraced he said, "So, you started without me."

"I got here early, brother, I thought I might as well start while I was waiting for you . . ."

"How are you Ragıp? You look a little drained, you're a little pale too."

"It's from the cold, brother, I walked a little."

"How's the front?"

"It's terrible, brother . . . We lost more men to cholera than we did in battle . . . There's sickness and filth everywhere . . . There's no medicine . . . we're burying dozens, hundreds of kids."

"What are the Bulgarians doing?"

"Cholera hit them too, they're writhing in the mud like us, they bury their men every day."

While they were talking Maksut brought more dishes to the table.

"When you're at the front you think the whole world has changed," said Ragıp Bey, "as if everyone was lying in the mud, being bombed, being shot, being brought down by cholera . . . Then when you get to the city you see that you're the only one who was facing bullets at the front and that no one cares . . . I don't think that the soldiers at the front should ever be given leave. It would destroy their morale."

"That's what being a soldier is like."

"You're right, brother, that's what being a soldier is like."

After he'd taken his first sip of *rakı*, Cevat Bey asked,

"Have you seen the conditions of the treaty?"

"I saw them, brother . . . Abasement . . . What else can I say?"

"Are you willing to accept this abasement?"

"How could I be willing to accept it? How could anyone be willing to accept it? But after all, these negotiations were conducted by a government whose army had fled. It's a reality that we fled twice, that we retreated as far as Çatalca . . . When you have an army like that the government won't be any better."

Cevat Bey paused for a moment, he speared an anchovy with his fork, brought it slowly to his mouth, then slowly put it back down again, Ragıp Bey realized that his older brother was about to say something.

"We're not willing," said Cevat Bey.

"Not willing to do what?"

"To accept this treaty, this abasement, this humiliation, to accept that the Ottoman Empire has fallen so low . . ."

"If we're going to talk about reality, it was the army's fault."

"We're not willing to accept the army being the way it is now either."

"What are you going to do about it?"

"We're going to change everything."

"How are you going to change everything?"

"First we have to change the government . . ."

"Brother, the soldiers at the front don't change their underwear this often, what are you talking about . . . This will be the third or fourth government in six months . . . I've lost count."

"Those were all the same, old pashas who can't think about anyone but themselves."

"Brother, six months ago your friends were in the cabinet."

"It's not enough to be in the cabinet, you have to be in charge of the cabinet."

Ragıp Bey stopped and looked at his brother . . . During the course of their conversation, the image of Dilara Hanım that had been chiseled into his mind disappeared from time to time, Ragıp Bey was getting swept up in what his older brother was saying, then the image returned with a great ripping sensation. After that last sentence, he suddenly focused more on what his older brother was saying.

"How is the sultan going to be willing to accept your friends taking over the government?"

Cevat Bey leaned towards his brother.

"This isn't a time to wait for him to be willing."

"Meaning?"

"It's all or nothing . . ."

He stopped for a moment to weigh whether he'd correctly understood what his older brother was saying, he touched his gun without letting anyone notice.

"You mean with this . . ."

"Yes."

"Isn't that dangerous, brother?"

Cevat Bey suddenly smiled.

"Since when have you started avoiding dangerous things, Ragıp?"

"Brother, war is one thing and politics is another . . . Weapons and danger are part of the nature of war, but politics . . . Politics is different, isn't it?"

"It's not, Ragıp . . . Here both war and politics are conducted with weapons. In a place with so many self-seeking swindlers it's even unclean to conduct politics without weapons . . ."

"So how are you going to do this? The army is divided, the moment the Committee makes a move the Halaskar Zabitan will take up arms, God forbid, they'll go at each other and the whole country will turn into a battlefield."

"That's your job now,"

"I don't understand, brother."

"We'll take care of the government in Istanbul . . . The moment the Halaskar faction makes a move at the front you'll be all over them, you'll catch them unprepared and trap them in a corner, they won't be able to raise their voices."

"You'd need quite a few men for that . . ."

"Our friends are talking to trustworthy officers at the front, not openly the way I am, they're making the situation felt."

"How are you going to take care of Istanbul?"

"The race is to the swift, don't you know . . ."

"What's going to happen to the First Army in Istanbul? Are they on board?"

"We'll have overthrown the government and set up another before they make a move."

"Who's going to be grand vizier? Talat Bey?"

"Mahmut Şevket Pasha."

"Is he on board?"

"The pasha said yes, I spoke to him myself."

Ragıp Bey gave a somewhat belittling smile.

"So the pasha really likes politics . . ."

"Ragıp, anyone who gets involved in this isn't going to be able to back out."

"How is he going to be able to trust your friends after what happened last time?"

"He said he wouldn't have Talat or Hacı Adil in the cabinet, and we agreed."

While they were talking, Maksut brought the quail kebab that was baked in large eggplants. Cevat Bey took a bite and said, "Delicious, that rascal Maksut really knows how to do this." Then he looked at Ragıp Bey.

"You're not eating anything, Ragıp . . . Is something bothering you?"

"No brother, it's just that I'm not hungry."

Cevat Bey looked at his brother with an almost fatherly concern as he tried to figure out whether or not he was telling the truth.

"After the dry bread at the front I would have thought you would have attacked this food."

"I'll eat later, brother."

"Ragıp," said Cevat Bey, "If you want we can have you transferred to Istanbul, you've been at the front for a long time . . . We can get the Ministry of War to issue a transfer, thank God we still have at least that much power."

Ragıp Bey froze almost instinctively.

"What are you saying, brother, how could I go off and leave my men in the mud?"

Then he worried that he might have sounded disrespectful to his brother, who was only trying to help him.

"Thank you brother, I don't want that now . . . You know that I like the front, I can't enjoy Istanbul when I know my men are there."

"It's up to you, but keep it in mind, if it starts getting you down we can take care of it."

Ragıp Bey changed the subject.

"I heard that Enver Bey has returned from Tripoli."

"He's back, like you he wanted to go to the front . . . They've appointed him as a staff officer in Hurşit Pasha's corps."

"Did you talk to him as well?"

"Not yet, but presumably he'll come to Istanbul in the next ten days to talk to his friends."

"What does he say?"

"I don't know yet, but I don't think for a moment that he'll say no . . . Anyway Talat Bey has already written to him to give him the necessary information."

Ragıp Bey was hesitant about whether or not to say what was in his mind, then he decided that it would be better to say it.

"Brother, if you won't consider it disrespectful, there's something I would like to say."

"Go ahead, Ragıp."

"Six months ago your friends were in power, you know too that things didn't go so well for the country."

"I told you, Ragıp, we were in the government but we weren't in charge of it."

"The Minister of War at the time, Mahmut Şevket Pasha, was very powerful, even you couldn't stand him, even you got sick of the way he was imprisoning and beating the opposition and you made him resign."

"We made a mistake . . . I was against it from the beginning. What happened, while we were getting rid of the pasha we ended getting left out of the cabinet."

"Won't the pasha be even more severe as grand vizier?"

"Ragıp, this country requires a lot of severity, you've seen how without it all of the traitors come out into the open, they complain, they criticize everything. They're against everything.

Those damned Halaskar have started playing all kinds of games in the military. They're worse enemies to us than the Bulgarians."

"Fine, brother, but what's going to happen to İsmail Hakkı Pasha from the quartermaster corps? He turned out to be a thief . . . Because of the quartermaster the army was left hungry in a place like Thrace. They didn't even send food, they took wheat out of the warehouses but didn't give it to the men . . . What's going to be done about that?"

Cevat Bey sighed.

"Look, you're right about that. I'm not happy about it either . . . We can't get rid of the man."

"Why not, brother?"

"Enver Bey says we can't . . . But I imagine we'll figure something out."

They drank their *rakı* in silence.

"When are you planning to do it, brother?"

"I suppose it will be done in the next two or three weeks . . . Some of our friends are dragging their feet a little, but after Enver Bey returns they'll change their minds. Together Talat Bey and Enver Bey will convince them."

"I hope it all works out, bother . . . Take care of yourself."

"Don't worry . . . At times like this you have to accept your destiny, you set out, and the rest is up to God."

Maksut's tavern had filled up, waiters were carrying trays of food to the tables, the smell of anise mixed with the smell of tobacco, bureaucrats, and gangsters sat at neighboring tables, regulars made comments and joked with friends at other tables, Ragıp Bey recognized and greeted a few people he'd known in the old days.

At one point, as if it had just crossed his mind, Ragıp Bey said,

"There's a French journalist, his name is Lausanne or something, Hasan Efendi mentioned him when I stopped by the *tekke* today . . ."

Cevat Bey thought for a moment.

"Yes, there is someone like that, he comes to our intelligence division as well, I've run into him a couple of times."

"I don't know, Hasan Efendi really doesn't like the man."

"What's Hasan Efendi's problem with this Frenchman?"

Ragıp Bey was about to say, "He thinks he's a spy," but he stopped himself, he'd suddenly realized he was going to inform on the man because he was angry at him over Dilara Hanım, and he was ashamed.

"I don't, it was just the way he talked, I thought you might know him."

"I've seen him, they say the articles he writes are favorable to us, he talks to ministers and so forth, they also say he has a lot of influence with the French government."

"Is that so?" said Ragıp Bey.

"That's what they say."

Then they started talking about old friends, childhood, their mother, once or twice Cevat Bey insisted that he eat some food but Ragıp Bey hardly ate anything.

They got up from the table towards midnight, Cevat Bey said, "it's late, I'm going to sleep at the Ministry, I have a lot to do in the morning. Can I drop you off in Karaköy?"

"No, brother, thanks, I'm going to walk a little, the fresh air does me good."

"Fine, Ragıp. Let's see each other before you go back."

As they were parting Cevat Bey looked at his brother carefully, there wasn't much of an age difference between them, but Cevat Bey always felt as if he were older, he behaved in a somewhat fatherly manner towards Ragıp Bey, he was worried about his lack of appetite and his dullness.

"You're well, aren't you?"

"I'm well, brother."

They embraced and parted.

Snow was sprinkling, the restaurants were emptying,

drunks were staggering, the round light of the gas streetlamps struck the pavement.

As he walked the faces and words of the Sheikh, Hasan Efendi and his older brother were fading and becoming indistinct, and Dilara Hanım's face was becoming clearer; Ragıp Bey was having trouble believing that such a beloved face had become the source of so much anguish; he realized in surprise that his pain augmented the light and brightness of this face, that the brightness of this face was dulling his entire memory and making all types of emotion insignificant.

Ragıp Bey was not a man who was easily anguished, heart broken or sorrowful, he turned these types of emotions into anger, with his outbursts he would leave his anger in the world like a freighter leaving its cargo in the harbor, but this time he wasn't able to do this, he couldn't be angry at Dilara Hanım or anyone else, he was angry only at himself for feeling this way.

As he was walking he realized at one point that he was repeating the same words to himself over and over again, "Why did you do it, Dilara, why did you do it Dilara," he was talking to himself, his words sounded like the moaning of a wounded man.

He stopped talking, but as he walked the same words kept echoing in his mind, "Why did you do it, Dilara," at the same time he was finding reasons to excuse Dilara Hanım, "I went away," he said, "I went away and left her," for some reason, Dilara Hanım having justifiable reasons for seeing another man refreshed him.

He didn't know how far he had walked, he walked without noticing his surroundings, as if nothing existed outside of himself, as if everything was in his mind, Dilara Hanım's face, what Dilara Hanım had said, Dilara Hanım's justifiable reasons for going to someone else; suddenly he sensed rather than saw that he was on a familiar street, something, a wall, a tree, a shadow warned him that he was in a familiar place.

He looked around.

He'd come to Dilara Hanım's street, "Like a dog looking for its owner," he grumbled to himself, but at the same time he was glad he was there, to be this close to Dilara Hanım, even if he wasn't going to see her it eased his pain. Later he said to Osman, "Why does loving make a person so miserable, why does it make a person so helpless?" Osman was not able to say, "That's not love, that's jealously," he pursed his lips and bowed his head.

The snow was getting heavier, the houses, the walls, the trees, the faded vines on the walls were all being silenced by a soft whiteness, Ragıp Bey leaned against a wall and looked at Dilara Hanım's mansion, all of the lights were out.

Ragıp Bey took shelter in the forgivingness of drunkenness, he'd made himself accept that he'd come here because he was drunk, it was only with this excuse that he could appease the shame and the anger he felt. He was staring at the mansion, snow was accumulating on his fur cap and on the shoulders of his coat, one or two cold flakes even went into his eyes.

His mind almost voluntarily accepted the sleepy waves of drunkenness, the only brightness within him was reflected from Dilara Hanım's face, as he stood there he felt he could spend his entire life there by that wall, yes, there, he could stand at the foot of that cold wall and look at the mansion, he didn't even have to see Dilara Hanım, he just wanted to know that she was near, to see everything she did, to record in his mind the times when the Frenchman came and left.

For a time he thought about going and knocking on the door, this was the thought that sobered him up, the thought was so terrifying that he sobered up in an instant, he saw himself, the street, the snow, he became aware of a miserable man waiting silently outside a house.

He walked quickly.

As he walked he cursed himself through his moustache, mumbling "Like a dog."

23

As soon as you entered Rukiye's waterfront mansion, you could tell that the people who lived there were happy," Nizam said to Osman once. "To tell the truth I don't know how I could tell, but you could tell as soon as you walked in, it was as if all the furniture was smiling."

The little flames that looked like burning orange peels in the fireplaces throughout the house radiated a honey-colored warmth that embraced all of the walls and heated them, there was a faint smell of wood incense, as if the house wanted to emphasize its feminine dominance by adding a faint scent of perfume and powder, hundreds of candles flickered in the engraved lamp-glasses in the many-armed chandeliers, the little flames danced in the slight breezes they created themselves, the shiny wooden floorboards absorbed the warmth, the large Isfahan carpets laid over them carried the warmth into their fibers, the curios on the mahogany tables between the velvet armchairs offered visitors new discoveries every time and gave the heavy furniture a playful cheer.

Nizam had named Rukiye's house "*l'empire de la lumière*" and the name "empire of light" suited the house, Rukiye's passion for light was revealed in every part of the house, there was no other house on the Bosphorus that had as many lights or whose lights could be seen from so far away, most of the other waterfront mansions were known by the names of their male owners, but everyone knew this house as "Rukiye Hanım's mansion."

Tevfik Bey had allowed Rukiye to decorate almost the entire house according to her wishes, whenever she asked his opinion about a change she was going to make, and she always asked, the young man would smile and say, "I like what you like," Rukiye would answer, "Say something," and he would say, "I said what I had to say at our wedding, I said 'I'm Rukiye Hanımefendi's slave,' and that was that." The young man possessed all of the confidence and peace of knowing that he was loved and, as Nizam said in a mocking manner, "He loved his wife like crazy," he felt an unending admiration for her intelligence and taste.

They were passionately bound to each other, they were one of those rare couples who melted their love in a bronze mold and turned it into a whole, the points of difference seemed to have disappeared, it was as if they'd merged with each other, it was impossible to distinguish between them; they loved each other by caring for and paying attention to each other, loving and being loved never became a matter of indifference, they addressed even the smallest issue with a natural carefulness, even when from time to time their opinions about politics, an article or a novel differed and they argued, each always believed that the other had something important to say.

Sometimes Rukiye would take Tevfik Bey's face between her hands and look lovingly at how handsome he was, there was a miraculous peace in their love, this peace had its source in loving with the same fervor and having the same urgent fear of loss, and being certain of not losing despite this fear. The rare equality in the feelings they felt for each other added a miraculous peace that could otherwise have turned into a spiny pain.

One night towards the middle of January, Nizam went to Rukiye's house for dinner, "I'll never forget that day," Nizam said to Osman, "of the thousands of ordinary days you've lived, one will become separated from the others, you don't know that it will become unforgettable, that it will leave a stamp on your life," then, both surprising and frightening Osman, his face darkened with one of those sudden explosions of anger that didn't fit at all with his cheerful appearance and he said something similar to what Rukiye would later say to Sheikh Efendi, "I hate destiny and the one who created destiny, this thing they call fate makes you live like a blind person, you don't see the sword that's moving quickly towards your face, and you're smiling like an idiot, I hate this thing they call destiny because it puts you in stupid situations, the way it makes you smile as disaster is approaching, the way it makes fun of you, the way it belittles you, the way it plays with you . . . I hate it." He paused for a while but then, unable to contain himself, he continued, "I would like to have punished destiny but they don't give you that right; I would have liked to strangle destiny, tear it to pieces, if destiny had a face I would have liked to beat that face to a pulp."

That night the sea was calm, there were flurries of snow, the air was frosty, as he approached in the launch, Rukiye's waterfront mansion looked from the distance like a fairy-tale house made from a pumpkin, Nizam's face burned from the cold on the short walk from the quay to the mansion, when he entered he was greeted by a pleasant-smelling warmth.

Rukiye hugged her brother tightly.

"You're frozen," she said, "you're as cold as ice."

"It's very cold outside, let's go sit in front of the fireplace."

Nizam looked at Rukiye's belly.

"My nephew is growing."

"It's not just your nephew, your sister is growing too, look at me . . ."

"Isn't Tevfik here?"

"He's upstairs, some documents arrived from the grand vizier's office, he's looking at them, he'll be down in a minute."

"How are you?" asked Nizam.

"I'm very well," said Rukiye, "Everything is so perfect that I get frightened sometimes."

"Rukiye, you've started talking like a worried old woman, is motherhood turning you into an old woman?"

Rukiye hit Nizam on the nose.

"Good God," she said with a laugh, "I'm pregnant, of course I'm going to be worried . . . You wouldn't understand . . . I'll see how you are when you get married . . . Are you hungry?"

"I'm hungry, we can eat when Tevfik comes."

"I had them make your favorite dishes, I sent a man to Beyoğlu in this snow to get foie gras, caviar and ham . . . You're going to eat it all, I'm going to feed it to you."

"Don't scare me," said Nizam, "If you're so eager to feed me I might fear that you'll slaughter me and eat me on the Feast of the Sacrifice."

Tevfik Bey arrived a little later, the two young men who loved the same woman in different ways were good friends, Tevfik Bey liked to laugh at Nizam's jokes and Nizam liked to laugh at his jokes.

At dinner, while she fed Nizam, Rukiye talked excitedly about her new discovery.

"Electricity is coming to Istanbul, I pleaded with Tevfik, we've already applied at the municipality, I'm going to wire the house, I'm going to hang lamps everywhere, Tevfik says I'm crazy, but I want to replace the gas lamps on the quay with electric lamps."

"You're crazy for illumination."

"I like lights, I like things to be well lit, dimness bothers me, I don't know how people can live with those dim lights, it brings a person down . . . A real home should be well illuminated."

"You miss Paris," said Nizam, "you miss the lights there . . . It's been twenty years since electricity came to Paris

and London, and you're still delighted that electricity is coming here . . . I don't understand you at all, I don't understand
my father either, why do you stay here? Why don't you settle
in Paris? The minute Mihrişah Sultan's decree of exile ends
I'm going back. I'm not going to wait here for electricity to
come, I'll go where there's already electricity . . . I don't know
how you can't understand something so logical."

"Tevfik's job is here."

"Let him not work, does he have to work? Do you need
money?"

"If I didn't work I'd get bored," said Tevfik Bey, "I'm used
to working . . . I think it's essential for a person to work, to see
the results . . ."

"The result is darkness," said Nizam in a mocking tone,
"you work and you work but there's no electricity. I'd rather be
lazy in the light than work in darkness."

"You'd prefer to be lazy everywhere," said Rukiye.

"Don't say that, sometimes I have fun until morning, is that
easy work? You're very hard-working but you can't have fun
until morning. You lie down and go to sleep because you're
lazy . . . And what was that Spanish proverb we memorized as
children: working is a waste of people's valuable time. I'm not
going to waste my valuable time."

"If you keep going this way you'll become the philosopher
of laziness."

"The food is delicious as always," said Nizam. "Where did
you find this cook?"

"Mihrişah Sultan found her."

For a time they talked about this woman they admired, they
talked about her beauty, her decisiveness, and her intelligence,
as always, Nizam imitated his grandmother, "Zeus' wife," he
said, "the goddess Hera," Rukiye played along with him, "I'm
sure she's still living on Olympus." "No one can bring her
down from there, should she wander among these miserable

people." As they spoke their voices were full of love and admiration for Sultan, at one point Rukiye said, "She never once treated me differently from her natural grandson," and Nizam immediately chimed in.

"What do you mean, she always treated you much better."

"Ingrate," said Rukiye with a laugh, "she bent over backwards for you . . . Do you remember how she brought a teacher from Japan so you could learn stick fighting?"

Nizam let out a laugh.

"Then later she wanted to send the man back the same day because he was so short . . . They had trouble talking her out of it because he was a great master."

As they talked in the freedom of youth like small, happy sparrows hopping from branch to branch, they ate with appetite.

Tevfik Bey was laughing and enjoying himself with them, but from the way he got lost in thought from time to time it was clear that his mind was preoccupied.

"Tevfik, you're very quiet, is anything wrong?" asked Rukiye.

"No, Rukiye dear, a council is going to meet about this treaty and I was thinking about that . . . The conditions of this treaty are very harsh. Let's see what they have to say about it at the council."

For a moment Rukiye feared that Nizam would make fun of Tavfik Bey's pensiveness and of the military defeat, she knew how upset Tevfik Bey was about the military defeat, if Nizam made fun of him he would be even more upset, but Nizam didn't say anything.

"Could something bad happen," asked Rukiye, "are you worried the outcome could be bad?"

Tevfik Bey, suddenly thinking that giving the conversation such a serious turn wasn't very polite, said, "Let's not talk about these things now, in any event I'm going to be hearing so much talk about this that there's no point in starting now."

Then to change the subject he said,

"Before you brought that up I was going to ask, you like light, you don't like dim places, but you always talk about the dim, shady garden at the *tekke* as a peaceful place . . . If the *tekke* garden was well-lit, wouldn't it be a more peaceful place for you?"

Rukiye didn't answer right away.

"That's different," she said.

Nizam laughed.

"Saying that's different is the same as saying you have no idea in the world what the answer is."

"I know."

"Say it, then."

"That place isn't part of this world, at least that's how I feel, the whole feeling there is different from the feeling outside, when you enter the *tekke* you feel as if you've entered a different realm. That garden is part of an unseen power, that's why shade suits that garden better than light."

"Would that invisible power be invisible in the light?"

"You know that's not what I'm saying, Nizam."

"I think you'd like that *tekke* no matter what it was like. I don't think it has to do with the *tekke* itself but with your father the Sheikh."

"One day I'll take you there, you can see for yourself."

Nizam asked in amazement,

"You're going to take me to the *tekke*?"

"Why not?"

"Rukiye dear, if I heard any talk about invisible powers I'd burst out laughing."

"You can't laugh at my father the Sheikh."

"Why not?"

"You've never met my father, have you?"

"No."

"I'm definitely going to introduce you one day . . . Don't

forget that our goddess Hera, Mihrişah Sultan, who looks down on the world, sat at Sheikh Efendi's feet like a little girl. Indeed if you ask me she fell in love with my father."

"Really? Mihrişah Sultan fell in love with someone other than herself?"

"That's what I felt."

"Look, I trust your feelings, if that's what you felt I believe you . . . But I'm suddenly surprised . . . It would never have occurred to me . . ."

Nizam thought for a moment.

"Sometimes I want to be able to see the entirety of life . . . Like how when you look at Paris from the Eiffel Tower you see the whole of the city, I'd like to look at life from a place like that, to see everything that was going on."

Rukiye laughed.

"Read a novel . . . That's the only place you can see the entirety of life the way you want. Literature is life's Eiffel Tower . . . When you climb up there, you can watch the whole of life, you can see all of the people, all of the streets, all of the houses. If you ask me there's no other place from which you can see all of life."

Tevfik Bey, guessing how Rukiye would react, assumed a very serious expression as he spoke.

"But don't people seem a bit small when you see them from the Eiffel Tower?"

"Bravo Tevfik," said Nizam, "a little more of that and I would have started reading novels again."

"That's why they put binoculars there, my dear Tevfik and my dear Nizam . . . You can see the entire city, and you can use the binoculars if you want to look at something more closely . . . I should get you to start reading novels again. See life, see people, see the entire city, see individual houses, individual people . . ."

Rukiye suddenly became serious.

"In fact wouldn't it be frightening to see all of life at the same moment?"

"Do you get frightened when you read a novel?" asked Nizam.

"Sometimes . . ."

"So in fact you're afraid of life . . ."

"Sometimes . . ."

"Rukiye, you're not afraid of anything," said Tevfik Bey, "I've never seen you afraid, why are you suddenly talking about being afraid? The goddess Hera's step-granddaughter, didn't you kidnap me by daylight with your promise to marry me?"

"I don't know, wouldn't being able to see everything that's happening at once be like being able to see destiny? Destiny needs time to get prepared, it takes a piece from here and a piece from there as if it was building a bird's nest, shaping life the way it wants to . . . The structure of life, to witness its construction from moment to moment, to watch that preparation . . . A word spoken here, an action there, a fight over there, to watch all of these being gathered together in preparation for a completely different outcome without being able to prevent what's going to happen . . . I don't know, it suddenly seemed frightening to me. I can't decide whether or not I'd want that."

Rukiye turned to Nizam.

"So, would you like to see destiny's preparations?"

"I would."

"Why?"

"At least I'd know what was going to happen to me and why . . . I would have experienced the luxury of not being surprised . . . And I already know my destiny for the long term."

"What destiny is that?"

"A hundred years from now, no one who's alive today will be in the world . . . Not just people, except for a few species, no animals will be alive, the trees will die too . . . I always say that people take life far too seriously, it's not something to be taken seriously. In the end what they call life is a miserable imposter that conceals its own simple truths through constant repetition. It presents itself as more important than reality. It's no different from a swindler. And we're the swindler's victims . . . We keep getting tricked."

"So what are we to do?"

"Don't take life seriously and have fun until morning."

"You mean we should be like you."

"Yes . . . I think I'm the most authentic . . . I know that life is an imposter, I'm not being tricked, I don't get surprised, in fact life is nothing, and I live in accord with it by not being anything."

Rukiye laughed.

"What ideas, my master."

"I've found the truth," said Nizam with a laugh. "People who haven't should think about it, people who go to work every morning . . ."

This time Rukiye turned to Tevfik Bey.

"Our master has solved the mystery of life, so would you like to be able to see destiny's preparations?"

"No," said Tevfik Bey in a very certain tone.

"Why?"

"I believe that there's a logic to life, if it conceals the future from me it's not just doing this to make itself seem important, it's doing so to protect me from being terrified . . . To live being able to see what's coming and not being able to do anything about it would make a person a miserable victim."

"So what kind of victim does not being able to see make you?" asked Nizam.

"An innocent victim."

"That's like asking for a blindfold when you're facing the firing squad."

"Yes."

"I would never wear a blindfold."

Tevfik Bey looked at Rukiye.

"So, have you made your decision, do you want to see or would you rather not see?"

"I've made my decision . . . I'd like to be able to see and to intervene."

Nizam shouted in French as he used to do when they were playing as children.

"*Tricheur . . .*"

Then he continued.

"Cheater . . . That's cheating . . . You had two choices and you made up a third . . ."

"Why is it cheating to add a third impossible choice to two other impossible choices?"

"Demagogue."

"Do you know any other insulting words, *mon petit*?"

"Do you remember what I would do to you when you did something like this to me when we were children?"

"Yes, you'd jump on me like a little horse and knock me to the ground."

On that snowy winter night in the light of hundreds of red-tongued candle flames they made fun of themselves and of life with all of the frivolity of youth, at the very time they were occasionally frightened by what they'd said and laughing at what they'd said, the leading members of the Committee for Union and Progress were meeting at Emin Bey's house in Vefa to decide on a date for the coup.

These large-bodied, frowning men, some in uniform and some in frockcoats, were having trouble deciding when they were going to stage their "coup." Talat Bey and the organization's gunmen were in favor of getting into action at once, the others wanted a plan to be made, for everyone's duties to be made clear, and to proceed in an orderly manner. In fact there was a hesitance among those who wanted a "plan," their heads would roll if they didn't succeed.

Those who defended staging the coup immediately wanted Enver Bey to arrive as soon as possible, they knew his courage and decisiveness would sway the entire group.

Talat Bey said softly to Adapazarlı Mümtaz Bey, who was very close to Enver Bey,

"Where is Enver Bey, if he doesn't come right away we're going to leave here tonight without having reached a decision."

"He said he was going to come, he'll be here soon."

At that moment Enver Bey, for whom they were waiting impatiently, was not far away in a house in the dark and labyrinthine streets of Kocamustafapaşa. He was trying to learn about the future from a fortune-teller named Hadiye who everyone called "Hodja Hanım." Enver Bey, who had strong superstitious beliefs, had great faith in "Hodja Hanım," he always wanted to have his fortune read by her before any major event.

Hodja Hanım, a short, stocky woman, had known what Enver wanted and expected from the future from the day she met him, she'd grasped that he needed a reliable foundation for his courage and adventurousness. She always encouraged Enver Bey in all matters.

That night Enver Bey had asked the fortune teller,

"Hodja Hanım, if I undertake a hazardous exploit for the sake of the nation, will I be successful? Should I undertake an exploit like this? What does the future show us?"

"Let's look and see, my lion," said Hodja Hanım.

She filled a copper bowl with water and placed it on the table between them. She put her finger in the water, smeared it on Enver Bey's forehead, then she stirred the water with the same finger and started looking at the ripples on the surface. The ripples on the surface of the water glowed in the light of a small lamp on a console nearby.

"There's good news, my lion, I can see great successes . . . Move forward, don't hesitate at all . . . All of the doors before you will open, you will dominate the world. You'll be commander of the armies, the day will come when you wear the crown of sovereignty . . . You were created to be a great conqueror, your fortune is as bright as daylight, none of your enemies will remain standing, people will carry you on their shoulders."

Enver Bey left Hodja Hanım's house with dreams of being a great ruler, the courage he'd already possessed since birth had been sharpened, the "good news" of great success had strengthened the confidence he already had, he wanted to get into action as soon as possible.

When Enver Bey arrived, the meeting was becoming disorderly, despite all of Talat Bey's efforts, the insistence and decisiveness of those who wanted to delay the coup had led to a serious slackness, everyone was talking among themselves, the meeting had lost the seriousness of its aim.

When Enver Bey opened the door and came in, everyone suddenly revived and pulled themselves together, this young and ambitious officer was still only thirty-two years old but his courage, adventurousness and sternness affected a number of the men in the room who were older than him, indeed he frightened them.

Even though he was a small, narrow-shouldered man he always stood perfectly straight, even when he was sitting he didn't let himself go, his moustache, which was twirled upwards, seemed too large for his handsome face and his eyes carried both arrogance and melancholy, perhaps on his own he would not have been so impressive, but when his legendary bravery was combined with his decisiveness and adventurousness he was able to dominate everyone around him.

Talat Bey's face lit up when he saw Enver Bey.

"Where have you been, we've been waiting for you."

"There was something important I had to do, I was obliged to take care of it . . . Have you reached a decision?"

There was silence in the room.

"We haven't been able to reach a decision," said Talat Bey, "some of our friends have some worries about staging the coup right away. They propose waiting. They propose making long and detailed preparations . . . I say that the agreements this government has made have ruined the Ottoman Empire, and that we need to intervene no matter what happens . . . When you arrived we were still discussing this."

As he listened, Enver Bey's face darkened and he frowned.

Everyone in the room had fallen silent, they were waiting curiously for what Enver Bey would say.

"I'm astounded by what I'm hearing," Enver Bey said, "We all know and trust each other and we all put the interests of the nation before everything. But now I'm hearing you don't find it right to interfere with this government, everyone has given a reason, I don't know the reasons you put forward . . . There's just one thing I'd like to ask everyone, if you believe that this government will save the future of the nation then there's no problem. Let us not meet here to gossip needlessly, let us disperse and go about our business. If we do not believe that this government will save the future of the nation, let us not get lost in theoretical arguments and remain indecisive. Let us find a solution immediately and overthrow the government."

Everyone at the meeting spoke at almost the same time.

"No, by no means do we trust this government," they said.

Enver looked each person in the face.

"Then what are we waiting for . . . Let's get into action tomorrow at the latest."

When they heard the words "tomorrow at the latest" the people in the room once again became hesitant.

Emin Bey said, "Let's do what has to be done, Enver Bey, but who's going to do it? Who is going to overthrow the government?"

Enver Bey stood up.

"I'll do it . . . With sixty self-sacrificing comrades by my side, I can achieve a fruitful result and overthrow the government . . . There's no need for anything more . . . Now we'll get into action immediately, we'll go to our friends' homes and invite them to take part, Kara Kemal Bey will undertake that, someone can find me a good horse, I'll get on that horse and go to Bab-I Ali and overthrow the government."

"Can you do it?"

"I can do it . . . All I need is for all of the comrades to be convinced that there's an urgent need for this and not be hesitant."

There was silence. Adapazarlı Mümtaz Bey suddenly spoke in a loud voice.

"Friends, there's nothing to fear, nothing to keep quiet about, nothing to be hesitant about . . . We're talking about doing something good here . . . If necessary lives will be given, one life isn't something to be afraid about."

Talat Bey feared that the people in the room might get angry.

"There are no cowards among us, Mumtaz Bey, no on here is afraid, our friends just want to examine all of the particulars in detail but we don't have that much time . . . I think we should make a decision and get into action without dragging it out any further."

Cemal Bey asked the most important question.

"What are we going to do about the troops that are guarding Bab-I Ali? It won't be possible to get past them with only sixty men."

Hacı Adil Bey asked,

"Which battalion is stationed there?"

Everyone looked at Enver Bey but Cevat Bey answered the question.

"The Uşak battalion . . . The commander is a friend of ours . . . If we make a decision I'll go and speak with him right away. As far as I know, he would fully support a patriotic endeavor such as this."

"Then go and see him right away," said Talat Bey, "you can fill me in on the details later . . . If he doesn't agree we'll think of another solution."

The time to decide was approaching, their willingness and their hesitation increased to the same measure, they were dazzled by the possibility of taking over the administration of a vast empire, but the dangers of going into action with so little preparation made them think.

Enver Bey, sensing that if this thinking went on too long they would begin discussing delaying the coup, rose to his feet.

"Friends, this is a matter of national importance, what more is there to think about . . . We'll give our lives if necessary but we can't sit here and do nothing to save our nation. This is not the place or time for delaying and foot dragging . . . Let's make a decision immediately. If anyone is frightened or hesitant they can withdraw, the rest of us will carry on . . . Is there anyone who wants to withdraw, if there is they should leave now."

No one said anything.

"Then the decision is made," said Enver Bey, "We're overthrowing this government, now let's start preparing right away . . . Let's save the Ottoman Empire from the abominable situation they've dragged it into."

Talat Bey said, "Let's start dividing up the duties, let's decide who's going to go talk to which comrades . . . Alright friends?"

"Alright."

This was how the decision was reached to stage a coup that would lead to change and upheaval not only in the Ottoman Empire but throughout the world and that would start a chain of developments that would affect the Middle East for the next hundred years.

Those who had attended the meeting left the house silently and dispersed into the city to carry out their duties.

24

D espite Rukiye's insistence, Nizam didn't stay at the waterfront mansion that night, without paying attention to the fierce north wind that was blowing down from the Black Sea, he crossed to the far shore in the dark of night in a launch that bobbed up and down on the waves.

He went to see Anya every day without fail, there was no need to make a decision to go, when the hour came he would set out like an animal instinctively returning to its den. There were no clear ideas about Anya in his mind, "At the time I didn't realize how dangerous it is to not think at all about a woman you go see every day," he said to Osman, "of course I didn't realize that she'd become so much a part of me that there was no need to think about her."

The love between these two strange people was developing through their indifference and their certainty that they wouldn't fall in love. Without thinking, and imprisoning their feelings in a darkness where they couldn't see them, they opened a boundless field in which their love could develop, each day this emptiness was filled with a slightly strengthened attachment. Their belief that they could change their minds at any moment acted like a silent guide leading them along paths that would bring them to a place where they could never give each other up.

With their fear of becoming attached to anyone and of allowing anyone into their lives, the certainty they felt that nothing like that would ever happen was like the darkness at the point where two lights collide with the same force, they were nearly imprisoned within a blindness where they couldn't see what was happening.

They didn't know what they were feeling and experiencing in those days, because they didn't encounter any obstacles or doubts that would force them to think or feel, they flowed towards each other without uneasiness and without any warning about how what they were experiencing was changing.

"People set traps for themselves and then fall into those traps," said Nizam with a maturity that surprised Osman; their minds really were setting traps for them. Like all people, their denial of their feelings for another person, of the need they felt for a warmth that had its source in the soul rather than in the body, didn't destroy this need. These two people's minds were bringing them towards the "promised" land that would satisfy this need without letting them notice, without their suspecting, appeasing them with quietness, with the magnificent calm that prevented them from turning to look at their own feelings. The confidence this quiet gave them was the bait for the trap their minds had set for them.

They were so convinced that they weren't obliged to make a decision that they didn't experience any indecisiveness when they approached each other. Their love didn't go through the indecisive phase, they didn't go down any of those great waterfalls, they flowed towards each other like calm streams. They didn't try to learn each other's secrets, they didn't follow the traces of each other's thoughts and feelings like hunters. They accepted each other as they were, with pasts full of uncertainty and futures full of uncertainty.

Once Nizam asked,

"You're never going to tell me, are you?"

"No."

"Why?"

Anya stared at the wall and didn't say anything, Nizam

thought she wouldn't answer, but he heard her speaking as if she was talking to herself,

"The woman who could have told anyone about it is dead . . . As for me, I don't know anything."

There were no great gestures in the development of their love, they increased their attachment to each other with very small, very little, almost unnoticeable gestures and facial expressions. The way Anya smiled slightly, how Nizam slowly embraced her after making love, how he left her house a few minutes later each time, the way Anya gently put her arm through his as they walked to the carriage, the way they snuggled against each other a bit more in the carriage . . . These little gestures bound them closer to each other, like two animals in a vast emptiness becoming accustomed to each other's smell and warmth.

When the carriage turned on to the gambling den road late that night, Nizam had the feeling that he'd arrived in a familiar land, the crackling curls of the flames that flickered in the wind now reminded him of Anya, of her weary smile and of the notes that drifted from her piano.

There were a few people talking in the lower room, as always Anya was playing with her flawless technique without even glancing around. Nizam was uncomfortable with Anya working in a gambling den, he thought it was very unfair to her, he was uncomfortable when other people spoke of her in a condescending manner, once he'd asked Anya, "Would you like to stop playing the piano at the gambling den?"

"No," said Anya in a completely flat tone.

"Why not, you're not that kind of pianist."

"I don't want to."

"You could even give concerts in Paris."

"I don't want to."

Nizam smiled at the way she answered like a stubborn and willful child.

"What do you want, then?"

"Nothing."

"Nothing isn't something you can want."

Anya shook her head.

"Sometimes nothing is a great luxury . . ."

Then she sighed and said,

"But I don't want you to ever have to learn this truth."

The tone of her voice when she said this was less that of a lover, of someone who was in love, of someone being flirtatious than it was motherly, like that of a mother who was worried about her son.

Nizam never brought the subject up again, he'd told her to stop working at the gambling den. To say it again would mean that he "expected" this of her, whereas they never expected anything of each other, if they asked for anything they would be obliged to give something, they knew that to want anything would be to give something, and neither of them were willing to give anything of themselves or their lives.

The road that was bringing them together was woven from their endless acceptance of each other's lives and decisions, the confidence they felt that they would not have to give anything or give up anything was what brought them closer.

Nizam looked at the people in the room, they weren't even aware of how extraordinary Anya's playing was, they were talking loosely and laughing from time to time. As Nizam was entering the room he saw Madame Cheriz coming down the stairs, the woman saw him and smiled.

"How are you Monsieur Nizam?"

"*Merci Madame* . . . How are you? You're leaving the game early tonight."

"I'm not leaving, I'm just taking a break. My luck isn't so good tonight, I thought I'd go downstairs and smoke a cigarette, maybe my luck will change . . . We don't see each other very often."

"Yes, you're right."

Madame Cheriz looked over at Anya.

"I heard you have new friends."

Nizam looked at the woman, "The curiosity these provincial people have," he thought to himself, they want to find out everything they can about the people they know, instead of answering he just smiled.

"Come to dinner some evening," said Madame Cheriz. "My family has sent me some very good wine."

"I'd love to,"

He saw Anya move her head slightly and glance towards the door, it was as if she'd sensed his arrival, he'd never seen any sign of jealousy, complaint or hurt feelings in Anya, but for whatever reason it made him uneasy for her to see him speaking to another woman, he was surprised by his uneasiness, this too was a feeling he was not accustomed to.

Just then, Kamil Bey also came down the stairs.

"What happened, I suppose the game is boring tonight, everyone's coming downstairs."

Kamil Bey nodded his head.

"The game is fine, it's just that they cleaned me out."

"Do you want a loan?"

"No, my good man, thank you, I'm being clever today, I've lost my allowance for the day, I don't want any more than that."

Then Kamil Bey turned to Madame Cheriz.

"Did you lose too?"

"Not yet, I came down for a cigarette in the hope that my luck would change."

"I'm so unlucky tonight," said Kamil Bey, "that if I ran around the woods five times my luck still wouldn't straighten out . . . What is this thing they call luck, I truly wonder about this on the nights when I lose, why do I get good cards on some evenings and bad cards on other evenings? Why to me and not the person next to me? Is it the same way in life? Are we lucky on some days and unlucky on others?"

He laughed and looked at Nizam.

"Don't you think that unlucky gamblers can make good philosophers? I've never heard a gambler who has won speak in a meaningful manner, but gamblers who lose always have some very interesting questions about life."

"Losers always ask," said Madame Cheriz, "They want to know why they lost . . . People who win never wonder why they won. Why should they. They've won, after all."

As he listened to them, Nizam was watching Anya out of the corner of his eye as he listened to them, she was sitting perfectly straight and playing as always, she didn't turn her head to look again.

"This whole business of luck nags at me . . . Sometimes I think, do you know, the people who tell me to stop gambling, I think their lives are a gamble . . . Tell me, my good man, can anything that contains an element of chance become gambling? Doesn't luck play a very important role in life? So? What makes it different from gambling . . . You have the freedom to play your cards any way you want, but you don't know what cards you're going to get, isn't life also like that, you have no idea how luck is going to treat you . . . What people call life is a game of chance that you play with the cards luck deals you."

Kamil Bey laughed and lit a cigarette.

"The more I talk to you the more convinced I am that what I'm saying is true. There's a very strong influence on me, my good man . . . I wonder if I should tell my father about this, tell him that in fact we're doing the same thing in different ways, I wonder if he'd respond in a mature manner or whether, in a twist of luck, I would become a child who was shot by his father."

Madame Cheriz laughed.

"I don't think you should tell your father, fathers don't understand these things . . . But I have to say that I think you're right. Whatever the game you're playing is called, if it has an element of luck in it it's gambling. If we look at it that way, those who play the game of life best are gamblers. The ones who make the best guesses about how the cards will be dealt and which cards will come and who bluff the best are the ones who win . . . What do you say, Monsieur Nizam?"

"Whatever the game you're playing is called, if there's an element of luck you're going to lose."

"That's a very pessimistic view, isn't it?"

"I'm a liar to those who say that the gambling den always wins. *madame* . . ."

In a joking rush, Madame Cheriz said,

"Wait a minute, wait a minute, I'm confused . . . Who is the gambling den in this philosophical metaphor?"

"Whoever deals the cards, whoever makes the luck . . ."

"Who makes luck, Monsieur Kamil?" asked Madame Cheriz looking at Kamil Bey.

"Ah, *cher madame*, if I knew who made it I would like to have a private word with him. I have one or two small complaints about his gambling den . . ."

When the sound of the piano stopped just then Nizam turned at once to look into the room, he saw Anya get up and walk over to the window. Madame Cheriz noticed where he'd looked, and with the elegance that French women love to carry and think suits them so well, said:

"I'm going back upstairs now, I'm sure that all of this philosophical talk has changed my luck . . . Don't forget the wine, Monsieur Nizam."

"Of course, madame, how could I forget . . ."

Madame Cheriz tapped Nizam's hand with her fingertips and headed for the stairs.

"I should get going too," said Kamil Bey, "let me go and

read the life of Socrates one more time, let me understand what happens to philosophers . . . Good night, Nizam Bey, and good luck to you."

It bothered Nizam that people knew about his relationship with Anya, people treating him like "a young man in love" and showing him understanding, he was bothered by the very idea that he was having a "love affair" with a woman who played the piano in a gambling den. He didn't want to be seen this way or treated this way . . . He always thought that there was something pitifully, indeed tragically ridiculous about love, he looked down on people who were in love. If he'd been asked why he thought this he wouldn't have been able to explain, but he was aware of his desire to be a person that no person or emotion dominated. Since childhood, the idea of being a person who everyone admired but who didn't admire anyone had always appealed to him; "I don't know," he said to Osman, "perhaps I was influenced by Mihrişah Sultan, everyone was in love with her but she wasn't in love with anyone, if she'd fallen in love with someone I don't think it would have suited her, it would have made her ridiculous . . . I suppose there are people whom being in love suits . . . But there are people it doesn't suit . . . It wouldn't have suited Mihrişah Sultan for instance . . . On the other hand being in love suited my father, but you know what happened to him. He allowed his wife to run off with a ne'er-do-well and he shot himself. Which would you rather be, Mihrişah Sultan or Hikmet Bey?"

During the brief moment he'd glanced at Anya a number of thoughts collided, broke pieces off of each other and shaped each other as they wandered through his mind; at first he thought of leaving at once, then it occurred to him to go upstairs and gamble without saying hello to Anya, he was disturbed by the idea that people thought he was in love with "a woman who plays the piano at a gambling den," and he was ashamed that he felt this way, he regretted feeling something that made him ashamed, and he was shaken by a feeling of debt to Anya, he was curious about how their relationship seemed to other people, he imagined people talking about him behind his back, once again he felt the desire to leave and in the end he walked calmly towards the piano.

He didn't know how or why he'd made this decision, he was aware that he was frightened and suspicious of this "thing" that hadn't chosen any of the dozen thoughts wandering through his mind and had decided to do something he hadn't thought of doing.

As he walked towards the piano he felt, perhaps for the first time in his life, the need to ask himself "What's happening?" for the first time he was curious about his feelings, for the first time he felt distressed by the question of whether or not he was fooling himself. In that brief moment his mind, which was never lively when it came to emotions, was bringing these questions to life, but he managed to conceal all of this beneath a shell.

He leaned on the piano and looked at Anya, when she looked up he saw her weary and helpless smile, Nizam was more affected than he would have guessed by the seemingly endless loneliness of this woman who had given up on life before she died.

The dereliction and desolation of a body that doesn't belong in any realm struggling to carry a dead soul . . . This woman, who was equally sick to death of her dead soul and her living body, never complained, never asked for help and mourned her dead alone . . . Nizam felt all of these things while he was looking at her, and he wished, not out of goodness but only to show other people that this was "extraordinary" and for them to grasp that what they were experiencing was not a relationship to be belittled, and at the very least for her to show other people this through the piano, but he didn't say anything.

He just looked at Anya.

"What's up?" asked Anya.

"Nothing."

"What's up?"

Nizam shook his head and didn't say anything.

"Tell me," said Anya.

This was the first time Nizam had seen her insist on anything. In a weak voice, as if he was whispering, he said,

"Play something."

As Anya continued to play the piano she stared straight ahead, and Nizam sensed rather than saw that there were enigmatic shadows playing across her face, like a very old, faded film, moving jerkily, with lines and scratches appearing and disappearing on the surface.

Then Anya raised her head and looked at him, in her eyes Nizam saw the look of someone who was preparing to commit suicide, someone who had already left the world spiritually, someone who had cut herself off and distanced herself from this world and was simply dragging her body behind her. For a moment he was frightened, as Anya was preparing to say "I've changed my mind," she smiled as if she was smiling at someone Nizam couldn't see, then her smile became younger and there was a liveliness in her expression.

She abruptly ended the piece she was playing and started to play the Moonlight Sonata, from the very first notes that liveliness, those emotions gushing from deep within her body, could be felt, she could have been dying or coming back to life, there was a feeling in her playing that evoked both, even the gamblers sitting in the room felt they were encountering something extraordinary and listened in silence for a moment before returning to their conversations.

After she'd played for a while she looked at Nizam with a smile, then she returned to the piece she'd been playing before, the emotional luster in her playing was gone.

All Nizam said was, "Thank you."

When Anya started playing the way she used to play, Nizam realized that he had to leave.

He went to the gambling room upstairs, sat when he was invited to a table and started playing, he was playing in a slap-dash manner, he wasn't keeping track of the cards, he didn't get into exciting skirmishes, he didn't bluff, he didn't raise.

He was bored by gambling, if it hadn't been for Anya he wouldn't have come to the gambling den. Nothing gave him the same excitement for very long, like a handsome bee, he sucked the excitement out of each thing, place or person that could give him excitement, then when he'd had his fill he sought another source of excitement. Sometime later he might have found excitement in gambling again, but for now gambling had lost its attraction, his attention was awake to the entire world, he knew that Anya was playing the piano in the room downstairs, gambling couldn't make him forget that.

He felt strange emotions that surprised him, he thought about how Anya was completely alone downstairs and that this loneliness was an anguish for her, and he was saddened by her loneliness; he somehow couldn't understand why he thought of her as all alone, he grasped that his thoughts and feelings were meaningless, but he still couldn't get rid of those thoughts and feelings, he couldn't get rid of the idea that leaving Anya alone downstairs constituted some kind of betrayal.

His mind, which usually softly swept thoughts and feelings he didn't want into the depths, wasn't helping him, it didn't or couldn't erase these thoughts.

Nizam didn't know what was happening to him, for a while his head began to spin, it was as if he was sliding away from the table, he held on to the edge of the table. His brow was covered in perspiration.

"With your permission," he said, getting up and leaving his cards on the table.

He hurried downstairs, Anya was as he'd left her, playing the piano, her playing was a bit strange, the notes weren't flowing, it was as if they were being dragged, they struggled away from the keys like exhausted centipedes.

He went out in front of the gambling den, the two Africans in tuxedos were standing perfectly still on either side of the door with an extremely serious bearing, their stance made it seem as if they were guarding a temple rather than a gambling den. He descended the five steps and leaned against the marble bannister.

The torches were burning, a faint smell of saltpeter and paraffin spread through the cool smell of trees and snow that wafted from the woods, Nizam felt the cold and lit a cigarette. He was feeling his way like a blind man feeling his way around a room he was accustomed to, he was trying to understand his feelings, these sudden convulsions, he sensed that there were some things "in his room" that he didn't know, but he couldn't see them and wasn't able to name them.

His mind was like a large and well-ordered station, thoughts and feelings arrived from opposite directions, a station master who was able to conceal himself managed to get them through the station without colliding, he would send them someplace that for Nizam was truly unknown, he generally wouldn't feel these contradictions. But now the station was in confusion, the emotions that were coming from opposite directions were crashing noisily, causing great confusion and panic.

The heaviest of these feelings was the strange anguish that was nourished by his belief that Anya was feeling alone and helpless inside. He didn't understand why he felt this way, this feeling had suddenly appeared out of nowhere; knowing that this wasn't real never lessened the anguish, it just made this anguish meaningless and unsettled him.

At the same time it surprised him to feel this confusing fluttering of tenderness, this sadness for a lady pianist he didn't really know anything about, and for this he was angry and looked down on himself.

Perhaps to be seized for the first time by the lure and vortex of anguish rather than excitement was alien to him, Anya's presence and her loneliness brought anguish rather than excitement seeping into him. This didn't prevent him from seeing other truths and beings, on the contrary this led him to see everything including himself more clearly, and he wasn't happy about what he saw.

He started walking pensively down the garden road. From time to time his attention was caught by the flames of the torches and their chemical flickering, he derived a childish joy from watching them. This inexplicable cheer amidst that strange anguish resembled those torches in the darkness, they illuminated and warmed their surroundings, but they made the vast darkness more intense and manifest.

Without thinking about where he was going, he followed the narrow, pebble garden path towards the back, there were no torches here, it was dark and smelled of damp wood and food.

As he was walking in the dark, he saw a shadow in a military coat emerge from a small door in the back of the mansion and walk away.

Soldiers did come to the gambling den, but they came and went by the front door. It was unusual to see an officer leaving secretly by the back door.

Just then he heard a threatening voice behind him.

"Are you looking for something, Nizam Bey?"

He gripped the handle of his cane tightly as he turned around.

He saw Lütfullah Bey standing there, half of his body in the dark and half illuminated by the flickering reflections of the torches. With that fiery light playing across half his face, he looked like a large devil.

Struggling to not allow his irritation to be sensed, he said,

"I was just walking."

"It's dark here, if you like, walk on the torch-lit road, Nizam Bey, it's safer."

As he said this he moved slightly to one side to make way for Nizam, it would have been strange to say "No, I want to walk in the dark," so Nizam had no choice but to walk past Lütfullah Bay towards the front of the mansion.

Lütfullah Bey disappeared as abruptly as he'd appeared.

Nizam didn't think much about his sudden appearance, his threatening tone or the officer he'd seen in the back, his mind was on Anya.

A purple light appeared above the woods and intruded on the darkness of the night, morning was about to break, Nizam wanted all of the customers to leave as soon as possible so he could take Anya away from there; it was as if he would only find the answers to this strangeness and these questions when he was alone with Anya, he was seized by a feeling like this. He made his way under the trees so as not to meet any of the customers, there was snow on the ground, spots of the light from the torches had penetrated the trees and were reflected on the snow, Nizam felt the cold as he walked on the soft, crunching, red-tinged snow. He didn't turn around a look at the carriages that were leaving, he liked being lost among the trees.

When he'd decided that all of the carriages had left, he emerged from the woods, the door of the mansion was open, the Africans had disappeared, he walked slowly into the mansion, he stamped his feet to get the snow off his boots.

When he looked into the room he saw Anya standing by the window smoking a cigarette, she seemed a bit pale, when she saw Nizam she smiled. She looked weary and lonely.

Nizam went over to her.

"Are you well?"

"Yes."

"You look a bit tired."

"I am a bit tired."

"Let's go," said Nizam.

They went out together, Nizam's carriage stood pitch-black in front of the mansion, in the twilight of that dawn, where the darkness of night mixed with the lights of dawn and the cold white of the snow mixed with the flames, it was as if they'd entered a fairy tale. Nizam was seized by the feeling that when they entered the carriage it would fly and bring them to unknown lands.

They got into the carriage, both of them were silent. Anya looked out the window.

As they were nearing the end of the torch-lined road, Anya said something hurriedly in Russian.

"What is it?" asked Nizam.

"Tell him to stop the carriage, tell him to stop the carriage for a minute."

Nizam didn't understand what was going on but he called to the carriage driver to stop.

The carriage stopped. The horses, unhappy about this sudden stop, neighed and shook themselves.

Anya hurriedly opened the door and got out, she lifted the hem of her coat and started running back, Nizam leaned out and watched her go. The sky had become purple, the trees were buried in a deep green shade, the lakes of light at the base of the torches had paled. Anya picked up a bird at the base of a torch that was fluttering and trying to fly, she stroked it, tried to get it to fly, but it couldn't fly.

She returned to the carriage holding the bird in her cupped hands.

"Its wing is broken," she said.

It was the first time Nizam had heard this kind of tenderness in Anya's voice, later he said to Osman, "I suppose it was then that I first thought that she was coming back to life."

The bird she'd found was a small sparrow, you could see its

heart was beating in fear even through the feathers, "It's very frightened," said Anya, she said something in Russian as she stroked the bird and tried to calm it.

"It's very frightened," she repeated.

As she stroked the bird she blew lightly on its wings to try to warm it. There was a very innocent, childlike smile on her face, Nizam thought she wasn't aware that she was smiling.

"How did you see that bird?" he asked.

"I saw its fluttering."

Anya was saying something as she stroked the bird, from the rhythm of her voice Nizam realized she was reciting a poem.

"What are you saying to the bird?"

"I was reciting a poem by Pushkin . . . Poetry will soothe it."

"You really are a Russian . . . Just like the French officer Pierre said in Tolstoy . . . Recite the poem to me too . . . The bird and I can both listen."

"It's difficult to translate . . ."

"Just translate as well as you can."

Anya, stopped, thought, weighed words in her head, perhaps she was trying to remember the French translation, then she began reciting in a voice that Nizam had never heard before, a voice that flowed like shiny ivory keys.

Naught of labor, naught of sorrow
On God's little bird doth rest
And it questions not the morrow,
Builds itself no lasting nest.

She squinted her eyes, stopped and thought, she was trying to find the right words.

On the bough it sleeps and swings
Till the ruddy sun appears,
Then it shakes its wings and sings,

When the voice of God it hears.

After Spring's delightful weather,
When the burning Summer's fled,
And the Autumn brings together
For men's sorrow, for men's dread,

Mists and storms in gloomy legions;
Then the bird across the main
Flies to far-off, southern regions,
Till the Spring returns again.

Then, as if she was embarrassed, she said:
"Something like that."

When they went into the house she threw her coat into a corner and ran in, she took out bandages, she bandaged the bird's wing, she filled a small bowl with water and put it next to the bird, she spoke Russian while she was doing so, sometimes she sounded as if she was reciting a poem and sometimes she sounded as if she was singing, she stroked the bird tenderly.

The bird seemed soothed, it was sitting calmly, it seemed to realize it was safe, Anya gave it some breadcrumbs too, she tilted her head to one side to watch it eat them with its small beak.

Then she went and opened the living room curtains.

The light of the sunny winter morning cheered the room as it filled it, it was as if it increased the warmth of the tiled stove.

She took Nizam by the hand and sat him across from her, she gave him a loving look, then a look of rebuke, and then she smiled.

"You're bringing me back to life," she said, "what's going to happen now?"

"You're going to live," said Nizam with a laugh.

A peaceful shadow fell across Anya's face.

"You don't know how difficult and painful that is, do you?"

"It's not that difficult."

"It is that difficult."

Anya lowered her head and looked at her hands as she thought, she seemed as if she'd forgotten Nizam was there, then she raised her head and looked at Nizam.

"Alright," she said.

Nizam didn't understand what Anya had said.

"Alright what?"

"Alright, I'm going to live, again, I'm going to live again . . . I'll tolerate the pain, you don't know how painful it is for me live, to take part in life again, you can't possibly know, but I'm going to do it, I'm going to do this for you."

She fell silent, then repeated softly.

"I'm going to tolerate the pain of living."

She said it one more time as if she was trying to convince herself of her decisiveness.

"I'm going to tolerate this . . . Perhaps this is what God wants."

Nizam didn't say anything, his instincts grasped that he shouldn't say anything, he sensed that even a small joke could sent Anya back into the darkness from which she was trying to emerge, he looked at Anya almost without moving.

"Are you hungry?" asked Anya.

She stood without waiting for Nizam's answer.

"I'm going to make breakfast for you, let's see what there is to eat in the house."

She went into the kitchen. They were going to have breakfast together for the first time.

Nizam didn't know what to do, he was frightened, he realized that Anya had made an important decision, but he didn't know why it was an important decision, at one point he'd wanted to say, "I didn't ask anything like this of you," but he realized this would be rude and didn't say anything.

He didn't want Anya to change anything in her life for him, he was frightened by the responsibility this placed on him, he felt this clearly. He didn't want any responsibility placed on him, and he didn't want another person to change her life for him, this was too much for him, it amounted to needlessly adding another person's life to his own, it wasn't an emotion he was prepared for. There was another weaker but more pleasant emotion alongside this frightened reluctance, it was the delight brought about by the intimacy of Anya having decided to change her life, that she was doing this for him, and that he was able to experience a woman transforming in front of him. Next to the burning feeling of reluctance and fear, this delight had an uncommon warmth and this warmth rose above the burning of the fear and prevented him from getting up and leaving.

"What did I do for Anya to decide I wanted her to change her life, I never knew that," he said to Osman later, "this remained a mystery for me . . . It's difficult to confess but in fact I wanted to run away that morning, I wonder why I didn't flee, I felt that what Anya had said was very heavy, I felt that it would affect my entire life, but why didn't I flee, why didn't I get up and go while she was making breakfast, I could have gone, I would never have seen her again . . . I've asked this question so many times . . . I might have been too lazy to flee, fleeing always requires strength, I think I just didn't have the strength that morning, I might also not have cared about my feelings, I might not have paid attention to the instincts that were warning me, I might have thought that nothing would happen . . . My mother always said that my self-indulgence would get me into trouble . . . Of course there was also the feeling brought about by seeing such a cold woman who described herself as dead miraculously come to life before my eyes," here Nizam smiled, "I might also have seen myself as someone important like Jesus Christ who could bring the dead back to life . . . Or it may have been the result of witnessing that magnificent transformation, of the tremendous feeling of intimacy and closeness of seeing a life transform in front of you . . . Whatever the reason, the result was that I didn't leave, my decision of that moment changed all of our lives."

Anya had set the breakfast on a small, round table

"I've lit the samovar too," she said, "try some Russian tea, see if it's anything like yours."

They ate their breakfast without talking too much.

Towards the middle of breakfast, Anya said, as if she'd sensed Nizam's fear,

"My returning to life doesn't place any responsibility on you, I'm the one who's making this decision. You mustn't feel responsible for me or for my decision . . . This would be very humiliating for both of us."

"I won't feel responsible," said Nizam.

Then he let out a laugh and repeated the last three lines of the poem Anya had recited.

Then the bird across the main
Flies to far-off, southern regions,
Till the Spring returns again.

Anya looked at him in surprise.

"How were you able to memorize that right away?"

Nizam shrugged his shoulders.

He was looking at the tapestry on the wall, it looked as if it was from the period of Louis XV, a curly-haired, porcelain-skinned fairy in a green forest, she was leaning down with one knee bent and her foot behind her, she was looking at something unseen on the ground; Nizam had seen a similar tapestry in Mihrişah Sultan's dressing room.

When Anya saw what he was looking at she smiled.

"It belonged to my great-great-grandfather."

When Nizam said, "it looks like the tapestries from the

period of Louis XV," Anya was surprised, she looked at him carefully.

When she realized that he knew about tapestries she added,

"It was a gift from the king of France."

This was the first thing Anya had ever said about her past, and now it was Nizam's turn to be surprised.

They were surprising each other, these surprises had the belittling affect brought about by hardly knowing each other at all, knowing nothing about each other's lives or pasts; for Nizam, Anya was a pianist at a gambling den, for Anya, Nizam was a young, wealthy, charming Ottoman gambler.

Now, with only one sentence each, they each realized that the other came from a much different background than they'd supposed, they were looking at each other in surprise and delight like two antiques enthusiasts finding something valuable in a shop that sold junk, they had an air of not believing, of doubting, that they'd found something "valuable" in this "shop." But they'd each realized that the other was "worthy of being curious about," they were examining each other as if they were trying to understand whether the conversation had actually occurred.

"How do you know about Louis XV tapestries?" Anya asked, "are you an antique dealer?"

Nizam let out a real belly laugh.

"God, look at the arrogance in that question," he said.

Then, with the confidence of realizing that Anya came from a completely different background and that she would never be wounded by a joke like this, he added,

"A pianist at a gambling den is asking me how I know about tapestries."

"Really, how do you know?"

"Do you think it's very important to know this?"

"To recognize a Louis XV tapestry at a glance, eh, that's not bad . . . How do you know it's not a tapestry from the Le Brun period?"

Nizam let out another laugh.

"My grandmother would have killed me if I'd mistaken a Louis XV tapestry for a Le Brun tapestry . . . Le Brun tapestries are hung in the reading room, Louis XV tapestries are hung in the dressing room."

"What next?" said Anya with a laugh, "You're making this up . . ."

"So who was your great-grandfather anyway? How did he know the king?"

Anya suddenly fell quiet, a shadow fell across her face, she had an expression of regret that resembled the regret of having gone too far.

"Perhaps some other time," she said in a pensive tone.

They drank their tea in silence.

Then Anya rose to her feet and took Nizam's hand.

"Come."

There was a confidence and authority in her voice that Nizam had never heard before, the softness of a woman's promising desire could be felt in that voice. Nizam's sensitive ears immediately noticed how many intonations had been concentrated in a single word, all of these voices could only take shelter in such a short word when an accumulation of knowledge and experience was filtered through hundreds of years of tradition.

They went inside together.

The light of the winter sun seeped past the edges of the curtains to form thin lines on the ceiling of the warm room, in the dimness of the room, the light that forced itself against the curtains from outside made them seem to fill like white sails.

Anya started to undress calmly, Nizam watched her, she'd lost the air of inexperience she'd had before, her hands were undoing her buttons as if they were dancing, her fingers had the experienced agility of a secret joy, with every article of clothing she removed he could see Anya change, she was like a water lily moving on the surface of a stagnant pond.

In bed, Nizam left himself to Anya, he sensed that there would be magic, that another woman would emerge from beneath the soft curves of the woman next to him.

That woman emerged.

Nizam learned what it was like to make love to a Russian aristocrat. He'd been with many women, women from all classes and of all nationalities, but none of them were like this.

It was like long winter nights on the Russian steppes; the snow falls gently with a soft whisper, windstorms tear at roofs, windows and moldings, the howls of wild animals can be heard, the windchimes in front of the doors of isolated winter mansions tinkle, large ovens and fireplaces roar inside the mansions, the snow is beginning to form drifts, the world disappears behind and vast, bright whiteness that is besieged by the blackness of the night.

"I went through a door from which there was no return," Nizam said to Osman later, "and I didn't want to return."

25

On January 23rd, 1913, the history of the Ottoman Empire and of the world was inalterably changed within half an hour by five people who drew their revolvers.

A cold rain was falling that morning.

The inhabitants of the city whose streets were deserted and that was being oppressed by an iron-colored sky were hiding in blackened wooden houses and government offices with dirty walls.

On Bab-ı Ali hill, which was usually crowded, there was no one to be seen except a few people walking quickly.

Only the *gazino* directly across from Bab-ı Ali and the coffee houses of Sirkeci had more customers than usual, nobody noticed these crowds playing backgammon, checkers and cards in these coffee houses that smelled of waterpipe tobacco and wet cloth, they seemed like people who had sheltered there temporarily from the rain.

Chief Inspector Mirilay Cemal Bey's office in the General Inspectorate Building just across from the Committee for Union and Progress building in Nuruosmaniye was crowded. Talat Bey, Enver Bey, Major Halil Bey, Mümtaz Bey, Hilmi Bey, Sapancalı Hakkı Bey, and Cevat Bey were chain smoking in irritable silence. The excitement could be felt when one of them occasionally took a deep breath or cleared his throat.

The time to move into action was approaching, but the

sixty volunteers Enver Bey had been expecting were nowhere to be seen. Talat Bey turned to Sapancalı Hakkı Bey and said, "Hakkı, come, let's go take a look around."

A little later, two members of the group that was preparing to overthrow the government of the Ottoman Empire pulled up the collars of their coats and opened their umbrellas, they passed the Cağaloğlu Pharmacy and started walking downhill, they glanced into the *gazino* across from Bab-ı Ali, they saw that there weren't too many of the men they'd been expecting, they moved on to the Meserret Coffeehouse, there too there were fewer men than they'd hoped for, then they took a look at the other coffeehouses in Sirkeci.

Hakkı Bey said in an irritated tone,

"Where are Enver Bey's volunteers, I only saw our civilians at the *gazino*, and there weren't too many of them."

Talat Bey made a face.

"What can we do, if that's the way it is, so be it . . ."

They returned to Bab-ı Ali. The gates were open, occasionally someone entered or left.

"It's time," said Talat Bey, "go tell our comrades to come out. I'll wait here. Here goes . . ."

Hakkı Bey hurried up the hill, struggling as he did so to protect his umbrella from the wind.

He opened Cemal Bey's office door without knocking.

"Come, comrades," he said, "everything is ready, come on out . . ."

From there he ran to the Headquarters building just across the street and called inside to the comrades who were irritably pacing and smoking cigarettes in the entry hall.

"Come on, we're moving out," he said, "be quick, the others are already on the move."

One of them rushed upstairs to tell those who were waiting in the conference room, and they all went out together.

Enver Bey went out with the others, they'd brought a grey

horse for Enver Bey, it was a large animal. It was stamping its front hoof on the pavement, making a strange sound.

Enver Bey said, "In the name of God the compassionate, the merciful," and jumped onto the horse, he took hold of the reins and squared his shoulders, stepped firmly into the stirrups and looked around.

With a disappointment he attempted to conceal, he asked, "Where are the sixty volunteers?"

No one answered, meanwhile the horse began to move, just behind Enver Bey's horse walked Yakup Cemil Bey, Mümtaz Bey, Mustafa Necip Bey, Sapancalı Hakkı Bey, these were the organization's boldest men, Cevat Bey was moving alongside them and behind them came the civilians under Kara Kemal Bey. It was not an impressive crowd.

They came out of the narrow street and turned on to Bab-ı Ali hill, the group paused for a moment between the Iranian Embassy and the Ministry of Public Works, Bab-ı Ali could be seen five hundred paces away. The rain was getting heavier.

A disorderly group of about sixty or seventy people who had received Talat Bey's signal in the coffeehouses were moving up from below.

"Long live the nation . . . Long live the Committee for Union and Progress . . ."

They were shouting to attract passersby and make the crowd seem larger. There was something about the scene that was reminiscent of enthusiastic market vendors trying to attract customers, they repeated the same words over and over.

"Honorable Ottomans . . . Honorable citizens . . . Saintly comrades . . . My soldier brothers . . . Long live the nation . . . Long live the Committee for Union and Progress . . ."

Passing young students, hodjas in turbans, officials in frock coats, toughs with the backs of their shoes pressed down gathered around to look at this strange man, as he moved on they began to follow him. A strange crowd had gathered around Enver Bey's horse.

They were on their way to overthrow the government of the Ottoman Empire and to take over the administration of the empire.

Enver Bey was still looking around carefully for the volunteers who were supposed to have come. From time to time one of the horse's shoes would slip on the wet pavement, Enver Bey was pulling the reins to keep his horse from sliding.

Ömer Naci Bey was walking in front of the group shouting excitedly.

As they approached Bab-ı Ali he became so excited by his own shouting that he started to foam at the mouth, fainted and fell flat onto the pavement.

They put him in a passing carriage.

In the garden of the prime ministry, the men of the Uşak Redif battalion who had been assigned to guard the grand vizier's office were sitting with their rifles stacked in front of them, they stood when they saw the crowd, if they'd wanted they could have gathered everyone up and taken them away, but the men didn't move, they just watched the crowd. The commander was nowhere to be seen.

The gates to the prime ministry garden were open, Enver Bey and his companions felt a moment's hesitation when they saw the soldiers looking at them but after that there was no turning back, Enver Bey jumped off his horse.

"Come on," he said.

Enver Bey, Yakup Cemil Bey, Mustafa Necip Bey, Hilmi Bey and Hakkı Bey ran into the garden and rushed up Bab-ı Ali's broad marble steps. Seeing that there were so few of them, Cevat Bey ran after them.

Meanwhile, Monsieur Lausanne was in Foreign Minister Noradikyan Efendi's waiting room, waiting for the foreign minister to finish his meeting with the Austrian Ambassador and drinking the coffee he'd been offered and to which he'd become quite accustomed out of a tiny porcelain cup.

The Grand Vizier Kamil Pasha was in his office with the Palace Chief Clerk Ali Fuat Bey, as the pasha was reading a telegram, the chief clerk heard the noise in the street and went to look out the window and saw the strange crowd that had gathered outside the prime ministry.

"Was there a rally scheduled for today, your excellency?" he asked.

Kamil Pasha answered without looking up from the telegram he was reading.

"No, there was nothing like that," he said

When Enver Bey and his comrades entered the prime ministry's large entrance hall, they ignored the two or three janitors standing there. When they entered the corridor that led to the grand vizier's office, they encountered two armed sentries. One or two of the janitors rushed forward. One of them blocked their way.

"Where are you going? This is off limits."

Hakkı Bey shouted, "Get out of our way, move back."

When the armed sentries saw Enver Bey's uniform they snapped to attention and the janitors retreated.

They went down the corridor and entered the large hall, there they came across a chief inspector, when he saw the armed men he immediately pulled out his weapon, "Stop," he said, "who are you, where are you going?"

Without even answering, Mustafa Necip aimed his gun and fired, the chief inspector was hit and as he fell to the ground he made a last effort, aimed his gun and shot Mustafa Necip in the heart, when Nazım Pasha's aide Nazif Bey and Tevfik Bey, who happened to be with him, heard the gunshots, came out into the hall and saw the guns and the chief inspector on the floor, Nazif Bey immediately pulled out his gun, but Yakup Cemil Bey shot Nazif Bey in the forehead with a single bullet. Tevfik

Bey was looking on in terror, he was holding a file he'd been bringing to the grand vizier, he wasn't armed but Yakup Cemil turned and fired at him too. The bullet entered Tevfik Bey's throat.

As Tevfik Bey tried to ask "Why?" his throat filled with blood, he collapsed on the spot and the papers he'd been holding were scattered about.

Those who'd come to the prime ministry building with Enver Bey had taken control of the gate and weren't letting anyone in, Talat Bey, Mithat Şükrü Bey, and Cevat Bey were waiting in the building's large entry hall.

Enver Bey jumped over the four dead bodies on the floor and headed for the grand vizier's office. The guards and the janitors had disappeared, everyone hid when they heard the gunfire.

He quickly opened the padded door, and he and Hakkı Bey entered the grand vizier's office, seventy-five-year-old Kamil Pasha looked at the young major who'd entered brandishing a gun.

"Your Excellency, the people don't want you, write your letter of resignation immediately," said Enver Bey.

Kamil Pasha remained perfectly calm. He gestured to the armchair in front of his desk.

"Fine, I'll write it, please sit down."

Enver Bey was not in the mood to sit, he didn't have time to sit, he shouted in a harsher tone,

"Write it, sir, write it quickly, this is no time to be sitting."

Kamil Pasha went completely white when faced with this rudeness, without saying anything he reached for the paperholder on his desk, took a sheet of paper with gilded edges and wrote a brief letter of resignation as Enver Bey watched him

To the serene and sole protector of the caliphate,
at the behest of the military,

I ask to be relieved of my duties as grand vizier.
The imperial decree rests with the Sultan.

Grand Vizier Kamil

Enver Bey grabbed the letter of resignation, read it, and put it back in front of the pasha.

"Say that it is at the behest of the public and the military, the people don't want you, it's not just the army . . . ."

"Fine," said Kamil Pasha.

He took the letter, wrote "at the behest of the public and the military," and handed it back to Enver Bey.

As Enver Bey took the letter of resignation from the grand vizier, the Committee members in the garden started entering the prime ministry building.

Just as Monsieur Lausanne was getting up to see what the commotion was about, the foreign minister's door opened and two men dragged the interior minister into the room, beating him as they did so, passed in front of the foreign minister and the Austrian ambassador and went out the other door.

As the ambassador watched the men drag and beat the minister, Lausanne heard him say politely to the Foreign Minister, "I'd better be going."

Lausanne also left the office and went to the door of the large hall.

There was a large, round table in the center of the room.

Talat Bey, Mithat Şükrü Bey, Yakup Cemil Bey and Mümtaz Bey were standing by the head of the table, just then Enver Bey and Hakkı Bey came in, Mümtaz Bey asked excitedly,

"Did you get the letter of resignation?"

As Enver Bey said, "I have it," one of the doors on the other side of the room opened and the large-bodied Minister of War Nazım Pasha came out, after taking a look at the men standing at the head of the table, he walked over to them with a surprising degree of calmness.

Lausanne saw the seven men talking at the head of the table. There didn't seem to be any air of hostility between them. Nazım Pasha was saying something to them.

Just then there were sounds of a commotion outside, Lausanne saw Nazım Pasha hurriedly take a step back and reach for his gun as if he feared he'd fallen into a trap, at the same moment Yakup Cemil Bey raised his gun and shot Nazım Pasha in the temple.

Enver Bey turned to Yakup Cemil.

"What have you done, you madman," he said.

Yakup Cemil shrugged his shoulders.

"He was talking too much."

Nazım Pasha's had collapsed next to the table, and the men were arguing next to his body.

Talat Bey turned to Enver Bey and said,

"Go to the palace right away and give the sultan this letter of resignation, meanwhile let's get things organized around here."

Enver Bey took Hilmi Bey and Mümtaz Bey with him and hurriedly left the prime ministry building, there was an automobile in front of the gate, "Whose car is this?" he asked.

"It's the Shayk Al-Islam Cemallettin Efendi's car, sir," said one of the janitors at the gate.

"Good, I'm taking the car."

Just as he was about to get into the car, some of his comrades came running out and said,

"That madman Yakup Cemil is wandering around the building brandishing a gun and saying, "I shot Nazım Pasha, I'm going to shoot the interior minister too'."

Enver Bey became annoyed and made a face.

"Tell him to come here," he said.

A minute or two later Yakup Cemil came, still holding his gun.

"Put that gun in your pocket and get into the car," said Enver Bey, "we're going to the palace, and you're coming with me."

They got into the car and the driver moved off.

All of these events had taken place within fifteen minutes.

As Enver Bey and his comrades left for the palace, Talat Bey said to Azmi Bey, one of the comrades who'd come with him:

"Go to the police headquarters immediately and assume control."

After sending him to police quarters, he went down to the prime ministry's telegraph office. With no authority to do so, he sent telegrams to all of the governors informing them that "the cabinet has resigned on the sultan's command," then gave them instructions about what they were to do.

All of the governors obeyed these instructions without question.

Within half an hour the Istanbul Police and all of the governorates were under the Committee's control.

When they arrived at the palace, Enver Bey was immediately granted an audience with Sultan Mehmet Reşat V.

Enver Bey got straight to the point.

"Your highness, the cabinet has resigned on the wishes of the people."

In a calm voice the sultan said,

"Congratulations, my son. Do you have any ideas about the new grand vizier?"

"Mahmut Şevket Pasha is a suitable candidate, your highness."

"I think so as well."

The sultan called a clerk and had him write up the necessary order for Mahmut Şevket Pasha to become grand vizier.

During the coup, Nazım Pasha, who had been commanding the army in place of the sultan, who was commander in chief of the army, under the title "deputy commander in chief," had been killed, and someone had to be appointed to replace him immediately.

"Who are you considering for deputy commander in chief?" asked the sultan.

"Ahmet İzzet Pasha is qualified for the position."

"Yes, I think he's qualified as well . . . He's a serious and capable officer."

Enver Bey didn't remain in the sultan's presence for long, he had to get everything organized and assume control of the state as soon as possible before people had time to think.

He and his comrades immediately went down to the palace chief clerk's office. From there he telephoned Mahmut Şevket Pasha's house . . . Ali Rıza Bey had gone to the pasha's house in the morning and was waiting there with him for the news.

Ali Rıza Bey answered the telephone on the first ring.

"Who is this?"

"It's Enver . . . Is the pasha there?"

"We're together . . . What's the situation?"

"Tell the Pasha that I offer him my congratulations, a little while ago his highness the sultan appointed him grand vizier . . . Go to Bab-ı Ali with the pasha, get going immediately, don't waste a minute. His excellency the pasha can assume control of the government and begin his job."

"We'll leave at once."

As Mahmut Şevket Pasha set out for Cağaoğlu, Enver Bey got a sheet of paper and wrote a letter addressed to Ahmet İzzet Pasha.

> *To his excellency İzzet Pasha, chief of the General Staff of the Army, it is the eminent Sultan's request that he accept the position of deputy commander of the Sultan's armed forces. Public order has been secured.*
>
> *Enver*

He sent the letter to İzzet Pasha, when İzzet Pasha saw that he was being promoted to commander in chief by a major he became annoyed and turned the offer down, but he recovered from his irritation ten days later and accepted the position on Mahmut Şevket Pasha's request.

As Enver Bey was returning to Bab-ı Ali, Mahmut Şevket Pasha was on his way to assume the position of grand vizier.

Now the streets were packed with thousands of people shouting, "Long live the people! Long live the Committee for Union and Progress!" As soon as the coup was successful all of the Committee members had got into action, they'd dragged their supporters out into the streets and influenced the crowds.

This coup that had been carried out by five people was now being celebrated throughout the Ottoman Empire with cheers, speeches, and rallies.

On the way back Enver Bey turned to Mümtaz Bey and said in a calm voice:

"The empire is now ours."

Mümtaz Bey smiled with glee.

"Because of you."

Envery Bey didn't answer, he was content to look out the window at the crowds.

Mahmut Şevket Pasha had arrived at Bab-ı Ali with great fanfare.

First they took the necessary measures to assure public order, in any event Azmi Bey was already police chief, and Mahmut Şevket Pasha appointed Cemal Bey Guardian of Istanbul.

Within two days a cabinet was formed, the cabinet was composed entirely of Committee members. The Committee had seized power.

The Ottoman Empire was now the property of these ambitious men, the oldest of whom was forty years old, they'd achieved enough power to make whatever decisions they wanted.

No one stood against them.

As for the five dead bodies lying in their own blood, they were forgotten.

26

Forgive me for saying this, but this country is a madhouse."

This sentence echoed in Monsieur Lausanne's mind the whole way to Dilara Hanım's house . . . He was thinking of starting his story with that, because that's exactly how he felt.

After writing news of what he'd witnessed at Bab-ı Ali and sending it from the Galatasaray Post Office, he'd come straight to Dilara Hanım, he thought that an event like this gave him the right to show up uninvited.

What he'd seen had terrified him, but there was a side of him that would be pleased to face any kind of terror of it meant he could see Dilara Hanım, even as he watched people being killed, he thought about the article he would write and how he would tell Dilara Hanım about it . . .

As he hurried to go write his article and then see Dilara Hanım, he had to make his way through bloodstained corridors and halls, he didn't know that the young man with the file in his hand over whom he had to jump was Hikmet Bey's step son-in-law, he would never even have guessed that this would directly impact people he knew.

When Dilara Hanım, who was reading a novel in the reading room and occasionally looking out at the winter persimmons hanging from the leafless trees, glowing like orange light bulbs against the leaden twilight of the rain, was informed that Monsieur Lausanne had arrived, she knew that something extraordinary had happened and she became alarmed. But she greeted Monsieur Lausanne as always with a polite smile, as if his arriving at that hour uninvited was the most ordinary thing in the world.

"Welcome," she said, "it's very cold outside, shall I have them make some hot tea for you? Or are you hungry?"

"Some terrible things have happened," Lausanne said, as if he hadn't heard her questions.

Like everyone who carries the same fear with the same secret anxiety, when Dilara heard him say "terrible things," she thought that what she had always feared had come to pass, that "something had happened" to Ragıp Bey, for a moment her face went pale, she leaned against the armchair next to her, but within seconds she realized that Lausanne didn't know Ragıp Bey, that it wasn't possible that he was bringing her news about Ragıp.

"What happened?"

"There was a coup."

"What coup?"

"The Committee overthrew the government in fifteen minutes with five men, they've seized power . . . People have been shot . . . I was at Bab-ı Ali at the time, I was waiting to see Noradikyan Efendi . . . I saw everything."

"How could they stage a coup with five people?"

"I don't understand it at all . . . Even the janitors outnumbered them, there were police there, there was a battalion of soldiers in the garden, but five men pulled their guns and walked in and took over the government."

"How is that possible?"

"I don't know, I've never seen anything like this in my life, I've encountered a lot of surprising things, but I've never witnessed a coup as strange as this."

"Come, let's go to the living room, I'll have them bring you something hot, I daresay you haven't eaten anything amidst all of this turmoil, you can eat as you tell me about it."

As they made their way to the living room, Dilara Hanım heard sounds in the distance and asked Lausanne, "What's happening, what's that sound?"

"They're celebrating the coup."

"How quick . . ."

Dilara Hanim had ordered the servants to prepare food without saying anything, using only her eyes, and as they entered the living room the servants were already setting the table.

They sat at the table.

"Aren't you going to eat?" asked Lausanne.

"I've already eaten, I'll have some tea with you . . . You can eat as you tell me what happened."

Lausanne repeated what he'd been thinking on the way.

"Forgive me for saying this, but this country is a madhouse."

Dilara Hanım laughed aloud.

"You look surprised," she said, "Everyone who lives here already knows this . . . We live in a madhouse. We're mad. Now tell me what these madmen did."

"Five armed men, there was an officer leading them, ran into Bab-ı Ali, they shot a chief inspector, two civil servants and the Minister of War, meanwhile one of them was shot, then they forced the grand vizier to resign and they left. The whole thing lasted fifteen minutes. Then they went to the sultan and asked him to appoint a new grand vizier . . . Mahmut Şevket Pasha is the new grand vizier . . . I wrote all of this down and sent it to the newspaper, but I'm afraid they're not going to believe me in Paris, that they'll think I made it all up. Who would believe that five people could take over an empire?"

"It really is strange . . . Didn't anyone resist them?"

"No, there was a battalion of soldiers in the garden but they just watched. The ministers didn't object either . . . They beat them and took them away . . . They took them into custody but they say they're going to release them. Only there's one minister Mahmut Şevket Pasha is angry at, I suppose they had a disagreement in the past, they say they're not going to release him, Mahmut Şevket Pasha is said to be a very vindictive man."

"I've heard that as well."

Monsieur Lausanne laughed.

"Meanwhile some amusing things occurred as well, the censors were very confused about what to remove from my article . . . You should have seen the man's face, his face was beet red because he didn't know who was in power, or who would get angry at what, I thought he was going to die . . . Then he allowed the entire article to pass as I'd written it."

He paused and took a bite of food.

"And you should have seen the Austrian ambassador as well . . . They dragged a minister into Noradikyan Efendi's office and beat him, the minister had been talking to the ambassador, both of them watched as the man was being dragged past, then the ambassador said he'd better get going, but you should have seen his face when he said this."

As Monsieur Lausanne was telling the story he imitated the ambassador's expression, seeing Dilara Hanım laugh out loud made him happier than anything else could manage to do, he felt a strange sense of victory for succeeding in making her laugh. Once he'd told Dilara Hanım that "Alexander didn't feel as much a sense of victory when he conquered Egypt as I feel when I make you laugh," then Dilara Hanım laughed and said, "See, now you've captured Egypt yet again."

As they were laughing about the ambassador the telephone rang, Dilara Hanım was startled, she too was having difficulty becoming accustomed to this new instrument, especially to the way it rang so suddenly. She got up and said to Monsieur Lausanne "It's probably Dilevser, I suppose she wants to ask me something, continue eating, I'll be right back,"

As Lausanne was eating he could hear Dilara Hanım's voice. "Yes, Dilevser."

". . . . . . ."

"What happened, my daughter, why are you crying?"

". . . . .."

"Good God, how could that have happened . . . What does Tevfik Bey have to do with any of this?"

". . . . ."

"God damn them . . . How is Hikmet Bey?"

". . . . ."

"Yes, I understand, let me throw something on and I'll be right over, my daughter."

When she came back in her face was red with anger.

"One of the young men you saw shot was Rukiye's husband Tevfik Bey, he worked at the prime ministry . . . When you were telling the story it didn't even occur to me that something could have happened to him . . . He was such a decent young man, such a polite person . . . May he rest in peace, I'm so saddened by this . . . Poor Rukiye must be devastated, the girl is pregnant . . ."

Monsieur Lausanne didn't understand who Rukiye was.

"I'm sorry," he said. "I don't understand, who is Rukiye?"

"Hikmet Bey's step-daughter."

"Oh no..."

With an inexplicable and unhealthy curiosity, Monsieur Lausanne was trying to figure out which of the two bodies he'd seen on the floor had been Tevfik Bey's.

"Wait here a minute," said Dilara Hanım, "I'll put something on and we can go to Dilevser."

"Do you think it's appropriate for me to come?"

"Of course, you're the one who saw what happened, in this painful time you're perhaps the most valuable person . . ."

They went out together, they moved close to each other under the umbrella that Monsieur Lausanne was holding, they walked towards the little gate between the two gardens, they could feel each other's warmth.

When they reached Hikmet Bey's house, Dilevser opened the door for them in tears.

"Mother dear, how could something like this happen, how cruel they are . . ."

"Don't cry, my daughter, don't cry . . . This country is like that . . . God damn them . . . Where's Hikmet Bey?"

"He's upstairs getting ready . . . We're going to go to Rukiye, she must be a wreck, oh mother dear, it can't be easy, and she's pregnant too . . . She loved her husband so much, I can't tell you . . . May God not allow anyone to suffer this . . . How can anyone bear this pain?"

"Where's Nizam? Does he know?"

"The news arrived just as he was getting home, he rushed off straight away without changing his clothes."

"Are you going too?"

"Of course."

As she said this her face flushed slightly, waves of pink spread towards her temples, she wanted to go help Rukiye, to console her, but at the same time she guessed that Mehpare Hanım, Hikmet Bey's former wife, would also rush to her daughter's side. She thought that Hikmet Bey should not be left alone on such a painful day, but at the same time there was the thought of seeing that woman. "But it's always like that, isn't it," she said to Osman, "a person can have so many different feelings and thoughts at the same time, is there any such thing as a pure thought or a pure feeling, when we talk about our thoughts and feelings aren't we talking about the largest and brightest of a cluster of feelings? Don't other emotions reveal themselves beside that emotion . . . It's not just me who's like that . . ." From the state she was in, Osman realized that even though no one else had noticed it, she was ashamed that a thought like this had passed through her mind.

No one said anything, but Monsieur Lausanne got into the carriage with them.

Hikmet Bey was stricken, from the redness in his eyes it was clear that when he'd gone upstairs to dress he'd cried, he'd been fond of Tevfik Bey, he knew how much his daughter had loved her husband, he feared that she might not be able to bear this sorrow.

Dilara Hanım said, "Monsieur Lausanne was at Bab-ı Ali when it all took place, he saw the people who were shot."

"Were you there?" asked Hikmet Bey, "did you see the fighting?"

"I saw Nazım Pasha being shot, but the others were already dead by the time I got to the hall where the fighting had taken place . . . I didn't see how they were shot."

"So did you see Tevfik?"

"To tell the truth, I can't say I saw everything in great detail, there was a chief inspector, in any event he was in uniform, and there were three young men lying on the floor, two of them were holding guns . . . One of them was still holding a file."

Hikmet Bey asked with an illogical haste, as if Monsieur Lausanne having seen Tevfik Bey's body would solve a great problem and Tevfik Bey would be saved.

"Ah, that would be Tevfik, in any event he didn't have a gun . . . Were you able to see where he'd been shot?"

"I was in a bit of a panic at the time, they were still holding guns, the one who was carrying a file was lying face down, I couldn't be quite sure but I think he was shot in the neck, blood was flowing from his neck to his chest."

Monsieur Lausanne was talking exactly like a journalist, Dilevser and Dilara Hanım began to cry, as they listened to Monsieur Lausanne, the reality of Tevfik Bey's death became clearer to them.

As they crossed to the other side in the launch, sitting facing one another in silence, the rain became heavier, the waves were swelling with the rain, the sea and the sky had taken on an ashen color, occasional bolts of lightning seemed to shake the sky.

When they got out onto the quay, they saw that the doors of the waterfront mansion were open and that people were moving around inside.

As they passed through the open doors they saw three dervishes sitting side by side just in the entryway, the dervishes placed their hands on their chests in greeting.

The door to the room to the left of the entry hall was partly open, inside there were serious-faced men in frock coats, they were very probably friends and colleagues from Tevfik Bey's workplace, Nizam was talking to them, it was as if he'd suddenly aged and matured, there was an air of gravitas about him.

In Rukiye's home they did not practice the usual custom of dividing the house into different sections for men and women, "I won't have any part of that nonsense'" Rukiye had said, this young couple who were so devoted to each other didn't receive many guests, and because they didn't attract attention with flamboyant gatherings, the "Sheikh's daughter's eccentricities" weren't noticed much. Like a number of wealthy families in Istanbul, they were like small islands surrounded by the sea of the public's traditions, and they lived lives that were quite different from those traditions.

A servant showed them up to the top floor, opened the door to the room with a bay window and made way for them to enter.

Rukiye was sitting on a divan in the corner.

Her face was completely white. It looked like the face of a corpse. As if all of the blood had been drained out of it.

She was weeping.

Her eyes seemed to have grown larger as well, she was staring straight ahead as she used to do when she was a child, as if at something no one else could see.

Tears were streaming from her eyes but she didn't sob, she didn't sigh, she didn't speak, she didn't moan, she didn't move, the tears streamed down her face constantly like thin, shiny strings.

It was only when she saw Nizam that she embraced him tightly and said, "Oh, Nizam, I'm dead."

After that she didn't speak again, didn't move from her seat.

Seated right next to Rukiye was Sula, the nursemaid Mehpare Hanım had brought with her from Salonica, Sula's large body looked like a huge, black rock, she was holding Rukiye's hand, saying something in Greek in a singsong voice as if she was singing a lullaby.

Mehpare Hanım was sitting in the winged chair next to them, she was grasping a silk handkerchief, but she wasn't weeping, she was just staring pensively as if she was thinking about something.

After they'd looked at Rukiye, everyone turned to Mehpare Hanım at the same moment, looking at this woman about whose legendary beauty they'd heard aroused different emotions in each of them, Dilevser looked at her with jealousy, Dilara Hanım with surprise, Hikmet Bey with pain and Monsieur Lausanne with admiration. Hikmet Bey averted his eyes the moment he looked, but the other three couldn't take their eyes off her, they looked at her as if in disbelief, as if they wanted to memorize her face, and they did so with the full knowledge that what they were doing was contrary to all rules of politeness.

Without getting up, Mehpare Hanım said, "Welcome Hikmet," and as she gave the others a slight nod of greeting, Monsieur Lausanne asked in a whisper, "Who is this lady?" and Dilara Hanim whispered her answer, "Rukiye's mother." As she said this, the jealousy that she felt on noticing Monsieur Lausanne's admiration caused her to feel little tongues of flame burning in her chest. Seeing such admiration evoked by another woman was not an emotion that was easy to bear.

They were ashamed to feel these feelings in a house of mourning, but it was impossible to prevent it. Emotions of different shapes and colors were revolving like a propeller around the shared anguish.

Monsieur Lausanne didn't know what to do so he sat quietly in an armchair near the door, he tried not to look at Mehpare Hanım but he couldn't help it, from time to time he glanced at her and tried to record the beauty he saw in his mind.

When they came in Rukiye tried to get up but Hikmet Bey put his hand on her shoulder and said, "Don't get up, my daughter," everyone was more moved by the way Rukiye was weeping than they would have been by any manner of wailing, shouting, moaning, or outbursts.

After they'd sat together in silence for a moment, Hikmet Bey pointed out Monsieur Lausanne to Rukiye.

"Monsieur Lausanne is a newspaper correspondent, my dear Rukiye," he said, "he was present at Bab-ı Ali during that fateful event, he saw what happened."

For the first time there was movement on Rukiye's face, she looked at Monsieur Lausanne.

"You saw the incident, Monsieur?"

"Yes, madame."

Rukiye's lips trembled.

"Was Tevfik frightened?"

It was clear that Rukiye was not asking this to measure her husband's courage, but to learn whether or not he had left this world in fear. She'd asked the question like a mother in panic that her child might be frightened, it was clear that she was hoping that at the very least he had died peacefully rather than in a spasm of fear. Without realizing it, she was seeking small consolations in the face of the vastness and endlessness of death.

Monsieur Lausanne looked at Dilara Hanım, he hadn't seen Tevfik Bey's murder, but he chose to lie, feeling that it might ease Rukiye, if only a little.

"No, madame, he didn't have the chance to be frightened, he was caught completely by surprise when he was shot."

"Did he suffer?"

"No, madame, his death was very quick and sudden."

"Where was he shot?"

Monsieur Lausanne sighed.

"In the neck."

"So how did it happen, Tevfik didn't have a weapon, why did they shoot him?"

"I don't know, madame, he was carrying files, during the course of the fighting they shot him too."

"Who shot him?"

"I didn't see that clearly, madame, there were armed men in the room, they were shooting, I didn't see which of them shot Tevfik Bey."

"He didn't suffer, did he? You're certain, aren't you?"

"Yes, madame, it happened very suddenly."

She remembered how on that evening when they were speaking with Nizam he'd said, "I wouldn't want to see."

"Did he realize that they were going to kill him?"

Monsieur Lausanne spoke with confidence, as if he knew the true answer.

"No, madame, he didn't . . . He didn't see that he was being shot at."

Rukiye didn't say anything more, there was a deep silence in the room, Rukiye was weeping again and her face was completely motionless, no one could think of anything to say and they looked straight ahead in silence. As Dilevser, Dilara and Monsieur Lausanne occasionally glanced surreptitiously at Mehpare Hanım, Hikmet Bey just looked at Rukiye. Mehpare Hanım was acting as if she wasn't aware that there was anyone else in the room, when they'd come in she'd briefly sized Dilevser up but she hadn't taken an interest in anyone else. As for Dilara Hanım, she was examining Monsieur Lausanne out of the corner of her eye, she could see that he was looking at Mehpare Hanım in admiration and disbelief, and that he couldn't stop looking at her.

They were all wrapped up in their own emotions, from time to time they could hear what Sula was saying to Rukiye in Greek.

Nizam came in and looked around the room in surprise, it was clear that he hadn't expected to see his parents and his stepmother together in the same room.

"They've gone," he said to Rukiye.

Rukiye blinked her eyes but didn't say anything.

"Do you want anything?" Nizam asked his older sister, "you haven't eaten anything, shall I tell them to bring you something?"

Rukiye shook her head.

"You really should eat something, Rukiye."

Again Rukiye shook her head to say she didn't want anything.

Nizam didn't insist, it was clear that he was very upset and that he was worried about Rukiye, his air of mocking indifference was gone, the cheerfulness that always evoked a sense of artificiality had been replaced by a genuine anguish, it was as if that anguish had suddenly matured him, this helped him take care of everything in the house with a skill that wouldn't have been expected of him, his whispered commands kept the house running smoothly.

He went out, spoke briefly with the servants, then came back, a little later the guests were served coffee from silver trays, there were miniature pastries served with the coffee.

Nizam sat next to his mother.

"How are you mother?" he asked softly.

"How do you think I am, my son . . ."

"Do you want anything?"

"No, thank you . . . Don't wear yourself out too much . . . Have you eaten?"

"I'll eat when the house calms down, I don't want anything now."

At that moment they felt a strange breeze, they all looked at the door, there was no one there. Later Dilevser said to Osman, "I swear I felt that breeze, I asked my mother and she felt it too."

When they looked up again a few seconds later, Sheikh Efendi was standing in the doorway in his long black robes and with anguish in his black eyes. His face seemed to have become even more transparent. He glanced very briefly at Mehpare Hanım, their eyes met for a just a moment, then they both turned their heads.

When Rukiye saw her father she jumped up and embraced him, "Father dear" she sobbed and trembled as she wept, Sheikh Efendi held his daughter gently and pressed her to his chest.

"They killed Tevfik, father . . . they shot Tevfik."

Like a little girl she was complaining to her father about the people who had done this, as if she expected him to find a solution, Sheikh Efendi stroked Rukiye's hair without saying anything.

He didn't say anything to try to console her, he sensed that at that moment any soothing words would cause Rukiye to rebel, he just held her to his chest.

Then he sat her back in her seat, sat next to her and took her hand in both of his hands. Rukiye asked him tearfully,

"Why did they do this . . . He was so cheerful when he left the house this morning . . ."

No one in the room could look anyone else in the eye, everyone had thoughts going through their minds, in that room full of bereavement, everyone was trying to free themselves from embarrassing emotions.

Death had brought together these people who life had separated and not allowed to see one another. Rukiye had said to Osman, "Of course death is more powerful than life, that night my parents saw each other for the first time since they'd separated, my father and Hikmet Bey saw each other for the first time there, that night Dilevser finally got the chance to see Mehpare Hanım, about whom she'd been so curious, we all gathered around a death . . . Life has the power to separate people but it doesn't have the power to bring people together . . . Only death can bring people together."

In an otherworldly tone, Sheikh Efendi said to Rukiye.

"Stay here tonight, my daughter, say farewell to your house . . . Tomorrow after the funeral I'm having you brought to the *tekke*. You can stay there for a time . . ."

"Fine," said Rukiye.

Sheikh Efendi looked at Mehpare Hanım, then at Rukiye.

"Who is going to stay with you tonight?" he asked.

"Nizam is going to stay."

Sheikh Efendi gave Mehpare Hanım a look of rebuke.

"I'm going to stay here tonight too," said Mehpare Hanım.

"Good," said Sheikh Efendi, "The dervishes are going to stay here tonight as well. If you need anything let them know."

Rukiye began sobbing again.

"Please tell them to recite the Koran on the bottom floor . . . Tevfik believed . . . If he can still see what's going on here he would be pleased . . ."

"They're already doing so."

"I'd like to be able to hear it."

"Of course, my daughter, I'll tell them, they'll recite louder."

Just as in the face of Mehpare Hanım's compelling beauty Dilevser had no other recourse but to accept this reality,

Hikmet Bey felt the same feeling in the face of Sheikh Efendi's power, Sheikh Efendi hadn't said anything significant, he hadn't recited prayers, he hadn't offered consolation, but his presence brought everyone peace, everyone had found a strange sense of resignation. The naturalness of his acceptance of death, the genuine belief that Rukiye heard when he later told her "We come from a divine light and we return to a divine light, my daughter" had infected everyone, if even only for a moment this shared resignation freed them from the terrifying helplessness that the reality of death brings.

Nizam was looking at the Sheikh in amazement, he was struggling to understand how he created this sense of confidence, how he'd managed to get everyone including himself under his influence. He sensed that Sheikh Efendi wasn't afraid of death, that he didn't find it terrifying, that for him it was no different from rain or a cloud. "This wasn't courage," he said to Osman, "this was not feeling the need for courage, it was even more effective than courage. He had no need for courage because he didn't see death as something to be afraid of, and everyone around him could feel this. No one was afraid then. He destroyed fear."

A few minutes passed in silence as everyone glanced at one another surreptitiously, trying to conceal their jealousy, their yearning, their regrets, their desire for revenge and the various thoughts that were passing through their minds.

Sheikh Efendi stood.

"I'll be going now, my daughter."

"Let me see you out, sir," said Rukiye.

Before leaving the room Sheikh Efendi took one last quick look at Mehpare Hanım, then wished everyone in the room "Good evening" and went out with Rukiye.

When they reached the lower floor he said something softly to the dervishes.

At the door Rukiye embraced her father again.

"How am I going to bear this pain, what am I going to do? How am I going to live without him?"

"Rukiye, my daughter . . ."

She looked up at her father, the lines of Sheikh Efendi's face had deepened and frozen as if they'd been chiseled out of marble with a heavy hammer, she saw that her father, who saw death as a "reunion," who didn't fear death and indeed longed for it, was helpless in the face of his daughter's suffering.

No words, prayers or verses that Sheikh Efendi could have uttered to try to console his daughter could have affected Rukiye as much as this.

Rukiye was learning how love turns into anguish by living it, now the anguish she saw in her father's face was as powerful as the anguish she felt in the face of death; what she felt in the face of death, her father felt in the face of his daughter's suffering, suddenly she thought "If something were to happen to me my father couldn't bear it," at a completely unexpected moment this thought simply appeared, shattering all of her thoughts and feelings.

They were in front of the open door, there was a strong wind and the rain had turned into a downpour, the skirts of Sheikh Efendi's cloak flew in the wind, the spray of the rain struck their faces.

Rukiye embraced her father one more time and breathed in the smell of laurel.

"Go already," she said tenderly, "you'll get cold . . . Don't worry about me . . . I'm going to suffer this pain, I'm going to bear this pain."

After Rukiye had seen her father out and was going back upstairs, the dervishes began reciting the Koran out loud.

The people waiting for Rukiye upstairs hadn't spoken since the grieving woman and Sheikh Efendi had left the room, there was a strange, tense silence, everyone was glancing surreptitiously at one another, then they quickly averted their eyes. None of them looked each other in the eye.

They heard the shutters banging in the strengthening wind and the drumming of the raindrops on the quay, the sound of the Koran being recited downstairs brought grief, anguish and consolation, they sensed the endlessness of death, but they couldn't prevent their thoughts and feelings from swimming like tiny fish in this endlessness. They were experiencing the distress of their every feeling, whether it was jealousy, fear, worry or admiration, being rendered meaningless in the face of death.

Knowing that a young man who the previous night had been sitting in one of those chairs was now lying naked on a marble slab with a red hole in his neck made life and emotions meaningless, but it did not negate them. "I must confess," Dilara Hanım said to Osman, "just as we felt the helplessness of life in the face of death that night, we also felt how resilient life is in the face of death, yes, it made our feelings seem meaningless but they continued to exist. Death smothered us and the realm of our feelings like a wool cushion, made our feelings smaller and meaningless, but we all knew that the moment death's shadow retreated they would all be as they were before."

They heard their own silence within the sounds that came into the room, within this silence that wrapped them so intensely, each of them was seized by a strange worry that their emotions were shining like a single star on an inky black night and were visible to everyone, this worry, which was one of the reasons they hesitated to look at each other, was the desire to conceal their eyes and their feelings.

Strangely it was Nizam who behaved in the most natural and sincere manner, he was the one who shared Rukiye's pain most genuinely, because he was the one who felt the same pain there was no meaning in wearing a false sadness, he didn't look at anyone in the room because he didn't feel the need to conceal his feelings from anyone.

"Are you hungry?" he asked the others in the room, "shall I have some food prepared for you?"

Everyone murmured "no," they really didn't want to eat, they didn't have the strength to eat, all they wanted was to look at the person they wanted to look at for a few minutes without being noticed.

Dilevser was the one who suffered most, seeing Mehpare Hanım's beauty before her ignited the fires of jealousy, she knew that she could never compete with this beauty, as she surreptitiously examined Mehpare Hanım she was looking not at her beauty, she was searching for some imperfection in her behavior, something about her that she could criticize or blame her for, but it was impossible to see any hidden fault behind Mehpare Hanım's ice cold façade. On top of that, because she was conscious that she was feeling these things in a house of mourning she blamed herself, she found herself ugly and mean-spirited. For Dilevser, "meanness" in human nature was a shame that should never be forgiven, and now she could clearly see this shame in herself.

Dilara Hanım had also been shaken by Mehpare Hanım's beauty, she was annoyed by the admiration with which Monsieur Lausanne looked at her, but these emotions didn't shake her as deeply as they shook Dilevser. She was just displeased.

Hikmet Bey was more worried about his young wife, because he knew what she might feel he felt the desire to ease and console her, but he grasped the strangeness of paying head to jealousy in a house of mourning, in the place where the person who'd died was being grieved. As always when he saw Mehpare Hanım he'd thought, "How beautiful she is," this was a beauty that had once shared his home and his bed, but it was also this beauty that had brought him to the brink of death. He told himself that if he had to make the choice again he would still choose Dilevser, this thought was sincere, but within this sincerity it was impossible to say that his attraction to that beauty was completely gone.

All of them left Rukiye's house wounded in some way, the sincere grief they felt for the young woman's loss made the other emotions seem larger, made these emotions cling to their flesh.

In the rocking launch that bobbed up and down in the waves, Hikmet Bey saw that Dilevser was shivering and grasped that this was more from emotional upheaval than from the cold, he asked "Are you cold?" then took off his coat and put it around her shoulders.

As for Dilara Hanım, she gave Monsieur Lausanne a mocking look and said,

"Mehpare Hanım is very beautiful, isn't she?"

"Yes, she really is very beautiful."

"Were you very impressed?"

"Beauty is impressive, Dilara Hanım, but on its own its affect is never lasting . . . For a man to be affected for more than half an hour requires something more than just beauty."

"Don't worry, Mehpare Hanım has those things too."

"What things?"

Dilara Hanım said in an irritated tone,

"I don't know, I just said that . . . This incompetent captain can't seem to manage to dock the boat."

27

Ragıp Bey was among those who were most pleased by the coup.

All of the Committee officers in the army were pleased by the coup, but Ragıp Bey wasn't pleased because "our side is in power now," Ragıp Bey hoped that the coup plotters would start the war again.

He'd been very restless since returning from leave, he hardly slept at all, day and night he wandered the trenches like a rogue horse, inspecting the men, drilling them until they were exhausted, there was always a cigarette in his mouth, even when he was standing next to barrels of gunpowder. Once, the sergeant said, "Commander, if you keep smoking like that, the infidels are going to see the smoke and think we've dragged ships onto the land like Mehmet the Conqueror," indeed you really could tell where he was just from the fragile, twisting plumes of smoke. He only lay in bed when he was on the point of fainting from exhaustion, indeed he fainted rather than slept, he'd wake up an hour or two later with the same name echoing in his mind, then he would start smoking immediately.

He didn't eat, when the sergeant insisted he would have a couple of spoonsful of tasteless soup, take a couple of bites of stale bread and say, "I'm full."

He kept losing weight, he'd become quite pale, his cheeks were hollow, and there were purple rings under his eyes

He would climb out of the trenches and look at the Bulgarian positions for a long, long time, among themselves the men said that "this defeat has driven the commander mad," they thought his irritability was due to the defeat, that's why they felt a respect mixed with fear.

The days that were most difficult to bear were the days when the rain became fierce, when it beat the entire plain, the days when both armies tried to hide under tarpaulins in their positions; he paced back and forth in a small shack that was heated by a wood stove, he looked out the windows, smoked cigarettes, muttered unintelligible sounds, in the end, unable to bear it, he would rush outside, walk the length of the muddy trenches, reprimanding the men, wearing himself out, getting plastered with mud from head to foot.

The cholera epidemic had been slowed by the arrival of winter cold but it still continued, he personally supervised the burial of the victims, of the black and yellow bodies with protruding ribs, sometimes he would wrap the bodies in the white burial shrouds that no one wanted to touch and place them in the mass graves with his own hands.

It was no longer possible to say that what he was feeling was simply pain or jealousy; he couldn't give it a name or grasp what it was, there was an exasperation in his chest like a wild and cloudy river rushing against a dam. This exasperation, which came from no longer wanting to exist and from the anguish that was ready to explode within him, as it grew within him his body could no longer tolerate it, it was trying to destroy him with its unending blows. There were times when he thought his stamina wouldn't suffice, that he would die, his pulse raced, his eyes became dark; at those times he became frightened, not of death itself, he was terrified of the idea of dying from his hatred for a man he didn't know, of the jealousy he felt for a woman, of such shameful weakness.

He didn't want a death like that, the idea of dying in shame upset the entire balance of his mind, fantasies of being hit by a bullet or blown apart by shrapnel seemed like the most peaceful fantasies in the world for him. Sometimes before drifting into a stupor-like sleep he would fantasize about the moment he was shot, he would picture the wound opened by a bullet piercing his heart or the shrapnel tearing through his body, this fantasy helped him sleep for a few hours.

Strangely, during these days when he had an almost insane desire to lose his life, the only things he didn't want to lose were the three crumpled letters in the inner pocket of his jacket, it was as if those letters provided a link between the isolated hell in which he was imprisoned and the world and the billions of people living in it, they prevented him from becoming completely cut off from humanity, those letters were the only air hole in the wall against which he'd pressed his face. Now those crumpled envelopes didn't remind him of the jealousy and anger he felt towards Dilara Hanım, in an incomprehensible manner they reminded him of her tenderness and her compassion.

He would take the envelopes out and look at him, there would be a softening within him, a relaxation of the tense emotions that were trying to destroy him. He didn't do this often, he rarely took those letters out and looked at them, he would leave these letters that could slightly soften the growing rigidity within him for the last moment, he didn't touch them until it became unbearable, until he reached the point when he thought about shooting himself; at that last moment he took them out and put them in front of him, then the formless emotions within him became ordered, the anger that had seemed so forsaken lessened, Dilara Hanım's smiling, loving face appeared, he remembered "the good old days." At those moments Dilara Hanım was no longer a devil whose facial features had been erased and who was making love to a French journalist, the intelligent, attractive woman he loved would reappear.

He would put the letters back in his pocket knowing that

the pain would begin again the moment he did so, he feared that if he looked at them too long they would lose their effect.

Later, with a modesty that surprised Osman, who was accustomed to always seeing him angry, he said, "Throughout my life everyone praised my bravery, whatever front line I fought at, my colleagues, my commanders and my men all respected my courage, I didn't besmirch my name once, I never experienced a moment of hesitation, I never once fled from death, I laughed at death, I pitied cowards, I belittled them, I blamed them, God knows that I never boasted about my courage but I felt genuinely pleased by this, I'm not going to deny that, I was pleased with my courage and with myself, perhaps I was secretly conceited about my bravery, God asked, are you becoming conceited by your bravery and fearlessness, just take a look at who I'm going to send against you, then he sent myself against me, he frightened me with myself. I was never afraid of anyone but I was afraid of myself, I was frightened by that confusion within me, I was frightened by my lack of stamina and my weakness, no one knew that I was frightened, but I did. I knew that I was frightened of looking at a letter too long, God showed me myself, go ahead and look, that's what you are, he said. If you ask me when and where I behaved courageously I won't remember, if you ask me when and where I was frightened I can tell you in detail, I'll relate every moment. A person can forget everything except having felt fear."

During the period when Ragıp Bey was making himself miserable every day with his own fears and weakness, he received an order transferring him to the Bolayır Corps under the command of Fahri Pasha.

In those days nothing could have pleased him as much as that order, when he asked around and found that other units had also been transferred he said, "Congratulations sergeant, we're going to war again. We're being sent to the Bolayır as reinforcements."

"We were getting bored here," said the sergeant, "the infidel stares at you, you stare at the infidel, what kind of war is that . . . Let's hope for the best, commander . . . When are we leaving?"

"We'll be going within a few days . . . You get everything ready . . . If you could just hand me my cognac . . . Let's celebrate the war."

Ragıp Bey had guessed correctly, the war was going to begin again. After seizing power in the world's strangest coup, Enver Bey became the sole ruler of the Ottoman Empire and he wanted to show the people some heroism.

He and his comrades put pressure on the Deputy Commander of the army Ahmet İzzet Pasha and the new Grand Vizier Mahmut Şevket Pasha and forced them to issue orders for a counterattack against the Bulgarians at Çatalca.

Experienced pashas were saying, "The Çatalca plain is covered in mud, the men won't be able to maneuver in that swamp, the moment a counterattack begins it will be cut down by machineguns."

These statements annoyed Enver Bey and his comrades, Major Enver Bey was conducting inspections of the corps without any official authority, he was pressing the pashas who commanded the corps to support the idea of a counterattack.

During one of these inspections that made the pashas mad with anger, though they remained silent in the face of the "young major's" power, he went to "visit" Abuk Ahmet Pasha, who was commanding the left wing of the Çatalca line.

Right away he said, "Our comrades are becoming impatient, Pasha."

"To tell the truth, I think they're right, I'm grieved by this situation as well . . . We overthrew the government with a sacred purpose, we promised the people that we would counterattack immediately and take back Edirne . . . Meanwhile days have passed and we haven't advanced an inch . . . We're in a shameful position regarding public opinion . . . Give us an answer pasha, how long is this going to continue?"

Mahmut Şevket Pasha had previously warned all of the pashas to behave calmly when Enver Bey and his comrades spoke this way, even though Ahmet Abuk Pasha was annoyed at being spoken to so disrespectfully by this major, he heeded Şevket Pasha's warning and answered as calmly as possible.

"Enver Bey, my son, you're a hero of liberty. You've earned the reverence of the people . . . If I were in your position, I would retreat from political and military life. I would leave everything to experts and skilled professionals and give up on interfering with everything. Only in times of danger would I come forward to lead the self-sacrificing masses. Don't be offended . . . It's only because I love you more than my own son that I'm obliged to give you this advice . . . More correctly, I would like to see you distance yourself from this business of gossip."

At first Enver Bey was fooled by Abuk Pasha's calm voice, but he slowly became aware of how harsh his words were and he turned bright red in anger. When the pasha had finished speaking, he jumped up and took two steps towards the pasha.

"What are you saying pasha, do you even hear what you're saying?" he shouted.

The comrades who were with Enver Bey also jumped to their feet, Abuk Pasha remembered how they'd shot the Minister of War without batting an eye during the raid on Bab-ı Ali and put his hand on his gun, Enver also reached for his gun.

One of Abuk Pasha's staff officers, Major Mahmut Bey, stepped in immediately, he took Enver Bey by the hand, said "Come, Enver Bey, this doesn't become you," and led him out of the room.

Everyone in the army soon heard about the incident, and Enver Bey returned to Istanbul and told the grand vizier to put pressure on the army to get into action.

And Grand Vizier Mahmut Şevket Pasha issued a helpless decree.

"The government undertakes to seek peace in accordance with the hopes of the nation. The army must move to facilitate this undertaking on the part of the government. Accordingly the army must immediately show strong signs of life."

All of the commanders in the army gave the same response to this decree, "To attack the Bulgarian forces from the center in this season would be suicide."

When Enver Bey and his comrades realized that they weren't going to be able to convince the pashas to go on the offensive, Enver Bey said, "Since it's not possible to attack the enemy at the front, why don't we hit the enemy from behind?"

When, at a meeting with him on this matter, Mahmut Şevket Pasha realized that he was not going to be able to convince Enver Bey, the grand vizier said,

"Enver Bey, make a plan of attack with your comrades, then we'll go over the plan and make a decision."

When he came a week later with the plan, Enver Bey said to the pasha,

"Pasha, we've put together a plan, with your permission I submit it for your consideration."

Attempting to conceal his reluctance, the pasha said,

"Go ahead, Enver Bey, I'm listening."

"Pasha, you know that the Provisional Corps under the command of Fahri Pasha is in Bolayır . . . At the moment there's no fighting on the Çatalca front, it appears that there won't be until the season changes, both sides have retreated to their positions. We can move some of our units here to Bolayır as reinforcements. They'll prepared to make a land assault, the Hurşit Pasha corps, where I served as chief of staff, will be brought by ship and landed at Şarköy. That way they'll be behind the Bulgarian forces at Çatalca . . . When two corps attack at the same time, the Bulgarian forces will be caught in a pincer and we can push them back and clear the way to Edirne."

This plan didn't sit well with the pasha, but instead of expressing this openly, and to gain time, he said,

"Explain your plan to Deputy Chief Commander İzzet Pasha, Enver Bey. Let's see what he has to say about it."

The following day Enver Bey went to İzzet Pasha. He explained the plan to him.

İzzet Pasha wasn't convinced by the plan either.

"Enver Bey, for this plan to work it's essential for the two corps to move at the same time and in a very well-planned manner. God forbid, if either corps' is out of synchronization with the other it could lead to a disaster."

"Nothing like that could happen, Pasha. With good leadership and management we can make it work . . . Both corps will move at the same moment and squeeze the Bulgarians into a corner. There's nothing for you to worry about."

İzzet Pasha realized that he wasn't going to be able to get through to this young major, that he wasn't going to be able to convince him. Enver Bey, who in effect had taken over the administration of the state and the army, needed to achieve a military success to prove the "Bab-ı Ali raid" justified in the eyes of the people. This desire had turned into a passion for him, throughout his military career he had never achieved a significant military success; he was brave, he was audacious, he was a good organizer, but he always achieved success in individual actions. Now he wanted to put this plan into action and achieve his military success. He wanted the people to come out into the streets again and shout "long live Enver."

In the end the aging pashas were obliged to say "yes" to the plan.

Units from various areas, including Ragıp Bey's unit, were being moved to Fahri Pasha's corps in Bolayır. Major Fetih Bey, chief of staff of the corps in Bolayır, was a diehard

Committee member, Major Mustafa Kemal Bey was with him. Like a number of officers their age, Fetih Bey and Mustafa Kemal Bey weren't very fond of Enver Bey, they'd been against the staging of the Bab-ı Ali raid and later wrote a report condemning it.

Enver Bey was aware of this.

Two corps whose staff officers almost hated one another were beginning to prepare for a joint assault.

Enver Bey decided to take personal command of the corps in which he was chief staff officer. He got the ships and the units ready.

Fahri Pasha's corps had taken up position in sturdy fortifications that had been built by the English and the French during the Crimean War, they had numerical superiority over the Bulgarians, the Ottomans had a force of fifty thousand men, the Bulgarians only had ten thousand men on that front.

The ambitious young staff officers were aware of the numerical superiority, but they didn't really take into account that they had only 36 cannons while the Bulgarians had 78.

Ragıp Bey accompanied his unit to the new corps, all of the preparations were complete, he was impatient to get into battle as soon as possible, he was chomping at the bit like a young colt to get into action, he was waiting for the order to attack. He didn't sleep at all. He was constantly moving around the positions, checking on the men, climbing pale-faced out of the trenches to look at the Bulgarian positions.

The young staff officers of both corps also had their own dreams, they wanted success too, Ragıp Bey was in pursuit of a greater dream than success, he wanted to settle accounts not just with the Bulgarians, but with life itself. He wanted to smell the smell of death, to feel the insignificance of life and of all feelings amidst the gun smoke, among people being killed and bodies being blown apart, to touch death, to take shelter in death. He was going to show death in person that he didn't fear death, that because he didn't fear death he didn't fear life either, that nothing in life was of any use to him, he was going to prove to himself that his love, his yearning, and his jealousy were very insignificant next to this.

Day and night he wandered above the trenches with his binoculars.

"How are the men?" he asked the sergeant.

"Like a fresh groom about to go into the bridal chamber, commander," said the sergeant, "they want to get into battle as soon as possible."

Ragıp Bey laughed, "I feel the same way" he thought to himself, "I'm going to enter the bridal chamber with death, if I come out of it alive, the world is my oyster."

His appetite had returned, he ate soup from a metal plate, he cleaned his plate with his bread, he thought less about Monsieur Lausanne, less about Dilara Hanım as well, the flames of war had enveloped his soul, even if they hadn't been able to melt and destroy other feelings it had managed to push them far away into the depths.

Every morning he complained, "What are we waiting for, when are we going to attack?"

The corps' two young staff officers shared his impatience but they had different reasons, they didn't want to share the credit for any victory with Enver Bey.

Major Fetih Bey said to Fahri Pasha, "Pasha, right now we're superior to the Bulgarians, the longer we delay the more chance they have to bring in reinforcements, they've heard about our preparations as well, isn't it necessary to get into action as soon as possible?"

The pasha said, "We have to wait for Hurşit Pasha's corps to land, according to the plan we're going to go into action together."

"Commander, we'll be too late . . . After we've managed to push the Bulgarians back, Hurşit Pasha can hit the retreating

Bulgarians from behind. If we're late it will be much more difficult to push the Bulgarians back here."

Fahri Pasha was an easy-going, well-intentioned commander, in those days the aging pashas didn't have much authority over the young Committee officers, the army was cleaning house, anyone the Committee officers said was "useless" was immediately sent into retirement.

In the end the pasha wasn't able to resist the two young staff officers' pressure for long.

"Fine," he said, "Make your final preparations. We'll decide on the day to begin the attack."

When the units received the order to "be prepared," Ragıp Bey was pleased, he lit a cigarette and said, "Finally."

"Tell the men to be prepared, we're going on the attack at any moment," he said to the sergeant.

In the middle of the night, the order came to "attack at first light," the night was dark, Ragıp Bey visited each of the positions, he joked with the men, he inspected all of their rifles, cartridges and helmets, "This is where boys are going to become men," he said, "tomorrow it will be clear who's a man and who's a coward, in the morning both friends and foe must see us, the enemy must tremble that the valiant rams are coming, our friends must be pleased, we're going for our nation, our mothers, our fathers, our betrothed . . ."

He had difficulty holding on until morning, when an indigo light appeared behind the far hills he squeezed his bandolier, pulled on his fur cap and called to the sergeant.

"If I die, get the letters from my pocket and burn them . . . If I'm wounded, hide them, if I recover you can give them to me, if I don't recover you can burn them."

"You told me that before, commander."

"Good, and I'm telling you again . . . Go be with the men, we'll be going out in a little while as soon as the order comes."

When the sergeant was gone, he looked at the sky, "Oh, Dilara," he murmured, "why did you do this?"

He didn't say this in jealousy or anger, he knew that he was saying farewell, in order to say farewell more lovingly he had to feel the closeness of the old days and complain.

He went into the trench and stood by the wooden ladder that had been placed so the men could climb out, no one spoke, in the silence everyone could hear everyone else breathing, the men's lips were moving, they were all praying, they knew that they were all going to move out together but that fewer of them would return.

When the order to "attack" came, Ragıp Bey took out his gun.

"My brave men," he shouted, "My brave rams, today is the day, this is the hour . . . God be with you, may your holy war be blessed . . . Attack!"

Ragıp Bey was the first one out of the trench, the men were coming out after him, the other units had come out of their trenches, with shouts of "God, God," thousands of soldiers ran towards the Bulgarian positions.

The rattle of machine guns came from the Bulgarian positions, they heard a ceaseless rattling, the men rushed forward over those had fallen as they shouted, "Ah, I've been hit" . . . There were small red holes in the chests of those who'd been hit.

Behind them, cannons began exploding.

Ragıp Bey's unit was among the forces attacking the right flank of the front, in the first attack they pushed the Bulgarians back, the Bulgarians were also moving back on the left flank, but their center was holding.

It was beginning to grow light.

They saw the retreating Bulgarian units, they were attacking with great enthusiasm, everyone seemed to be beside themselves, it had turned into a *zikr* ceremony on a battlefield to the sound of gunfire, the men were in such rapture they'd forgotten their own existence.

Their belief that they could defeat the Bulgarians grew stronger by the moment.

Suddenly the Bulgarians disappeared, a sudden fog descended on the plain.

It wasn't only the Bulgarians they couldn't see, they were having difficulty seeing each other. They ran through a grey could of smoke, unable to see anyone.

The Bulgarian machineguns were now firing mercilessly, Ragıp Bey heard the sound of an artillery shell exploding not far in front of him, a severed arm flew past at the level of his face, veins were hanging from it like purple threads.

Ragıp Bey shouted, "Let's not lose contact with each other."

Screams and commands were heard, artillery shells fell one after another into the densely packed Ottoman units, five or six men were blown apart at a time, human bodies were being scattered like red lines in the thick grey smoke of the fog.

With the rattling of the machine guns, men were leaning against each other as they fell like grass leaning away from the wind.

Hundreds, thousands of men were being shot in the fog.

The Ottoman units had lost contact with each other.

They didn't know where the Bulgarians were either, they only heard the sound of gunfire and the last shouts of the dying.

"The men are being cut down, commander," shouted the sergeant.

Ragıp Bey didn't hear him.

"Attack, my brave men," he shouted and ran towards the sound of the machinegun fire.

Suddenly he was struck in the chest as if by a large stick and flung into the air, he flew quickly into a red darkness.

He could hear his own voice saying, "I've been hit."

He fell onto his back in the mud.

The right side of his fur cap was covered in blood.

He tried to say, "sergeant, the letters . . ." but he was unable to complete his sentence.

28

E ven in those bleak days, Mihrişah Sultan's arrival in the city turned into a festive occasion. When the Khedive of Egypt's daughter, the former wife of the sultan's physician, now aging, her magnificent beauty slightly wrinkled, alit at Istanbul harbor with her extraordinary style, her young Parisian ladies in waiting, her Ethiopian butlers, her Italian musicians, her French cooks and hundreds of leather suitcases, a scent of perfume wafted through the city that smelled of death and cholera, people lined the streets to watch this fairy-tale princess.

Hikmet Bey and Nizam had come to greet her at the harbor, with her usual likeable ill temper she said to her son, "You've really aged, Hikmet," then she turned to look at Nizam and said, "and you've become very pale, you look like flowers that have been forgotten in a vase."

As she got into the shiny black landau that had just been varnished, she said, "What's this, you're still going around in a horse carriage, you haven't bought yourself a car, you've become really miserly, find me an automobile, I can't go around in this carriage."

Everyone who came to meet Mihrişah Sultan felt as if they'd been caught up in a storm, even though they were accustomed to her, her son and her grandson felt the dizzying effects of the storm.

"How is Rukiye?" asked Sultan.

"She's very sad," said Nizam, "She's staying at her father

the Sheikh's *tekke* but she cries every day, sometimes I fear that she's not going to get over this."

Mihrişah Sultan had never discriminated between her step-granddaughter Rukiye and her natural grandson Nizam, she'd been very devoted to her since she was a child, as soon as she heard that her husband had been shot she boarded the first ship and came to Istanbul.

"Of course she's going to mourn her husband, she's going to be sad, but there's no need to blow things out of proportion, she's going to have a child, she has to think about that. It's egotistical for a pregnant woman to be too sad . . . What is Sheikh Efendi up to . . . Is he still in love with your former wife?"

In surprise, Hikmet Bey said, "I don't know."

"I'll go to the *tekke* tomorrow," said Mihrişah Sultan, "I'll talk to the girl, did you just leave her there like that?"

"Nizam goes every day," said Hikmet Bey as if he was apologizing.

"Is your going of any use then?" asked Sultan, turning to Nizam.

"I don't know, grandmother, sometimes it seems as if she calms down a bit, but she's very sad, very shaken."

Nizam paused for a moment, his expression was frozen.

"Whoever did this needs to be punished, I want that man to die, the price must be paid, his family should suffer the same pain."

Mihrişah Sultan gave Nizam a worried look.

"I don't imagine you're the one who's going to mete out this punishment, are you an executioner?"

"I won't, but no one else is going to either, the men who shot Tevfik are wandering the streets as heroes, she doesn't say anything, but I think Rukiye is very upset by this situation, this is an unbearable situation, it makes the pain so much worse."

"You're not confusing the poor girl by talking nonsense like this, are you? She has enough pain to deal with, there's no sense in adding more pain by telling her there's no revenge, no justice. I don't want to hear about this again . . . Anyone who comes to this country of idiots becomes an idiot within two weeks. It's clear you've become an idiot too. He's going to mete out punishment . . . All we need now is a blood feud. What are you, a Bedouin chieftain?"

Nizam didn't say anything.

It wasn't very easy to talk in Mihrişah Sultan's presence, with a single glance or word she could make you look like an idiot; from birth destiny had bestowed upon her an extraordinary fortune and extraordinary beauty, kings, princes, counts, crown princes and sheikhs had been smitten by her, she managed to wear her arrogance like a jewel that had been embedded in her beauty, when faced with her mocking and distant stance, people quickly became "admirers."

"Fate has two hands, Crazy Osman Bey," she said to Osman once in her belittling manner, "however much it gives you with one hand, it will take away with the other. If you see that someone has too much of one thing, you can be absolutely certain that he's lacking something else to the same degree. I was a very wealthy and very beautiful woman, yes, but never in my life have I experienced a love that a doorman's wife might experience. I was surrounded by people day and night but I always slept alone and I woke alone. I was a goddess for many people, but I was never a woman for anyone, they were so busy admiring me that they didn't have the opportunity to love me. Am I complaining, no, but this is the truth, I always saw the truth."

She paused and thought about something.

"Still, I suppose I would have liked just once to have fully experienced this thing called love, then at least I would have understood what these miserable little people are so madly obsessed with."

There'd been many men who'd wanted to experience a love with her, but it was Mihrişah Sultan herself who wouldn't allow them into her life, she had such a tremendous admiration for herself that she'd never found any man, and there were kings among them, to be her equal, to love any man, to take any man seriously, seemed to her a betrayal of her beauty, she was in love with her own beauty. This was best expressed by a young count in Paris as he writhed in pain.

"No one can love Mihrişah Sultan as much as Mihrişah Sultan loves herself. No one can compete with the love she feels for herself. Mihrişah Sultan could never love anyone as much as she loves herself."

There had been one exception to this, Mihrişah Sultan had wavered when she met Sheikh Yusuf Efendi, it was only in his presence that she felt powerless, she'd feared she would become attached to him and she'd fled. A strange flame had passed between them that they'd never spoken of and would never speak of, no matter how much they each tried to extinguish this flame, whatever they felt for other people, they both knew that the embers were still glowing, that a single breath would ignite them, no one else but the two of them knew this truth.

"What is the geezer doing?"

Nizam and Hikmet Bey looked at each other, trying to figure out who the "geezer" was.

"That's right, there are two of them now . . . One lives in Yıldız and the other lives in Beylerbey . . . The new sultan is a real idiot I suppose, look how two gun-toting kids took the man's empire away from him. At least the other one was smarter, it took something like a revolution to bring him down from the throne . . ."

"You're talking about Abdülhamid," said Hikmet Bey, "he's well, he's in Beylerbey, he's just sitting there waiting, hoping that it will be his turn again . . . The commander of the unit assigned to guard him is an old friend of mine, I get news from him once in a while."

Mihrişah Sultan, who had referred to Abdülhamid as "that geezer" even when he was still sultan, was perhaps the only person who hadn't been afraid of him. She was always certain that she was untouchable, and she really was untouchable, it would have been impossible to touch her without causing an international scandal, it wasn't just Egypt, a lot of old friends in Europe, including a number of kings, would also have become involved.

"That geezer will never stop dreaming about the throne . . . Still, he was better than these gun-toting murderers. I used to say that no one could be worse than Abdülhamid, but these people turned out to be worse. Are these your old friends?"

"I know some of them from Salonica . . ."

"And you used to call them your friends, these murderers . . . They came and extinguished poor, dear Rukiye's life . . . Oh, Hikmet, you didn't just ruin your own life, you ruined your children's lives too, you should have lived in Paris where these children could have established honest lives for themselves . . . He was going to bring liberty to his country . . . Has liberty come to this country?"

Hikmet Bey sighed.

"Mother, that tyrant had to be overthrown . . . Would you have wanted him to stay in power forever?"

"Are these people any better? They're murderers, they're gun-toting executioners . . . Hikmet, things will never get any better here."

"I suppose that on this subject I have to say you're right, to tell the truth I have very little hope left . . . You bring one down, another replaces it . . . I imagine it will be years before this place is free of tyranny . . . Sometimes this place seems to me like a child that was born crippled, whatever you do it remains crippled."

"I'm angry at you, but I think my real mistake was to marry an Ottoman. I should never have come to these lands, it smells of death here. I smell this smell every time I come here."

"Mother, I think you're a bit too angry, this is a beautiful country, I love it here."

"And you're always loving the wrong things, Hikmet . . . You've wasted your life on these wrong loves, and now you say you still love this place."

"That's what loving is like, mother . . . There's no right or wrong about it . . . You just love."

"You really become a boring man when you say such idiotic things, you were more fun when you were young . . . How is Dilevser?"

"She's fine, but she was very shaken by what happened."

"Seeing Mehpare will have shaken her."

When they heard her say this they knew that Mihrişah Sultan had heard about everything, Hikmet Bey blushed.

"Sometimes you can be really merciless, mother."

"When I tell the truth?"

"Sometimes telling just one among many truths can be cruel, and it means forgetting other truths . . . Dilevser loves Rukiye very much, she understands her pain and her sorrow . . ."

Mihrişah Sultan turned to Nizam without even feeling the need to answer this.

"What are you up to, how are you?"

"I'm well, thank you, I'm very upset about Tevfik's death . . . And I'm very worried about Rukiye."

"From what I hear, this worry doesn't prevent you from hanging out at gambling dens all night . . . In any event, I'm going to have to have a talk with you."

Nizam laughed.

"I suppose you're going to exile me from here too . . . Am I going to go into exile again?"

"In fact I'm going to send you to the cotton fields in Egypt, but . . . You'll just do something indiscrete there too."

In the garden of Mihrişah Sultan's large mansion, where the

servants, butlers, and gardeners waited at the ready as if she could arrive at any moment, different flowers were planted in every season, they saw that red azaleas had been planted on one side of the garden, they'd placed clusters of purple and white hyacinths among the azaleas, on one side there were winter roses of a faded yellow that was almost white waving at the ends of their thin stalks, a fresh, bracing smell wafted from the flowers, the greenery of the pine forest that stretched behind seemed to want to make people forget that it was winter.

A long convoy of carriages entered the mansion garden, everyone got out laughing and talking in French, Italian, Turkish and Arabic, Mihrişah Sultan told the housekeeper who came to greet her to "settle everyone in properly."

Nizam was with the French ladies in waiting, he was talking to the ones he knew from Paris, he was hearing the sounds of a life he missed, he was making the girls laugh, as she watched them from a distance, Mihrişah Sultan said to Hikmet Bey, "how much like you he is," she said, "I remember how when I came to Istanbul when you were young, you would talk to the ladies in waiting cheerfully like that."

Hikmet Bey laughed, "I remember," he said, "I felt as if Paris had come to me."

"Come, let's have some tea, then I'll rest . . . Nizam can stay here tonight. Tomorrow morning I'll go to the *tekke* with him and see Rukiye. Tomorrow evening you can come to dinner with Dilevser."

Hikmet Bey left after they'd had their tea. Mihrişah Sultan retired to her room to rest . . . Nizam plunged into the gossip of Paris with the girls, he asked about what his friends and his enemies were doing.

In the evening Mihrişah Sultan and Nizam had dinner alone together.

"So tell me," said Mihrişah Sultan, "What have you been up to in Istanbul?"

"I'm not really doing anything."

Mihrişah Sultan looked at Nizam carefully.

"What about this gambling den you go to every night?"

"I get bored, where can I go? . . . There are no proper restaurants, there are no cafes, no one here goes anywhere with women, everyplace is filled with men. There's no theater, no opera. I go to the gambling den out of boredom, I don't play such high stakes. I haven't become a gambler and I won't . . ."

"Who is that Russian girl?"

"Are you having me watched?"

"Ha, you've forgotten your manners too, you're answering my question with a question, is that it? I ask you a question and you ask me a question . . ."

"Forgive me," said Nizam, ". . . She plays piano at the gambling den."

"Are you in love?"

"No . . . I don't think so . . ."

"You're not in love but you go to see the girl every night . . . You feel compelled to see her . . . Is that it?"

"I don't have anything else to do."

"So does she play the piano well?"

Nizam suddenly became excited.

"You wouldn't believe it, you've never heard anyone play the piano like that . . . Even in Paris I never encountered anyone who could play like that."

"You know that I don't like hyperbole."

"I'm not exaggerating."

"If she's that good, why is she playing piano in a gambling den in Istanbul?"

"I don't know . . . I said it to her too, she could give concerts anywhere in the world but she doesn't want to . . . She has an air of being embittered by life, but I don't know the reason . . . She's a very introverted woman."

"Does her family live here?"

"She never talks about her family, when I ask she doesn't answer, she just tells me not to ask . . . But I saw a Louis XV tapestry in her house, the king of France gave it to her great-grandfather as a gift."

Mihrişah Sultan laughed out loud.

"Is that what she said?"

"Yes."

"Did you believe her?"

"Yes . . . Anya wouldn't lie."

"How do you know she wouldn't lie?"

Nizam stopped and thought.

"No, she wouldn't lie . . . Anyway, she doesn't say anything, she's not the kind of person who would try to brag . . . You have to care what people think in order to lie, don't you, and she doesn't care at all what people think."

"Strange . . . You bring this girl along to see me, let me have a chat with her."

"What am I going to say to her, shall I tell her that Mihrişah Sultan has summoned her? She wouldn't come . . ."

"Put it to her this way, if she doesn't come here, I'll go to the gambling den."

"This would frighten me . . . Not her."

"If she loves you it will frighten her too . . . In any event you'll understand . . . Tell her what I said to you . . . Are you going to the gambling den tonight?"

"No."

"Why, did seeing the French girls make you forget the Russian girl?"

"No, since it's your first night I thought it would be more appropriate for me to stay here."

A little smile appeared on Mihrişah Sultan's face, Nizam realized that his grandmother was pleased by this.

"I'm going to bed, I'm tired," said Mihrişah Sultan, "don't stay up late having fun with the girls, don't let the girls stay up late either, they're tired too . . . In any event we're going to the *tekke* in the morning."

After Mihrişah Sultan had retired to her room, Nizam gathered all the girls in the living room, he had the Italian musicians brought, admonished them not to play too loudly and gave a "little ball" amidst the laughter of the girls who said he had "established his harem." He knew that Sultan would hear about this in the morning, but he also knew that his grandmother would have guessed he would behave this way and would ignore this slight self-indulgence.

As he danced with each of the girls in turn and flirted with them, he realized how much he missed "women," he wasn't thinking about having a relationship with any of the girls, but he'd missed the "presence" of women, the way women spoke, the way they danced, the way they laughed, the way their perfume wafted through the air, the harmony of their movements, a multitude of bodies whose softness could be sensed, flirting, the girls' glances, their delicate teasing, their gossip, their laughter. "I don't know quite how to explain it," he said to Osman, "of course there are women in the Ottoman Empire, but the presence of women isn't felt, I don't know if I can explain it, there's no smell of perfume in the air, there's no aimless flirting, no joking . . . And imagine it, there isn't even a place where men and women can go eat together."

They danced, talked and laughed until daybreak. From time to time he thought of Anya, he thought of her playing the piano alone at the gambling den, but he couldn't free himself from the gravitational pull of the amusement, Anya's glances kept getting lost among the crowd of women.

When the girls asked, "When are you coming back?" he answered, "Whenever sultan says my exile is ended," but as he said this he realized how much he missed Paris, how much he felt he had been torn from the world that belonged to him.

When he sat wearily at the breakfast table, Mihrişah Sultan said, "You look a bit drained, didn't you sleep well?"

Nizam muttered something like, "I slept well, I don't know," and Sultan didn't press him any further.

They set out after breakfast, Nizam sensed that Sultan was a bit excited, as they neared the *tekke* Mihrişah Sultan covered her hair with a white lace cloth that suited her very well.

Nizam laughed.

"You look like the Virgin Mary."

Mihrişah Sultan smiled slightly and said, "Don't talk non-sense."

Rukiye met them at the *tekke* gate. She hugged Mihrişah Sultan like a child.

"You came all the way here for me," she said.

As she said this she began crying.

"Don't cry, my girl, don't cry my dear Rukiye, of course I came, did you think I would leave you alone at a time like this? Are you alright, my girl?"

"I'm not well . . . I'm not at all well, I'm having a lot of trouble coping with this pain . . . It's very difficult to become accustomed to death . . . I didn't know it was going to be so difficult."

Rukiye stopped suddenly.

"Forgive me, I've kept you standing here, come, let's go inside, you'll get cold."

"Is Sheikh Efendi here?"

"He said that we should talk a while first and that he would come welcome you later."

Rukiye embraced Nizam as well, "Welcome, my dear Nizam, and you come here every day."

They went together to the room at the front of the *tekke* that had been prepared for them.

"It's always so melancholy here," said Mihrişah Sultan, "I don't know, was Sheikh Efendi's decision to bring you here right?"

"Talking with my father the Sheikh eases me a bit, and anyway I like the melancholy atmosphere here, the shade, I like the way that this seems like another realm."

"Never mind, my girl, living within this melancholy all the time won't help you to forget your pain."

"It doesn't make any difference where I am anyway . . . Reality is the same everywhere . . . Tevfik is dead, there's no place on earth that will change this reality, that will make me forget this reality."

Coffee was brought for them, Mihrişah Sultan drank her coffee in silence to give Rukiye time to calm down.

"Come here, sit next to me," she said to Rukiye.

Rukiye sat next to her and Mihrişah Sultan held her hand.

"You're a strong girl, Rukiye, you're strong by nature and I also raised you to be a strong woman . . . The pain of death is difficult, like everyone else I've experienced this pain, I know the feeling of helplessness . . . But, my girl, we need our strength at times like this . . . You're going to have a child . . . You can't let your child be born like this, you can't allow your child to be born amidst this pain. Do you want the shadow of the anguish you're feeling now to fall on your child for the rest of its life? What sin has your child committed to deserve that?"

She stopped and looked at Rukiye.

"You're going to bury your grief and anguish now, you're going to forget the past, you're going to think about your child and the future . . . My child, losing someone you love is the worst blow that fortune can deliver, of course it is, of course it will turn your world upside down . . . But do you want the people who killed your husband, who did this evil to you, to also do evil to your child? If you don't want them to touch your baby, if you don't want their evil to infect your child, you're going to dust yourself off, my dear Rukiye. If you want to create a cheerful, happy world for your baby rather than a world full of mourning, if you want that child to experience happiness, you're going to

436 · AHMET ALTAN

emerge from your mourning this very day, when I come here tomorrow I'm going to see you smiling . . ."

Rukiye was weeping without making a sound, just as she had on the day Tevfik was shot.

"Promise me, Rukiye, tonight you'll go to bed thinking about Tevfik, but tomorrow morning you'll wake thinking of your child . . . Promise me that . . . I came here from Paris to hear you make that promise . . . If you promise to do it you'll be able to do it, I know you."

Rukiye was weeping silently, Mihrişah Sultan and Nizam were looking at her.

"Oh, this is so difficult . . ."

"I raised you to be a woman who could do difficult things . . . When you give birth I'm going to come get you and your baby. We'll raise your child together. Together we'll make your child a strong person, one day when your child is in pain you'll hold his hand, you're going to tell him to be strong."

Rukiye continued to weep silently.

Then, in the authoritative tone that the two siblings knew so well Mihrişah Sultan said,

"Rukiye."

"Yes."

"Are you going to be unfair to the child Tevfik bequeathed to you? Are you going to find your own grief more important than your child's future?"

Mihrişah Sultan's voice softened again.

"My dear Rukiye, you have to do this . . . You have to bury your grief . . . Do you understand this?"

"I understand."

"Are you going to do as I say?"

"Yes."

"Do you promise?"

Rukiye remained silent for a moment, then she raised her head and looked at Mihrişah Sultan and took her hands.

"You came all the way here for me, I'll never forget that."

Mihrişah Sultan didn't say anything.

Rukiye sighed.

"Fine," she said, "I'll do what you told me to do, I'll bury my grief . . . I'm giving you my promise, the next time you won't see me like this."

Mihrişah Sultan hugged Rukiye and pulled her to her chest, "Oh my beautiful girl, I know it's very difficult but you have to do it, my dear Rukiye, otherwise I wouldn't have pestered you at a time like this."

"I know, ma'am."

"Good," said Mihrişah Sultan, "We should get going, cry as much as you want today, but when I come tomorrow I want you to greet me with a smile . . . Your father the Sheikh is busy I suppose, I'll see him some other time."

Just then the door opened.

A woman said, "If it's convenient, his excellency the Sheikh would like to come."

"Tell him to come," said Sultan.

As they waited in silence for Sheikh Efendi to arrive, Mihrişah Sultan absent mindedly adjusted her headscarf, there was an ambiguous uneasiness in the way she sat, the way she touched her collar.

When the door opened and Sheikh Efendi appeared with his usual air of peace, Rukiye and Nizam stood, Sultan and the Sheikh looked at each other, it was as if they were trying to see what had changed over the years, "Welcome," said the Sheikh.

"Thank you, your excellency."

The Sheikh turned to Nizam.

"How are you, Nizam?" he asked.

"I'm fine, sir, how are you?"

A strange friendship had begun between the Sheikh and Nizam, who came to the *tekke* every day to visit Rukiye; at first, even though he didn't express it openly, and with an enjoyment particular to young people, Nizam made it clear that he didn't attach any importance to a man of religion who was respected throughout the empire, not showing any respect and behaving in a superficially polite manner. He possessed the ease of not knowing the value of the person he was speaking to, he was never rude, but it was clear he hadn't internalized the genuine admiration and respect. He treated the Sheikh like the father of a stepsister he loved very much, he had no significance for him beyond that. Because he had no special interest in religion or religiosity, everything that the Sheikh represented was unimportant to him. As he told Anya later, he found something ridiculous in the *tekke*'s shady garden, the mystical atmosphere, the grave cypress trees, and the reverential dervishes.

"It's like the next world there," he said to Anya, "but if you go a little way out the gate there are carriages passing. Think of the next world being so close to the avenue . . ."

The Sheikh's experienced eyes immediately saw the way Nizam looked at him with indifferent rebelliousness and concealed disrespect, this situation interested him in the way a wild horse might interest a horse-trainer, but he didn't act, he left him to his own devices.

What brought them closer was the great love they had for Rukiye and their joint efforts to heal her, what impressed Nizam was the calm anguish the Sheikh felt when faced with his daughter's pain, he could see that he was deeply saddened, that he was doing everything in his power to heal his daughter, that he felt helpless, that he closed himself in his room and prayed.

While this helplessness propelled the Sheikh to seek shelter in prayer and God, it propelled Nizam towards a dangerous and uncontrollable anger.

Nizam didn't even know what helplessness was, he had so little experience with the emotion he felt that he didn't even know what to call it, he wanted the people who'd hurt his older sister and killed his brother-in-law to be punished, he believed in the rightness of this desire, but when he saw that this was impossible he believed he was encountering a disrespectful assault not just on his older sister but on himself as well. The desire for revenge was growing within him. He didn't understand why the murderers weren't being punished, it was unjust, and not being able to speak out against this injustice led to this anger settling into his soul and growing steadily.

Once, with a strong sense of rebellion, he said to Hikmet Bey,

"I don't understand this, it's clear who the murderers are, why aren't they being punished?"

In a weary and exhausted tone, Hikmet Bey said,

"The murderers are in power, my son, they're now both murderers and judges, how are they going to be punished?"

"So this murder will just be left unpunished?"

"I'm afraid that will be the case . . . There's not much that can be done about it."

"Are we just going to accept this?"

"At the moment there's nothing that can be done, Nizam, look, Parliament has been closed, they're suppressing all opposition, they're silencing the press, they control the army, they control the police . . . We have to wait . . . They're going to become more violent, they have no other choice, each time they'll be a little more violent, in the end they'll become victims of their own violence."

"Is that what we're going to wait for? For them to become victims of their own violence?"

"Yes."

"I can't accept that, father, forgive me . . . And I don't understand how you can be so placid. How can you not protest this, you rose up against the sultan's tyranny, now you say we should wait in silence."

"The situation is very different."

"How is it different, I don't understand what's different about it."

"At that time there was an organization to overthrow the sultan, now that organization is in power and there's no other organization to overthrow them. The nation's hope itself became the nation's scourge, there's no other hope at the moment."

"In the sultan's time we had hope, but now that hope is gone, is that right?"

"Yes."

"If only you hadn't overthrown the sultan, at least then there'd be hope, at least there would be hope that the sultan would be punished for the crimes he committed. So look, there's no hope . . ."

In order to take out his anger at Hikmet Bey and to hurt him as cruelly as possible for not being as eager as he was to avenge Rukiye, Nizam said,

"That means you made a mistake, it would have been better not to have overthrown the sultan. You struggled for nothing. Nothing changed and there's no hope left."

"That's the way this country is," said Hikmet Bet, struggling to conceal his anger, "it won't be easy to straighten out. The sultan is gone, after a while you'll see that these people are going to go too, the people who replace them will go too, but this country will always suffer. The miserable people here don't find tyranny objectionable. It's as if they think that tyranny is part of the natural order . . . They don't know any other way of life. Those who know that a way of life other than tyranny is possible have to do their best to tell the people."

"Then what will happen?"

"One day things will be straightened out."

"Are you going to live to see things get straightened out?"

"No."

"Am I going to see it?"

"No."

"If I have children will they see it?"

"I don't think so."

"Their children?"

"They probably won't see it either . . . Nizam, this place won't be easy to straighten out but we have to live in the hope that one day it will be, we'll do our best. This country is like a child that was born crippled, it won't be easy to heal it but this reality won't prevent us from loving it, it won't make us give up on trying to heal it."

"Forgive me, father, but what you say doesn't make me feel any better . . . What kind of country is this? The murderers are always in power, there's no hope that things will get better, and we're supposed to love this place?"

"It will get better one day, my son."

"One day doesn't have any meaning for me, father, tell me about the present . . . I'm living in the present."

"Life isn't a struggle to get what we can get right away, sometimes you have to be willing to take the first steps towards something that will only be successful much later, stairs rise step by step, one day you reach your goal . . . To be enlightened is to accept that there's something called tomorrow . . . Beyond this is to accept that there's such a thing as a day . . . Even further beyond this is to accept that there's such a thing as a day."

"To be enlightened is to have every day except today, I suppose . . . I'm not that kind of enlightened person. I'm not even an enlightened person. I'm living in the present, my brother-in-law was murdered in the present, my older sister is weeping today, the punishment should be meted out today."

"If you don't have the strength to bear the truth you'll suffer throughout your life, you'll live without hope, you'll live in desperation . . . The truth hurts us today, we can't change this, but we can't stop hoping for tomorrow."

"That would be an empty hope, father, you know that as

well. This isn't hope, it's an empty consolation . . . The Ottoman Empire is finished . . . That's the reality . . . As far as I can see it's not going to come back to life again. Every time you try to revive it you'll see the face of its corpse. I'm not going to try to bring the dead back to life, I'm not going to fool myself. That's not the kind of person I am. I'm not the kind of person to wait next to a corpse in the hope that it will resurrect one day. Father, don't fool yourself, this dead body is not going to come back to life. While you try to bring it back to life it will just keep rotting, the flesh will fall off the bones, it will smell, and people like you will wait hopefully for it to come back to life . . . You're wasting your life trying to resurrect it."

Hikmet Bey was unable to keep himself from laughing.

"So what should we do then, son?"

"Bury it . . ."

"And then?"

"You'll suffer for your dead nation for a time, you'll accept this reality, let it become part of nature again beneath the earth, perhaps one day it will come to life in a completely different form . . . There's no other hope for this country . . . The only hope is to obey the rules of nature."

That day, Hikmet Bey decided to send Nizam back to Paris with Mihrişah Sultan, his anger worried him, he was also sad that he had no love for these lands. If he had said the same things about the country and "the people who've never known anything but tyranny" with a bit more sadness, the bond between them might have strengthened, but Nizam's lack of love, his coarse realism, undermined the bond between father and son.

Hikmet Bey said to Dilevser, "Even if what he says is true, shouldn't he say it with a little sadness? His lack of love makes me sad, he talks as if he doesn't love anything, it's as if everything is his enemy, why doesn't he love anything?"

"It's not that he doesn't love," said Dilevser, "he loves you very much, he loves Rukiye very much, he loves Mihrişah Sultan very much, I'm not quite sure but I suppose he loves his mother very much too . . . He even loves me . . . It's just that the way he loves is different from what we're accustomed to. Perhaps he sees loving as a kind of weakness . . . I'm not completely sure but I know that he loves."

Dilevser had inherited her mother's sharp tongue but seldom resorted to it, she laughed as she added,

"And he loves himself very much."

"I'm not even sure of that," said Hikmet Bey. "Sometimes I think he's angry even at himself."

Nizam was a little more careful about what he said when he was talking to Sheikh Efendi, he wasn't as hurtful as he was when he spoke to his father, but he still couldn't keep himself from expressing his anger. But the really surprising thing was that Nizam was the only person who could make Sheikh Efendi laugh, Nizam's nonchalance, his concealed disrespect, the wit that was nourished by this nonchalance and concealed disrespect, created a space between then that neither of them was accustomed to, an enjoyable space with lose boundaries.

Sometimes, when Rukiye wearied of her own pain and fell asleep, they talked about what they could do for her together, then they became two troubled people, they sought consolation not in each other's ideas, beliefs or status but in the common love they felt for Rukiye.

For two people who were not at all alike, who were indeed almost the complete opposite of each other, to be saddened about the same person, to love the same person so intensely, to be so troubled about the same person, in fact surprised them both, once Sheikh Efendi said to Nizam, "God connected all of his creatures together with a hidden bond, when you touch one person, you touch many more people than you could possibly imagine."

"The Lord tells all of his creatures that other people are

your destiny . . . All of your fates are bound together . . . None of you are going to be saved alone, if you are going to be saved, you'll all be saved together, if you are lost you will be lost together . . . Perhaps this is the greatest test, for the sons of Adam to understand this bond . . . Our Lord is waiting for the creatures he created to understand this . . . He wants his creatures to reach this perfection, to become this mature."

"Your Lord is going to have to wait a long time to see this."

"Our Lord has endless time . . . He is timeless . . . Time is for us creatures . . . But why do you think that?"

"People will never reach that level of maturity. Don't take this as disrespect, your excellency the Sheikh, you and my father are always expecting something from the future. You don't expect anything from today. In my opinion, you both see in different ways that there's nothing to expect from today. I differ from you in that I don't see anything much changing in the future. I don't expect anything from the future. However bad today is, that's how bad the future will be . . . And why is your Lord always waiting for us to understand things instead of just telling us openly."

"He told us but we didn't understand."

"What did he say?"

"'You must descend as enemies, and stay on the face of the earth for a time and get along . . . You'll live there, die there, then resurrect and leave . . . ' This is what our Lord commanded in the Araf Sura . . . The sons of Adam were sent to this earth to atone for a sin, in order to atone they have to pass a test, to reach the level where all of this enmity and evil is left behind and we realize all of our fates are bound together, we're here to earn the right to return to the place from which we were expelled . . . You talk about today, yes, today is important for all creatures, today we'll take our own test, today we will save our souls from torment by doing what has to be done, however, the future is much more important for all of us, we look to the future for the day when people will be freed one by one from their sins, their mistakes, their enmity and their evil, when they will reach that maturity and be saved, yes, we look to the future to fulfill that common destiny I spoke about . . . It won't happen today, but it will begin today. It will begin again tomorrow, it will begin again the day after that, the future will begin again every day and every day people will understand that they have a common destiny and they will reach that perfect destiny, we were sent here as enemies, but we will walk knowing that we will only be able to get out of here if we become friends."

Partly from the callowness of youth, partly from his self-indulgent nature, and partly because he didn't know Sheikh Efendi's merit, Nizam came out with a question that no one else but him would have had the courage to ask,

"And if there's no God . . ."

"This doubt is a very heavy load to carry within you, you can carry this load if God helps you . . . I am certain of God's existence, I see him everywhere I look, even in you who asks this question . . . But since you've asked, let me put it this way, if there's no God then there's no future for humanity. No matter how many people live, no matter how many people pass through this world, the entirety of life will be no more than a person can live, it will only last as long as a person can live . . . Eighty, maybe ninety years . . . The same ninety years repeated . . . That's all. All of humanity, these billions of people, would amount to a single miserable creature imprisoned within ninety years. All of history, the past that stretches behind us, would amount to ninety years. The entire future would amount to ninety years. There would be no redemption, no hope for humanity . . . When you look around at this world, could all of this have been created for ninety years? Does this seem possible to you? The future is what makes life

what it is, it consists of those who will come after you, it consists of those who will come after them . . . What gives this
unending repetition meaning is that this voyage is directed
towards that goal."

Nizam didn't say anything as he thought for a while about
what Sheikh Efendi had said, then in a stubborn tone he asked,

"So, if God does exist, what's going to happen to today's
murderers?"

"God will make his judgment concerning them . . . They are
both staining their own souls and delaying humanity's common
future, their punishment will be meted out when the time
comes."

"No, I can't accept that their punishment will be left for
some unspecified time, I don't understand how to accept this."

"One day you'll understand . . . I entreat God that the day
will come when you understand . . . I pray for you."

"Why are you praying and supplicating for me?"

"I pray for everyone, and besides, you're a good boy."

Nizam laughed.

"No one else but you knows that I'm a good boy, how do
you know this?"

"You're suffering, my son . . . I see that you're suffering . . . That's how I know."

Perhaps the primary reason Sheikh Efendi embraced
Nizam as if he was his own son despite all of his contradictions, strangeness, and concealed disrespect was the genuine
love this young man felt for his older sister, the desire he felt
to ease her pain and the great anguish her anguish caused
him. The attachment Nizam felt to Rukiye gave Sheikh
Efendi confidence. This selfish young man came to the *tekke*
every day, sometimes he sat for hours with his older sister
without uttering a word, he insisted that she eat, he struggled
to cheer her up just a little.

Once he said to Rukiye about Nizam,

"Your anguish is taming him. You anguish is teaching him the reality of life."

Nizam became someone whose arrival not only Rukiye but the entire *tekke* awaited, his blameless, sinful, self-indulgence amused everyone, sometimes when he encountered the water man in the garden he would good-naturedly help him carry his water cans, sometimes he would joke with the old woman who brought sherbet, sometimes he would have philosophical arguments with the dervishes and surprise them.

Nizam was surprised by their tolerance, on one occasion he asked Sheikh Efendi,

"They know that I'm a sinner but they're not angry at me . . . I've become the sinful dervish of the *tekke* . . . Sometimes I'm surprised by the friendly way they accept me."

"The *tekke* door is open to everyone," said Sheikh Efendi, "we greet everyone who comes through the door with the same love. Our duty is not to punish sinners, it's not even our place to decide who is a sinner and who is not, this is between you and your Lord . . . Our duty is to show you the correct path . . . If you find that path, that's good, we'll be pleased, if you don't find it we'll feel sorry for you . . . And a good Muslim won't ask "is he a sinner," he'll ask "is he a good person," we believe that whoever you are, if you're a good person, one day you'll become a good Muslim . . . You're on the wrong path, yes, but you're not harming anyone but yourself, you haven't infringed on anyone's rights, you didn't cheat anyone of their rights. They see this as well, they're not just accepting you into their *tekke*, they love you, they're hopeful that you'll become a good Muslim, they pray for you."

"I don't want to lie to you or deceive you . . . I don't want to deceive anyone . . . You know that I won't be able to become a good Muslim, don't you, your excellency the Sheikh?"

"No one can know that, Nizam, not even you can know that."

Nizam didn't give up his sins and his sinfulness, but just as he went to the gambling den every night, he went to the *tekke* every morning, and as he struggled to heal Rukiye he found a peace there that he didn't find anywhere else.

Sometimes he asked Sheikh Efendi childish questions.

"It's very peaceful here, is it this peaceful because you don't commit sin? Is your secret not committing sin?"

Sheikh Efendi laughed.

"No," he said, "The reason it's so peaceful here is that we don't judge anyone."

One of the most important reasons Sheikh Efendi loved Nizam was that he occasionally asked questions like this, he found a reassuring innocence in this childish curiosity. He also knew that Nizam wasn't so innocent, but Sheikh Efendi wasn't surprised by contradictions in people, he knew that he went to the gambling den every evening but he greeted him every morning without rebuke and with the same friendliness.

That morning Mihrişah Sultan had also noticed the way Nizam was received at the *tekke*, "they all know you," she said, and Nizam laughed and said, "I'm going to become a dervish too."

From the moment Sheikh Efendi entered the room Sultan noticed the love he felt for Rukiye and the closeness he showed Nizam. This both reassured her and caused her to feel a strange jealousy, as if she was going to lose "the children's love."

The excitement of seeing Sheikh Efendi pushed these feelings back, Sultan always saw the Sheikh as a man, she saw him that way now too, she wasn't at all interested in his religiosity, his belief, his devotion, she admired the power, decisiveness and untouchability that made his calm more apparent, as well as, though she didn't admit this to herself, his handsomeness.

Of all his traits, the one she found most interesting was his untouchability, kings, sultans, grand viziers, and shayk al-islams could be touched, they saw that they were being touched, but Sheikh Efendi was untouchable, that's how Mihrişah Sultan felt. She couldn't quite find the answer to why he was untouchable, she was trying to understand what made this man untouchable, "I suppose it was his belief that made him untouchable," she said to Osman, "he was so attached to God that no human could touch him, could approach him, it was as if his faith made him a part of God . . . At least he evoked that feeling in people."

These words explained why Mihrişah Sultan had the kind of interest in Sheikh Efendi that she'd never had in any other man, there was no man who could counterbalance the magnificent arrogance with which she looked down on people, but Sheikh Efendi's apparently "divine" untouchability and loneliness led her perhaps for the first time to see a man as her equal, and indeed even her superior. Her soul, which was full of the love and admiration that constantly flowed from herself towards herself, and which was weary of itself, chose the Sheikh in order to direct these feelings outwards, to be free of them, to slough off her attachment to herself, to feel the warmth of a human emotion.

The inevitable interest that these two people who were isolated by their own strength felt for each other was whipped up by the impossibility of anything coming of it. They never said a word to each other about this, they only allowed their feelings to be reflected through surreptitious glances, words emphasized differently and vague gestures. To reflect these signals in a manner that they and no one else could see was extraordinarily difficult, but to the same degree very exciting.

As the four of them sat and chatted, and as she repressed the excitement of this first meeting, Mihrişah Sultan kept adjusting her headscarf or her collar, Sheikh Efendi was more motionless than usual, he just glanced at Sultan from time to time, at those moments his eyes grew larger, or at least Sultan thought she saw his eyes grow bigger.

Rukiye seemed not to notice any of this, at another time she would have sensed what was going on before anyone else, but that day she was full of her own pain, but for his part Nizam was watching them with a hidden smile. It amused him to see these two powerful people become powerless, childish and inexperienced, and struggling not to let this show.

"Let's walk in the garden a little, your excellency the Sheikh," said Mihrişah Sultan, "I like the *tekke* garden, we can talk as we walk."

"If you won't get cold . . ."

No matter how much she admired someone, it wasn't easy for Mihrişah Sultan not to be herself, and with the arrogant frankness that suited her so well she said,

"I won't get cold. I'm not accustomed to such ill-lit rooms, your *tekke* is very nice but it's badly lit . . . The light outside will make me feel better."

Sheikh Efendi smiled.

"As you wish."

Sultan said to Nizam,

"You sit with Rukiye, there are things I need to discuss with Sheikh Efendi."

They went out together.

The sky was overcast, a faint, pinkish grey light seeped between the gaps in the clouds, in places the deep green of the cypress trees glowed with this light, as the clouds moved so did the shadows. The Golden Horn was motionless, it had taken on the color of the sky, greys, blues, and pinks were floating side by side on the surface.

As they walked side by side, Mihrişah Sultan said,

"I didn't say anything to Rukiye, I tried to console her, to soothe her, but what's going to happen to these murderers who

killed Tevfik? These men have climbed to the top in this country, they're acting as if this murder never occurred."

"We've turned them over to God . . ."

"You mean they're not going to receive any punishment . . ."

"God's punishments are worse than any other kind of punishment . . . They took a life, they destroyed a being, of course
there's a punishment for this."

"Your excellency the Sheikh, your faith, your belief in the
next world, may be strong, but I'm not like that . . . I want
human justice before divine justice. Are these men going to
walk around like heroes? Aren't you going to do anything?"

"I will shelter in God from the desire for revenge . . ."

"But in fact you want to take revenge . . ."

"We're a miserable race, we're conscious of our misery and
our weakness . . . We're the descendants of a species that was
expelled from paradise and that is struggling to return to the
place from which it was expelled . . . We arrived crippled, and
we're struggling to return whole . . . Our souls, our bodies,
every particle of our being is crippled by weakness. Satan
doesn't invent sins for us, he doesn't create weaknesses that
weren't there, he just tells you to go along with your sins, you
get caught up in the temptation of your weaknesses . . . What
can this miserable human, this crippled creature, do? How can
we be freed from the depravity in our own souls? Our weaknesses appear before us in so many guises, sometimes it's an
anguish, sometimes it's a desire, sometimes it's an ambition,
sometimes it's anger . . . It's easy to get carried away by them.
Here we have a weeping child, how easy, how sweet it would be
to be carried away by the temptations of anger and the desire
for revenge . . . Revenge is the forbidden fruit, how easy it
would be to reach out, pick it, and eat it, how delicious it would
be . . . A word, a command, even a glance would be enough, it
would be a drink of water for your child's pain, a drop of balm

for your wounded heart . . . Is that what should be done? Should we ease our anguish with blood and revenge?"

He stopped, when he stopped, Mihrişah Sultan also stopped, he turned and looked at Mihrişah Sultan.

"Would you recommend that to me? Shall we pick that poisonous fruit, further crippling a soul that is already crippled by nature?"

"When you ask me like that, I suppose I've become Satan, your Excellency the Sheikh."

"Please . . . I didn't ask with that intention, I asked sincerely, as a friend. What would you recommend? Yes, we're capable of taking revenge, in this transitory word God has granted us that possibility . . . What should we do, should we use that possibility to go against God's commandment? They destroyed a being, should we destroy a being too?"

For a moment Mihrişah Sultan feared that if she said "yes," Sheikh Efendi would really do this, that he would take revenge, that with a single order he would set the gigantic power under his command into motion.

"No," she said in panic, "That's not what I wanted to say."

"What did you want to say?"

Then he realized that this question was rude and he continued immediately.

"You're in a lot of pain too, I know, I feel the same pain every day when I see Rukiye like that . . . There are times when I'm seized with anger, God knows that there are times when I want to take revenge, I want to find some consolation for Rukiye's pain . . . I don't say anything to anyone, I'm seized by the worry that anything I say could be misunderstood, that someone might think this was what I wanted and do something without my knowledge . . . I keep quiet . . . I can see in Rukiye's eyes that she's begging for a solution to her pain, I'm her father, she's expecting me to ease her pain. It's natural she would expect that, she's a child, when she has no strength left she'll take shelter in her father . . . What is her father to do? There are times when I'm frightened of myself, there are times when I'm frightened of my weaknesses, there are times when I'm frightened by my own power . . ."

Mihrişah Sultan could see that Sheikh Efendi was revealing a side of himself that he hadn't shown anyone, perhaps out of loneliness, perhaps out of desperation, perhaps because there was no one else he could share it with, perhaps because he could no longer bear the torment he was suffering, he'd shared his anguish and is anger with great sincerity. "Powerful men have moments of powerlessness," she said to Osman later, "I have to say this, neither power on its own nor powerlessness on its own can be as attractive in a man as this contradiction. The greatest gift a powerful man can give a woman is to reveal his powerless side, I'd never in my life received a gift as great as that, in any event I'd never encountered anyone powerful enough to give me that gift . . . At a moment like that, a woman feels all of her emotions, everything from maternal feelings to uxorial feelings, rebel. I don't know, is that something like this thing they call love?"

Mihrişah Sultan could see that Sheikh Efendi was caught between his anger and his belief, that he was suffocating from carrying alone the weight of the decision he would make at the intersection where the emotions he called weakness and the path he knew was right separated. The men who had killed his son-in-law had taken over the entire empire, it was impossible to punish these murderers even though it was clearly known who the murderers were, the people were shouting "long life" to the murderers and remembering them with love. He was faced with such clear injustice and unfairness that he was having difficulty convincing himself and those around him to accept it. He thought that Rukiye's eyes were constantly asking him "Why? Why were we subjected to an injustice like this, why did God find me deserving of this pain, is this God's justice?"

Everyone knew that with a single command he could right the broken scales of "justice," that he could reckon with this murder in kind, as he'd said to Sultan he was frightened by this "power," he had power but he couldn't use this power. "This is a test," he kept telling himself, "this is a test."

He retreated to his room and prayed for hours, "God grant me the strength to pass this test with honor, help this miserable creature whose soul is made wretched by weakness, God keep me from making the wrong decision and taking the wrong path, I take shelter in you, protect me from my own weakness."

When Mihrişah Sultan saw the pain the Sheikh was suffering and the helplessness he was experiencing, she grasped that she had been unfairly self-indulgent.

"This unexpected anguish has shaken all of us, sometimes we talk nonsense . . . Forgive me for what I said, consider it the impertinence of a grieving woman. What you said is true, punishing the murderers is not our duty, we have to look for ways to ease our girl's torment, we have to think about the child that is going to be born . . . That's our duty."

Sheikh Efendi looked at Mihrişah Sultan, the white, lace scarf covering her head, her dark blue dress, the star-shaped, diamond clasp that held up her hair, and the blue of the Golden Horn that was reflected here and there on her face among the dark green shadows gave her the look of someone out of a fairy tale.

They looked at each other in silence for a few seconds, it was a silence filled with words that hadn't been uttered, couldn't be uttered and wouldn't be uttered. During that silence they said so much more to each other than they could have said in a conversation, they heard every word that hadn't been uttered, they felt every emotion that passed within them. Their silence was like a magical elixir, as they drank it they felt enveloped by an intoxication that was full of emotions and shadows. They grasped body and soul that at no time and under no circumstances would the two of them be as close to each other, and tell each other as much as they did during that brief moment of silence.

A seagull took off from the Golden Horn and flapped its wings as it passed among the trees.

Sheikh Efendi sighed, they started walking again, they didn't speak, they didn't want to break the silence, they wanted to extend this brief period of time because it might never be possible to repeat it.

During that brief moment, they intensely felt the clash between the limitlessness of emotions and the limits of life. The almost drunken lightheadedness they were experiencing came from witnessing the small universe in which only the two of them were present being created by a violent clash and then beginning to slowly disappear. All of their emotions were created anew, had been brought to life with a bright fire that filled their entire beings. They'd seen everything, they'd heard everything.

Later Mihrişah Sultan told Osman, "Never in my life had I experienced what I experienced in that brief moment, I also learned that time is insignificant, it's not important how long you live, it's important what you live, I understood this. Sometimes a single second can be as long as a life."

After they'd walked a bit further and reached the shore of the Golden Horn, Mihrişah Sultan said:

"There's a matter I would like to speak to you about."

"Please."

"If you'll permit it, I would like to take Rukiye to Paris after the child is born. I think it would be good for her to get away from a country that's being governed by her husband's murderers, to get away from injustice and desperation. Let her spend some time there raising her child, finding consolation, calm down . . . I don't know what you say to this, do you find it suitable?"

"It's a good idea . . . I think you should bring Nizam too . . . He shouldn't stay here."

When Mihrişah Sultan heard this she looked at Sheikh Efendi in alarm, and the Sheikh felt the need to explain.

"He's very angry too . . . He's suffering a great deal of torment. I think it would be good for him to get away from here."

They didn't speak of anything else as they walked side by side back to the *tekke*.

29

Some nights Anya no longer went to the gambling den, she stayed home. She was trying to become accustomed to life and emotions like a baby just learning to walk, sometimes she stumbled, sometimes she fell, sometimes she wept, sometimes she retreated into silence.

"I don't know," she said to Nizam, "I don't know if you've done something good or something bad by drawing me back into life . . ."

"I didn't draw you back into life," said Nizam, "You weren't going to be able to pretend to be dead anymore, perhaps I might have helped a chick trying to get out of its egg to break the shell."

In these days of transition, the behavior of two different women could be seen one after the other, a Russian aristocrat and a gambling den pianist, neither had become completely real, and in their shadowy state they mixed together; when Anya saw the woman who cleaned the house and cooked the food make a mistake, she rebuked the woman in such a polite but decisive manner that Nizam was surprised by her natural authority; sometimes she turned and looked at Nizam in such a way that he could see a woman sitting at a sumptuous table at the Tsar's palace with all of her acquaintances; sometimes she retreated into such a timid silence that she possessed all of the paleness and frozenness of death.

She didn't speak at all about her past and Nizam didn't ask her, this was an unspoken agreement between them, sometimes the emotions that were coming back to life revived a memory, in delight she would mention an incident from her past, then with a sadness greater than the delight she would fall silent. From some of the things Anya said during those brief moments of coming to life, he learned that Anya had played the piano for the Tsar's family but that she was not a professional pianist, her father had recognized her talent when she was still a child and had hired the best teachers for her, but that he had never allowed her to perform in public.

Once Nizam asked her, "Have you ever wanted to play the piano before an audience and let everyone see how talented you are," and had laughed out loud at the way Anya said, "For the people?"

Nizam knew that she came from an aristocratic family and that due to some incident she'd experienced she'd had to flee Russia and kill her soul; sometimes it dizzied Nizam that Anya possessed the memories, identities and habits of two different women at the same time, that they were so intertwined, and that sometimes they seemed to multiply like two mirrors facing each other. Sometimes it was as if he was dancing an endless waltz, he turned with the woman in his arms, and with each turn the woman changed, had a different face and a different appearance, he didn't quite know who Anya was. The dark emptiness in Anya's past drew him in, he wasn't curious, there was no change in his selfish lack of curiosity, but he found excitement in the idea of bringing that dead darkness back to life, of witnessing that miracle. He wanted to bring Anya out of that darkness into the light, to help her regain her former identity. "I don't know why I wanted this," he said to Osman later, "I just wanted that . . . I don't know, perhaps what I really wanted was to prove to myself that I could do this."

On the nights when Anya didn't go to the gambling den, they ate together, sometimes Anya would play the piano for Nizam for hours. It's very difficult for a woman and a man to develop a conversation when one of their pasts can't be touched upon, most of their conversations hit this wall, it was difficult to make any progress, then their common love for music took the place of this past, their relationship developed more through notes than through words.

Not being able to describe their feelings to themselves, not possessing a clear consciousness of their own feelings, came perhaps from this wordlessness, they lived as if they were listening to music, without describing, simply by sensing, they abandoned themselves to the relationship as if they were abandoning themselves to music.

They weren't aware that they were living a love.

Nizam liked it when Anya sat at the piano and played in a manner he would not be able to hear anywhere else from anyone else, he thought that he was attached to that music, that he missed it; he was aware that it was a great privilege to be able to listen to that music, and he didn't want to lose this; he wasn't aware that through this music he was becoming increasingly integrated with Anya, that they were becoming inseparable.

Like Anya, he didn't talk much about his family, he worried that this might upset Anya; like Nizam, Anya only had small clues about his family, she guessed that his family was very wealthy but she didn't know where this wealth had come from. They were each always surprised by the other's knowledge of music and literature, in fact this surprise, which had its source in a concealed disdain, increased their love and attachment. Like explorers in a mysterious and unmapped landscape, they admired and were surprised and delighted by everything they saw, and they walked with increasing excitement, not knowing what they would find in the end.

Nizam told Anya about his Paris days, at these times it became apparent that Anya loved Paris and knew the city well, but Nizam's Paris went beyond the salons, restaurants, theaters, and music halls that Anya knew and turned in to the back streets and the darkness; Nizam told her about his adventures there in a manner that made Anya listen with her eyes wide open in amazement. Sometimes Anya squealed as she laughed aloud.

Tevfik Bey being shot was another turning point in their relationship, Anya became the only person to whom Nizam could show his true feelings without being guarded. He could talk about his anguish, his anger, and his desire for revenge with complete openness. Perhaps if he'd met her in a ballroom rather than at a gambling den he might not have been able to reveal himself with such ease, but the place where they'd met played a very important role in their relationship, even though they sensed each other's true identities they didn't know them fully, this gave them, and especially Nizam, an enormous freedom, they could wander naked in a land where no one knew them without caring much about what the people around them thought.

When Nizam talked about the pain Rukiye was suffering, Anya could see how much he loved his older sister and how he could love a person; the torment Nizam felt in the face of Rukiye's pain cracked the compassion and tenderness concealed like a seed in a secret pouch, this led to his compassion and tenderness enveloping Anya as well, to his wanting to protect her.

At another time these emotions might have surprised or indeed have frightened Nizam, he wasn't accustomed to nurturing feelings like this for a woman, but the tenderness he felt for Rukiye, and the genuine sadness he felt in sharing her anguish, showed him that what he felt for Anya was a natural emotion.

During those anguished days, Anya wrapped him in an almost motherly tenderness, she listened to what he said, eased his anger, consoled him and played the piano for him. They were experiencing a reality without even grasping that they were aware of this reality; contrary to what people thought, genuine love was not demonstrative. They didn't feel the need for great words or great gestures, they flowed like a babbling brook in the valleys at the peaks of unreachable mountains; thunder and lightning only occurred when that love was broken somewhere.

Nizam walked more willingly and less anxiously within this musical vagueness they'd created, Anya came step by step, feeling her way timidly; Nizam was falling in love but he wasn't even aware of this, Anya saw better than he did what they were beginning to experience, she was more doubtful than Nizam.

"If I didn't play the piano you wouldn't come here like this," she said to him once.

"Are you saying I love you for your piano?" Nizam asked with a laugh.

"I'm saying it's possible."

"I don't know," said Nizam, "I've never thought of you and the piano as separate entities . . . But I would have liked it if you only played for me . . . For you to play for people who don't understand is unfair to you."

"I only really play for you."

The jealousy in Nizam made itself evident through the piano, the excuse it chose to come out into the open was convincing, and Nizam was certain that this feeling was not jealousy.

He didn't know that at first jealousy poisons and numbs its victims like a poisonous spider, then slowly melts and swallows them; he couldn't name the feeling because he'd never felt jealousy about anyone before. He believed that destiny had been unfair to Anya in response to her talent.

Just as mentioning the past had been forbidden by an unspoken agreement between them, so too had talking about emotions had been forbidden, they didn't know how they had decided this but they never spoke about their feelings.

They feared their emotions, for different reasons they had

decided not to involve themselves with emotions and to live a life in which everything flowed on the surface and that didn't descend into the depths, and they weren't prepared for the possibility that this could change; one had been crippled by what she'd lived through and the other was crippled by a self-ishness that imprisoned him within a cold loneliness, they were almost certain that healing these deformities would bring them a lot of pain.

This emotional silence was reflected in great explosions of enthusiasm when they made love, they knew the freedom of experiencing every kind of emotion when they made love. The bed was like an oasis in a desert from which feelings had dis-appeared, they weren't aware that they'd come closer there, that they'd become inseparable.

In that shelter where the emotions hidden behind their bodies were allowed to emerge, they expressed all of their feel-ings with their bodies. This physical language was more effec-tive and lasting than words, they perceived each other's emo-tions through the warmth of each other's bodies, this led them to engrave those feelings within them with the private warmth of a body.

Their relationship experienced a strange contradiction, as they rejected the naturalness of their emotions and fled, their relationship's roots grew deeper like those of trees growing in arid soil, they were establishing themselves healthily, they were becoming more difficult to pull out, they were gaining a more natural structure by another route.

Words had been replaced by the sound of music and the great battlements of their bodies, love was growing in an unac-customed place in an unaccustomed manner, they chose not to be aware of it as they abandoned themselves to this love.

Mihrişah Sultan sensed what was going on because she knew Nizam very well, when she expressed her desire to meet Anya in a very firm manner, Nizam remained obliged to tell Anya.

"Mihrişah Sultan wants to meet you."

Anya had turned her back to get something from the table, he could see that her shoulders had tensed, that her body had become pointed and sharp like a large thorn. In a cold tone Anya asked,

"Why?"

"I don't know, but she wants to meet you."

"There's no need for this."

"Mihrişah Sultan has made up her mind."

"Tell her that I don't want to impose on her."

Nizam laughed,

"You don't know Mihrişah Sultan . . . Can someone in Russia whom the Tsarina wants to meet say there's no need?"

"She's a tsarina?"

"That's Mihrişah Sultan for you . . . If you don't go to meet her, she's going to come to the gambling den to meet you. Once she's made up her mind, there's no power on earth that can stop her."

"You're exaggerating."

"You can be certain that I'm not, you'll understand when you meet her."

"I don't want to meet another tsarina, Nizam . . . I don't want to see tsars and tsarinas anymore. I'm not ready for this. I have a simple life and I don't want to move outside that life."

"There's no reason to be afraid."

"I'm not afraid . . . I just don't want to."

"Fine, if you don't want to I won't insist . . . Mihrişah Sultan will come to see you."

"How is she going to come?"

"She'll come to the gambling den with her entire entourage . . . She's made her decision, no one can change her mind . . . I don't know the reason but she wants to meet you, it's impossible to prevent this."

"She's going to come to the mansion?"

Nizam smiled, Anya played the piano at the gambling den but she couldn't bring herself to call it a gambling den, she referred to it as the "mansion."

"She'll come to the mansion,"

"She shouldn't do that."

"Anya, if there was anything I could do, I don't want this either, I don't want you to have to experience anything that would make you uncomfortable, but Sultan won't listen to me, if the sultan himself came she wouldn't listen to him either."

Anya sighed and repeated what she'd said.

"She shouldn't come to the mansion."

Nizam didn't answer.

"She shouldn't come to the mansion," repeated Anya, "I don't want her to see me there."

Nizam listened without saying anything.

"I'll go to her."

Two days later they went to see Mihrişah Sultan together.

Anya was very restless and quiet in the carriage, she'd shrunk into a corner. At that moment, she regretted everything that had happened from the moment she'd met Nizam, it was clear from the tension in her face, the way she bit her lip and the way she stared vacantly that if it were possible she would be willing to return to the days when she hadn't known Nizam. The hands she'd left on her lap seemed like dead hands, but the knuckles on the fingers she'd interlaced were white.

She was wearing a very elegant dress that Nizam hadn't seen before, she was wearing a pearl necklace that she'd never worn before, she was wearing mascara and had applied a little rouge to her cheeks, she'd taken pains to get ready for this meeting, it was clear that she'd opened the trunks and taken out the clothes she'd been able to bring with her and keep. She'd taken out and put on clothes that perhaps she'd thought she would never wear again but had kept in the trunk because it represented a bond with the past, but doing so had made her uneasy. Nizam sensed that Anya perceived this meeting as a kind of return to the past and that this was why she was so uneasy.

When they entered Mihrişah Sultan's garden, Anya raised her head and looked outside, the garden, flowers, trees, and the size of the mansion gave her an idea about its owner.

An Ethiopian butler in a frock coat opened the door, immediately afterwards a French lady in waiting greeted them with a cheerful politeness, she kissed Nizam, nodded to Anya and said, "her ladyship will be down shortly."

All of this wealth, magnificence, the elegance of the furniture in the house, the selective taste with which it had been arranged, the large carpets on the floor, Chinese vases the size of a man placed in the corners, fresh flowers that had been cut that morning and arranged, the smell of the house, the warmth that spread from the fires in the fireplaces, made Anya's head spin as if she was being pulled into the dark abyss of the past she had fled.

Nizam sat Anya in a large, winged chair and held her hand, he was afraid that anything Mihrişah Sultan said might hurt her. He noticed that her face had gone pale. This house contained everything that Anya wanted to forget.

There was a light flurry of snow outside.

The living room door opened, Mihrişah Sultan, in a light blue silk dress, entered like a goddess who had descended from the heavens, two ladies in waiting came in behind her.

Anya and Nizam stood when she entered.

"I've brought Anya," said Nizam in a cheerful tone that attempted to conceal his anxiety.

Almost instinctively, Anya curtseyed as she'd been taught as a child, greeting Mihrişah Sultan elegantly and naturally as if she was greeting a tsarina.

Sultan tenderly stroked Anya's hair as if she was stroking a child.

"This profligate finally brought you," she said, "You're very beautiful."

For some time Mihrişah Sultan had treated everyone apart from a few people as if they were children, she sought a secret consolation for her anger at old age, adding her age to her beauty and power to put people down.

Anya's face flushed.

"Thank you, madame."

It was clear from her expression that Anya was impressed by Sultan's beauty, by her face, which was still impressive despite being slightly wrinkled, her eyes and her stance, she grasped that Nizam came from a wealthier and more established family than she'd guessed. Her behavior had changed almost entirely, she'd become a mature Russian aristocrat, both liveliness and melancholy were reflected in her eyes.

"Nizam tells me you play the piano beautifully," said Sultan, "I hope that one day I'll have the opportunity to hear you."

"He exaggerated, madame."

"Nizam doesn't exaggerate much when he speaks, it's his attitudes that are exaggerated . . . Sometimes I get angry at what he does, but I always believe what he says."

Anya smiled and looked straight ahead.

After they'd had their coffee, Mihrişah Sultan said to Nizam in her nonchalant manner, "Go on and talk to the girls, they've missed you."

Nizam hesitated and turned to Anya, it was clear he was worried she would be uneasy if she was left alone, "Go," said Sultan again, "don't worry, we're just going to talk alone for a little while."

After Nizam had left, Sultan asked, "Would you like another coffee?"

"No thank you, madame."

"It's not my habit to interfere in these things," said Sultan, "however this time the situation is a little strange."

Anya placed her knees together and elegantly pulled them under the armchair, her back was straight, she'd lost her bashful manner, she looked at Sultan with an elegance that made it felt she would not tolerate any kind of disrespect. In fact she wanted to warn Mihrişah Sultan, to tell her she wanted to finish this conversation without it being dragged into a course that would be unpleasant for both of them, but Sultan wasn't someone who worried about warnings like this.

"As I suppose you can guess, Nizam has had many inappropriate liaisons, those were casual liaisons, they weren't serious, but I see now that even if he isn't aware of it he has formed a bond of affection with you . . ."

Sultan paused for a moment and sighed.

"Despite being a very good pianist, you play the piano at a gambling den, in a place that's not quite appropriate for you."

"What do you want from me, madame?" Anya asked in a cold tone.

"You could give a concert in Paris, I could arrange that."

"*Merci* madame, I don't want to give concerts."

"Are you afraid of appearing before an audience, of encountering people who know you?"

"No, madame, I'm not afraid of anything, I just don't want to. If you'll permit it, I want to decide what I'm going to do. I'm content with my situation, I don't want to change it."

Mihrişah Sultan chose to pretend not to notice the sternness in her manner.

"I can protect you," she said, "While I'm alive, no one can do anything to you."

"I don't want anyone to protect me, madame."

"But Monsieur Gavril protects you . . ."

Before continuing, Sultan took a deep breath to let it be known that a solid blow was coming.

"And even if you're not aware of it, Count Rodovski is also protecting you . . ."

Anya went completely red, her eyes widened, she looked at Sultan almost in terror, Sultan had known that she would be surprised like this and she continued in a calm tone.

"I know the whole story, Anya, I even know the things you don't know . . . I possess the means to find out whatever I want to find out . . . I want you to leave that gambling den . . . Monsieur Gavril might not be aware of it, but the Special Organization is watching his activities, Cheka is also watching him, and so are the sultan's men . . . Your clever Gavril thinks that if he lights fires around the place no one will see what's going on at the gambling den, but everyone sees. You are not safe there. Just as you're not safe, Nizam isn't safe either."

Anya was having trouble breathing, as she tried to catch her breath she asked,

"How do you know Count Rodovski?"

"As I said, I possess the means to find out whatever I want to find out . . . I know who you are, Anya . . . I know what you've been through too . . . Don't worry, I'm not about to tell Nizam anything. This is between you and me, as long as you don't tell Nizam, he won't learn the truth about you."

"You had no right to do this."

"What didn't I have the right to do?"

"To come into my life like this, to look into my past, to remind me of the things I wanted to forget . . . You had no right to do that, madame. My past, my present life, the work I do, madame, none of these give you the right to come into my life so impudently. I took shelter in a gambling den so as not to encounter anything like this, for my past to be raked up, for anyone to try to protect me, for anyone to try to teach me how to live, now I see how right I was, until I met Nizam I was living like a dead person, yes, like a dead person, but I was at peace, but now . . . Madame, you've done a very bad thing to me . . . With your permission I would like to leave . . . I don't want to see either you or Nizam again . . . I have suffered a great deal, but never once in my life have I encountered such disrespect as I'm encountering now."

Anya stood, Mihrişah Sultan stood as well and took hold of her arm.

"Please sit," she said.

Anya looked at Sultan, once again Mihrişah Sultan said, "Please, please sit down."

After hesitating about what to do for a moment, Anya sat down again, Mihrişah Sultan resumed her seat across from her.

"My aim is not to interfere in your life or rake up your past, and I never intended any disrespect, my girl, why should I behave disrespectfully to you, I don't think you're someone who deserves this . . . I know that you've suffered and that you've paid your penance, I just want to help you and Nizam, I have no other aim, you can be certain of that . . . I don't know how long your liaison will last, but Nizam seems to be smitten by you, if you continue to die in that gambling den, then at least for a time he will live, so to speak, a dead life with you . . . There's no need for this . . . I can establish a new life for you."

"Madame, I already had the kind of life you want to establish for me, I don't want that life anymore . . . I don't deserve that life . . . In fact I don't even deserve life . . . Why don't you just leave me in peace where I am?"

For a moment Mihrişah Sultan thought Anya was going to cry, but Anya didn't cry, there was a look of pained decisiveness on her face.

"Anya, I'm asking you as an old and worried grandmother, so please don't see this question as disrespectful, as an attempt to interfere in your life . . . Do you love Nizam?"

"I don't know," Anya answered in a stern tone.

"In my opinion, Nizam loves you and is not going to leave you. He'll remain with you in a dangerous place. The gambling den where you work is full of dangers and threats . . . Of course I understand your anguish, your torment, but now you're not just punishing yourself, you're punishing another person . . . Come with me, I'll rent a small house outside of Paris, you can remain distant from the crowds, you can stay there as long as you like, then you can leave whenever you want to go in a different direction, but as long as I'm alive I will see you as my daughter, as long as you want my support you will have it."

Mihrişah Sultan continued in a calm, mature tone.

"We can't be both gods and sinners in our own lives . . . We've all made mistakes, we've committed sins, we've caused other people pain, we've come to terms with our conscience, but turning into a god and meting out punishment to ourselves, that doesn't work. This isn't penance, it's an arrogant sinner playing god . . . We're not gods, we can't be . . . If you really want to suffer, isn't it more appropriate for you to suffer alive? Let go and allow me to help, live more peacefully in a safer place, don't deny the power of fate, see that fate is granting you a new opportunity, live with the acceptance that both torment and happiness are part of fate . . . I'm just telling you this."

"I'm not ready for this, madame . . . I'm not trying to be a god, I'm not trying to be anything . . . And I don't want to talk about any of this with anyone . . . I came here because Nizam said you would come to the mansion if I didn't . . . I came to visit you because I didn't want to experience a scene like that . . . Look, madame, I see that you're very wealthy and very powerful and that you want to help me with good intentions, I'm grateful . . . But I don't want this . . . I think you'll also accept that continuing this conversation beyond this point will strain the boundaries of respect for both of us."

While uttering this last sentence, Anya's voice, tone and emphasis changed considerably, she ended the conversation not like a woman who played the piano in a gambling den, she spoke like someone who had been accustomed to authority from a young age, like a decisive woman who had learned to keep people outside her boundaries, and with a somewhat superior and imperious manner.

Mihrişah Sultan was not accustomed to being spoken to like this. Her voice changed as well, from the tender voice of a grandmother to the threatening voice of a princess who was accustomed to demonstrating her power.

"Countess Rodovski," she said, "are you aware that by taking this attitude you're placing a life other than your own in danger? I can see that you are not going to take responsibility for yourself, but are you choosing to be this irresponsible with another person? Do you believe that this is an acceptable attitude?"

Hearing her name after so many years, the name she'd thought she would never hear again, was as if she had suddenly been assaulted by the past she wanted to forget, the terrifying events, the fires, the sound of gunfire, murders and an unforgivable betrayal, Anya was seized by the feeling that she was besieged, that she couldn't break free; her face went white, as if all of her blood was draining out through an invisible wound, her breathing became shallower, her head began spinning and she had to hold on to the corner of the armchair. She bit her lips as she tried to gather strength, after a moment of silence she stood, it took all of her strength to keep from staggering.

"This conversation ends here, madame," she said, "I hope I never encounter you or anyone from your family again . . . I see that you don't understand the harm you've done to me and I don't want to encounter anything like this again."

She walked towards the door without waiting for Mihrişah Sultan's answer, she was making a great effort not to show her powerlessness, she wanted to get out of that room as soon as possible.

Sultan realized she'd gone too far, that she'd touched a

nerve that shouldn't have been touched, and she regretted it, but there was no longer anything she could do about it. To put the distraught woman at ease, she said in a cold tone,

"You can be assured that I won't share your secret with anyone."

As she held the doorknob, Anya answered without turning around.

"You got hold of a secret you had no right to know, madame, how you use it is your problem."

She opened the door and went out.

Nizam had been talking to the young ladies in waiting in the next room, when he look towards the room where Anya and Mihrişah Sultan were he saw Anya leaving, he left the girls and rushed over to Anya, when he saw the state she was in he asked "What happened?" in panic.

"Nothing happened, if you'll permit me I'm going to take your carriage, I'll send it back when I get home."

"I'm coming with you."

"Please don't come."

Anya said this in such a decisive manner that Nizam didn't say anything, Anya climbed into the carriage and closed the door without looking at Nizam.

Nizam went back to Mihrişah Sultan.

"What happened, Anya was in a bad state, she didn't want me to come with her."

"Your pianist turned out to be very sensitive . . . She couldn't even bear to talk."

"What did you talk about?"

Mihrişah Sultan was angry at Anya for being disrespectful and for refusing to heed her suggestions, but at the same time she knew that she'd been unfair, and that she'd pried into another person's life without permission. Her pride prevented her from accepting her unfairness, she couldn't do this, but she was uneasy because she knew she'd been unfair.

"I wanted to help her but she didn't want this . . . She didn't accept any of my offers of help."

"It was already clear that she wouldn't accept this, if she was she would already have accepted my offer . . . Why was she in such a bad state when she was leaving? Did you say something bad to her?"

"Where did that come from, why would I say anything bad to her . . . Don't talk nonsense, Nizam."

"So what happened? Why did she leave in such a hurry, why did she tell me not to come with her?"

"I don't know . . . Perhaps because she's lived a solitary life for so long she's not accustomed to talking to people."

For a moment Nizam remained undecided, he was thinking about what to do.

"If you like, go, talk to her," said Mihrişah Sultan, "but there's something you need to know very well . . . If you want to be with that woman, she has to leave that gambling den, it's a dangerous place for both of you. If that woman doesn't leave that place, if she's going to maintain her meaningless insistence on remaining there, you have to stay away from that place."

"Why?"

"I told you why, that place is dangerous . . . That man they call Gavril has some strange connections, and you could get into trouble just by being there."

"What kind of trouble?"

"I don't know how it's going to happen but I know that you're going to get into trouble, Nizam . . . I'm not in a position to give you too many details but you must take what I said seriously, you either have to leave that woman or she has to leave the gambling den.

Nizam thought in silence.

"I don't know, for whatever reason, Anya refuses to leave that place."

"Talk to her . . . If you talk to her in a clear manner perhaps she'll change her mind."

"I'll give it a try, but I'm not very hopeful."

As Nizam got into the carriage, he saw that it was snowing more heavily and that the snow was beginning to accumulate on the ground, the horses hooves made a full sound on the deserted streets that were quickly being covered by snow.

Nizam didn't like distressing situations like this at all, he didn't know what to do, he didn't know what to say, he was angry at Anya, he was angry at Mihrişah Sultan, he was angry at himself, he was angry at everyone who was involved in this complicated situation; that wasn't enough, he was angry at life, at fate, at this nonsensical luck.

He hit the carriage ceiling with his cane, the driver opened the sliding window and looked in.

Nizam told him to go to Madame's house.

He didn't know how, when or why he'd made this decision, but when he told the driver to go to Madame's house he'd felt a huge sense of relief; he believed that everyone had been unfair to him, that everyone had caused him unnecessary difficulty and distress, and he was angry at everyone who had been unfair to him.

He leaned back, it was as if by making this decision he had distanced himself from everyone, from all the people he knew, from the city, all of the problems had been left behind, those calm piles of sand were flowing in his mind, they were covering all of his troubles and concealing them, life was once again becoming completely empty and calm.

He closed his eyes and smiled.

At Madame's house he was greeted with great fanfare, Nizam teased everyone, joked with the girls, the house was empty at that hour of the day, the girls were lounging around in the living room. Evangeliki said. "Oh, I didn't think you were ever going to come here again."

"How could I never come here again?"

"I don't know, it's been so long since you were here, you didn't call . . . I said that Nizam Bey has forgotten us."

They went upstairs together.

The girls in the living room giggled as they listened to Evangeliki's screams, then there was silence. When Evangeliki returned with a smile on her face, the girls asked,

"What happened?"

"He's sleeping," said Evangeliki, "he told me to wake him in the evening."

Nizam woke towards evening, he ate the food Evangeliki brought, he'd forgotten what had happened that day, his mind was once again at peace when he left the house.

Darkness had fallen, the snow was falling heavily, as the snow fell, the city whitened and became beautiful, the muddy streets, the crooked houses of blackened wood, the shapeless roofs were melted and erased by that soft whiteness, the silvery smoke rising from the chimneys, the thin minarets, the umbrellas of light from the gas street lamps, the snowflakes fluttering like confetti within these umbrellas of light, brought out another fairy-tale city that didn't actually exist.

The carriage driver was driving slowly, Nizam could hear a crunching sound as the wheels moved over the snow, he remembered the question his philosophy teacher in Paris had asked, "What is reality, and is there a reality that isn't real?" "There is," thought Nizam, "at the moment this city is a reality that isn't real, tomorrow morning it will change completely, it will be wiped away, it exists now but it isn't real, it's just an image."

The reality he'd fled in the afternoon became more real as he neared Anya's house, and the peaceful piles of sand that covered his consciousness began to collapse slowly, the problem that had to be solved was growing steadily, and Nizam's distress began to increase again.

He had to make a decision but he didn't want to make a decision or even think about making a decision. Later he gave up on trying to make a decision. He would behave however he felt like behaving.

In fact he knew that this wasn't his real decision, later he said to Osman, "The human mind is a trickster, it fools itself with all kinds of games." He was fooling himself, he knew this but he pretended not to know; he'd decided to leave Anya, go back to Paris with Mihrişah Sultan and Rukiye and to forget this strange country and this woman full of mystery. He didn't want to be aware of this decision and to carry its weight.

When he arrived at Anya's house, the aging servant answered the door.

"Madame is unwell, she doesn't wish to see anyone," she said.

Nizam gently pushed the woman aside.

"Let me take a look," he said.

When he went into the living room, Anya was sitting in an armchair wearing the same clothes she'd worn that morning, it was clear that she hadn't even changed, that she'd collapsed into the armchair when she came home and hadn't moved since.

She looked up at Nizam and asked in an exhausted tone,

"Why did you come here?"

"Why did you leave?"

"There wasn't anything left to talk about . . . I told you that I don't want to talk about the past . . . I also told you that I didn't want to come back to life . . . To insist is disrespect . . ."

"I didn't insist."

"Mihrişah Sultan is insisting."

Nizam repeated what he'd said.

"I didn't insist."

Anya's face was still completely white, her eyes were as empty as they'd been when he first met her, she was looking at him as if he were a corpse.

"Does it matter who insisted, Nizam? The moment I make a move to come back to life, my past confronts me . . . The past is there . . . It's part of life . . . I don't want to come back to life, the moment I do my past confronts me, I don't want to remember the past . . . I don't want anything . . . I want to stay like this . . . Please leave . . . Don't come back . . . Don't harm me."

Fortune had presented Nizam an opportunity to carry out the decision he'd made on the road and concealed even from himself; he tried to wipe the pleased smile off his face, he didn't want Anya to see that smile.

As he turned towards the door without answering he took a last look at Anya, he saw her lips, they were trembling.

Her lips were quivering like the wings of a frightened little bird.

Nizam was shaken by this small detail that was barely visible, it was as if his consciousness had been torn by that faint trembling, whatever was hidden beneath came pouring out through those cracks, a plethora of contradictory feelings shattered his consciousness like an earthquake and turned his mind upside down, even though he could hear a voice shouting "Don't you dare do that," he turned and sat across from Anya.

"I'm not leaving . . . I'm not going to leave."

Anya looked at Nizam in great surprise, she hadn't been expecting this. She'd been certain he would want to leave as well. The moment she was pleased that he had stayed, she became frightened as she thought about what was going to happen.

In a pleading tome she said.

"Please leave . . . I ask you."

"I'm not leaving."

"Nizam . . . Please . . ."

Anya began to weep, her lip began trembling even more.

"Nizam, please don't . . . It hurts me . . . You don't know . . . I can't take this . . ."

Nizam was surprised by what he'd done, but he was also impressed by what he'd done, he felt delighted and pleased to have behaved this way. All of his emotions had become sharper, he'd decided to sacrifice himself with a feeling of compassion he'd never known.

"If you want to live this way, fine, I'll live this way with you, I'm not going to pressure you . . . If one day you want to return to life, I'll return with you . . . But right now I'm not going to leave you alone."

"Nizam, you're going to ruin your own life too . . . Mihrişah Sultan was right, I can't take that responsibility."

"I'm making my own decision . . . There's no need for you to feel responsibility for this."

"This isn't going to be good for either of us."

Nizam shrugged his shoulders.

"So be it."

"This isn't a game, Nizam."

"I know."

"You don't know . . ."

Nizam reached out and took Anya's hand, "Don't cry," he said, "don't cry anymore."

He was pleased that he'd stayed, but he also felt a deep regret, he wanted to find consolation by seeing that Anya was happy.

Anya took Nizam's hand, brought it to her face, and smiled.

"You're going to destroy both of us . . ."

30

When he opened his eyes, he saw a pleasant, smiling face through a slowly settling blurriness. Slightly slanted green eyes, thick, shapely eyebrows, dimpled cheeks, lips parted slightly in a cheerful smile, hair covered by white muslin.

In a soft, tender voice with a slight accent, she asked,

"Are you awake, colonel?"

"Where am I?"

"In the hospital . . . Did you think you were in heaven when you saw me?"

"What city am I in?"

"Istanbul . . . Now let me ask some questions . . . Do you have any pain?"

"No."

"Good . . . You're lucky, the bullet broke your ribs but it didn't reach your lungs . . . You'll be out of bed soon, you'll be able to put on your attractive uniform.

When the waving in front of his eyes began to clear up, Ragıp Bey could see the nurse who was looking at him more clearly, she was what people used to call "small and lively," she was small, all of her lines were round, she was full of life, everything about her and everything she said reeked of femininity, a woman who was both tender and scornful.

"Do you want anything?"

"Where are my things?"

"They put everything you had with you in the drawer next

to you . . . Seeing as your property is so important to you, let's take a look and see what you have . . ."

She reached and opened the drawer of a white commode next to the head of Ragıp Bey's bed.

"Your cigarette case, your lighter, your wallet . . . Should I look in your wallet, do you want to know how much of your fortune is left?"

"Are there any letters?"

"No."

Ragıp Bey tried to sit up in bed.

"My letters should be there."

The nurse slowly held his shoulder and lay him back in the bed.

"Stop, stop . . . I said you were doing well but you're not doing that well."

"Where are my clothes?"

"You don't have any clothes . . . They must have been left behind in the hospital tent at the front . . . They were probably torn apart when you were shot and they're not fit to wear anymore."

"There were letters in my jacket . . ."

The nurse slowly touched his shoulder.

"Fine, calm down . . . I'll go see now, I'll ask around if you have any more things, perhaps they brought your uniform and I didn't see it . . . You just lie here quietly . . . I'll take a look and come back."

When the nurse left, Ragıp Bey raised his head and looked around, beds with white rails at the head and foot were lined up across from each other, on each side of the beds were white screens that were open at the front, only the one at the very end was closed, a white commode had been placed next to each bed, the beds were full, the black-and-white tiled floor was spotlessly clean, it smelled of soft soap and Lysol.

Leafless trees and softly falling snow could be seen through the wide window that reached as far as the ceiling at the end of the ward. The sky had taken on a purplish color.

From time to time, moaning could be heard.

When he felt the pain in his chest he lay down again, "I didn't die," he thought in anguish, having lost the letters increased the loneliness he felt at that moment, as if there was nothing left in life for him to hang onto, as if he'd been left all alone in a void, he was seized by a feeling of shrinking and drying out as he fell into an abyss.

All he wanted at that time was his letters, there was no logical reason but he didn't even want Dilara Hanım, he just wanted those letters, if he found them, the loneliness and desperation he felt at that moment would end. He struggled to remember the moment he was shot and to figure out what could have happened to the letters, he must have fallen into the mud when he was shot, his jacket had probably been covered in blood and mud. They might have cut the jacket off of him, or the medics might have thrown the jacket and the letters away when they undressed him.

His hair stood on end at the thought that suddenly occurred to him that someone had found the letters and read them, he immediately rejected this thought, in all of that confusion, who was going to take letters out of a bloodied jacket and read them?

Perhaps the strangest thing about it was that these letters, which were of almost life-sustaining importance to this lonely officer and were the only thing in the world he wanted to see at that moment, had gained value by representing the love and longing he felt for Dilara Hanım; those letters were valuable in themselves, they'd become part of his life. When he didn't have them he felt as if something was missing.

He didn't know what was written on those pieces of paper, they wouldn't bring him any news of life, at that moment those pieces of paper were life itself.

As he lay motionless with thick bandages on his chest in that hospital ward that smelled of Lysol, life seemed to have taken everyone with it and left, there was nothing left to remind him that he was alive except the pain in his chest.

He looked out the window at the purplish sky and the slowly falling snow.

He'd faced death many times, he'd felt the danger of death many times, many times death had rubbed itself against his body and moved on, but on none of those occasions had he felt the anguish, fear and loneliness he felt as he lay in that hospital bed. "If they were to ask me to choose between death and the loneliness I felt in that hospital room," he said to Osman later, "I would choose death without batting an eye."

He drifted off to sleep again.

One day during the period when he was drifting in and out of deep and restless sleep, when the door opened and the cheerful nurse came in, Ragıp Bey noticed that there was another shadow behind her.

"I couldn't find your letters but I did find you a visitor," said the nurse, "I said you were lucky . . ."

"Get well soon, commander."

When he heard the sergeants voice he turned his head in excitement, he had difficulty keeping himself from asking about the letters.

"Thanks, sergeant. How are you?"

"I'm well commander, I kept something for you, I brought them with me."

He put his hand in the inner pocket of his jacket and took out three crumpled envelopes.

"Your letters."

Ragıp Bey took a deep breath.

"Where did you find them?"

"When you were shot I was right behind you, I carried you to the medics' tent, I remembered what you'd said, I got the letters out of your pocket before they undressed you . . . Did I do the right thing?"

"Good for you, sergeant, you did well."

He took the letters, opened the drawer and put them in.

"What was the outcome of the battle?" he asked, "did you capture the positions after I was shot?"

"No, commander, hardly, it was a huge bloodbath . . . The Ottomans lost a lot of men, we retreated . . ."

"We were defeated again?"

"We were defeated . . . Ah, what can we do, we were defeated again, the corps just retreated . . . After us Hurşit Pasha's corps retreated as well."

"God damn it . . . How are the men?"

"What do you expect, commander, morale has been completely destroyed . . . How could there be any morale left when we couldn't even defeat a handful of Bulgarians. Whatever, commander, the real question is how are you? The nurse lady told me that my commander would be on his feet soon."

"That's what she says, I suppose I will be . . ."

"Do you have any orders, commander, the nurse told me not to stay too long."

"No, there's nothing at the moment . . . Well done about the letters, sergeant, you did the right thing, thank you."

The sergeant was pleased to be congratulated, as he left with a smile, the nurse came to Ragıp Bey's bedside.

"Come on, let's change these bandages . . ."

She spoke as she changed the bandages.

"Are you pleased, look, your letters turned up."

"I'm pleased," said Ragıp Bey as he tried to smile.

"You kept going on about those letters, why don't you read them?"

"I'll read them later . . . Is this a military hospital?"

"The French Hospital . . . They brought some of the wounded here."

Ragıp Bey looked at the nurse in amazement.

"Are you a nun?"

The nurse put her hand over her mouth to keep from laughing out loud.

"Me? A nun? God forbid . . . Do I look like a nun? When they received so many wounded, they borrowed nurses from other hospitals in the area . . . I'm only here temporarily."

"What's your name?"

"Efronia."

"Efronia?"

"I'm Armenian, if that's what you're asking."

"No, dear, that wasn't what I was asking, I wasn't sure if I'd heard your name right . . . your accent is difficult to understand."

"Were you the battalion imam?"

Ragıp Bey was surprised.

"Me? An imam?"

The nurse laughed.

"Eh, it seems to me that a man would have to be an imam to think that I was a nun . . ."

As she chatted away to distract Ragıp Bey to lessen the pain while she changed the dressing, her expert fingers changed the bandages; there was a pleasant and reassuring contrast between her cheerful face and vivacious talk and the seriousness with which she looked at the wound and the bandages.

When, as she was changing the bandages, Ragıp Bey started in pain, she first said "Don't move" in a stern tone, then later asked tenderly,

"Does it hurt?"

"No."

"Bravo, my hero, even if you were in pain you would never tell a woman, isn't that so? Because you're a man . . . But look, you can tell a nurse. If you tell me that it hurts I'll do it more slowly . . . I'm almost finished anyway."

Ragıp Bey, was clenching his teeth in pain and his face had yellowed a bit, but still once again he said, "It doesn't hurt."

For a brief moment Efronia looked up from the wound at Ragıp Bey's face, saw his face tensed in pain and said "I'm finishing up now" in an affectionate tone.

After she'd changed the bandages she laid Ragıp Bey back down in bed, wiped the sweat from his brow and said, "Sleep now" in a soft voice, "have good dreams, good dreams will heal you more quickly."

Ragıp Bey drifted back to sleep, he had complicated dreams, he'd been shot in battle but somehow he didn't die, he was bleeding profusely as he walked, he asked the crowds about someone, he couldn't hear whom he was asking about, no one answered, everyone except him was dead but they were walking.

He would wake up, he would see the darkness outside the window and the pale glow of the night lights, each time Efronia would be at his bedside. "It's O.K.," she would say, "it's O.K., everything is going to be alright, I'm here."

She wiped his brow.

Sometimes he saw Dilara Hanım, but she spoke like Efronia, she joked with him, changed his bandages, then suddenly her voice changed, she began speaking in her own voice, and sometimes Efronia spoke like Dilara Hanım.

Dilara Hanım suddenly pulled away towards the ceiling, then she vanished, then he would shout "Dilara" after her, when he shouted, Dilara Hanım came back, she wiped his brow the way Efronia did, said "Fine" the way she did, "it will pass, you have to dream nice dreams, nice dreams will heal you more quickly."

He held her hand so she wouldn't disappear again. He felt the warmth of her hand.

"Don't go," he would say.

"I'm not going anywhere, I'm here, I'm always by your side, don't worry."

"Your letters are lost."

"No, dear, we found them . . . Look, they're sitting in the drawer . . . The sergeant brought them, remember?"

"Yes . . . I didn't read them."

"I know."

Then everything was blood and mud again, the dead were walking, none of them answered Ragıp Bey, "We lost the war," Ragıp Bey was saying, "God damn it, we lost the war, you all died, I've been left behind, you left me behind."

Once he saw Dilara Hanım among the walking dead, this frightened him a great deal, "Dilara," he shouted, "Dilara."

Dilara Hanım turned, looked at him and smiled.

"Did you die?"

"No, dear, I'm here, I didn't die."

"Good . . . Your letters are lost."

"We found your letters, look in the drawer."

"Yes . . . please don't leave."

"I'm not going anywhere, I'm here."

He slept and slept and then slept again, every time he woke he saw Efronia at his bedside, when he pulled himself together a bit, Efronia joked with him and tried to cheer him up as she changed his bandages.

"Are you a colonel?"

"No."

"This paper says you're a colonel."

"It's a mistake."

"I think being a colonel would suit you, when you're released you can say you're a colonel, this paper says so . . . I can back you up and say you're a colonel . . . Does it hurt?

"No."

"Are you a liar, colonel?"

"It doesn't really count as pain."

"How much pain do you have to be in for it to count as pain?"

Ragıp Bey didn't answer.

"Are you married, colonel?"

"Doesn't it say so on my paper?"

"I looked, it doesn't . . . They didn't write the most important thing . . . Is there anyone you want me to send news to, to call?"

"No."

"If there's anyone you want to see, let me know and I'll send word to them."

"There isn't."

"Isn't there anyone you'd be happy to see?"

"No, there isn't."

"Colonel, you're a liar, but it's not important . . . All colonels are liars."

"How do you know that colonels are liars?"

"All of the colonels I know are liars . . . Stop, don't move, it will hurt much more if you move."

As Ragıp Bey made a face and waited for the pain to pass, he asked:

"How many colonels do you know?"

Efronia looked up from the bandages for a moment and smiled at Ragıp Bey.

"One."

"One, huh, and he's not even a colonel."

"Now this is going to hurt a bit, but it will be over very quickly, I promise, I'll take care of this in a jiffy . . . Are you an important person?"

"No."

"But colonel, every day we send personal updates about you to the Ministry of War."

"Who sends it?"

"The chief physician."

"Good God . . . Why?"

"If I knew I wouldn't have asked you . . . But you don't

know anything either . . . You don't know that you're a colonel and you don't know that you're an important person . . . Don't be wrong about your marital status . . . Don't be giving me false hopes."

Ragıp Bey didn't understand the joke.

"Am I giving you hopes?"

Efronia laughed.

"Of course . . . Every night you're here with me . . . Now I'm finishing up, colonel, I'm wrapping it around one more time then I'm tying it up . . . I told the doctor to give you medication to help you sleep."

"Why?"

"You're not sleeping well."

"How do you know?"

"I told you, I'm here with you every night."

"I don't want that."

"My dear colonel, this isn't a barracks, this is a hospital . . . What I say goes, not what you say . . . Fine, it's finished . . . Lie down now."

Ragıp Bey was sweating from the pain and she wiped his brow again, "Did that tire you out?" she asked, "no it didn't."

"Fine. Get some sleep . . . Rest."

Ragıp Bey spent his days sleeping and waking up, lurching from dreams to fantasies, pursuing Dilara Hanım in his dreams and finding Efronia, every time he shouted Dilara's name in his sleep Efronia came running to his bedside, he would hold Efronia's hand thinking that it was Dilara's hand.

Every time he woke he looked out the window, sometimes there would be heavy snow, sometimes a leaden sky, sometimes there were dry branches covered with snow, sometimes the dark of night, sometimes the lavender light of dawn.

Some of the screens around the beds were closed, then they were opened again, then another one would be closed, he sensed what this meant, but because his mind was clouded by medication he couldn't grasp it. Sometimes he heard moaning. Sometimes he would come face to face with one of the officers who was recovering and could get out of bed and move around, they greeted each other in a distant manner, as if they didn't want anyone to know that they were partners in crime.

One morning when he woke up feeling a little better, he saw Cevat Bey come in through the door.

When he tried to sit up, Cevat Bey rushed over and said, "Don't make yourself uncomfortable," grabbed him by the shoulder and sat in the stool next to the bed.

"How are you Ragıp?"

"Thanks, brother, I'm fine."

"You frightened me."

"There's nothing to be frightened about, you see I just don't die . . . Everyone around me dies but I don't die."

"Why are you saying that, of course you're not going to die, this country still needs you."

"How are you, brother?"

"I'm fine, Ragıp, thanks."

"What happened in the battle, brother? The sergeant came by, he said something about how we lost . . . Were we defeated again?"

"Unfortunately we were defeated."

"When I was shot we were attacking, we had numerical superiority, the Bulgarians were retreating . . . How were we defeated again?"

Cevat Bey sighed.

"It was because of Fethi Bey and Mustafa Kemal's recklessness . . . They decided to attack before Enver Bey so he wouldn't get credit for the victory and this messed up the plan, the two corps were supposed to attack together, when they each made separate assaults the plan was ruined. And while you were attacking a fog descended, the units lost touch with each other . . . . As I told you before, Ragıp, we lost this war before it even started . . . This last time Enver Bey's plan could have worked, but individual ambitions and jealousies got in the way . . ."

"So what's going to happen now?"

"We're back to talking about conditions for an armistice."

"Brother, didn't you stage the Bab-ı Ali raid because you were against the treaty, now you're negotiating a treaty?"

"There's nothing we can do, Ragıp . . . Enver Bey is reorganizing the army now, he's getting rid of all the pashas who still have the old mentality. We're starting over from scratch. We're restructuring all of the armies and the corps, even down to the squadron level."

"How much is that worth after having lost the war?"

"The war will continue . . . The Ottoman Empire will get its revenge . . . Enver Bey is bringing in advisors from the German army, we're distributing the generals and officers they send to the units . . ."

"So we're putting ourselves under German command?"

"No . . . How could we? But we're learning about all of their innovations from them, and the foundations are being laid for a solid alliance."

Just then Ragıp Bey noticed his older brother's epaulettes, "congratulations, brother, you've become a colonel."

"Thanks, Ragıp, I was transferred to the assistant undersecretary's office at the Ministry of War, the promotion came with the transfer."

"Hah, the nurse here said that information was being sent to the Ministry of War . . . Was that you?"

'Yes . . . I get an update every morning . . . I came a few times but you were always sleeping, that sweet little nurse wouldn't let me in . . . I have some good news for you too . . . Your uniform was torn and lost at the front, I had a new one made for you and I brought it for you . . . Let's see if you like it."

When he turned to the door and signaled, the soldier who'd been standing at attention next to the door brought the uniform he was holding. Cevat Bey held the jacket under the arms so the epaulettes were showing and handed it to Ragıp Bey.

"Why don't you try it on and see how it fits."

Ragıp Bey took the jacket and started to put it on when he noticed the epaulettes.

"Brother, this must be your uniform, they brought the wrong one, this one has a colonel's epaulettes."

"There's no mistake, Ragıp . . . Congratulations. You've been promoted to colonel . . . But I wanted to tell you in person . . . If only our mother could see this . . . The two of us were promoted on the same day."

"How could this be, brother? Don't you have seniority? How could we both be promoted to colonel on the same day?"

"Ragıp, we're living in dangerous times, at times like this there are going to be exceptions, a lot of pashas and officers in the army are being forced into retirement, and a lot of young and accomplished officers are being promoted . . . You deserved this more than any of us."

Ragıp Bey held the jacket but didn't put it on.

"What's wrong, Ragıp, aren't you happy about this? I thought our staff colonel would be pleased . . ."

"What do you mean, of course I'm pleased . . . But it just seemed strange after such a rout . . . What accomplishments have there been . . . We've lost all of the battles I've been in . . . We did hold out for a while at Çatalca."

"You did everything you could, Ragıp . . . From now on you'll do even better . . . You shouldn't have to pay for the mistakes the pashas made, this army expects a great deal from you . . . Look at your promotion in that light."

"Thank you, brother."

"Go ahead, try it on."

Ragıp had trouble moving his arm as he put the jacket on.

"It looks good on you," said Cevat Bey, "congratulations, colonel."

"Thanks, brother."

"I'd better get going, Ragıp, I have a lot of work to do, I'll come again . . . And you get better and get out of here as soon as you can, we really need officers like you."

"I want to get out of here as soon as I can too, brother, it's very depressing just lying here."

After Cevat Bey had gone, Efronia came with a smile on her face.

"Your new uniform has come."

"Yes."

"Did you ask whether you were a colonel?"

"I asked, it seems I'm a colonel."

"I told you so . . . Give me the jacket and lie down, colonel . . . Rest a little . . . You'll be better soon, so enjoy this place while you can . . . You're getting better now, your uniform has come too, tomorrow we're moving you to a single room . . . Don't be upset, I'm still going to be taking care of you . . . You said you weren't a colonel but you turned out to be a colonel, you said you weren't an important man but you turned out to be an important man . . . God willing you won't turn out to be married."

Ragıp Bey laughed.

"No, I know that, I'm not married."

"We'll see, your older brother came and we learned part of the truth, if your wife comes tomorrow we'll learn the rest . . . Come on, lie down, colonel."

The following day they moved Ragıp Bey to his own room, Ragıp Bey was aware that this was the result of his brother's new position and the new situation in the country and this made him uncomfortable, but it seemed a bit childish to insist on "not going to the room" so he was obliged to accept it. He was experiencing the privileges of having a relative in an influential position for the first time, and this would put him in an embarrassing position before the other officers. As he left the ward he struggled not to make eye contact with anyone, he was also angry because this was the first time he'd been put in an embarrassing situation like this.

He no longer had to spend all of his time in bed, he spent the better part of the day sitting in an armchair in the room and looking out the window. He slept better despite all of the nightmares.

When he spent the day alone and motionless, he constantly faced his own emotions, his jealousy and his anguish rebelled. He had no way to escape himself or distract himself, he tried to read books but he couldn't give his attention to the books, every sentence reminded him of his own anguish.

Efronia was his only savior during those days. He waited eagerly for her to come and distract him. His mind was looking for a way to escape the torment that his emotions were creating, he was looking for some relief, and Efronia provided that, "In order for a person to get free of himself, to escape himself, he definitely needs someone else to help him," he said to Osman, "I learned this then. You need someone to pull you out. Otherwise you drown in yourself . . . What an unfortunate sea a person's own soul is. It's the source of all your anguish."

Sometimes they spoke at night as well. Because they didn't have many common interests to talk about, they began talking more about themselves and their lives.

"Are you married?" Ragıp Bey asked, at any other time and with any other woman he would not have asked that question, but in that room he reached the point where he could talk about everything.

"No."

"Were you ever married?"

"I was."

"Why did you separate?"

Efronia was pensive for a time. She answered just as Ragıp Bey was beginning to regret having asked the question.

"My husband was a lieutenant . . ."

She paused and sighed.

"We were from the same neighborhood, we were childhood sweethearts . . . We sang hymns together in the church choir . . . in any event I didn't even know anyone else . . . I loved him very much, I always loved him . . . He was a courageous man like you . . . Like you he wouldn't say anything if he felt pain."

"So what happened?" asked Ragıp Bey excitedly.

"During the last uprising, a day before the Movement Army entered the city, he was shot at the entrance to the Galata Bridge . . . He went out alone to stop the mutineers . . . First they shot him with their rifles then they used their bayonets on him . . ."

Efronia suddenly fell silent.

"He was a brave man," said Ragıp Bey.

"He was."

"My condolences . . ."

That day Ragıp Bey saw the always cheerful Efronia's eyes fill with tears, he saw how she stopped talking, he saw the pain she carried. This pain made Efronia's cheerfully joking manner all the more precious in Ragıp Bey's eyes, he decided that she was a much stronger and more trustworthy person than he'd thought, "For whatever reason," he said to Osman, "anguish gives a person more confidence than cheerfulness, isn't that strange?"

They never brought the subject up this again, but Ragıp Bey asked some officers he knew and learned that Efronia's husband had been well liked by his colleagues and his men and that he was a truly courageous officer. In a strange way this increased Efronia's esteem in Ragıp Bey's eyes.

When he was alone he thought about Dilara Hanım, now

when he was bored he put his coat over his shoulders and walked in the garden, the aching within him had not eased, but when Efronia came he forgot his troubles and his past.

One day as Efronia was changing his bandages she said, "Your wound is closing."

"You'll be returning to your unit soon, colonel."

Ragıp Bey didn't say anything.

"The war is over."

Then Efronia paused and added,

"And I'm not going to worry about you . . . And anyway I'll be going back to my own hospital soon . . . The wounded are being discharged one by one . . . We'll be able to relax until these crazy soldiers start killing each other again."

Ragıp Bey couldn't control the excitement in his voice.

"When are you going?"

"Don't worry, colonel, I won't go until you're discharged."

Then Efronia smiled.

"Were you sad that I was going to leave?"

That evening as darkness fell a light rain began, Ragıp Bey opened the windows, outside there was a smell that told of the coming of spring, the rain fell with a soft whisper, he felt a strangeness that surprised him but he couldn't figure out what it was, for a moment he thought it might have to do with the weather getting warmer, later he felt that some things were rolling within him, some things were getting mixed up, some things were changing form, that confusion lasted a minute or two and then a reality that surprised him was reflected brightly in his mind. He missed Efronia. He was waiting for her to come.

The feeling that came after that was even more surprising. He felt a deep anguish not because he missed Dilara Hanım but because he missed Efronia . . . Even though it had caused him pain for so long he wanted this yearning to continue, he wanted the pain to continue. He was weary of his own emotions, he'd struggled to escape himself, but now just when he was about to be free he was saddened by the prospect of freedom. Beneath the thick shell of his anguish, his soul had struggled to change itself without letting him know, it was only after he'd changed that it revealed itself. As Ragıp Bey realized later, "Sometimes the pain you suffer for one person prepares you for another person."

He'd long since accepted that he would never see Dilara Hanım again, but as long as he missed Dilara Hanım the relationship continued, at least in his mind, he'd become accustomed to this relationship, this yearning, this pain, all of these emotions had become an important part of his life, he'd lived with these emotions for a long time. Now realizing that he missed another woman was like a real parting for him, it was a moment like the scab of a wound coming off, the wound was closing, but it hurt Ragıp Bey that this wound he was so accustomed to was closing.

This parting in his mind, this breaking away, caused him so much pain that he suddenly wanted to go to Dilara Hanım, to see her, to hold on to this pain. He knew that if he didn't go that very moment he would never see Dilara Hanım again, that he would part from her in that hospital room, and this shook him deeply.

Osman, watching him writhe in his hospital room, looked on with an air of condescension towards humanity's misery, as these miserable creatures live they have no idea what the future is preparing for them, they think that the moment they're in is endless, they don't know how life is playing with them, how amused it is by them. At that time Ragıp Bey didn't know about the terrible events he would live through with Efronia, or how he would meet Dilara Hanım again in a time of darkness, he had decided that he would certainly never see Dilara Hanım again.

Ragıp Bey had no idea about the future or about what

meeting Efronia, who would soon enter his room, would bring to his life, he was leaning out the window smoking a cigarette, feeling the deep melancholy of the moment when he could see with an almost lucid clarity that he was breaking away from the past and becoming attached to the future. He could also sense that this melancholy was temporary and that the delight concealed beneath it would emerge into the open and grow stronger by the day.

Suddenly he heard Efronia's cheerful voice.

"What's this, colonel, you haven't even turned on the lights . . . Here you are moodily smoking in the dark . . . Are you sad that you're going to leave the hospital?"

Ragıp Bey quickly turned towards her.

"I was just lost in thought . . ."

Efronia turned on the lights in the room.

"Spring is coming, colonel . . . I could smell it in the garden just now . . ."

"Yes."

Efronia could hear the strangeness in Ragıp Bey's voice and suddenly became serious.

"Are you alright? . . . Do you have pain anywhere? Or did you do something to your wound, did your wound open again?"

"No, no, I'm fine . . ."

"So what's the matter with you then, colonel?"

"There's nothing the matter with me, I just got lost in thought as I was smoking a cigarette . . ."

"Come on, come on . . . You're such a liar, colonel, I realized that from the very first day . . . Come on, tell me why you're upset, you're upset because you won't see me again . . . He suddenly felt melancholy because he's not going to see Efronia again . . . What can we do, colonel, that's life . . . You meet people, then you go your separate ways."

"Perhaps we'll see each other again . . ."

"Where would we see each other . . . If you think that I'm going to join your unit just so I can see you, you're very much mistaken, let me tell you . . ."

Ragıp Bey looked at Efronia without saying anything.

"Put on your coat, let's go out into the garden," said Efronia, "there's a very lovely spring rain . . . We can sit in the pergola for a while."

They went out into the garden together without speaking, there was a fresh smell, the smell of the rain had blended with the smell of the earth and of the trees that were coming back to life.

They sat next to each other on the wooden bench. Efronia suddenly shivered and wrapped her black cape around her. The pale light from the hospital that filtered through the dry vines that had not yet come back to life struck her face, illuminating her eyes and her lips and leaving the rest of her face in darkness.

There was a strange melancholy in her eyes and a lively cheerfulness in the curve of her lips, it was as if her eyes and her lips belonged to two different faces, it might not have been so noticeable if her entire face could be seen, but seeing them separately like this, the two separate emotions could be seen quite clearly.

After they'd sat in silence for a time, Efronia realized that she was going to have to take matters in hand.

"Yes, colonel . . ."

"Are we going to see each other again?"

"If you want to see me again you're going to have to say so openly, you're not going to see me by asking questions whose meaning is so vague."

Ragıp Bey liked it when Efronia spoke like this, the way she was always in command of the situation, this combination of authority and a cheerfulness whose source he couldn't determine. He couldn't keep himself from smiling.

"You mean it won't happen unless I say something . . ."

"No, it won't."

"What am I supposed to say?"

"Say whatever you want to say."

"Fine . . . I'd like to see you."

"Holy Mother of God, it took a lot for you to say that . . . Was it that difficult for you to say this?"

"No it wasn't . . . So, how are we going to see each other?"

"I looked at your papers, you're going to be going back to Çatalca . . . I'll come to Çatalca, we'll find a place to stay nearby . . . And anyway when you come to Istanbul it will be easy for us to see each other."

Ragıp Bey couldn't contain himself.

"What will people say?"

Efronia took Ragıp Bey's hand between both of hers.

"I don't even care what people say . . . I've paid my dues to both people and God . . . I've been through hell, no one can make me live through anything worse . . . If you care about what people say you can just go and leave me right now."

"And if I do go?" Ragıp Bey asked with a laugh.

"Then I'll break every finger on your enormous hand one by one."

Ragıp Bey laughed so loud that his laughter echoed throughout the hospital garden. He couldn't even remember the last time he'd laughed so fully.

"You can be scary."

"Yes . . . If you knew how scared you should be you would have fled a long time ago."

Efronia nestled against Ragıp Bey, she was very soft.

"Tomorrow morning when you're discharged from the hospital, leave your belongings with me . . . The following morning you can go from there to the vicinity of Çatalca . . . After you've left your things, let's go to Kağıthane . . . Spring is coming . . . We'll wander around a bit . . . It's been years since I've been anywhere . . . I'm not even sure if Kağıthane is still there . . . You can stay the night with me, I'll cook for you . . . You'll see what kind of cooks Armenian women are."

Ragıp Bey couldn't contain himself.

"What about the neighbors?"

"You weren't afraid of the Bulgarian army but you're afraid of my neighbors? The courage of heroes is a bit strange . . ."

"I was thinking of you."

"Don't you worry about me . . . I'll be fine."

"Fine . . ."

They listened in silence to the sound of the rain on the leaves.

"I'm glad the war is over," said Efronia softly, "I wouldn't have been able to send you to war."

"I'm not supposed to worry about you but you're going to worry about me?"

Efronia's voice sounded very anguished.

"You're a man, men don't know how to protect themselves . . ."

Ragıp Bey's voice changed, perhaps for the first time since he'd met Efronia he was speaking with his true voice, his true identity.

"I'll protect myself, Efronia . . . I'll protect you too . . . There's no need for you to fear anything . . . Anything."

"I won't be afraid."

Ragıp Bey noticed that her voice sounded strange and he turned and looked.

Efronia was crying.

"Why are you crying?"

"I'm just being silly, I'll get over it . . . Don't look at me . . . Women cry from time to time, did you know that, colonel? We occasionally cry to make you look more courageous and heroic, to make you look sterner . . . Just a little favor . . ."

Ragıp Bey could see Efronia's eyes in the light that filtered through the vines, they were still wet, the moisture made them seem large and clear.

Efronia wiped her eyes.

"That's enough . . . Don't worry, colonel, I don't cry often . . . Just once in a while."

She was quiet for a moment, then she stood.

"Stand up, colonel, you're still the hospital's property, I'm in charge of you, I can't let you get cold."

Ragıp Bey stood as well.

When they went into the hospital, Efronia asked in her usual cheerful manner,

"Are you going to be able to find your room on your own, colonel?"

Ragıp Bey laughed.

"I imagine I'll find it."

When he got to his room he sat on the bed. He lit a cigarette. He opened the drawer next to him. He took out the letters and looked at them for a long time as if he didn't know what to do.

Then he got up slowly and put the letters carefully in the pocket of the jacket that was hanging on the wall.

31

A t almost exactly the same time, at Dilara Hanım's mansion in Nişantaşı not very far from the French Hospital, another conversation about "the war has ended" was taking place. As Monsieur Lausanne said, "When it begins, as it continues and when it ends, war possesses the power to change people's lives," the lives it had changed as it began were going to be changed again as it finished.

On account of that spooky web of intelligence gathering particular to women, Dilara Hanım had learned that Ragıp Bey had been wounded and was being treated in the French Hospital, when she first heard this she thought he was going to die and it occurred to her to rush to the hospital right away, but when she learned that the wound wasn't deadly she decided to wait.

What she was waiting for was a little note that said, "Come."

For nights she fantasized about this, she'd even decided what she was going to wear when she went to the hospital, she'd set those clothes aside in a different part of her closet so she could get dressed and go right away if he should suddenly summon her.

That note never arrived.

She observed Ragıp Bey's slow recovery with both hope and disappointment. She was aware of Efronia's existence but she couldn't quite figure out if there was anything going on between the nurse and Ragıp Bey, when she learned that she was a nurse who took close interest in her patients she thought that it might be a nurse-patient relationship.

All of the emotions that were thought to make love what it is were present, yearning, desire, jealousy, but there was also another emotion that could damage even the greatest love; the desire to be independent.

On the one hand she wanted to be with Ragıp Bey for the rest of her life without ever parting from him, on the other hand she knew that a relationship like this would kill her soul and her independence and leave a bitter taste in her mouth. If she hadn't had that desire for independence, Dilara Hanım would have gone to the hospital and "taken" Ragıp Bey, the reason she didn't make a move despite her great desire to do so was this duality within her.

If Ragıp Bey had summoned her or come to see her, she might have given up on her desire for independence, but that desire wasn't going to go away on its own.

"I never understood why they think this is a feeling particular only to men," she said to Osman, "this is a feeling that everyone has, some feel it more, some feel it less, like all feelings it was distributed to people in different amounts. I got a larger share, a part of me is happy about this, another part of me thinks that it was a curse."

That evening she greeted Monsieur Lausanne with some disquiet, she knew what he was going to say to her.

Monsieur Lausanne said what she'd expected him to say in the middle of dinner.

"The war is over, madame."

"I know . . . You sound as if this makes you sad."

"You can appreciate better than I that every event reverberates in people's lives in a different manner . . . Of course it's good that the war ended, young lives will be saved, fewer will die . . . But it carries a very different meaning for me . . . I have to return to my country . . . My ship sails tomorrow morning."

Monsieur Lausanne paused and waited for Dilara Hanım to say something. Dilara Hanım didn't say anything.

"Sometimes you can be merciless, madame."

"Why do you say that?"

"Do you know that your silence is deadly?"

"What do you want me to say?"

"I know what I want you to say to me, you know as well . . . The question of interest here is what you want to say . . . In fact your silence says it all . . . But, oh, this ridiculous hope . . . Lovers and poets never lose hope . . . Isn't hope the reason they spend their lives with knives in their backs and somehow can't take those knives out?"

Lausanne paused and smiled.

"That was a somewhat dramatic way to put it, madame, I'm aware of that . . . But to tell the truth one is disturbed by the mortification of hanging on to a hope . . . At least it disturbs me. I'm not like that. I'm not one of those people who hang their lives on the hook of hope . . . Perhaps this is a professional habit, I like life and people to be open and clear."

"Women as well?"

"Especially women . . ."

"Have you met many women who are open and clear?"

"Madame, you mock me."

Dilara Hanım suddenly became serious.

"No, I'm not mocking you, Stephan, sometimes a person can't be open and clear, because feelings aren't open and clear like that, you know this better than I do . . . The human soul is not an item of news or an event, a single murderer isn't always guilty of a murder . . . What can I say to you? Yes, I enjoy you being in Istanbul, seeing you, talking to you, laughing at your jokes, listening to what you have to say . . . If you were to have remained in Istanbul I would have been very pleased, when you leave I will be truly saddened . . . But is all of this enough to make me ask you to stay? I don't think so . . . And you don't think you need to learn my thoughts before deciding whether to stay or go . . . If you'd found that it was enough you would have stayed without asking me . . . But you're asking . . . Because this isn't enough for you either . . . The reason you can't stay without asking is the same reason I can't ask you to stay . . ."

When Dilara Hanım finished speaking, there was a silence, they both became pensive, again it was Dilara Hanım who broke the silence.

"Perhaps if it had been a different time . . ."

"Please don't, madame . . ."

Dilara Hanım looked at Monsieur Lausanne to try to understand what he was objecting to.

"I don't deserve such pathetic consolations . . . Even though love, and especially unrequited love, makes me as desperate as it makes everyone else, I've never allowed myself to become this desperate . . . At the moment some other time doesn't concern me . . . I'm concerned with the present, with today."

"At this moment we're here, talking . . ."

"This is our last conversation, madame . . . We're never going to see each other again . . . Sometimes this absolute a truth is a heavy load to carry . . . I will never see you again, never hear your voice, never see your smile. Never notice the way you bite your lip when you're excited . . ."

"Why are you being so drastic? Life . . ."

"The future is uncertain, yes . . . But not always . . . Both of us know that this will be our last conversation . . . It's just that this truth saddens me more than it saddens you . . . This is another absolute truth."

There was another silence, they listened to the patter of the rain on the window.

"Spring is coming," said Lausanne, "I never thought I would be saddened by the arrival of spring and the ending of a war . . ."

Dilara Hanım smiled.

"Here war never ends, you know this better than I do . . ."

"The next war will be the war that separates us . . . German officers are being assigned to the Ottoman army . . . I suppose you know what this means . . ."

"No."

"If war breaks out in Europe, our two nations will be enemies, madame . . . This war will be a war that separates us completely."

"Is war going to break out in Europe?"

"I can't give a definitive answer at the moment, but all of the signs are pointing to it . . ."

They were silent for a moment, then Lausanne laughed.

"Who is going to bring you news from the front this time?"

Dilara Hanım sighed before answering.

"I told you before, your importance to me, yes, perhaps in the beginning it was because of the news you brought me but later it wasn't like that . . . It saddens me that you're leaving, we spent some very difficult times together . . . You were always supportive of me . . . You made me laugh during the most painful times . . . Don't think that the idea of never seeing you again doesn't sadden me . . . No, on the contrary reality hurts me, perhaps more than either of us could have guessed . . . I would have liked life to continue this way."

"Life requires change, madame . . . No time ever lasts, no moment continues . . . You either change life or life changes you . . . One of you must change . . . I would have liked the two of us to change life, that would have made me a happy man . . . But I know and I see that this is not the way it's going to be . . . Life is going to change us . . . And this is what helplessness is, madame . . . Helplessness is not being able to change life . . . When you love someone, you lose the power to change life, you're left in need of another person to be able to change life, your own will is of no use . . . Loving shouldn't have been like this, it shouldn't have been something that makes a person weak, helpless and miserable . . . On the contrary it should have been something that strengthens people . . . But it isn't . . . I've never in my life felt as weak and helpless as I do at this moment."

Lausanne suddenly stopped and laughed.

"You know that reducing a man to a state like this is a great sin, don't you madame? To make a powerful man power-less . . . To be a Delilah who cuts Samson's hair . . ."

Dilara Hanım was listening to Lausanne voice as it mixed with the sound of the rain, she thought that she liked the way he spoke, the way he would make a joke to lighten the atmos-phere when he was talking about the most painful matters, the way he expressed his emotions so openly, the examples he gave; at that moment Lausanne wasn't aware of it, but Dilara Hanım was weighing what life with Lausanne would be like, he could stay here, she could go to Paris, could Lausanne give her the space and freedom she wanted, would she get bored, when she got bored would she be able to tell Lausanne to "leave," wouldn't saying "stay" entail a serious responsibility, all of these questions were going through her mind. Could she for-get Ragıp, more importantly was she prepared to accept the reality that she and Ragıp would never be together again, could she make the possibility that they would never come together again a part of her life? Could she stand this? Not seeing him was one thing, parting from him was another thing, but it's something altogether different to say, "there will never be any possibility of us ever being together again." All of these ques-tions were passing through her mind, her decisions changed almost moment by moment.

This was one of those moments when your destiny wobbles like a raindrop at the end of a branch; the course of a life was bound to a single word, and that word kept changing shape.

Lausanne wasn't aware that the woman he was with was struggling to make a decision, that his future could change at any moment, he just saw a woman listening to him, but he didn't understand what was going through her mind. He thought that Dilara Hanım had already made her decision, he'd even given up on trying to convince her, he was just trying to extend this last night, these last hours, these last minutes, he was reproaching himself for not being able to leave.

"I'm afraid I'm not the only victim in your life, I'm not the only man to have been taken by you . . . I won't even have a special place on your list of victims . . . Being a victim is bad, but you don't even have at least the consolation of being the only victim . . . Are you going to remember me as one of your victims?"

He was trying not to be reproachful, not to reveal his weakness too much, but he kept coming back to the same subject, he was complaining with an anguished smile. He was fully aware that this would not gain him anything, but he couldn't manage to stop talking.

"You're being unfair to me and to yourself," said Dilara Hanım, "I'm not Delilah and you're not part of a crowd of victims . . . If you think you didn't have a special meaning for me you're mistaken . . . My . . ."

Monsieur Lausanne couldn't contain himself and asked a question before Dilara Hanım had finished speaking.

"Why, then?"

If Monsieur Lausanne hadn't been in such a hurry to ask that question, the conversation might have developed differently, Dilara Hanım had been about to say something that would have affected both of their futures. That question gave her pause, she looked at Monsieur Lausanne as if she'd just woken from a deep sleep, and like Lausanne she decided that there wasn't any future for the two of them. There was a possibility that Dilara Hanim's decision was influenced by Lausanne's "early decision" that "this isn't going to work out," and later Lausanne would think about that moment a great deal, he would always be curious about what Dilara

Hanım had been preparing to say but hadn't after she'd said "my."

"I don't know."

"May I ask something . . . Since this will be our last conversation perhaps you can see my wanting to ask this question not as disrespect but as a condemned prisoner's last wish," said Lausanne with a slight smile. "After all, these kinds of farewells are a kind of death . . ."

"Of course you can ask, there's no need to make such a chilling comparison."

"Has there ever been anyone you asked to stay?"

Dilara Hanım thought for a moment.

"No."

"Has there ever been anyone you wanted to ask to stay?"

"Yes."

"Why didn't you ask him to stay?"

"I don't know . . . Perhaps because I'm so accustomed to being alone, perhaps because I worry about being dominated by a man . . . I'd like to know the answer to this as well."

"Do you regret not having asked?"

Dilara Hanım made a face and nodded her head.

"Yes . . . And a great deal as well."

"If you had the same opportunity again would you ask him to stay this time?"

"I don't know."

"You say this despite your regret?"

"Yes . . . I say this despite my regret."

"Your life will be full of regret . . ."

"I imagine so . . ."

"Doesn't this sadden you?"

"What can I do?"

"Ask someone you want to stay to stay."

"When you say it like that it sounds very logical . . . But for whatever reason I don't behave logically . . . This is the problem that needs to be solved, why don't I behave logically . . . Otherwise I'm also aware that asking someone to stay would be the intelligent thing to do . . ."

Out of professional habit, Lausanne was practically turning a conversation about love into an interview, but as he asked his questions, Dilara Hanım became more aware of the strangeness of her decisions and actions, and, more importantly, she realized that other people could see this.

She could clearly see that amidst the disintegration in her soul and in her mind, there were two different emotions existing side by side. She loved Ragıp Bey and she would always love him, of this she was certain. Despite all of the pain it caused her this feeling made her happy, to succeed in being able to love someone like this, to be able to love like this, to be able to miss someone like this, to be able to feel pain like this, after a period of what amounted to almost years of emotionlessness and indifference, this created the stormy blessing that her soul needed. Emotions were creating new emotions and multiplying, this was a multiplication that pleased and excited a person, like the greening of the earth.

But there was another emotion next to this emotion.

One couldn't even call this another emotion, there was another woman carrying on her existence in her soul, despite all of the love this woman felt she could not countenance the idea of living in the same house with a man, she couldn't even think about a man taking over her life and asking her questions, that possibility seemed like a disaster to her, the end of life, like drying out and becoming arid again, and this brought her to another impasse: not experiencing any love fully. If she loved someone she couldn't live with him, if she lived with him she couldn't love him. The suffocation and boredom that living with someone created in her soul would kill love.

Later she would tell Osman in an anguished voice, "I became a victim not of my feelings but of my mind, while I wanted to experience my emotions, my mind always reminded me of what I would experience later, before I even began to experience anything, my mind would experience what it guessed I would experience and wear itself out. My feelings never diminished but my willingness was destroyed. No one who hasn't experienced it can know what a terrible contradiction this is."

After thinking for a while, she said with the frankness that suited her so well, "I don't know, perhaps there was no need to explain it in such a complicated manner, perhaps it's that sneaky greed that's thought to be particular to men, wanting everything all at the same time and not being able to possess anything . . . If I wasn't wealthy, if I didn't have money, if I didn't have a house with high walls where I could live the way I wanted far from prying eyes, I might not have been so greedy, it would have been more possible for me to think of living a different kind of life and I could have experienced my love." Later, as if Osman was somehow responsible for all of this, she said with a mocking smile, "From all of this, do we arrive at the conclusion that money is to blame for my not being able to find happiness?"

"You're lost in thought," said Monsieur Lausanne.

"Yes . . . I was thinking."

She looked at Lausanne, she liked talking to him, discussing politics, war, the news and literature with him, learning what was going on in the world from him, knowing that he was in love with her; if she was with Ragıp Bey a relationship like this would not have been possible.

Now she was saddened that he was leaving, that he was departing her life, never to return; she thought about whether, if she asked him to "stay," she would be able to live both by herself within her boundaries and with Lausanne outside those boundaries. She knew now that she'd lost Ragıp Bey, this was perhaps the real reason her thoughts about Lausanne had become stronger.

When Monsieur Lausanne was gone, she was going to be

very much alone. Long nights alone at home, distress . . . She would think about Ragıp Bey more, in her loneliness she would miss him even more.

"If I ask you to stay will you really stay?"

"I will."

"Won't you regret it?"

"I don't know . . . We'll think about that later . . . If I think about whether or not I'll regret it from the very beginning I won't be able to do anything . . . If I do regret it, I'll think about it then."

"You're right."

"Are you very frightened of regret?" asked Monsieur Lausanne.

"Yes . . . All the time, too."

"Don't you regret having a fear like that?"

Dilara Hanım laughed.

"Yes . . . All the time."

"You're deathly afraid of regret but you invariably feel regret . . . Is that so? Madame, you've fallen into a frightful trap that you've set for yourself . . . And you don't ask anyone to help you free yourself from it."

"I don't know . . . In fact when you put it like that it sounds a bit mad, I'm aware of that . . . But you can be sure it's not madness, perhaps it's too much cleverness."

"Sometimes there's not much difference between the two, madame."

It didn't distress Dilara Hanım to talk about herself, her problems, her troubles, her impasses and "the traps she set for herself," on the contrary she found it appealing to share her troubles, to talk to Lausanne as he described those troubles. There was no one she could have had this conversation with except Monsieur Lausanne. She was becoming increasingly aware that his departure would leave a greater void in her life than she had imagined.

"The thing you describe," said Lausanne, "is an unending indecisiveness . . . You must be unable to make any decisions concerning your private life . . . Like a lily floating on the water . . . Forgive me for saying this, but beautiful and rootless . . . Whereas you appear to be very decisive."

"I am a decisive person."

"On the subject of remaining indecisive?"

Dilara Hanım laughed out loud.

"I suppose I'm losing esteem in your eyes . . ."

"Nothing could cause you to lose esteem in my eyes, madame, of that you can be certain . . . What I said was nothing more than the admonishing reproach of a desperate man . . . Otherwise I know very well what a strong person you are despite all of this . . ."

Towards midnight Monsieur Lausanne said,

"It's now time for me to bid you farewell."

Dilara Hanım didn't want Lausanne to go, but she was aware that asking him to stay was a momentous decision and that she was not going to be able to make this decision.

She thought about asking him, "Stay here tonight," she truly wanted this. This wasn't just a physical desire, on the one hand there was the thought that she owed him this "last night," on the other hand, even if she didn't admit it to herself, there was another aspect of this thought that resembled a desire to leave an indelible mark.

Monsieur Lausanne stood but Dilara Hanım remained seated, she was thinking in an indecisive manner.

Finally she stood.

"Fine," she said, "I'll see you out."

Monsieur Lausanne would never know what had passed through Dilara Hanım's mind. Even though she'd wanted very much to do so, Dilara Hanım had been unable to grant Lausanne this "last night," she'd feared that it would sever all of her links with Ragıp Bey, that it would be an infidelity from which she could never return. Perhaps if she hadn't liked Lausanne so much that night, if she hadn't felt something resembling love, she wouldn't have hesitated to say, "stay here tonight," but she was frightened by what she felt for him.

They stood facing each other in front of the large door.

It was chilly outside. A drizzle was falling.

"Spring is coming," said Monsieur Lausanne, "I will pass this spring without seeing you . . . While I'm alive I'll pass many springs without seeing you . . . This will be the last time I see you, knowing this so certainly makes me shudder."

"That's life, you never know."

Monsieur Lausanne kissed Dilara Hanım's hand. He smiled.

"I loved you, madame . . . I think that I will continue to love you for a long time . . . Just as you made me very happy, you have also caused me grief . . . I leave here an unhappy man . . . Still, I want to say this to you . . . If one day you should need me for whatever reason, all you need to do is let me know . . . I will come."

"I know, Stephan . . . And I will never forget you . . . Know that . . . Always know that . . . If only it could have been different . . ."

Monsieur Lausanne opened the carriage door and got in without saying anything.

He took a last look at Dilara Hanım out the window.

The carriage suddenly started moving.

As the carriage moved, Dilara Hanım felt something quake within her.

She waved her hand.

A gloved hand emerged from the window of the speeding carriage, she saw the hand waving in a final farewell.

She returned to the living room.

She sat in an armchair. The house seemed very empty to her.

She was very anguished.

"I'm all alone," she thought, "I'm all alone."

32

The *tekke*'s thick walls echoed with the cries of a new-born baby.

Thick-eyebrowed women dressed in black were running down the corridors in an accustomed rush, carrying hot water, muslin, and towels.

The man had all disappeared.

Mihrişah Sultan leaned down towards Rukiye, who was covered in perspiration, "You have a son, my girl," she said.

She was about to say, "May God grant that he grow up with a mother and father," but she swallowed and remained silent.

Rukiye opened her eyes with difficulty, took a deep breath and asked, "Is he healthy?"

"He's healthy and beautiful. May God grant him good fortune."

One of the older women swaddled the baby and put him in Rukiye's arms, "He's like a little lion," she said, "may he have good fortune."

Rukiye took the baby in her arms and looked at his face, there were swollen, red patches on his face and his breath was shallow and strained.

"He can't breathe," she said in panic.

The women laughed.

"He's trying to get used to it, he'll be alright soon."

One of the women tied Rukiye's hair, which was drenched with perspiration, in a red muslin cloth, another was reading the Koran by her bedside. A frowning old woman was softly reciting the Jawshan in a corner of the room.

Sheikh Efendi and Nizam were walking in the garden, trying to appear calm, under the bright March sun the Golden Horn was flowing like a large blue bird about to take flight, a slight wind was blowing through the trees.

A dervish came and whispered something into the Sheikh's ear.

Sheikh Efendi smiled and turned to Nizam.

"It's a boy . . . May God give him love and assistance . . . May his life be fortunate."

"How is Rukiye?"

"She's well . . . They're both well, they're in good health . . . Don't worry."

"Aren't we going to go see them?"

"Let them catch their breath a little, my son, let Rukiye rest a little, then we'll go see them . . . There's no rush, let's walk a little, let the women take care of things, in any event they'll call us when it's time."

Since morning Nizam hadn't been able to keep still, he was afraid that something might happen to Rukiye, at one point they heard the screams echoing off the walls, Nizam's face went completely white, after Sheikh Efendi moved his lips as he recited a prayer, he held Nizam's arm and said, "Don't be afraid."

"Helping God to create a new living being is not an easy task . . . The most important duty entrusted to humanity . . . This magnificent duty was given to women, that means they were created to be more robust than we are if they were chosen for this blessed duty. They say women are weak, if they were weak would they have been given this tremendous duty? Every pregnant woman carries God's command in her belly, when you see a pregnant woman you see that command. God creates the creatures he wants to create through women . . . Just think, God

could have created all of his creatures himself the way he created Adam and Eve, what a great duty this is . . . Every time a
baby is born people witness once again the difficulty of creating a living being, then you'll think, if bringing a human being
into the world is this difficult, how glorious and difficult a task
it is to create the vast realm of people, the earth, and the vast
universe . . . Here you see the Lord's power, he was able to perform such a glorious task with so little effort . . . Every time a
baby is born, humanity's faith is refreshed, they see the power
and the glory and they believe."

"Aren't you worried?" asked Nizam suddenly.

Sheikh Efendi was surprised.

"About what?"

"That something might happen to Rukiye."

Sheikh Efendi thought.

"No, evil also comes from God . . . I take shelter in him."

"You know as well that you haven't always made the right
decisions . . . Yes, I know, he knows as well . . . Don't you
worry when you hear those screams? Aren't you afraid that
something bad might happen to her?"

Sheikh Efendi had become accustomed to Nizam exceed-
ing the limits of disrespect when he was upset or worried, he
knew that this was how he was expressing his worries and he
responded in a tolerant manner.

"We're all human, of course we have all of those fears and
worries, no one can be free of these . . . That's how we were created . . . The important thing is what you do when you feel that
worry, if there's anything you can do you do it, if not, take shelter in God rather than rebelling needlessly, trust in him, beg for
blessings . . . He who gives troubles also gives the remedy."

"There's no remedy for death."

"That depends on how you see death . . . If you think of it
as returning to the place from which you came, you won't be
as frightened."

"That's what you say, but when Tevfik died I saw that you were very upset too . . . You were as upset as I was . . . You went and prayed, I burned with anger . . . But both of us were upset."

Sheikh Efendi thought.

"We all have weaknesses that we're obliged to deal with . . ."

Just then Mihrişah Sultan arrived, her face was radiant with delight.

"I suppose they've given you the news . . . She gave birth to a leonine boy . . . What are you doing?"

Sheikh Efendi smiled.

"Nizam is questioning my faith."

Mihrişah Sultan gave Nizam a shaming look.

"Please . . . How could he do that . . . Nizam, how can you be so disrespect—"

"He's not doing it with bad intentions, don't worry . . . And you have to look not at the one who's questioning but at the one who's being questioned . . . That means there's a mistake or a deficiency that required me to be questioned . . ."

Nizam was ashamed.

"Please," he said, "I would never have asked with that intention, your excellency the sheikh . . . Forgive me . . . I was just trying to understand . . . I never thought you would take it that way, you can be certain that's not what I meant."

Sheikh Efendi smiled at Nizam.

"I know, my son . . ."

Then he turned to Mihrişah Sultan.

"How is Rukiye? How is the baby?"

"They're both very well . . . Rukiye is a bit tired . . . Come, let's go, I came to get you, come see Rukiye and the baby."

Sheikh Efendi and Mihrişah Sultan were almost taking pains to avoid being alone together, they were frightened of themselves and of their emotions, they were trying to protect themselves from the impasse of impossibility.

Whenever they met, either Nizam or Rukiye was always with them, in a strange way this made them a kind of family, in their nameless closeness, both Sheikh Efendi and Mihrişah Sultan found peace and happiness within this family that they found themselves part of.

With the secret and powerful desire that was becoming apparent between them, this calm reassuring "family" environment freed them from the obligation to restrain their feelings. They were pleased to be able to see each other every day without having to worry.

They approached each other with emotions that oscillated between the heavy anguish occasioned by a terrible death and the delight of an anticipated birth and that were sharpened by this contrast, every day they were a bit more impressed by each other's strength, intelligence and wisdom.

Rukiye had passed the month before giving birth more calmly within the great wave of tenderness that surrounded her, she'd kept the promise she made to Mihrişah Sultan, she'd suppressed her grief as much as possible, she'd directed all of her attention towards her unborn child, she didn't weep in front of anyone again.

Nizam became the family's naughty, rebellious son who entertained everyone.

In fact during those short, intense, and confusing days between death and birth, the four of them experienced the family life they'd yearned for all their lives, the warmth and closeness created by love, tenderness and respectful care.

Sheikh Efendi and Mihrişah Sultan didn't bring up the subject of revenge again, it was as if Mihrişah Sultan had forgotten what she said that day, it was as if she'd changed her mind about revenge, Nizam was the only one who brought the subject up, once when he attempted to talk about "revenge" in Mihrişah Sultan's presence, Sultan gave him such a withering look that he was obliged to remain silent.

Once or twice when she was alone with Sheikh Efendi she brought the subject up, "The murderers are going about their lives comfortably," she'd said, "the murder has even been forgotten, it's as if people had never been killed, life is going on as if a murder like this had never been committed. And on top of that the murderers are governing the country."

Each time, Sheikh Efendi wrapped himself in silence before he answered, he too was angered by this clear unfairness, this injustice, the pain his child suffered, his grandson being born without a father, but unlike Nizam, he spent hours in the *zikr* room praying to be freed from this anger, he begged God for help in freeing himself from this anger, this sin, this rebellion, "God, free me from this anger, keep me from this sin, help me."

He was trying to calm Nizam without mentioning his own feelings. They had long conversations. "Any undertaking whose outcome is not auspicious only serves evil," Sheikh Efendi would say, "an act of revenge will not bring about an auspicious outcome."

"If you try to take revenge you become an accomplice to murder, the murderers can point to the victim's crime as an excuse for their own crime."

As he generally did, he would stop and think for a moment and the add as if he was talking to himself.

"People haven't learned how to die, but they've learned how to kill . . . They don't believe that they're going to die but they believe they can kill . . . If they knew they were going to die, if they remembered that they were going to die, they wouldn't kill, only someone who has forgotten that their existence is ephemeral could kill a person . . ."

Nizam would oppose him, not just because what Sheikh Efendi said didn't make sense to him but also in order that the Sheikh would continue trying to convince him, the things he said relieved him somewhat, but he didn't succeed in extinguishing the sudden fires of anger that flared up within him. Perhaps it was because he felt himself to be a part of a whole, because he felt himself to be surrounded by a family, that these fits of anger occurred less often that they had in the past.

Sheikh Efendi received news from the four corners of the empire, he had knowledge of all developments. "A terrible calamity is coming the like of which has never been seen before," he said once to Mihrişah Sultan and Nizam. "This time the war is going to be very extensive."

On the one hand he didn't want Mihrişah Sultan and the children to leave the *tekke* at all, on the other hand he wanted them to get away from the calamities that were going to envelop the empire as soon as possible and reach someplace safe. Thus one more conflict was added to the conflicts that almost entirely filled his soul.

"If you were to go somewhere far away," he said once, "somewhere calm."

"Once the baby is able to travel we'll think about it," said Mihrişah Sultan.

They were also experiencing scenes that seemed unimportant but that left traces on their souls, once when the three of them were walking and talking in the garden, Mihrişah Sultan said to Sheikh Efendi, "You're going to get cold, why don't we tell them to bring a thicker cloak for you to wear."

Sheikh Efendi flushed slightly and looked straight ahead, then smiled and said, "Thank you, there's no need, I'm accustomed to it."

It was Mihrişah Sultan's habit to soon see any place she went as her home, and she soon acted as if she owned the *tekke*, at first the taciturn, black clad women of the *tekke*, with its thick walls, small windows and murky corridors, were discontent with her presence, they complained about her in whispers, they'd been cold and distant towards her, but in time they'd submitted to her natural, genuine authority. As Nizam said to Osman in his usual joking manner, "My grandmother believed that God created the world just for her, she saw any place in the world that she went as her own garden, she treated the people she encountered there as guests, some of whom she liked and others of whom she didn't like," for his part Sheikh Efendi, one of the quietest of the talkative dead who made various comments about each other, never said a single word about Mihrişah Sultan.

The first of the women of the *tekke* to establish a relationship with Mihrişah Sultan were the older women, as they talked about Rukiye's pregnancy, grief and health, the common love they felt for Rukiye brought them closer, they were impressed by Sultan's magisterial strength, and she was impressed by their humility and wisdom.

Once when she was talking with these elderly women who used examples from fairy tales, legends and hadiths, she'd said with a laugh, "How many sayings you know!" The women had laughed and said, "We don't know anything, in the end these are all God's words."

The women, who at first were secretly jealous of the closeness Sheikh Efendi showed to Sultan, were impressed by Mihrişah Sultan's respectful attitude towards the Sheikh, they chose to believe that she would "find religion on account of the Sheikh." Sultan was very interested in the knowledge that the women of the *tekke* had about that closed world that belonged to women, they knew what to do when someone was sick, upset or troubled, they found a remedy at once. She was surprised to learn so much at her age about the details of "the state of being a woman," so many problems and remedies, not from Paris society but from the women of the *tekke*.

Indeed sometimes when there were no young people around, a mocking smile would appear on their wrinkled faces, they told Sultan things that made her laugh out loud in amazement. She was also impressed by how the same women recited the Jawshan with such great tenderness and faith when Rukiye was sick, and how they beseeched God to heal Rukiye. And the women of the *tekke* admired the way Sultan looked on life and on men from on high.

They had no tastes in common, their personalities, the way they had been brought up, the way they had been educated and their inclinations were completely different, but during those days in which they lived between pain and hope, they developed a friendship in the shared waters of womanhood. They didn't dance to Sultan's tune.

Rukiye spent the last part of her pregnancy in the magical climate, like a warm, inland sea, created by these two very different peoples, she lived feeling her wound heal day by day among the *tekke* walls that whispered "life is ephemeral," the tender smiles of the women, the sounds of the Jawshan and the Koran being recited, the smile that appeared on Mihrişah Sultan's authoritarian face, which seemed to say "I'll find a solution for everything," Nizam's jokes and Sheikh Efendi, who said "How are you, my daughter?" and whose anguished eyes made it clear that he felt her pain even more than she did.

It was a strange period of catharsis for the four of them, in the warmth of this "family" climate that defied description, Sheikh Efendi distanced himself from his inarguable power, Mihrişah Sultan distanced herself from her unshakable and unrivaled authority, Nizam from the selfishness that was shaken by sudden crises of self-sacrifice, and Rukiye from the pervasive anguish in the depths of her soul, as they made amends to each other for past sins, they learned the happiness of living in an environment where these sins were not present.

It was a period during which they forgot the past and the future and lived only in the present, later Nizam said to Osman with the clever and enthusiastic cheerfulness that had always been part of his personality, "I don't remember a time before or after that was as peaceful as the time I spent in the *tekke*."

During this brief period when they pretended not to see the distressing worries they had about the future, their emotions were almost exactly the same, a passion that was perhaps more intense and constant than could be seen in a real family, the desire to see each other, to hear each other's voices, to take shelter in each other. The pain they wanted to ease became for them a fire around which they gathered on a cold night, around that fire they were both consoling each other's pain and warming their own souls with that consolation. In the *zikr* room, in the shadowy light of the red-tongued candles, Sheikh Efendi said to Nizam as if he would never mention those days, "When you ease someone else's pain, you ease a pain within yourself, the other persons pain is a means to ease your own pain, as you do good deeds you will get better, you find salvation . . . The person who deserves gratitude is not the one who does a good deed but the one who accepts a good deed."

They arrived at that bright March morning when the baby was born in the narrow corridor of history that began with one war and stretched towards another within the happiness they'd created from their anguish, with the birth of the baby this happiness was transformed into a celebration.

"Come on," said Mihrişah Sultan, "stop dragging your feet, Sheikh Efendi, your grandson is waiting for you."

Sheikh Efendi moved slowly, as if he knew that this happy birth was going to be the end of something, he turned slowly and said, "Let's go."

They passed among the cypresses and entered the door of the room in which Rukiye had given birth.

Rukiye was lying in bed with a red cloth on her head, red cheeks and eyes glowing with joy, the baby was in her arms, it was as if she'd been reborn while giving birth, she'd become beautiful, she'd been renewed.

"How are you, my daughter?"

"Thank you, sir, I'm very well."

"How is the baby?"

"He's very well too, thank God."

At the *tekke* Rukiye had become accustomed to using religious phrases without even realizing it, phrases like "thank God, thank heavens and god willing" appeared at the end of her sentences of their own accord.

She handed the baby to her father.

Sheikh Efendi took the baby timidly into his arms, the red-faced baby swaddled in white was like a light against the blackness of his grandfather's cloak.

Mihrişah Sultan turned to Rukiye and asked,

"What's his name going to be, Rukiye?"

Rukiye looked at Nizam, Mihrişah Sultan, realizing that they'd talked about naming him Tevfik, that they'd thought about naming the baby after his murdered father, jumped in out of fear that the child would live his life with the stamp of a death, that his mother would always be reminded of the murder.

"If Sheikh Efendi finds it appropriate, I think his grandfather's name is suitable . . . Of course if you find it suitable."

Mihrişah Sultan had guessed that Rukiye wouldn't reject this suggestion in her father's presence, and it happened as she'd guessed, Rukiye looked first at her father and then at Nizam, it was clear from the look on his face that he was also pleased with this idea.

"What do you say, father?"

"Whatever you think is suitable, my daughter, he's your son, you name him."

Rukiye smiled.

"Let his name be Yusuf, sir, may he be as intelligent and astute as you are."

"Is this Yusuf going to be a sheikh as well?" asked Nizam, "I suppose everything is starting over again. A little sheikh efendi."

Rukiye looked at Sheikh Efendi.

"Would you say his name please, sir."

Sheikh Efendi gently lifted the baby up, recited the call to prayer softly into his ear and repeated his name three times.

A new life had been born.

They were all happy, they'd left their pain behind.

People look towards the future with hope in the happy blindness they've been granted, they don't know that a terrible disaster waits at the door.

33

During those strange days, Nizam moved among the strange oscillations and tides of emotion, sometimes his feelings for Anya seemed like an undying love and sometimes they seemed like an oppressive nuisance, but they weren't either of these things, they were constantly changing form. It was nearly impossible for Nizam, who didn't like emotions and who indeed wasn't at all accustomed to this kind of thing, to understand his feelings for Anya and to describe them. It was as if a harness had been placed around his neck, a harness that was made of a combination of those two terrible emotions, pity and admiration, as he shook himself like a thoroughbred horse it got tighter, slowly it was becoming a part not just of his emotions but of his body.

It wasn't possible for him to consciously discover his feelings, every time, his consciousness came up against one of these two emotions, he couldn't see beyond them. Admiration brought on the fear of losing Anya, and pity meant always worrying about her and not wanting to leave her alone, when these two terrifying bonds came up against the selfish side of him that didn't want to be attached, it caused him distress, and a feeling of having been caught. Nizam could not countenance being distressed. Without being aware of it, he was flailing to free himself from this.

When his emotions, wants, fears, and habits began to clash, Nizam experienced a transformation within him, though he never understood what had happened or how it had happened.

When a love composed of pity, admiration, worry, habit,

and yearning, the like of which Nizam had never before experienced, wanted to develop and came up against the boundaries of fear and distress, it hid and changed shape like an intelligent creature. It disguised itself as curiosity. When he didn't see Anya, he was curious about what she was doing, whether or not she was upset, whether she was alone, whether or not she'd gone to the gambling den. He believed that he could go, satisfy his curiosity and return, that's why he went to see her without feeling any fear.

Mihrişah Sultan's warnings and the warm family atmosphere at the *tekke* made it possible for him to go a few days without seeing Anya, but then he would go running to see her again.

Anya didn't ask why he'd come, why he hadn't come sooner or what he was doing. She didn't talk about her feelings at all, she didn't complain. She was like a closed room that didn't reveal what it contained, and this increased his curiosity.

He never knew where he would find Anya, sometimes he would go to the gambling den only to learn she hadn't come, sometimes he would go to her house only to be told that she was at the gambling den. Anya was also shaken, Mihrişah Sultan's cruel reminders of her past just as she was struggling to come back to life with Nizam had opened all of her old wounds, at the same time, the days she spent with Nizam led her to become aware once again of the attraction of life, now she could neither return to her former state nor manage to live under the new conditions. The entire order of her life was upset, her decisive retreat from life had been unsuccessful.

When he went to the gambling den towards morning one night after not having visited for several days, he saw Anya and Kamil Bey standing next to the piano talking, and he saw Anya smiling. This surprised and angered him greatly.

Without realizing it, he'd come to believe that being able to make Anya smile was a privilege that belonged to him alone, this belief was shattered by a man being able to make her smile, it made Nizam feel as if he'd been betrayed.

He thought that this smile was a kind of ingratitude . . . As if Anya owed him a debt of gratitude and couldn't smile with anyone else.

When Kamil Bey noticed Nizam he suddenly stopped talking to Anya and came over to him with a diffidence that made him even more angry.

"Where have you been, my good man, you've been missed."

In a cold tone, Nizam said, "I've been busy."

"Anya and I were talking about the denizens of the gambling den . . . I was saying that those like you should be put in the ghost category, they appear and disappear, they suddenly show themselves in various corners of the mansion, then they disappear into nothingness behind the curtains . . . Then there are the ones like me, they're like the windows, doors or roof of the gambling den, you know you'll find them there, if they're missing it's as if part of the mansion is gone . . . Of course there are the ones who are like the fireplace, during certain seasons they appear regularly, for a long time they come frequently . . ."

Nizam wasn't listening to what Kamil Bey was saying, he was looking at Anya, Anya was looking at him steadily with that blank expression, without even the slightest movement on her face, the insistence in her glance and the lack of expression in her eyes made Nizam uneasy, it was as if he had encountered a code he didn't understand, he wondered what this contradiction could mean.

He heard Kamil Bey say, "Well I'll be off, you're not much in the mood for chatting, my good man."

"Have a good evening," he said.

Anya was still looking at him.

He walked completely straight, they didn't say anything, together they turned and left the mansion, the sky was turning grey, the smell of soot and smoke from the torches mixed with the smell of daffodils, gillyflowers and the pine trees in the forest.

They got into the carriage together. Anya seemed to shrink inside her coat. He heard her sigh once or twice.

Nizam got out at the door to Anya's house, helped Anya out, then got back into the carriage.

After that he didn't go to the gambling den for three days, every morning he went to the *tekke* and stayed there until everyone went to bed. He loved the baby, he called him "Dragonfly," Rukiye pretended to get angry, "don't say that to the boy, it makes him sound like an insect . . ."

"Don't you think Yusuf is a big name for the boy, he's a little dragonfly, in any event all Yusufs are born as Dragonflies, they become Yusuf when they get older."

"Oh, Nizam, that's enough nonsense . . ."

Nizam carried his curiosity about Anya within him like a closed iron box, he didn't reveal his feelings to anyone, as a part of that peaceful milieu he tried to keep Anya out of his mind.

Once, when no one else was around, Rukiye asked,

"What happened to that Russian lady?"

"She's fine."

"Do you see each other?"

"Occasionally."

"Do you love her?"

"No."

"Mihrişah Sultan said that gambling den is dangerous but you still seem to be going. Why do you go if you don't love her?"

"Because it's fun . . ."

Rukiye looked at him.

"You're lying, aren't you?"

Nizam smiled and shrugged his shoulders. "Be careful," said Rukiye, "you're always getting yourself into trouble, don't leave me obliged to be saddened about you as well. Look, I wouldn't be able to bear that now."

"Don't worry."

Despite all of the warnings, Nizam didn't believe that he faced any danger, a part of him was completely cut off from reality, in part of his mind there was a dreamy state, as if he believed that the world and the people living on it were far from him and his family, and that no one could touch them. He'd been this way since childhood, nothing he'd experienced had been enough to overcome this delusion. The greatest obstacle that frustrated the establishment of a relationship with Anya, or with any woman for that matter, was this delusion, when establishing a serious relationship with "one of them" clashed with this delusion, he preferred to perpetuate the delusion, in order to perpetuate this delusion, he refused to form a real relationship with a "person."

Perhaps the most important reason he was so fond of those days he spent at the *tekke* with Sheikh Efendi and Mihrişah Sultan was that these two powerful and untouchable people had a stance that nourished this delusion.

Once when Mihrişah Sultan asked Sheikh Efendi, "What's that old geezer doing?" Sheikh Efendi, who'd become accustomed to the way Sultan spoke, smiled and asked, "Which one?"

"It's not worth asking about the one who's sitting on the throne now, he's a complete puppet, he's afraid of men who are the same age as his grandson, he grovels before them . . . They say he's terrified of Enver . . . I'm asking about the other one, the crafty one, he would never have allowed himself to be debased like that . . . What's he doing in Beylerbey, does he have any plans to ascend to the throne again?"

"They say he's aged a great deal, I imagine he was very hopeful when he first came, but I suppose that after what happened he doesn't have many hopes left concerning the future . . . Though with him hope springs eternal . . . They recently allowed his daughters to visit him, the royal ladies went to Beylerbey . . . I don't know whether it was to bid farewell . . ."

"Sheikh Efendi, what do you say, where is this all going to lead? The murderers are in power, do you think that anything good can come out of this?"

Sheikh Efendi shook his head.

"In my opinion it won't . . . This nation is unlucky."

Mihrişah objected in an irritable tone.

"It's not bad luck, it's stupidity . . . Can you call consenting to so much evil bad luck, your Excellency the Sheikh, they got themselves out of one mess, they imprisoned that tyrannical geezer, then they went and brought in new tyrants . . . These lands can only produce tyrants . . . Sometimes I wonder if I'm not thinking that things were better in the old geezer's time . . . Why do we keep ending up with tyrants, why are there so many murders in this country?"

"I worry that much worse things can happen," said Sheikh Efendi.

A few months later Grand Vizier Mahmut Şevket Pasha would be shot and killed in his carriage in Beyazit, preparations were being made for this murder that would be committed soon, Sheikh Efendi had heard one or two things about what might happen. Hasan Efendi said that those who had been planning the murder had been caught but that Talat Bey had had them released. Monsieur Gavril's name was mentioned during this conversation.

"Once I see you all leave this place safely as soon as possible I'll be less worried," said Sheikh Efendi.

Preparations for the journey had begun slowly, they mentioned the journey often, they took an anguished pleasure in talking about this, as if they were rubbing places that hurt. They knew that this parting would be their final parting, that they would never meet again. This feeling of happiness that they'd experienced recently, which was never spoken of, never mentioned, that was never told and never would be told, would remain with them for the rest of their lives as a secret. Sometimes they missed each other as if she'd already set out on that journey, at those times they were frightened of the days before them.

All of Nizam's emotions were mixed together, he experienced them as if they were seasons, it would seem like winter before noon and like spring after noon, no emotion existed on its own, none of them proclaimed sole leadership, every emotion was constantly changing places with another, during those uncertain days he suddenly encountered an emotion that he tried to conceal from himself, that he felt growing within him even though he denied it: jealousy.

Late one afternoon, an image that had been hidden in the back of his mind suddenly and without warning became visible; he remembered how Anya and Kamil Bey had smiled together. It occurred to him that this wouldn't be confined to a single occasion, that they might have smiled together before, then he thought that she might smile like that with other people as well. "She's changed," he said to himself. Nizam had believed that Anya would never change, that she would always distance herself from the world and reject life, this belief had always made him feel secure, and now he was seized by great fear and anger.

The possibility that Anya could be with another man, that she could go with another man shook and stupefied him and led to a great fear of loss. He felt regret for having brought Anya back to life, the moment she came back to life she left the man who had brought her back and smiled with another man, he found this unfair and ungrateful and it made him angry.

At midnight that night he got up and went to Anya's house, he was pleased to find she was at home and without saying anything he sat across from her and looked at her face, he struggled to find some signs or hints there. Then he got up and left.

Anya noticed perhaps for the first time that night that Nizam had changed.

The attitudes and habits that until then no event or emotion had changed, the personality traits he thought would never change, began to change quickly, later he said to Osman in a manner that combined anguish and shame, "I became another person, there was another person inside me, I'd never even noticed this."

That free, joking, witty, indifferent young man was gone, he had been replaced by an inquisitorial, long-faced, angry man who asked questions. He started going to Anya's house and to the gambling den at completely unexpected hours, these raids were intended to uncover the truth he believed was being concealed from him. For no reason he began to behave in a hostile manner towards Anya, he was unnecessarily peevish, from time to time he made fun of her, he made untoward implications about the past he knew she was so sensitive about.

Because he wasn't accustomed to it he didn't know how to deal with jealousy, he didn't know how to get this emotion under control, he saw that he was turning into a boring man, each time he promised himself he wouldn't behave like that again, but each time he thought of Anya or saw her, his suspicious anger flared up.

He wasn't just suspicious about the present, about what she'd experienced that day, he was also suspicious about Anya's past, it didn't stop with suspicion, he invented pasts for her in his mind, one of these became increasingly convincing for him, there was no rational reason to believe this, but in those days he had few remaining bonds to logic.

He thought that she had been a high-priced prostitute, that she'd fooled wealthy people with her silence and her piano playing and taken their money, she'd been obliged to flee because she'd robbed or killed one of them, Gavril, who found wealthy customers for her, had fled with her, he increasingly believed this and accepted that it was true.

He now saw Anya's every action and every word in light of this fantasy that he believed was true, he found signs in every word that proved this belief. He behaved towards her in a manner he had never and would never behave towards a real prostitute, with almost shameless disrespect, he made shameful implications and said derisive things.

Anya couldn't quite grasp what was happening, she couldn't imagine that Nizam would be jealous of her, she couldn't figure out how to behave in response to this sudden change, increasingly she was closing herself off and becoming more silent.

She thought about leaving Nizam, but because she felt she wouldn't succeed in getting Nizam out of her life and returning to her former "death," she couldn't do this; she could neither return to her former "death" nor countenance living without Nizam, nor could she become accustomed to Nizam's strange disrespect. She was seeking a way to calm Nizam down.

That soft and deep love that they'd never acknowledged or named, that healing emotion, had been broken by Nizam's jealousy, it had lost all of its peace, confidence and brightness. Both of them were aware that their emotions and their relationship had been stained; this made Nizam even more angry and aggressive, and it made Anya more helpless and quiet. Except for a few instances when Anya had happy memories, they didn't smile anymore.

Nizam had never asked questions before, but now he frequently asked questions about her past, Anya began to think that this strangeness that had emerged at such an unexpected time had to do with the secret concerning her past.

Once she'd told Nizam, "I don't like conversations like this," and Nizam had left without saying anything.

Another time when she said, "This kind of behavior doesn't suit you, Nizam," the same thing happened, once again Nizam left the house without saying a word.

When he was gone, Anya missed him.

At times like that she realized that she loved him in a stronger manner than either she or Nizam would have supposed, that she'd made him the center of her life, just as Nizam was facing his jealousy, she was facing her love, and like Nizam, she didn't know what to do either. She was stuck in a labyrinth, she couldn't find a way out, she couldn't break free, they were losing each other increasingly more frequently within the same labyrinth. Anya began to fear that on one of these occasions when they lost each other, they wouldn't be able to find each other again.

Because Nizam was the one who had brought her back to life, he represented almost everything people possess in life, he was her son, her father, her husband, her brother and her best friend, to lose Nizam would mean losing everything she had in life once again, Anya didn't have the strength to bear a second loss.

Sometimes they sat for hours looking at each other's faces without uttering a single word, each was curious about what the other was thinking, Nizam looked at her with jealousy and hostility, and she looked at him with fear and love.

Sometimes Anya sat at the piano and played pieces Nizam liked in order to try to calm him, but in time she felt Nizam wasn't listening with the same admiration he used to, that he was fidgeting with distress in his seat, and she suddenly stopped playing.

Nizam no longer wanted her to play the piano, he wanted her to talk, he wanted her to explain, he wanted to hear everything about her past, her emotions, whether or not she loved him. Nizam expected from Anya what was most difficult for her to do, but Anya slowly began to think that her not talking would kill the relationship, that she would lose Nizam, and that she would be forced to return to her own death. Even though she thought she wasn't ready for this, she grasped that unless she was able to put to rest Nizam's suspicions about the past, they weren't going to be able to walk towards the future, when she realized this she behaved rudely towards Nizam with an anger she couldn't express. As her belief that she was going to have to talk strengthened, so did her anger at Nizam.

As she thought about relating her past in order to save their future, another worry appeared within her, after she'd told him everything, would she be able to forgive Nizam for forcing her to tell him, she didn't know if she would be able to love him as much as she had. She was afraid of not loving Nizam.

Despite these fears, she believed that she wouldn't be able to heal Nizam in any other way, she thought it was his doubts about her past that had changed him like this. She couldn't think of any other reason why an incurious, polite cheerful man could transform into such a crude, curious, disrespectful person.

One evening Nizam came earlier than usual, "I just dropped by, I won't be staying," he said. He couldn't stay away from Anya, but he couldn't be at ease when he was with her, he found reasons to be suspicious in her every gesture, in her every glance, in every modulation of her voice.

As he perched on the edge of the armchair, ready to leave, in silence, without looking at Anya, he suddenly looked up at the wall and said in a hostile voice,

"In fact a wealthy friend gave you that tapestry as a gift, isn't that so?"

Throughout his life Nizam had been a man who was never coarse or ugly, now he didn't mind being coarse, or rather he couldn't prevent himself, even as he knew he shouldn't do it, as if there was someone inside him who wouldn't listen to him, he turned into someone who wasn't at all like him and said things that made him ashamed.

Anya looked at Nizam.

"Are you certain that you want to learn about my past, Nizam? Is this what you want?"

She was looking at him the way she had the night she'd let her dress fall to her feet and asked, "is this what you want?"

Nizam saw that look, he remembered that scene, he prepared himself to say "No" as he had that night.

"Yes," he said.

He was even more surprised than Anya by what he'd said but he wanted to know, he wanted to learn everything, to know everything, to understand, to be certain. For her to tell him about her past would be an indication of love, it would mean acceptance, Nizam wanted to be certain of that love, of being loved, that Anya was willing to change for him.

"So be it."

Anya didn't say anything. For quite some time they sat in silence. From the patter on the windows they knew it had begun to rain.

Anya stood, went inside, and came back with a carafe and two small crystal glasses.

"If I'm going to talk, and if you're going to listen, we're going to need to drink a little."

She poured vodka into the little crystal glasses, she knocked back the vodka in a way Nizam had never seen anyone do before and poured herself another.

"I . . ." she said.

Then she fell silent again, she hadn't fully decided yet.

Then she began talking in a hoarse voice that seemed to come from the depths, from within, from her lungs.

"I was born in Petersburg . . . in a mansion similar to your grandmother's mansion, perhaps it was a little bigger . . . My name is Countess Yulia Mihaylovna Rodovsky . . . My father was Count Rodovsky, a distant relative of the Czar . . . He was a tall, handsome man, my mother died giving birth to me, I never knew her . . . My father loved music . . . Sometimes you remind me of him, when we first met at the mansion and you said, "You're not playing with feeling," I was very surprised, my father used to say that to me when I was a child, "You're not playing with feeling, play with feeling.""

Anya stopped and drank another glass of vodka.

"I had no siblings . . . My father recognized I was a talented pianist when I saw still very young . . . I took lessons from the best teachers in Russia . . . There was one teacher . . ."

Anya smiled.

"He was a strange, somewhat befuddled man, but when he played the piano it was as if he became another person, I admired him. He had a son about my age, he would bring his son to the lessons, he would listen in silence, he had huge black eyes, thick, stubborn, and silent lips . . . He was a morose boy . . . Piotr . . . He would stare at me, he would watch me. Then he would suddenly smile, you wouldn't believe the way his face changed, it was suddenly another child's face, he would light up. He was very handsome. I fell in love with him, and he fell in love with me. We would write letters to each other . . . Sometime later I started giving recitals at home for my father's acquaintances . . . My father was very proud of me, sometimes I'd look at him when I was playing and see that he was very happy . . . He listened in the same way you listen . . . I was always surprised by the way you listen to the piano, you always reminded me of my father . . . I was invited to the palace a couple of times, I played for the Tsar and the Tsarina. The Tsar said to my father, "Congratulations, Count Rodovski, the young countess has become a superb pianist." I'll never forget how happy my father was that night. On the way home, in the carriage, he took my hand and said, "My dear Yulia, you are the greatest gift that's ever been bestowed on me.""

Anya was now talking as if she'd forgotten Nizam was there.

"I was seventeen years old, one evening we were invited to the palace again. That evening the Tsar invited some other people. Prince Nikolay Steponovitch, one of the Tsar's cousins, was also there . . . Or rather I learned later that he was there. He was an undersecretary at the Ministry of the Interior . . . He fell in love with me, or perhaps he fell in love with the way I played the piano, I don't know . . . . He told the Tsar he wanted to marry me. The Tsar summoned my father and told him. My father couldn't say no to the Tsar . . ."

Anya sighed.

"I married Nikolay. He was a stern man. But he always treated me well, I always remember him fondly. I always felt guilty that I didn't love him. We had two children one after the other . . . two boys . . . Nikolay was in love with me but he worshipped his sons. He would tell me his dreams and plans for them, he never got tired of talking about the children . . . At night we'd go and watch them together, I'll never forget how they looked when they were sleeping."

Suddenly her voice became shaky, Nizam thought she was going to cry but Anya continued without crying.

"I wasn't happy but I wasn't unhappy either . . . I played the piano, I took care of the children, I played with them, I played pieces on the piano for them . . . When I was playing they would come and hit the piano keys . . . This made them laugh a lot . . . Sometimes I played the piano for them just so that they would do this and laugh . . . You should have seen how they giggled, they never got tired of doing this . . ."

She paused and sighed.

"Years passed . . . Placid, calm years . . . Things were complicated in Russia but our house was calm. Nikolay never talked about politics, sometimes he would suddenly be called in the middle of the night, and he would go at once. At that time there were a lot of explosions and assassinations in Russia, but Nikolay succeeded in keeping all of this out of our house . . . One day I heard that my piano teacher was ill and I went to visit him. He was in bed, he had pneumonia . . . Piotr was there too. At that time he was in his last year of medical school. We realized that we were still in love with each other . . . He still went around with a long face, then he would suddenly smile . . . I couldn't resist that smile, I wanted to see that smile all the time . . ."

Nizam was inwardly tense as he listened to this part . . . Anya, who had been silent for years, was now letting herself go like a river flooding its banks.

"We met once or twice at his house but it was very dangerous, it was impossible for me to go to his house without being seen, without being noticed . . . Our mansion had a very large garden, in the grove at the back there was a small house full of gardening tools, old junk, old closets and beds. I gave Piotr the key to a small gate on the side that was seldom used. There were always guards standing at the large front gate, but not many people knew about the small gate, it was difficult to see among the vines . . . At night Piotr would come in through that gate and go to the little house, I would go there too, we'd meet there, I would go back before it got light.

Anya closed her eyes.

"It seems we were two traitors . . . We were both betraying . . . I was betraying Nikolay, and Piotr was betraying me . . . He'd never mentioned it to me but he'd become a Narodnik . . . He'd joined them when he was in medical school . . . One night he opened the gate for his comrades and secretly got them into the house . . . My cousin was giving birth to her first child, I was with her, I wasn't at home . . ."

Tears began to fall from her eyes.

"They killed Nikolay, the guards came, there was a skirmish, meanwhile, I don't know how, a fire started . . . The guards shot Piotr and his comrades . . . During the fighting the children had been forgotten . . ."

Anya's face had changed, it had become stony and white, the lines on her face seemed sharper and deeper, as if they'd been drawn with a pencil. It looked like a wax death-mask.

"The children burned to death . . ."

Anya had covered her face with her hands and shook as she cried, but she made no sound, she was doubled over, she'd shrunk in the armchair, she looked tiny. Nizam didn't know what to do, he was looking at her in pity, he thought of going and holding her hand, but he realized he shouldn't touch her then. Now he understood why she'd killed herself while she was still alive, why she didn't talk to people, why she looked at people as if they were dead, what kind of past he'd brought back to life with his disrespectful questions, why Anya had said, "Sometimes nothing is a great luxury, I hope you never come to understand this."

They didn't know how long they remained in silence like that.

Anya swallowed, took her hands from her face and looked at Nizam, then she poured herself another vodka and drank it.

"They suspected me . . . The next day Monsieur Gavril came, he took me and a few things . . . We went to Crimea, and from there to Istanbul . . . My father never spoke to me again, he never called, he never wrote, she had never received news of him."

Nizam knew that he shouldn't say anything, but he couldn't resist asking,

"Why did Monsieur Gavril help you?"

Anya blinked her eyes as if she was trying to understand what it was that Nizam was asking, then in an indifferent voice she told him.

"My father and grandfather raised Monsieur Gavril together and sent him to school, his parents had been killed in a bandit raid in my grandfather's village . . . He was a military doctor . . . And he was a very famous doctor . . . When Ignatiev, the Russian ambassador in Istanbul, fell ill, he was sent to Istanbul with a team of doctors . . . That's when he met your grandfather, they became good friends . . . Later, during the Russo-Japanese War, while he was on his way to Vladivostok as Admiral Rojetsvensky's personal physician, the Japanese bombed the fleet, the admiral's ship sank, Monsieur Gavril got into a lifeboat with some wounded soldiers, but all the sailors died on the way. He was at sea with the dead soldiers for six days with no food or water. Then he reached the shore and a villager found him, he brought him to his shack and gave him bread and milk . . . After that incident he became a national hero in Russia . . . And he ruined his life in order to save me. I think he gave up his entire future to pay a debt of gratitude to my family . . . I suppose my father sent him . . . He had some military acquaintances here, he opened the gambling den with their help . . . In any event he used to gamble when he was young, "All seamen are gamblers," he used to say.

Anya sighed again as she tried to pull herself together.

"Monsieur Gavril found this house and set me up here . . . At first I thought about killing myself, I thought about it a great deal . . . In fact I didn't really have any other recourse . . . But I realized that this would be an escape, that it would be a deliverance I didn't deserve, I didn't allow myself to escape punishment for what I did . . . I knew I had to suffer that punishment every single day, I suffered it, I am suffering it, I will continue to suffer it . . . But no punishment is enough . . . I don't have the right to either live or die . . . I know this . . . Oh, Nizam . . . Oh, Nizam . . . You should never have come . . ."

She wiped her eyes with the back of her hand.

"I was the one who proposed playing the piano at Monsieur Gavril's mansion . . . Otherwise I would have gone crazy in this house . . ."

Nizam silently stood, took Anya's hands and pulled her to her feet, then he hugged her, he hugged her tightly. He didn't know what to say, he didn't know what the right thing to say was, he regretted having forced Anya to tell him these things, he felt ashamed.

"Would you like to play the piano?" he asked.

"No."

"What would you like?"

"I want to sleep a little."

Nizam brought Anya to the bedroom as if he was bringing

a small child, he lay her on the bed in her clothes, then he lay next to her and hugged her.

As Anya was drifting off to sleep, he asked the question he'd wanted to ask from the beginning but that he knew would be untoward and impolite, he asked in a whisper, even as he asked he wished in fact that she wouldn't hear it.

"Did you love Piotr very much?"

Before falling asleep Anya answered with a whisper that sounded like a candle being extinguished.

"Very much."

For the next three days Nizam stayed with Anya, he didn't even go to the *tekke*. It was as if Anya was ill, she didn't get out of bed, she slept all the time, she didn't speak, she didn't eat; Nizam covered her, wiped away her perspiration, tried to feed her the soup that the old woman made, he lay next to her and stroked her hair, he whispered "My dear Anya" into her ear. Sometimes Anya opened her eyes and looked at Nizam as if she didn't recognize him, then with a strange surprise she would say, "Nizam," and fall back to sleep.

A man Monsieur Gavril sent came by a few times to ask about Anya and to see whether or not she needed anything, they told him Anya had "a cold" and sent him away.

Nizam had been shaken by what he'd heard and what he'd learned, he realized he'd been terribly unfair, that he should not have obliged Anya to tell him these things, he was deeply upset; However, seeing that she loved him enough to tell him this terrible secret, to relive that pain, being with her every minute in a manner that left him no need to be jealous, was good for Nizam's soul, it calmed him, indeed as he told Osman later, "it made me happy."

Three days later Anya got up, her face was pale, there were rings under her eyes, it was as if her eyes were "looking at dead people" just the way they'd been in the days when Nizam first met her. In a cold and distant voice, as if she didn't recognize either Nizam or the housekeeper, she said, "I'm going to the gambling den," it was the first time Nizam had heard her say "gambling den."

She got ready without speaking.

Nizam brought her to the gambling den, she said "Thank you" as she got out of the carriage, she went into the gambling den without looking back, there was a crowd in front of the gambling den, carriages were coming and going, suddenly Nizam didn't want people to see he'd brought her there, he couldn't think of what to do. Anya had already gone into the gambling den, he knew that if he went to her she wouldn't speak to him.

The way the woman with whom he'd spent three days in the same bed feeling such great love and tenderness had turned into a complete stranger, the way she hadn't looked at him, the way she hadn't spoken to him, indeed the way she'd behaved if she didn't know him at all, inflamed the jealousy that had been temporarily subdued, he thought she didn't love him because he'd forced her to tell him, that she would never love him again. He didn't know what to do, he hit the roof of the carriage and told the driver "Let's go." He didn't know where he was going to go.

He needed to find shelter somewhere, with someone.

The heaviness of Anya's memories, her willingness to talk about those memories and the complete nakedness with which she'd demonstrated her love for Nizam, the tender love he'd felt as he listened and for three days afterwards, the jealousy that was becoming manifest within him again, were turning Nizam upside down, he didn't know which emotion to hang on to, which emotion to possess, he was being torn apart by an almost unhealthy yearning, he now wanted to be with Anya at every moment, he wanted to embrace her, to talk to her. But the state she'd been in that evening had shown him that Anya didn't want this.

He told the carriage driver to go to Mihrişah Sultan's house.

He'd decided that was where he would find the women's voices and the old memories that would console him, that would reinforce his strength, cheer and arrogance. When they entered the garden he saw the bright lights of the mansion in the distance, as they approached he became aware of the sound of music, the entire garden smelled of flowers and trees.

They were preparing to sit down to dinner, a long table had been set, the ladies in waiting where giggling and chatting among themselves in groups, the Italian musicians were playing entertaining pieces, the butlers were rushing back and forth putting the finishing touches on the table.

Mihrişah Sultan greeted Nizam by asking, "Where have you been?"

Even this reproachful voice was enough to calm Nizam, he felt as if he'd returned home from a long journey, he was tired but happy.

"I've been busy, ma'am."

"With what?"

Nizam didn't know how to answer this so he didn't say anything. Mihrişah Sultan didn't drag it out but she said,

"You're not listening to my warnings, you're making a mistake. And you look as if you've come from a war, go pull yourself together, straighten yourself out and come down to dinner . . . Hurry, everyone is hungry . . ."

He went up to the room that was always kept ready for him whether he came or not and where his ironed shirts were hanging in the closet, when he looked into the mirror as he prepared to wash with the hot water the servants had brought, he understood what Mihrişah Sultan had wanted to say, his beard had grown, his cheeks were sunken, his eyes were hollowed, his face had taken on a black and yellow color. He washed, shaved, changed his clothes, and went down to dinner.

Everyone was seated at the table, they were waiting for him, the girls, risking Mihrişah Sultan's displeasure, greeted him with applause, "Monsieur le Sultan has finally graced us with his presence," they teased, when Nizam arrived they began serving the food, dishes arrived on covered silver trays, the lids were removed on the table, the smell of the food and the wine was enough to soothe Nizam. He forgot everything in a moment. Anya, her memories, that dim room in which they'd lain for three days, Anya's voice, her eyes, the absent-mindedness with which she'd left him, were all erased from his mind by the piles of sand, his mind was illuminated and purified, he left behind all of his troubles, all of the heaviness. This miracle revived Nizam, led him to see his former emotions, his love, his yearning, and his jealousy as nonsense.

At the table he became the old Nizam, he joked with the girls, he teased each of them in turn, he made them laugh, he ate with appetite, he mocked everything, provoking the ladies-in-waiting with puns without letting Mihrişah Sultan hear him.

He'd been healed. That's how he felt, he must have been so shaken and blinded by what he'd experienced, if he hadn't wanted so much for his mind to be numbed and to not be able to notice anything, perhaps he would have been suspicious that his recovery had occurred so quickly, but he'd missed the calm in his soul so much that it didn't even occur to him to be suspicious; in any event it was not his nature to tease out his emotions and be suspicious of them, in a very short time he'd become the old Nizam.

34

B ecause he lived among the dead, he was free of the future, of that unnerving vagueness, of that darkness; what had been lived became a known fact. This was the main reason Osman liked his dead and his friendships with his dead, there was nothing frightening about "what was going to happen," everything had already been experienced, everything was known.

Despite all their past might, beauty, and intelligence, among the dead he was the most powerful, he could see the future like a god, he knew what the dead were going to experience before they experienced it. There was no game that destiny could play to distract Osman, by jumping into the past over that thin line that separates today from yesterday, he had rendered life, destiny, and God meaningless, with this slight change of time he'd been freed from humanity's misery in the face of the future.

In order to achieve this power he'd given up the present; by giving up the present he was free from the future that spooked and terrified him, of the danger-filled unknowability of the future, he lived in a secure period of time in which he knew everything that was going to happen beforehand. None of the rewards of life could have been more precious to him than this, he was powerful and happy among his dead.

Living a life that ended at the boundary of the future and always remaining in the past gave him the extraordinary confidence of being able to see any moment again, brightly illuminated, whenever he wanted. He didn't understand why other people were so happy as they marched towards darkness, why they didn't hide, why they left themselves open to all of the dangers of the future. What could be nicer than a life in which there was no darkness at all, the answer he gave to this question was always the same: nothing.

Not seeing and not knowing was frightening, there was nothing else frightening in life. He was the master of the time in which he lived. He had a grasp on every moment. He knew every corner. In any event, the most wonderful thing about the past was this illumination and clarity.

Within that clarity he watched Nizam walking towards disaster, he watched knowing what would happen and without fear.

After their strange parting that day, Nizam didn't go to the gambling den for a week.

In the mornings he went to the *tekke* with Mihrişah Sultan, he talked to Rukiye, played with his nephew, he amused Rukiye by saying, "He looks like me, he's going to be handsome," he teased her with "so is he going to be a sheikh, since you can't be, the *tekke* is going to be left to little Yusuf," he made friends with the dervishes, he took walks in the garden amidst the smells of approaching spring with Mihrişah Sultan and Sheikh Efendi, he shared the common joy by talking about how Rukiye was recovering, in the evening he had dinner with Mihrişah Sultan and talked about preparations for the voyage, at night he would go home and have coffee with his father.

Life seemed frighteningly calm and normal.

Later he said to Osman, "who could have known that you're supposed to be frightened of tranquility?"

Preparations for the journey were being made slowly, but no one was in a hurry, everyone was dragging their feet; even Mihrişah Sultan's ladies in waiting, who with the coming of spring had become captivated by rowboat excursions, carriage rides, the deep green of the woods, the attention of the aristocrats who looked at them with admiration and wrote them letters and sent them gifts, the spice-scented mystery of the Grand Bazaar, the colorful brightness of the silk that was sold by the yard, the smell of the pepper trees in Kağıthane made their heads spin, the transparent veils they wore on their excursion to Göksu Stream made them feel as if they were in an Oriental fairy tale, were begging Mihrişah Sultan to stay in Istanbul a little longer.

Mihrişah Sultan smiled at them, pretended she was delaying the journey for them and warned them, "Don't become too accustomed to it, we'll be leaving soon."

"All of us had different reasons to want to delay," Rukiye said to Osman, "it didn't even occur to us that we would all have separate reasons to regret this."

Mihrişah Sultan was doing everything possible to delay the day when she would see Sheikh Efendi for the last time, Rukiye feared that leaving Istanbul behind would feel like leaving Tevfik Bey behind, Nizam was pleased to delay leaving, but he didn't confess to himself why he was pleased.

Sheikh Efendi knew that the day when his loved ones would all leave together was approaching, on the one hand he was glad the journey was being delayed, on the other hand a strange uneasiness made him want them to leave as soon as possible.

During that week, they enjoyed their fill of being together and experiencing that family happiness, deriving pleasure from every moment.

Osman watched their happiness with pity.

A week later, on the day they took the baby out into the garden for the first time, when he told Rukiye "I'll see you tomorrow morning" as he left the *tekke* and got into the carriage with Mihrişah Sultan, Nizam didn't know that he would never see his older sister again, that this was their last meeting, that he was leaving and never coming back.

As always, he ate with Mihrişah Sultan in the evening,

played cards with the girls after dinner, went home at night, drank coffee with his father, surprised Hikmet Bey by kissing him and said, "Good night, father."

He went to bed and slept peacefully.

He woke towards morning with a ripping sensation, it was as if his lungs were being torn apart, he must have begun thinking when he was still asleep, because when he woke the thought that "Anya is with someone now" was echoing in his mind, "she came back to life, she's in pain, she's surely found someone to console her."

Yearning and jealousy had become an almost physical pain and were tearing him apart.

The sky was turning grey, he jumped out of bed in terror, got dressed without even thinking about what he was doing, he woke the carriage driver at that hour, as the man rubbed his eyes he said, "Come on, hurry up, be quick," nearly pushed the man into the carriage, and said, "we're going to the gambling den."

The carriage driver was surprised, and he was frightened by the state Nizam was in, they were racing through the empty streets, Nizam had opened the windows, wind was blowing in, the weather was cool, the morning wind smelled of fresh leaves, but Nizam didn't notice any of this.

When they turned into the woods where the gambling den was, the torches had been extinguished but the gambling den's lights were burning, He jumped out of the carriage and ran inside, the room was empty, the piano lid was closed, he looked at the corner where Anya always stood, there was nobody there.

Nizam took a deep breath and looked around.

Then he thought that Anya might be in the kitchen downstairs, Monsieur Gavril ate breakfast at this hour. He opened the door behind the stairs, he could hear voices from below.

When he reached the kitchen door, he first saw Anya standing silently in a corner of the kitchen, Monsieur Gavril was sitting at the table eating his bread and milk, a large man was standing by the stove, looking at Anya and laughing, the way the man was looking at Anya and the arrogance of his voice exploded in his mind at the same moment.

"The Bab-ı Ali raid was terrific," the man was saying, "We took care of everything in fifteen minutes . . ."

He didn't know that the large man was one of Kara Kemal Bey's men, that he came by the gambling den every month to get money from Monsieur Gavril for the craftsmen's associations, that he was there that morning not just to collect money but also to learn whether or not he would hide Şevket Pasha's prospective killers who Talat Bey had rescued from the police, he didn't mention who they were, he just asked "Could you put a couple of our friends up for a while?"

At that moment Nizam couldn't decide whether he was more angered by the way the man was looking at Anya and smiling or by the way he'd praised the Bab-ı Ali raid.

Anya was the first to see that Nizam had arrived, when she saw the way Nizam was looking at the man she panicked and tried to take a step towards him, but somehow she couldn't move, then Monsieur Gavril saw Nizam.

The large man who was smiling at Anya didn't realize anyone had come on until he heard Nizam's voice.

"Did you take part in the Bab-ı Ali raid?"

All of the lights in Nizam's mind were going out, there was only the man's face before his eyes, his cleanly shaven, slightly reddened face, his moustache, his lips parted in a smile, his gloating eyes, his desire to impress Anya.

Monsieur Gavril saw the look in Nizam's eyes and knew what was going to happen, he shouted "Nizam Bey" at the same moment the man answered "yes."

Nizam almost flew at the man, he punched the man with all his strength but the man was very large, he wasn't going to be knocked down by a single punch, he just swayed a bit, but at the same time he put his arms around Nizam.

They rolled on the floor together.

Nizam was hitting the man with all his strength, he saw that his face was covered in blood but his anger didn't abate, he was vaguely able to make out that the man was reaching for his waist and trying to take something out, as he tried to hold the man's hand, the man had taken out his gun, the gunshot on the stone kitchen floor echoed with a deafening roar but the bullet passed Nizam's face and didn't touch him, Nizam was struggling to push down the hand that was holding the gun, the man was trying to get Nizam off him.

Then they crashed with all their weight against the stove, which was burning so hot that it made a roaring sound, the stove toppled over with a great crash, Nizam could feel the heat of the blazing logs that had been scattered about, he could hear the crackling of the flames from the rolling logs, from the corner of his eyes he could see that the curling flames had spread throughout the kitchen like fireworks. There was a smell of burning leather from the soles of his shoes.

The fire spread quickly through the kitchen that was full of dry rags, wooden cupboards, pine shelves and strings of onions and garlic, Monsieur Gavril, who had been struggling to separate them, left them and was trying to put out the fire, but in a very short time the fire had spread to the curtains and the walls.

As they were wrestling among the flames, Nizam shouted to Monsieur Gavril, "Get Anya out of here, get out of here, run."

The man took advantage of Nizam's momentary distraction, freed his hand and fired another shot, this time the bullet grazed Nizam's shoulder. Nizam got on top of the man again and tried to push him down. At the same time he was shouting, "Go Anya, get out of here."

Ever since Nizam had arrived, Anya had been looking at him motionlessly, Monsieur Gavril had grabbed her by the wrist and was trying to get her out of the kitchen, meanwhile the curtains and frame of the door that opened onto the garden had caught fire.

Monsieur Gavril had managed to drag Anya by the wrist as far as the stairs, Nizam saw out of the corner of his eye that they'd reached safety and gave all of his attention to the man, he forgot everything else and saw only him, the man fired again, Nizam could feel a burning in his shoulder but he didn't pay attention to it, they were rolling among the flames, they could hear the sound of crackling wood, toppling furniture and collapsing columns from the building. The flames had spread everywhere, the wooden mansion was blazing like the torches in front of the door.

As they were wrestling, Nizam saw a jar roll past them, he grabbed the hot glass even though it burned his hand, raised it and hit the man on the head with it, the man was shaken, when Nizam hit him again the man remained motionless.

Nizam shook himself free from the man's arms, rushed up the stone stairs, when he got upstairs he saw that the entry hall was in flames, he pulled his jacket over his head and ran through the flames, he rushed outside past the thick wooden doors that crackled as they burned, he took a deep breath of cool air.

Monsieur Gavril was not far away, on his knees, watching the burning mansion.

"Where's Anya?" he asked.

"We came out together but she went back in," he said, "I tried to hold her but she suddenly pushed me and managed to get in."

Nizam noticed that Monsieur Gavril was weeping but he didn't pay attention to this.

He turned in horror and looked at the mansion, there was a great crackling as it burned, smoke, and flames were rising into the bright sky, sparks were flying about, they could hear the sound of collapsing walls and shattering glass.

Monsieur Gavril realized what Nizam was going to do.

"Don't," he said, "You'll never come out again, it's too late to help Anya now . . ."

Nizam didn't even hear what the man said.

There was only one thing he wanted at that moment, to see Anya, to see her face.

He pulled his jacket over his head again and rushed through the door into the burning mansion, flames leapt at him from all sides, smoke was filling his nasal passage.

"Anya," he shouted, "Anya . . ."

Through all of the noise he heard something that sounded like a moan, he turned in that direction, she was lying on the floor near the kitchen stairs.

Nizam had never in his life felt such great delight. He went over to Anya.

"Get up," he said, "Let's get out of here, the building is about to collapse . . ."

Anya looked at him, from the smile on her face it was clear she was glad to see him, she seemed calm, almost happy, there was no sense that she was frightened.

"I sprained my ankle, perhaps I broke it, when I was running in to find you . . . You go . . . You can't carry me, both of us can't get out of here."

"You mean I should leave you, you're crazy . . ."

As Nizam took Anya in his arms and turned towards the door, the door collapsed in flames.

"We'll go out the back window," said Nizam.

He carried Anya into the room where the piano was, the window frames and the walls were burning, everything was bright red, Nizam wanted to turn back, but the frame of the door he'd just come through had collapsed in flames, creating what looked like a barricade of flames.

They were in the middle of the fire.

He carried Anya over to the piano, he took off his jacket

and put it over her shoulders as if it would protect her from the flames. The piano was still intact, it black surface reflecting the red tongues of fire that surrounded it.

They crawled under the piano.

"The piano will protect us," said Nizam.

They sat side by side, Anya was as calm as if she was sitting on the grass in a park, indeed she even seemed happy.

She lay her head on Nizam's chest. She took Nizam's face in her hand and turned it towards her, she looked at him and smiled.

"My name is Anya," she said with a smile, "I . . ."

Nizam was unable to hear the rest of what she said because of the noise, the ceiling of the room collapsed with a great crash.